Moorcock's Multiverse

The Michael Moorcock Collection

The Michael Moorcock Collection is the definitive library of acclaimed author Michael Moorcock's SF & fantasy, including the entirety of his Eternal Champion work. It is prepared and edited by John Davey, the author's long-time bibliographer and editor, and will be published, over the course of two years, in the following print omnibus editions by Gollancz, and as individual eBooks by the SF Gateway (see http://www.sfgateway.com/authors/m/moorcock-michael/ for a complete list of available eBooks).

ELRIC
Elric of Melniboné and Other Stories

Elric: The Fortress of the Pearl

Elric: The Sailor on the Seas of Fate

Elric: The Sleeping Sorceress

Elric: The Revenge of the Rose

Elric: Stormbringer!

Elric: The Moonbeam Roads
comprising –
Daughter of Dreams
Destiny's Brother
Son of the Wolf

CORUM
Corum: The Prince in the Scarlet Robe
comprising –
The Knight of the Swords
The Queen of the Swords
The King of the Swords

Corum: The Prince with the Silver Hand
comprising –
The Bull and the Spear
The Oak and the Ram
The Sword and the Stallion

HAWKMOON
Hawkmoon: The History of the Runestaff
comprising –
The Jewel in the Skull
The Mad God's Amulet
The Sword of the Dawn
The Runestaff

Hawkmoon: Count Brass
comprising –
Count Brass
The Champion of Garathorm
The Quest for Tanelorn

JERRY CORNELIUS
The Cornelius Quartet
comprising –
The Final Programme
A Cure for Cancer
The English Assassin
The Condition of Muzak

Jerry Cornelius: His Lives and His Times (short-fiction collection)

Moorcock's Multiverse

The Sundered Worlds
The Winds of Limbo
The Shores of Death

MICHAEL MOORCOCK

Edited by John Davey

Copyright © Michael and Linda Moorcock 1965, 1966
Revised versions Copyright © Michael and Linda Moorcock 2014
All characters, the distinctive likenesses thereof, and all related
indicia are ™ and © 2014 Michael and Linda Moorcock
Artwork Copyright © James Cawthorn 1964

The right of Michael Moorcock to be identified as the author
of this work has been asserted by him in accordance with the
Copyright, Designs and Patents Act 1988.

This edition published in Great Britain in 2014 by
Gollancz
An imprint of the Orion Publishing Group
Orion House, 5 Upper St Martin's Lane,
London WC2H 9EA

An Hachette UK Company

5 7 9 10 8 6

A CIP catalogue record for this book is
available from the British Library

ISBN 978 0 575 09258 7

Typeset by Jouve (UK), Milton Keynes

Printed and bound in Great Britain by Clays Ltd, Elcograf S.p.A.

The Orion Publishing Group's policy is to use papers
that are natural, renewable and recyclable products and
made from wood grown in sustainable forests. The logging
and manufacturing processes are expected to conform to
the environmental regulations of the country of origin.

www.multiverse.org
www.sfgateway.com
www.gollancz.co.uk
www.orionbooks.co.uk

Introduction to
The Michael Moorcock Collection

John Clute

H E   I S   N O W over 70, enough time for most careers to start and
end in, enough time to fit in an occasional half-decade or so
of silence to mark off the big years. Silence happens. I don't think
I know an author who doesn't fear silence like the plague; most of
us, if we live long enough, can remember a bad blank year or so,
or more. Not Michael Moorcock. Except for some worrying
surgery on his toes in recent years, he seems not to have taken
time off to breathe the air of peace and panic. There has been no
time to spare. The nearly 60 years of his active career seems to
have been too short to fit everything in: the teenage comics; the
editing jobs; the pulp fiction; the reinvented heroic fantasies;
the Eternal Champion; the deep Jerry Cornelius riffs; NEW WORLDS;
the 1970s/1980s flow of stories and novels, dozens upon dozens
of them in every category of modern fantastika; the tales of the
dying Earth and the possessing of Jesus; the exercises in postmodernism that turned the world inside out before most of us had
begun to guess we were living on the wrong side of things; the
invention (more or less) of steampunk; the alternate histories; the
Mitteleuropean tales of sexual terror; the deep-city London riffs:
the turns and changes and returns and reconfigurations to which
he has subjected his oeuvre over the years (he expects this new
Collected Edition will fix these transformations in place for good);
the late tales where he has been remodelling the intersecting
worlds he created in the 1960s in terms of twenty-first-century
physics: for starters. If you can't take the heat, I guess, stay out of
the multiverse.

His life has been full and complicated, a life he has exposed and hidden (like many other prolific authors) throughout his work. In *Mother London* (1988), though, a nonfantastic novel published at what is now something like the midpoint of his career, it may be possible to find the key to all the other selves who made the 100 books. There are three protagonists in the tale, which is set from about 1940 to about 1988 in the suburbs and inner runnels of the vast metropolis of Charles Dickens and Robert Louis Stevenson. The oldest of these protagonists is Joseph Kiss, a flamboyant self-advertising fin-de-siècle figure of substantial girth and a fantasticating relationship to the world: he is Michael Moorcock, seen with genial bite as a kind of G.K. Chesterton without the wearying punch-line paradoxes. The youngest of the three is David Mummery, a haunted introspective half-insane denizen of a secret London of trials and runes and codes and magic: he too is Michael Moorcock, seen through a glass, darkly. And there is Mary Gasalee, a kind of holy-innocent and survivor, blessed with a luminous clarity of insight, so that in all her apparent ignorance of the onrushing secular world she is more deeply wise than other folk: she is also Michael Moorcock, Moorcock when young as viewed from the wry middle years of 1988. When we read the book, we are reading a book of instructions for the assembly of a London writer. The Moorcock we put together from this choice of portraits is amused and bemused at the vision of himself; he is a phenomenon of flamboyance and introspection, a poseur and a solitary, a dreamer and a doer, a multitude and a singleton. But only the three Moorcocks in this book, working together, could have written all the other books.

It all began – as it does for David Mummery in *Mother London* – in South London, in a subtopian stretch of villas called Mitcham, in 1939. In early childhood, he experienced the Blitz, and never forgot the extraordinariness of being a participant – however minute – in the great drama; all around him, as though the world were being dismantled nightly, darkness and blackout would descend, bombs fall, buildings and streets disappear; and in the morning, as though a new universe had taken over from the old one and the world had become portals, the sun would rise on glinting rubble, abandoned tricycles, men and women going about their daily tasks as though nothing had happened, strange shards of ruin poking into altered air. From a very early age, Michael Moorcock's security reposed in a sense that everything might change, in the blinking of an eye, and be *rejourneyed* the next day (or the next book). Though as a writer he has certainly elucidated the fears and alarums of life in Aftermath Britain, it does seem that his very early years were marked by the epiphanies of war, rather than the inflictions of despair and beclouding amnesia most adults necessarily experienced. After the war ended, his parents separated, and the young Moorcock began to attend a pretty wide variety of schools, several of which he seems to have been expelled from, and as soon as he could legally do so he began to work full time, up north in London's heart, which he only left when he moved to Texas (with intervals in Paris) in the early 1990s, from where (to jump briefly up the decades) he continues to cast a Martian eye: as with most exiles, Moorcock's intensest anatomies of his homeland date from after his cunning departure.

But back again to the beginning (just as though we were rimming a multiverse). Starting in the 1950s there was the comics and pulp work for Fleetway Publications; there was the first book (*Caribbean Crisis*, 1962) as by Desmond Reid, co-written with his early friend the artist James Cawthorn (1929–2008); there was marriage, with the writer Hilary Bailey (they divorced in 1978), three children, a heated existence in the Ladbroke Grove/Notting Hill Gate region of London he was later to populate with Jerry Cornelius and his vast family; there was the editing of NEW WORLDS, which began in 1964 and became the heartbeat of the British New Wave two years later as writers like Brian W. Aldiss and J.G. Ballard, reaching their early prime, made it into a tympanum, as young American writers like Thomas M. Disch, John T. Sladek, Norman Spinrad and Pamela Zoline found a home in London for material they could not publish in America, and new British writers like M. John Harrison and Charles Platt began their careers in its pages; but before that there was Elric. With *The Stealer of Souls* (1963) and

Stormbringer (1965), the multiverse began to flicker into view, and the Eternal Champion (whom Elric parodied and embodied) began properly to ransack the worlds in his fight against a greater Chaos than the great dance could sustain. There was also the first SF novel, *The Sundered Worlds* (1965), but in the 1960s SF was a difficult nut to demolish for Moorcock: he would bide his time.

We come to the heart of the matter. Jerry Cornelius, who first appears in *The Final Programme* (1968) – which assembles and co-ordinates material first published a few years earlier in NEW WORLDS – is a deliberate solarisation of the albino Elric, who was himself a mocking solarisation of Robert E. Howard's Conan, or rather of the mighty-thew-headed Conan created for profit by Howard epigones: Moorcock rarely mocks the true quill. Cornelius, who reaches his first and most telling apotheosis in the four novels comprising *The Cornelius Quartet*, remains his most distinctive and perhaps most original single creation: a wide boy, an agent, a *flaneur*, a bad musician, a shopper, a shapechanger, a trans, a spy in the house of London: a toxic palimpsest on whom and through whom the *zeitgeist* inscribes surreal conjugations of 'message'. Jerry Cornelius gives head to Elric.

The life continued apace. By 1970, with NEW WORLDS on its last legs, multiverse fantasies and experimental novels poured forth; Moorcock and Hilary Bailey began to live separately, though he moved, in fact, only around the corner, where he set up house with Jill Riches, who would become his second wife; there was a second home in Yorkshire, but London remained his central base. *The Condition of Muzak* (1977), which is the fourth Cornelius novel, and *Gloriana; or, The Unfulfill'd Queen* (1978), which transfigures the first Elizabeth into a kinked Astraea, marked perhaps the high point of his career as a writer of fiction whose font lay in genre or its mutations – marked perhaps the furthest bournes he could transgress while remaining within the perimeters of fantasy (though *within* those bournes vast stretches of territory remained and would, continually, be explored). During these years he sometimes wore a leather jacket constructed out of numerous patches of varicoloured material, and it sometimes seemed perfectly fitting that he bore the semblance, as his jacket flickered and fuzzed from across a room or road, of an illustrated man, a map, a thing of shreds and patches, a student fleshed from dreams. Like the stories he told, he seemed to be more than one thing. To use a term frequently applied (by me at least) to twenty-first-century fiction, he seemed equipoisal: which is to say that, through all his genre-hopping and genre-mixing and genre-transcending and genre-loyal returnings to old pitches, *he was never still*, because 'equipoise' is all about *making stories move*. As with his stories, he cannot be pinned down, because he is not in one place. In person and in his work, it has always been sink or swim: like a shark, or a dancer, or an equilibrist...

The marriage with Jill Riches came to an end. He married Linda Steele in 1983; they remain married. The Colonel Pyat books, *Byzantium Endures* (1981), *The Laughter of Carthage* (1984), *Jerusalem Commands* (1992) and *The Vengeance of Rome* (2006), dominated these years, along with *Mother London*. As these books, which are non-fantastic, are not included in the current *Michael Moorcock Collection*, it might be worth noting here that, in their insistence on the irreducible difficulty of gaining anything like true sight, they represent Moorcock's mature modernist take on what one might call the rag-and-bone shop of the world itself; and that the huge ornate postmodern edifice of his multiverse *loosens* us from that world, gives us room to breathe, to juggle our strategies for living – allows us ultimately to escape from prison (to use a phrase from a writer he does not respect, J.R.R. Tolkien, for whom the twentieth century was a prison train bound for hell). What Moorcock may best be remembered for in the end is the (perhaps unique) interplay between modernism and postmodernism in his work. (But a plethora of discordant understandings makes these terms hard to use; so enough of them.) In the end, one might just say that Moorcock's work as a whole represents an extraordinarily multifarious execution of the fantasist's main task: which is to *get us out of here*.

Recent decades saw a continuation of the multifarious, but with a more intensely applied methodology. The late volumes of the long Elric saga, and the Second Ether sequence of meta-fantasies – *Blood: A Southern Fantasy* (1995), *Fabulous Harbours* (1995) and *The War Amongst the Angels: An Autobiographical Story* (1996) – brood on the real world and the multiverse through the lens of Chaos Theory: the closer you get to the world, the less you describe it. *The Metatemporal Detective* (2007) – a narrative in the Steampunk mode Moorcock had previewed as long ago as *The Warlord of the Air* (1971) and *The Land Leviathan* (1974) – continues the process, sometimes dizzyingly: as though the reader inhabited the eye of a camera increasing its focus on a closely observed reality while its bogey simultaneously wheels it backwards from the desired rapport: an old Kurasawa trick here amplified into a tool of conspectus, fantasy eyed and (once again) rejourneyed, this time through the lens of SF.

We reach the second decade of the twenty-first century, time still to make things new, but also time to sort. There are dozens of titles in *The Michael Moorcock Collection* that have not been listed in this short space, much less trawled for tidbits. The various avatars of the Eternal Champion – Elric, Kane of Old Mars, Hawkmoon, Count Brass, Corum, Von Bek – differ vastly from one another. Hawkmoon is a bit of a berk; Corum is a steely solitary at the End of Time: the joys and doleurs of the interplays amongst them can only be experienced through immersion. And the Dancers at the End of Time books, and the Nomad of the Time Stream books, and the Karl Glogauer books, and all the others. They are here now, a 100 books that make up one book. They have been fixed for reading. It is time to enter the multiverse and see the world.

September 2012

Introduction to
The Michael Moorcock Collection
Michael Moorcock

B Y 1964, AFTER I had been editing NEW WORLDS for some
months and had published several science fiction and fantasy
novels, including *Stormbringer*, I realised that my run as a writer
was over. About the only new ideas I'd come up with were miniature computers, the multiverse and black holes, all very crudely
realised, in *The Sundered Worlds*. No doubt I would have to return
to journalism, writing features and editing. 'My career,' I told my
friend J.G. Ballard, 'is finished.' He sympathised and told me he
only had a few SF stories left in him, then he, too, wasn't sure
what he'd do.

In January 1965, living in Colville Terrace, Notting Hill, then an
infamous slum, best known for its race riots, I sat down at the
typewriter in our kitchen-cum-bathroom and began a locally
based book, designed to be accompanied by music and graphics.
The Final Programme featured a character based on a young man
I'd seen around the area and whom I named after a local green-
grocer, Jerry Cornelius, 'Messiah to the Age of Science'. Jerry was
as much a technique as a character. Not the 'spy' some critics
described him as but an urban adventurer as interested in his
psychic environment as the contemporary physical world. My
influences were English and French absurdists, American noir
novels. My inspiration was William Burroughs with whom I'd
recently begun a correspondence. I also borrowed a few SF ideas,
though I was adamant that I was not writing in any established
genre. I felt I had at last found my own authentic voice.

I had already written a short novel, *The Golden Barge*, set in a
nowhere, no-time world very much influenced by Peake and the

surrealists, which I had not attempted to publish. An earlier auto-biographical novel, *The Hungry Dreamers*, set in Soho, was eaten by rats in a Ladbroke Grove basement. I remained unsatisfied with my style and my technique. *The Final Programme* took nine days to complete (by 20 January, 1965) with my baby daughters sometimes cradled with their bottles while I typed on. This, I should say, is my memory of events; my then wife scoffed at this story when I recounted it. Whatever the truth, the fact is I only believed I might be a serious writer after I had finished that novel, with all its flaws. But Jerry Cornelius, probably my most successful sustained attempt at unconventional fiction, was born then and ever since has remained a useful means of telling com-plex stories. Associated with the 60s and 70s, he has been equally at home in all the following decades. Through novels and novellas I developed a means of carrying several narratives and viewpoints on what appeared to be a very light (but tight) structure which dispensed with some of the earlier methods of fiction. In the sense that it took for granted the understanding that the novel is among other things an internal dialogue and I did not feel the need to repeat by now commonly understood modernist conven-tions, this fiction was post-modern.

Not all my fiction looked for new forms for the new century. Like many 'revolutionaries' I looked back as well as forward. As George Meredith looked to the eighteenth century for inspiration for his experiments with narrative, I looked to Meredith, popular Edwardian realists like Pett Ridge and Zangwill and the writers of the *fin de siècle* for methods and inspiration. An almost obsessive interest in the Fabians, several of whom believed in the possibility of benign imperialism, ultimately led to my Bastable books which examined our enduring British notion that an empire could be essentially a force for good. The first was *The Warlord of the Air*.

I also wrote my *Dancers at the End of Time* stories and novels under the influence of Edwardian humourists and absurdists like Jerome or Firbank. Together with more conventional generic books like *The Ice Schooner* or *The Black Corridor*, most of that work was done in the 1960s and 70s when I wrote the Eternal Champion supernatural adventure novels which helped support my own and others' experiments via NEW WORLDS, allowing me also to keep a family while writing books in which action and fantastic invention were paramount. Though I did them quickly, I didn't write them cynically. I have always believed, somewhat puritanically, in giving the audience good value for money. I enjoyed writing them, tried to avoid repetition, and through each new one was able to develop a few more ideas. They also continued to teach me how to express myself through image and metaphor. My Everyman became the Eternal Champion, his dreams and ambitions represented by the multiverse. He could be an ordinary person struggling with familiar problems in a contemporary setting or he could be a swordsman fighting monsters on a far-away world.

Long before I wrote *Gloriana* (in four parts reflecting the seasons) I had learned to think in images and symbols through reading John Bunyan's *Pilgrim's Progress*, Milton and others, understanding early on that the visual could be the most important part of a book and was often in itself a story as, for instance, a famous personality could also, through everything associated with their name, function as narrative. I wanted to find ways of carrying as many stories as possible in one. From the cinema I also learned how to use images as connecting themes. Images, colours, music, and even popular magazine headlines can all add coherence to an apparently random story, underpinning it and giving the reader a sense of internal logic and a satisfactory resolution, dispensing with certain familiar literary conventions.

When the story required it, I also began writing neo-realist fiction exploring the interface of character and environment, especially the city, especially London. In some books I condensed, manipulated and randomised time to achieve what I wanted, but in others the sense of 'real time' as we all generally perceive it was more suitable and could best be achieved by traditional nineteenth-century means. For the Pyat books I first looked back to the great German classic, Grimmelshausen's *Simplicissimus* and other early picaresques. I then examined the roots of a certain kind of moral fiction from Defoe through Thackeray and Meredith then to modern times where the picaresque (or rogue tale) can take the form of a road movie, for instance. While it's probably fair to say that Pyat and *Byzantium Endures* precipitated the end of my second marriage (echoed to a degree in *The Brothel in Rosenstrasse*), the late 70s and the 80s were exhilarating times for me, with *Mother London* being perhaps my own favourite novel of that period. I wanted to write something celebratory.

By the 90s I was again attempting to unite several kinds of fiction in one novel with my Second Ether trilogy. With Mandelbrot, Chaos Theory and String Theory I felt, as I said at the time, as if I were being offered a chart of my own brain. That chart made it easier for me to develop the notion of the multiverse as representing both the internal and the external, as a metaphor and as a means of structuring and rationalising an outrageously inventive and quasi-realistic narrative. The worlds of the multiverse move up and down scales or 'planes' explained in terms of mass, allowing entire universes to exist in the 'same' space. The result of developing this idea was the *War Amongst the Angels* sequence which added absurdist elements also functioning as a kind of mythology and folklore for a world beginning to understand itself in terms of new metaphysics and theoretical physics. As the cosmos becomes denser and almost infinite before our eyes, with black holes and dark matter affecting our own reality, we can explore them and observe them as our ancestors explored our planet and observed the heavens.

At the end of the 90s I'd returned to realism, sometimes with a dash of fantasy, with *King of the City* and the stories collected in *London Bone*. I also wrote a new Elric/Eternal Champion sequence, beginning with *Daughter of Dreams*, which brought the fantasy worlds of Hawkmoon, Bastable and Co. in line with my realistic and autobiographical stories, another attempt to unify all my fiction, and also offer a way in which disparate genres could be reunited, through notions developed from the multiverse and the Eternal Champion, as one giant novel. At the time I was finishing the Pyat sequence which attempted to look at the roots of the Nazi Holocaust in our European, Middle Eastern and American cultures and to ground my strange survival guilt while at the same time examining my own cultural roots in the light of an enduring anti-Semitism.

By the 2000s I was exploring various conventional ways of story-telling in the last parts of *The Metatemporal Detective* and through other homages, comics, parodies and games. I also looked back at my earliest influences. I had reached retirement age and felt like a rest. I wrote a 'prequel' to the Elric series as a graphic novel with Walter Simonson, *The Making of a Sorcerer*, and did a little online editing with FANTASTIC METROPOLIS.

By 2010 I had written a novel featuring Doctor Who, *The Coming of the Terraphiles*, with a nod to P.G. Wodehouse (a boyhood favourite), continued to write short stories and novellas and to work on the beginning of a new sequence combining pure fantasy and straight autobiography called *The Whispering Swarm* while still writing more Cornelius stories trying to unite all the various genres and sub-genres into which contemporary fiction has fallen.

Throughout my career critics have announced that I'm 'abandoning' fantasy and concentrating on literary fiction. The truth is, however, that all my life, since I became a professional writer and editor at the age of 16, I've written in whatever mode suits a story best and where necessary created a new form if an old one didn't work for me. Certain ideas are best carried on a Jerry Cornelius story, others work better as realism and others as fantasy or science fiction. Some work best as a combination. I'm sure I'll write whatever I like and will continue to experiment with all the ways there are of telling stories and carrying as many themes as possible. Whether I write about a widow coping with loneliness in her cottage or a massive, universe-size sentient spaceship searching for her children, I'll no doubt die trying to tell them all. I hope you'll find at least some of them to your taste.

One thing a reader can be sure of about these new editions is that they would not have been possible without the tremendous and indispensable help of my old friend and bibliographer John Davey. John has ensured that these Gollancz editions are definitive. I am indebted to John for many things, including his work at

Moorcock's Miscellany, my website, but his work on this edition has been outstanding. As well as being an accomplished novelist in his own right John is an astonishingly good editor who has worked with Gollancz and myself to point out every error and flaw in all previous editions, some of them not corrected since their first publication, and has enabled me to correct or revise them. I couldn't have completed this project without him. Together, I think, Gollancz, John Davey and myself have produced what will be the best editions possible and I am very grateful to him, to Malcolm Edwards, Darren Nash and Marcus Gipps for all the considerable hard work they have done to make this edition what it is.

Michael Moorcock

Contents

The Sundered Worlds

For Barry Bayley

Prologue

COUNT RENARK WAS *a wanderer in the galaxy for two years – but he was not lonely. Renark could never be lonely, for the galaxy was his omnipresent friend and he was aware of its movements. Even the peculiar control exercised on it by forces which he could not sense was as comforting as its presence. He moved about in it and contained awareness of every atom of it in his long, thin-boned skull. He wandered purposely through the teeming galaxy for two swift years and then, when ready, journeyed again towards the Rim...*

Book One

The Fractured Universe

Chapter One

H IS NAME WAS Renark von Bek, Count of the Rim, scion of an ancient family and keeper of more than one dangerous secret.

The three of them met, at last, in a terrible town called Migaa on the harsh, bright edge of a wilderness. Both town and planet were called Migaa and it was the last-chance planet for the galaxy's fugitives.

Count Renark disembarked from his cruiser, uncomfortable under the glare of the diamond-bright sun. He threaded his way through the great looming shapes of a hundred other ships, his mind searching the town ahead for his two friends. His skilled brain probed the shapes of streets and buildings, people and objects until at last he had located them, half a mile away on the other side of the town.

He strode briskly from the spaceport and there were no Customs officers to stop him here. He kept his friends' forms firmly fixed in his mind as he hurried in their direction. They were agitated and he guessed they might be in trouble.

People stared at him as he passed, a very tall, very gaunt man with deep-set black eyes in a long skull, a brooding face in repose. But they didn't stare at his face – they thought him remarkable mainly because he wore no apparent weapon. Almost all the men and women who came to Migaa came hurriedly – but they also came armed.

Only Count Renark walked purposefully along the metal-paved streets, through the glinting steel buildings. The others moved aimlessly, wearing dark lenses to ward off the glare of the desert reflected in the steel and chrome of the buildings. He noted little transport on the streets, and what there was moved lazily. He thought the town had an exhausted air – yet at the same time it possessed an atmosphere of expectancy. It was a peculiar mood – and it smothered Migaa.

He noted also a shared quality in the faces of the men and women, a set expression which tried vainly to disguise the hope lurking in their eyes. They seemed afraid of hoping, yet evidently could do nothing else. Migaa – or what Migaa offered – was their last chance. It was Renark's too, but for other, less selfish, reasons.

When he reached the building where he sensed his two friends were, it wasn't the tavern he'd expected. This was called the Last Break Inn, like hundreds of other taverns throughout the galaxy, but this one's name had a special significance.

He walked in to find tumult.

A fight was going on. He recognised several who could be either thieves or spacehands judging by the white, metal-studded plastileather overalls they wore. They were thick, brutal shouting men and they were attacking two others, not of their kind.

Renark recognised the pair. Paul Talfryn and young Asquiol of Pompeii, their backs against the far wall of the noisy, overcrowded public room. For a moment he felt the urge to leave them to it, confident that they would survive, but then he decided to help them. He wanted them to be as fit as possible for the forthcoming journey.

As he moved forward, a spacehand, using the whole of his metal-studded body as a weapon, launched himself at Renark. The spacehand had obviously learned his fighting techniques aboard ship or on a low-gravity planet. Migaa wasn't a low-grav world and the man's method of charging in an attempt to buffet Renark against the far wall didn't work. Renark skipped aside and the hand blundered past. Renark kicked against the base of the man's spine with a pointed boot. The spacehand collapsed backwards and Renark kicked him sharply in the head, knocking him out.

Swiftly Renark pushed towards his friends.

Talfryn looked almost panic-stricken as he warded off the blows of his attackers, but Asquiol – flamboyant, grinning and vicious – was enjoying himself. A set of knuckle-spikes gleamed on his right fist, and there was blood on them. One of Asquiol's opponents blundered back into Renark, clutching at a bleeding eye-socket.

'We're wasting time!' Renark shouted as the others saw him.

He moved into the crowd, pulling the tumbling spacemen aside with his large, ugly hands. Together, Talfryn and Asquiol punched their way towards him.

A growling giant swung a pocket-mace at Asquiol who ducked, crouched, then shot out his spike-covered fist deep into the space-hand's belly. The giant shrieked and the mace dropped from his hand as he fell to his knees.

The trio burst from the tavern and ran up a narrow side street until they saw the spacehands abandon the chase, shouting cat-calls from behind them. They turned into an alley, running between the backs of the buildings, their boots ringing on the metal.

'Which way to the Salvation Inn?' Renark said.

'Thanks for breaking that up,' Asquiol grinned. 'I thought you Guide Sensers could tell where anything was. It's this way. Not far.'

Renark didn't bother to use his space-sensing ability. The image of what he had done to the spacehand was still sharp in his mind. He didn't like violence.

Asquiol led them back onto a main way. As they walked, Tal-fryn turned to Renark, his expression embarrassed.

'Sorry about that,' he said. 'Those hands were looking for trouble. They picked on Asquiol because of his clothes. We had to fight. We managed to avoid a dozen others, but couldn't get out of this one. The whole damned town's the same – tense, nervous, impatient.'

'I'm afraid I encouraged them,' Asquiol said. 'Really, one can't have one's dress insulted by such a vulgar breed!' He collapsed his knuckle-spikes and put them away.

Lonely and time-begrimed despite his youth, Asquiol dressed with careful flamboyance. He wore a high-collared, quilted jacket of orange nyb-fur and tight slacks of purple stuff which fitted over his pointed, carbon-glass boots. His face was pale and tapering, his black hair cut short in a fringe over his forehead. He carried a slender, anti-neutron beamer – an outlawed weapon.

Asquiol had once been a prince – independent Overlord of Pompeii, before the Galactic Council enforced its extraordinary powers and brought the planet into the Union.

Renark remembered that Asquiol had lost his title and estates for protecting him, and he was grateful.

He noticed that the younger man had lapsed into a brooding mood. It was his usual reaction and because of it many people thought him unbalanced, though Renark knew that Asquiol was the very opposite. His was a fine, delicate balance which only his will maintained.

Talfryn, lean-faced like his two friends, sensitive and bearded, was an unlicensed explorer and therefore a criminal. He was dressed conservatively – sleeveless jerkin of unstained hide, blue shirt and black trousers – and carried a heavy power-gun. He looked curiously at Renark, but since he said nothing Renark remained silent.

Then he smiled. His thin, grim lips quirked upwards and he straightened his back, turning his long head and looking hard at Talfryn.

Talfryn seemed disturbed by the look, and felt obliged to speak so he said: 'When do we leave? I'm impatient to get started.'

Renark did not respond far a moment, and just kept looking.

Talfryn said: 'I can't wait.'

'I'm not sure yet,' Renark said.

As they reached the tall, many-windowed structure of the Salvation Inn, on the edge of town, Talfryn said to Renark: 'You told us we were wasting time back there. How much time have we, roughly?'

'Maximum, thirty-six hours,' the Guide Senser replied.

Asquiol looked up, startled out of his mood. He seemed troubled. 'Is that all?'

'That's all – probably less. I can feel it coming closer to this continuum all the time, but it's difficult to keep a fix on it always. It takes most of my energy.'

They entered the wide, high-roofed public hall of the Salvation Inn. Asquiol looked around him, seeking someone in the crowd, but was disappointed. The huge windows which stretched up one high wall lighted several tiered galleries and looked out onto the bright black-and-white carbon desert of the planet.

They pushed through the crowd of men and women of many types. There were richly clad men; ragged men; women who drank heavily and women who sipped at a single drink; vociferous men and quiet women. Here, as in the rest of the town, there was an air of tired, tense expectancy – an atmosphere which had lasted, this era, for thirty-seven years. All the residents glanced often at the big scanner screens suspended in the middle of the hall.

The screens would come to life only on particular occasions – when what they awaited entered the area of space on which they were always focused. When that happened – if it happened – there would be a rush for the spaceport and Migaa would be deserted again. Some people had been waiting in Migaa for over thirty years; others had died before their chance came.

The three climbed a narrow, winding stair until they reached a gallery occupied by a table and three chairs. They sat down.

'I had this reserved,' Asquiol said as he craned his neck to peer into the public hall.

Renark looked at him quizzically. 'I'm having the ship checked and re-checked,' he said. 'It's got to be ready very soon. The Shifter could materialise well before the maximum thirty-six hours I mentioned. Though it shouldn't be here for another twelve hours – judging by the rate it's been moving towards us since I contacted it twenty days ago.'

Renark paused, staring out across the terrible desert, screwing his eyes against the glare which penetrated even the darkened windows.

'We've got to be ready,' he said. 'I can't tell how long it will remain in this continuum. There's also the possibility that it will rip through the continuum at speed and we won't have a chance to get there before it travels on.'

'So we could have come to Migaa for nothing.' Talfryn shrugged. 'Well, my time's my own.'

'Mine isn't.' Renark did not expand on that remark.

He was the only man in the entire galaxy capable of knowing when the Shifter System would materialise. Others who came to Migaa took the chance that the bizarre, continuum-travelling system would appear in the space-time during their own life, but it was a gamble. This was the only reason Migaa existed, built on the nearest halfway habitable planet to where the Shifter would materialise. So the outlawed and the damned, the searching and the hunted came to Migaa when there was nowhere else to go. And they waited.

Renark knew he did not need to wait, for he was a Guide Senser with a peculiar instinct, developed to the level of a science. He could locate, given only the vaguest direction and description, anything in the galaxy, whether it was a planet or a lost penny.

Needing no maps or co-ordinates, he could lead a person anywhere they wanted to go. He was a human direction-finder, and because of this he knew the Shifter was coming closer, for he had trained himself to see *past* his own space and out into other dimensions lying beyond, where there seemed to be hazy ghosts of planets and suns almost, but not quite, like his own, each one replicating itself, level upon level, and each replica slightly different to the last, into infinity.

He had trained himself to see them, to prove a theory concerning the nature of the weird Shifter System which had been known to materialise – just suddenly *appear* in space and then vanish again without trace – only five times since mankind had reached the Rim.

Little else was generally known about it.

The few explorers and scientists who had managed to reach the Shifter before it vanished again had not returned. It was impossible to say how long it would stay at any one time. The mystery system seemed to have a wildly erratic orbit, and Renark's theory that it moved on a course different from the rest of the universe – a kind of *sideways* movement – had been postulated years before when, as Warden of the Rim Worlds, he had been given the responsibility of sensing it – as he sensed the worlds and suns within his own continuum.

The time of the Shifter's stay varied between a few hours and a few days. It was never certain when it would appear or disappear. The desperate men who came to Migaa were optimists, hoping against hope that they would have the luck to be there when the Shifter arrived.

Though the Shifter received its title from Count Renark's own theory, it had several other names – Ghost Worlds was a popular one – and certain religious-minded people ascribed some more dramatic significance to the system, declaiming that it had been cast from the universe for some sin its inhabitants had committed. These fanatics also had a name for the system – the Sundered Worlds.

And so a whole framework of myth had developed around the system, but very few dared investigate it for fear of being stranded. For the most part only criminals were willing to take the risk.

Count Renark stared down at the seething public hall. The Galactic Union's government machinery was near-perfect, its institutions difficult to abuse. This meant they could guarantee a greater degree of personal freedom for their citizens. But, because the government worked so well, criminals were hard put to escape the Union's laws. Migaa was their only hope. From Migaa they had the chance of escaping right out of the universe – unless the Galactic Police – the Geepees – made one of their sudden swoops on the town. For the most part the Geepees were content to leave well alone, but sometimes they hunted a criminal when he possessed some particular item or piece of information which they wanted. Then, if he eluded them long enough, they would come to Migaa looking for him.

Count Renark knew the Council sought him, that Musef Mordan, Captain in Chief of the Galactic Police, had his men scouring the galaxy for him. He wondered how long it would be before Mordan thought of Migaa.

Asquiol put his head in his hands and stared at Renark. 'Isn't it time we had your reasons for this trip, Renark?' He turned his head and searched among the crowd below. 'What made you quit your position as Rim Warden? Why wouldn't you tell the Council what you learned from that mysterious spaceship which landed on Golund three years ago? And why the passion to visit the Shifter?'

'I don't want to answer yet,' Renark told him. 'In fairness I should, but if I did it would give rise to further questions I can't possibly answer yet. All I can tell you right now is what you've guessed – I've been waiting three years to get to the Shifter, ever since I learned something of great importance from the crew of that spaceship on Golund. Indirectly what they told me caused me to resign as Warden. As for the answers I don't have – I hope the Shifter will give me them.'

'We're your friends, Renark,' Talfryn said, 'and we're willing to go with you for that reason alone. But if you don't find the answers you want out there, will you answer the original questions?'

'There'll be nothing to lose if I do,' Renark agreed. 'But if you decide you don't want to come, then say so now. It's dangerous, we know that much. We might perish before we even reach the Shifter, and once there we may never be able to return.'

Both men moved uncomfortably but said nothing.

Renark continued: 'I owe you both debts of friendship. You, Paul, helped me in my research on variable time flows and were responsible finally for crystallising my theory. Asquiol saved me from the attentions of that police patrol on Pompeii, sheltered me for six months and, when the Council found out, was forced, under the terms of his agreement, to give up his birthright. You have both made big sacrifices on my behalf.'

'I'm curious enough, anyway, to explore the Ghost Worlds,' smiled Talfryn, 'and Asquiol has nothing to keep him here unless it's his new-found attraction for Willow Kovacs.'

Willow owned the Salvation Inn. She was reputed to be beautiful.

Asquiol appeared displeased, but he only shrugged and smiled faintly. 'You're right, Talfryn – if tactless. But don't worry, I'll still go when the time comes.'

'Good,' said Renark.

A woman came up the narrow stair leading to the gallery.

She moved in full knowledge of her slim beauty and her lips were curved in a soft smile. She was wearing the spoils of her conquests – her emerald-coloured dress was covered with jewels mined on a thousand planets. They flashed brightly, challenging the very brilliance of the desert. Her hands, heavy with rings, held a tray of hot food.

As she reached the table, Asquiol looked up at her and took the tray, making sure he touched her hands as he did so.

'Thanks,' she said. 'And hello – you must be the famous Warden Renark von Bek.'

'Ex-Warden,' he said. 'And you're the young woman who has so disturbed our proud friend here.'

She didn't reply to that.

'Eat well, gentlemen,' she said, then returned down the staircase. 'We'll meet later, Asquiol,' she called over her shoulder as she made her way across the crowded floor of the great tavern.

Count Renark felt slightly troubled by this new intrusion. He hadn't been prepared for it. Although his loyalty to both his friends was great, he wanted Asquiol on the trip much more than he wanted Talfryn.

Asquiol was young, reckless, inclined to vindictive acts of cruelty at times; he was arrogant and selfish and yet he had a core of integrated strength which was hard to equate with his outward appearance.

But a woman. A woman could either complement that strength or destroy it. And Renark wasn't sure about Willow Kovacs.

Philosophically, and for the moment, Renark accepted the situation and turned his mind to the problem in hand.

'I think we should give the ship another check,' he suggested when they had eaten. 'Shall we go out to the pads now?'

Talfryn agreed, but Asquiol said: 'I'll stay here. I'll either join you out there or see you when you return. How long will you be?'

'I've no idea,' Renark said, rising. 'But stay here so that we can contact you if necessary.'

Asquiol nodded. 'Don't worry – I wasn't thinking of leaving the inn.'

Renark restrained an urge to tell Asquiol to be wary, but the Guide Senser respected his friend. It was up to the Prince of Pompeii to conduct his own affairs without advice.

Renark and Talfryn walked down the stairs, pushed their way through the throng and made for the door.

Outside there was a buzz of excited conversation. The two men caught some of it as they walked along the metal-paved streets.

'It seems there's a rumour that the Geepees are on their way in,' Talfryn said worriedly.

Renark's face was grim. 'Let's hope they don't get here before the Shifter.'

Talfryn glanced at him. 'Are they after you?'

'They've been after me for two years. Oh, it's not for any crime. But the Council came to the conclusion that I might know something of use to them and have been trying to get hold of me.'

'And do you know something of use to them?'

'I know something,' Renark nodded, 'but it's in their interest and mine that they don't find out about it.'

'That's part of your secret?'

'Part of the secret,' Renark agreed. 'Don't worry – if we reach the Shifter, I'll let you know it, for better or worse.'

He let his mind reach out into the void beyond the Rim. It was out there, coming closer. He could sense it. His mind trembled. He felt physically sick.

It was so wrong – *wrong*!

Implacably, the impossible system was shifting in. Would it stay long enough for them to get to it? And could they reach it? If only he knew a little more about it. It was a big gamble he was taking and there was just a slim chance of it paying off.

Only he knew what was at stake. That knowledge was a burden he had had to strengthen himself to bear. Most men could not have begun to bear such a burden.

As he walked along, glancing at the wretches who had so hope-fully come to Migaa, he wondered if it was worth the attempt after all. But he shrugged to himself. You had to accept that it was worth it, he told himself, and act on the understanding.

There were none there who might have been properly described as extraterrestrials. One of the discoveries humans had made when settling the galaxy was that they represented the only highly developed, intelligent life form. There were other types of animal life, but Earth, throughout the galaxy, had been the only planet to bear a beast that could reason and invent. This was an accepted thing among most people, but philosophers still won-dered and marvelled and there were many theories to explain the fact.

Two years previously Renark had suddenly resigned from his position as Warden of the Rim Worlds. It had been an important position and his resignation had given rise to speculation and gos-sip. The visit of an alien spaceship, supposedly an intergalactic craft, had not been admitted by the Galactic Council. When pressed for information they had replied ambiguously. Only Renark had seen the aliens, spent much time with them.

He had given no explanation to the Council and even now they still sought him out, trying to persuade him to take over a job which he had done responsibly and imaginatively. Space Sensers were rare, rarer even than other psi-talents – and a Guide Senser of Renark's stature was that much rarer. There were only a few G.S.s in the entire galaxy and their talents were in demand. For the most part they acted as pilots and guides on difficult runs through hyperspace, keeping, as it were, an anchor to the main-land and giving ships exact directions how, where and when to enter normal space. They were also employed on mapping the galaxy and any changes which occurred in it. They were invalu-able to a complicated, galaxy-travelling civilisation.

So the Council had begged Renark to remain Warden of the Rim even if he would not tell them who the visitors to Golund had been. But he had refused, and two years had been spent in collecting a special knowledge of what little information was known about the Shifter. In the end they had resorted to sending the Geepees after him, but with the help of Talfryn and Asquiol he had so far evaded them. He prayed they wouldn't come to Migaa before the Shifter materialised.

Renark had fitted his ship with the best equipment and instruments available. This equipment, in his eyes, included the dynamic, if erratic, Asquiol and the easy-going Paul Talfryn.

Several hundred ships were clustered in the spaceport. Many had been there for years, some for a century or more, their original owners having died, disappointed and frustrated, never having achieved their goal.

Renark's great spacer was a converted Police Cruiser which he had bought cheaply and illegally, rebuilt and re-equipped. It could be ready for take-off in half a minute. It was also heavily armed. It was against the law to own a police ship or to own an armed private vessel. The Union owned and leased all commercial craft.

The spacer required no crew. It was fully autosentient and had room for thirty passengers. Already, since landing, Renark had been pestered by people offering huge sums to guarantee them passage to the Shifter, but he had refused. Renark had little sympathy for most of those who gathered in Migaa. They would have received more mercy from the enlightened Legal Code, of which the Union was justly proud, than from Renark of the Rim.

Although Migaa itself was thick with criminals of all kinds, there were few in relation to the huge human population of the galaxy. For nearly two centuries the galaxy had been completely at peace, although the price of peace had, in the past, been a rigid and authoritarian rule which, in the last century, had thawed into the quasi-anarcho-socialist system which now served the galaxy.

Renark had no hatred for the Union which pestered him. He had served it loyally until he had acquired that certain knowledge which he had withheld from the Galactic Council. They had asked many times for the information he possessed, but he had refused; and he was cautious, also, never to let his whereabouts be known.

He glanced up into the blazing white sky as if expecting to see a Geepee patrol falling down upon them.

Slowly, the two men walked across the pad towards the cruiser.

Mechanics were at work on Renark's ship. They had long since completed their initial check and found the ship completely space-worthy. But Renark had not been satisfied. Now they checked again. Renark and Talfryn entered the elevator and it took them into the centre of the ship, to the control cabin.

Talfryn looked admiringly around the well-equipped cabin. He had the scientist's eye that could appreciate the ingenuity, the skill, the energy, the pure passion which had gone into its construction.

Once, a year ago, Renark had said in a talkative moment: 'Take note of these instruments, Talfryn – they represent our salvation. They represent the power of the mind to supersede the limitations of its environment, the power of every individual to control, for the first time, their own destiny.'

Renark hadn't been referring to his own particular instruments and Talfryn knew that.

Now, Talfryn thought, the mystique attached to science had made it at once a monster and a salvation. People believed it capable of anything, because they had no idea any more what it was. And they tended to think the worst of it. More men like Renark were needed – men who could not take the simple workings of a turbine for granted, yet, at the same time, could accept the whole realm of science.

Just then another thought occurred to Talfryn – a thought more immediately applicable to their present situation. He said: 'How do we know that our drive – or any of our other instruments – will work in the Shifter, Renark?' He paused, looking around him at the tall, heaped banks of instruments. 'If, as you think might be possible, different laws of space and time apply, then we may find ourselves completely stranded in the Shifter's area of space – cut adrift without control over the ship.'

'I admit we don't know whether our instruments will work out there,' Renark agreed, 'but I'm prepared to risk the chance that we share certain laws with the Shifter. Maybe I'll be able to tell when it's closer, but my judgement won't be infallible.'

As a Space Senser, Renark needed no equipment to heighten his powers, but he did need to concentrate, and he therefore used an energy-charger, a machine which replaced natural, nervous and mental energy as it was expended. It was equipment normally only issued to hospitals.

Now, as Talfryn studied the recordings which had been made of the Shifter and became increasingly puzzled, Renark got into a comfortably padded chair and attached electrodes to his forehead, his chest and other parts of his body. He held a stylus and a writing screen on the small ledge in front of him.

Calmly, he switched on the machine.

Chapter Two

R ENARK CONCENTRATED ALL his powers.
  He could feel the presence of the galaxy, spreading inwards from his own point in space; layer upon layer of it, time upon time, scale upon scale.

He was aware of the galaxy as a whole and at the same time felt the presence of each individual atom in its structure – each atom, each planet, each star, each nova, each nebula, each spiral. Through space, where matter was of minimum density, little cores of denser matter moved. Spaceships.

Faintly, beyond the limits of his own galaxy, he sensed the lesser density of intergalactic space, and beyond that he picked up faraway impressions of other galaxies.

There was something unpleasant happening out there – something he already knew about. Something he was pledged to challenge.

Then he adjusted his mind so that, instead of sensing the components of the galaxy, he sensed it as a whole. He widened his reception to take in a small area beyond the galaxy and immediately the entire structure of time and space, as he knew it, was flawed.

There was something there that was alien – something that did not fit. It was as if a body had moved through that small area and had torn a hole in the very fabric of the universe. His mind and body trembled as he sought to adjust to this new, unnatural factor. It was a binary star with eleven planets equidistantly encircling it.

It did not exist. Not in relation to the universe Renark knew. As yet, he could make no close assessment of its components. It was wrong! Renark controlled his mind against the thought and concentrated on judging the system's progress. It was, in relation to itself, travelling through space in the same manner as ordinary stars and planets travelled. But it also travelled through a series of dimensions of which

Renark had no experience whatsoever. And its course, its orbit through the dimensions, was bringing it closer to Renark's own continuum.

He opened his eyes, gasping.

Quickly, he jotted down an equation; closed his eyes and read-justed his mind.

It continued towards them. It shifted through myriad alien dimensions, moving through a whole series of continua, progressing imperturbably onwards in an orbit as constant as the orbits of its planets about its stars. Soon now it would be passing through Renark's own space-time.

But how long would it stay there? Renark could not tell without knowing a little of the universes which lay beyond his own – and of these he had much to find out. His future plans depended on it.

In less than twenty minutes, Renark was finished. He looked over Talfryn's shoulder at the records. 'She's coming closer,' he said. 'In twelve to fifteen hours she'll be here. That's if my calculations are right. I think they are. As far as I can tell, she's travelling at a regular rate. I can't explain why the periods spent in this continuum have varied so much, though, if her speed is as constant as it seems to be.'

'Well, you've narrowed it, anyway.' Talfryn's body seemed to tense.

'Yes.' Renark moved about the control room reading displays.

'And you're certain it won't miss this space-time altogether?'

'That's possible – but unlikely.'

Count Renark stared at a bank of gauges for a moment and then he moved towards a chrome-and-velvet chair which had a whole bank of manual levers and switches in front of it, a laser-screen above it. This was the gunnery control panel.

Again he began to move uneasily about the great cabin. Again he volunteered a suggestion.

'We don't know all the directions in which our own universe moves,' he said. 'It may also, for all we know, have a "sideways" movement through the dimensions at an angle different from the Shifter. This would explain to some extent any inconsistency in the length of time the system stays in our space-time continuum.'

Talfryn shook his head. 'I've never been able to grasp any of those theories about the system. I don't even understand your ability to sense its approach. I know that, with training, Space Sensers can locate planets and even smaller bodies in normal space-time, but I wasn't aware that they could sense things outside, beyond, in different dimensions – wherever it is.'

'Normally they can't,' Renark said, 'but many who have probed the perimeter of space outside the galaxy have mentioned that they have sensed something else, something not in keeping with any recognised natural laws. Others have had the illusion of sensing suns and worlds within the galaxy – where suns and worlds just can't be! This has given rise to the theory of the "multiverse", the multi-dimensional universe containing dozens of different universes, separated from each other by unknown dimensions…'

He paused. How could he explain in calm, logical words the sense of apartness, of alienness, he had received? How could he describe that shock, that experience which contradicted all he accepted with every sense he possessed, something that struck at the id, the ego, the emotions – everything?

He opened his mouth, trying to find words. But the words did not exist. The nearest way of expressing what he felt was to give vent to a shout of horror, agony – triumph. He didn't feel inclined to try.

So he shut his mouth and continued to pace the cabin, running his ugly hand over the firing arm of the big anti-neutron gun which had never been used. It was a savage weapon and he hoped it would never be needed.

Nuclear weapons of any sort made him uncomfortable. His strange sixth sense was as aware of the disruption of atoms as it was of their presence in natural state. It was an experience close to agony to sense the disruptive blast of atomic weapons. The anti-neutron cannon, beaming particles of anti-matter, was an even more terrible experience for him.

Once, as a child, he had been close to the area of a multi-megaton bomb explosion and his whole mind had blanked out under the strain of the experience. It had taken doctors a year to pull him back to sanity. Now he was stronger, better co-ordinated – but it was still not pleasant to be in a space fight.

Also, he loathed violence. It was the easy way out and, like many easy ways out, not a way out at all but only continuation of a vicious circle. So whenever possible he avoided it.

However, he was prepared, in this case, to use it – if it meant using it against anything in the Shifter which attempted to stop him in his avowed objective.

Renark had geared himself to drive towards one aim, and one only. Already he was driving towards it and nothing – nobody – would stop him. He was dedicated, he was fanatical – but he was going to get results if that was possible. If it wasn't possible, then he'd die trying to make it possible.

Soon, now – very soon – the Shifter would enter their area of space. He was going there. The Shifter offered the only chance in the universe of supplying him with the information he needed.

He glanced back at Talfryn, who was still studying the records. 'Any clearer?' he asked.

Talfryn shook his head and grinned. 'I can just understand how the Shifter orbits through dimensions hitherto unknown to us, in the same way as we orbit through time and space, but the implications are too big for me. I'm bewildered. I'm no physicist.'

'Neither am I,' Renark pointed out. 'If I were I might not be so affected by the Shifter. For instance, there's something peculiar about any system comprising a G-type binary star and eleven planets all equidistant from it – something almost artificial. If it is artificial – how did it happen?'

'Maybe it's the other way about,' Talfryn suggested vaguely. 'Maybe the planets all being the same distance away from the parent suns has something to do with the peculiar nature of the system. If they are a natural freak, could this have caused the Shifter's orbit?'

Renark nodded. He thought for a moment before he said: 'If you take for granted that Time is cyclic in accordance with the other known laws of the universe – although, as you well know, my own experiments seem to prove that there is more than one particular time flow operating in our own universe – if you take that for granted, however, we can describe the rest by means of circles.'

He walked to the chair where he had left his stylus and pad, picked them up and moved over the chart table.

'The Shifter orbits this way –' he drew a circle – 'whereas we progress this way.' He drew a half-circle cutting horizontally through the first circle.

'Imagine that we have a finite number of space-time continua, each with some mutually shared laws.' He drew a number of other half-circles below and above the first. 'They're all, like us, travelling this way. There is no contact between us but we exist side by side without being aware of each other's presence, all revolving in different sets of dimensions.'

Talfryn nodded.

'Imagine that the normal continua, as we understand the word normal, are orbiting horizontally, as it were. Then imagine that the Shifter is orbiting *vertically*. Therefore, instead of going its way without ever touching other alternate universes, its course takes it *through* them.

'But wouldn't it take millions of years to complete a cycle like that?'

'Not necessarily. We know it doesn't, because we can't use temporal and spacial values and apply them to something as different as the Shifter. It has rules of its own which seem chaotic to us but are probably as ordered in relation to itself as ours are to us.'

'You've got to take quite a bit for granted,' Talfryn sighed.

'Our scientists have been doing extensive research into the "multiverse" theory. They're pretty convinced.'

'Life and the universe,' said Talfryn, seating himself in a chair, 'are getting too complicated.'

Renark laughed shortly. 'One thing's clear, Talfryn – there are going to be a lot of mysteries solved and a lot of new ones started when we reach the Shifter. No-one has ever returned from it.'

He glanced up suddenly. A light was blinking on the control panel.

'That's the intercom,' he said. 'Might be Asquiol or one of the engineers. Could you deal with it, Paul?'

Talfryn walked over and picked up the instrument. He murmured a command but no picture appeared on the screen. He listened briefly and then turned back to regard Renark. 'Asquiol's here – and he's brought that girl with him.'

'What?' Renark for a moment lost his equilibrium. 'Why?'

'That's the other thing – that's why they came here so fast. The Geepees have arrived – they're looking for you!'

Renark pursed his lips. He should have been ready for a police raid but he had been too busy explaining the Shifter to Talfryn.

Asquiol and Willow Kovacs stepped out of the elevator.

Asquiol said nervously: 'Sorry about this, Renark – but these are my terms.'

Renark shrugged. 'Terms?' He leaned over the control panel adjusting dials. 'What's happening out there?'

'The Geepees are scouring Migaa asking if you're there. I got out as fast as I could. They'd be likely to recognise me and connect me with you.'

'Good.'

'You're willing to have Willow along on the trip?'

'You've told her the risks?'

'Yes.

Renark sighed. 'I thought this might happen – knowing you. But I want you with us.'

Renark forced away his irritation. There was no room for petty emotions in his plans. Only he knew what hung on his reaching the Shifter and discovering its nature and its cause. Matters of personalities could not be considered. Action, not argument, was required of him now.

He had to pray that the Geepees wouldn't discover him before the Shifter materialised. They'd have to sit tight and wait it out. With any luck the Geepees wouldn't make a search of the ships on the pads until after they had scoured the town.

Renark beamed a message to the engineers, telling them to

clear away their equipment and leave the ship in readiness for take-off.

Then he sat in his chair and waited.

An hour passed.

Willow seemed uncomfortable, sitting there in her immaculate sheath dress, listening to the men talking and going over the equations Count Renark had made, the records of the Shifter, theories which had been put forward.

Count Renark said: 'Rumour has it that *this* planet has a large human colony. I think we should head for that – number eight by my reckoning. You can see I've marked it.'

He glanced at Willow, who appeared pensive and moved nervously on her seat. Normally nothing could break her self-contained attitude – an attitude that had been necessary in a town like Migaa. But here, for the first time, she was in the company of those even more self-contained than she was. And it disquieted her.

At last Asquiol saw her discomfort and said half-apologetically: 'Anything troubling you?'

She smiled without amusement, then, shrugging, she left the control room.

Willow had always been curious about the Ghost Worlds, living as she had in their shadow all her life. But she had never seen them. For some reason the Ghost Worlds had allowed her to dominate all the many men in her life, for they had seemed to have a hunger which she could not satisfy – though they had sought in her that satisfaction and had, therefore, put themselves in her power, thinking she had a secret she did not, in fact, possess.

Now she was going to the Shifter... on Asquiol's instigation. She was glad. These men, all three, offered her something she was unused to. A strength of character, perhaps, that she had never found in all the others who had come to Migaa, a peculiar mixture of detachment and passion. She had acted impulsively, however, and was now not sure she wished to go with them. She wondered if what she felt was called 'fear'.

Looking up from the charts, Talfryn glanced at the scanner screen. He swore and moved towards the controls.

'Something's gone wrong with the V-screen. I'll try and...'

'Don't touch those controls!'

Renark's brain seemed to swell within his skull, excitement pulsing through him, his body pounding. He paused for a second, frowned, controlled himself and then said calmly: 'It's coming, Talfryn.'

He sent his mind out, probing. He felt the sudden presence of the alien system grow as it merged into his own space-time – a whole system plunging towards them out of the hazy twilight of the universe, rupturing time and space on its rogue orbit. Elation flooded through him as he ran towards the V.

The other two stood close behind him.

He watched as visible lines of energy swept across the area of space where his calculations indicated the Shifter would appear.

Space seemed to peel back on itself. Great, blossoming splashes of colour poured through as if from the broken sides of a vat, merging with the darkness of space and making it iridescent so that sections shone like brass and others like silver, gold or rubies, the whole thing changing, changing constantly, erupting, flickering, vanishing, reappearing, patterns forming and re-forming.

Then, faintly at first, as if through rolling, multicoloured clouds, the Shifter itself began to materialise, coming into sharper focus.

And then it was hanging there, as solid as anything else in the universe, the clouds which had heralded its approach fading away. A new system had joined the galaxy.

But for how long, Renark wondered, would the eleven planets hang, equidistant, around the blazing blue binary star?

He rushed back to the control panel, pressed a single stud activating the ship's automatic circuits.

The ship lifted. It shrieked away from the spaceport, away from the Geepee vessels, and within minutes was in deep space straining towards the Shifter.

Moving to a single-minded, pre-arranged pattern, Renark acted like a zombie, his eyes fixed on the weird system ahead, his body one with the streaking ship which leapt the space between the edge of the galaxy and the mystery worlds.

Willow came out, startled, saw the screen and began to tremble.

Asquiol looked at her, but she glanced away and hurried back to the passenger accommodation.

Renark seated himself in the pilot's chair, his arms stretched over the complicated control board, checking every slight tendency for the ship to veer away from the Shifter.

At this distance the planets seemed, apart from their ordered positions around the suns, to be no different from any other system in the galaxy.

Yet they glowed like carefully set diamonds around the sapphire suns. The ship sped closer and Renark could observe the rotation of the planets around the twin star. They appeared to be moving very slowly. Yet the closer they came the faster the planets seemed to move.

The other two had taken their places. The ship's drive, buried in the core of the ship, could be heard now, humming with the strain.

Renark shouted: 'Talfryn, keep all communication equipment on *Receive*. Asquiol, don't use those guns at random – wait until I order you to, if it's necessary.'

He turned in his seat for a moment, stared at Asquiol. 'And don't, on any account, use the anti-neutron cannon.'

Asquiol grimaced.

Talfryn flipped switches.

Willow reappeared, bewildered by the suddenness of events. She was frustrated, wanting something to do. The men worked, with concentration and efficiency, to their pre-arranged plan. Asquiol was oblivious of her presence.

The planets came closer. There was something peculiar about several of them, particularly one at nadir-south-east of the binary.

As the Shifter got larger on the screen, the communications panel began to squeal and moan.

'We're picking up its static, anyway,' Talfryn commented.

'They must be panicking on Migaa,' Asquiol grinned. 'The quicker we move the less chance we've got of getting caught up with the mob when they come out.'

'They'll be fighting the Geepees right now,' Renark said. 'They won't even let a fleet of battlewagons stop them reaching the Shifter after waiting so long.'

'That'll delay both sides for a while,' Asquiol said.

'Let's hope the delay will be a long one.' Renark stared at his screen. 'What's ahead of us to starboard, Talfryn? Looks like a small fleet of some sort.'

Talfryn moved dials. 'You're right. Spaceships. A kind I don't recognise. We'd better head for the nearest planet and try to escape them. They don't look friendly.'

The twin star was very close and bright now, blacking out the planets on Renark's laser-screen.

Asquiol broke the energy seals on the guns with the key Renark handed him.

About ten of the weird ships came jolting closer, the metal of their hulls giving off a peculiar, yellowish glint. They pulsed through space and there was something menacing in their approach. Then they veered away, describing a long curve, and began to circle the area through which Renark's cruiser would have to pass.

Then, with a jerk which ripped at their nerves and muscles and threatened to turn their bodies inside out, they entered alien space. They were in the Shifter's territory now. That was why the other ships had come no further, but awaited them. Their minds blanked momentarily. They felt dizzy, sick. Renark, his senses going, sent out a desperate tendril of mental energy, anchoring himself to the Shifter ahead. He felt the presence of the darting alien ships. The metal of their construction was unfamiliar to him.

Then, suddenly, his whole mind seemed to explode as the fabric of space was ripped apart.

He gasped with the agony, forced his eyes open. He looked at the screen, and the planets, no longer whirling so rapidly around the binary, were moving at a more leisurely pace.

An inhuman growl rumbled through the control room. Talfryn worked the receiver, trying to pick up a picture, but couldn't. The growl came again but the language was unrecognisable. The leading vessel of the yellow fleet moved.

It seemed to turn over on itself, described a couple of somersaults, and then sent a coiling blast of energy before the humans' ship.

Renark blocked his mind and tensed his body. 'Screens!' he yelled.

But Asquiol had already raised them.

The ship shuddered and the screens proved effective against the alien weapons – but only just. Asquiol aimed the energy-laden guns on the leading ship.

'The anti-neutron cannon would dispose of them quickly enough,' he said wistfully.

'And probably the system as well,' Talfryn added as Asquiol's rapid shots bit into the alien ship, and it exploded to form, almost immediately, nothing more than a ball of ragged metal.

Now the other ships came on in formation. But Asquiol bent over his guns and grimly pressed his fingers down on all studs. The ship took the enemy retaliation, but shuddered horribly. His own fire damaged two, which spiralled away from their comrades.

Then the whole fleet sailed up in the strange, somersaulting motion and fired together.

'We can't take this attack!' Talfryn screamed.

Asquiol's eyes were intent on the enemy craft. He sent another great blast of energy slamming through space as the force of the joint attack hit the cruiser.

The ship shook, shuddered, groaned and came to a dead stop. Lazily it began to spiral through space while more of the alien ships came flooding up from the nearest planet. Asquiol did what he could to halt them, but with the ship out of control it was difficult to aim.

Renark was fighting the controls.

'We took it,' he shouted, 'but it's thrown our circuits crazy. Talfryn, get down there and see what you can do with the Master Co-ordinator!'

Talfryn scuttled from his seat and entered the elevator, dragging a spacesuit with him.

Asquiol, eyes narrowed, aimed his guns carefully, cursing.

He cut down several more. But these ships didn't seem to care whether they were destroyed or not. Momentarily Asquiol wondered if they had living crews aboard.

Something was wrong with the quality of the void. It did not have its normal sharpness. Rivers of colour, very faint, seemed to run through, and shapes seemed to move just beyond the limit of his vision. It was tantalising, it was maddening...

Willow, pale and tense, clung to a bulkhead, her eyes fixed on the big laser-screen. Space was alive with boiling energy. It swirled and coiled and lashed through the disturbed vacuum. To her, it was as if the binary had suddenly gone nova, for she could not see through the multicoloured patterns of force which obscured everything but the yellow, darting shapes of the enemy ships.

Slowly the patterns faded, but the alien vessels came on.

Renark realised that the hideous nature of the void was not created by the force released in the battle. It was something else. Something much more ominous.

Asquiol kept up a rapid continuous fire. The screens took the brunt of the energy, but suddenly the ship was agonisingly hot.

Renark spoke into his PV. 'Talfryn, are you down there now?'

Talfryn's worried voice groaned back to him. 'I'm doing what I can. With any luck I should have fixed up most of the masters in five minutes.'

'Do it sooner,' Renark ordered, 'or you'll be dead.'

What were these aliens? Why were they so savagely attacking a ship when they hadn't even bothered to discover whether it was friend or enemy?

They came on with implacable ferocity.

Asquiol's lean face ran with sweat. Willow was on the floor now, her eyes wide, still fixed on the screens.

'Get into a suit, Willow,' he shouted. 'Get into a suit!'

She staggered up and walked unsteadily towards the locker from which she had seen Talfryn take a suit. Slowly she opened it, hissing with pain as the metal burned her hand, struggled to release a suit and clamber into it, its fabric automatically adjusting to the shape of her body.

Renark pulled on heavy gauntlets. The controls were now too hot for him to manipulate with bare hands.

Again and again the alien craft somersaulted and sent charges of energy towards the ship.

Asquiol felt his skin blister as he returned the fire and had the satisfaction of seeing another three alien ships collapse into scrap.

Then Renark felt the ship responding again to the controls. Talfryn had fixed the Master Co-ordinator. He sent the ship veering away from the alien vessels. 'Vardy Dan!' he commanded in ship's pidgin.

Talfryn came rushing from the elevator, tearing off his helmet. He flung himself into his seat.

'Christ!' he shouted. 'More of them!'

Another fleet, larger than the one that had already attacked them, was coursing in to join the fight. As it got nearer, Talfryn noticed that the ships were not of the same design as the first fleet. In fact not one of these ships was of identical design. The weirdly assorted fleet fanned out – to engage not their ship but the enemy!

Pale rays stranded out and twined around the enemy craft, which vanished.

'By God, they're on our side!' Asquiol cried joyously as Renark eased his ship away from the area of the fight.

Suddenly a clear voice came over the speakers. It began giving directions. Talfryn moved the keys. 'I can't find the source,' he said. The voice, speaking their own language, although a slightly archaic version, began to repeat the directions in exactly the same tone as before – velocity, trajectory and so forth.

The ship was beginning to cool. The people inside relaxed somewhat.

'Don't bother finding the source,' Renark said. 'It sounds like a recording, anyway – an automatic instruction to visitors. We'll do as it says.'

Following the directions they found themselves shooting towards a rust planet – small, ominous. The ships which had aided them now surrounded them, a motley assortment, but fast enough to stay with Renark's speedy cruiser.

When they were on course, a new voice broke into the taped instruction recital.

'Welcome to Entropium. We saw that you were in trouble and sent help. Forgive us for not doing so earlier, but you were then beyond our boundaries. You put up a pretty good fight.'

'Thanks,' Asquiol said softly, 'but we could have done with that help sooner.' Except in rare instances, Asquiol was not a grateful young man.

'That was out of the question,' the voice said lightly. 'But you're all right now, barring accidents…'

They sped down into the glowing red shroud of the planet.

'… *barring accidents*…'

Again and again they went through the same action, unable to do anything, trapped into it, as if they were on a piece of film being run many times through a projector.

Every time they appeared to reach the planet's surface they found themselves heading through the red mist again.

Then they were in the mist and motionless, the voice speaking amusedly: 'Don't worry, this will probably last a short while.'

Exhausted as he was, Renark had to use his special space sense to get some kind of grip on the situation. But it was virtually impossible. One moment he felt the presence of the rust planet, the next it was gone and there was nothing in its place.

Several times they repeated their action of dropping down towards the surface until, quite suddenly, they were flashing through the fog and emerged into daylight – pinkish daylight – observing the jagged face of a sombre-coloured planet which, in its wild texture, was like a surrealist landscape painted by an insane degenerate.

Willow lay on the floor in her spacesuit, her eyes closed, and even the men fought to control their minds and emotions as they jarred and shuddered at the sight of the alien planet. It was unlike any other they had ever seen, unlike any planet in the galaxy they knew.

Why?

It wasn't simply the quality of the light, the texture of the surface. It was something that made them uncomfortable in their bones and their brain.

It seemed unsafe, insecure, as if about to collapse beneath them, to break up like a rotten melon.

'Follow the scarlet vessel,' said the voice on the intercom.

Then Asquiol, Willow and Talfryn had vanished and only Renark was in the ship moving down once again into the red fog of the planet.

Where were they?

Desperately he quested around him with his mind, but the madness of disordered space and time was all about him – a whirlpool of *wrongness*.

Talfryn reappeared.

Renark said: 'Where were you – what happened?' Then Willow reappeared, and Asquiol reappeared.

And suddenly they were back over the surface of the planet again.

'Follow that scarlet vessel,' the voice instructed.

This time they noted a sardonic quality. Asquiol smiled, sensing that out there was a fellow spirit, as malicious as himself.

Willow had been seriously affected by the phenomenon, particularly when she had found herself momentarily alone in the ship. How many ships had there been in those few moments?

The scarlet vessel was at the point of the phalanx of slim, round, squat or square spaceships surrounding them. It broke away from the main fleet and headed across the planet in a southwesterly direction. Renark turned his own ship after it. The scarlet vessel slowed and Renark adjusted his speed. There was a break and for a few seconds the ship travelled backwards, then lurched and was moving forwards again after the scarlet ship. Ahead of them now they could make out the towers of a city.

The whole situation was taking on the aspect of a confused nightmare. Whether it was illusion or some physical distortion of reality, Renark simply couldn't tell.

Even the outline of the city ahead did not remain constant but wavered and changed.

Perhaps, Renark guessed, these hallucinations or whatever they were, were the effect of adjusting to the different laws which applied to the Shifter System. Their senses had been thrown out of gear by the change and were having to adapt.

He hoped, for the sake of his mission, that he *could* adapt.

'Entropium,' said the voice on the laser.

The scarlet craft arched upwards until it was vertical over the planet, and began to shudder downwards on an invisible repulsion field. Renark followed its example.

Cautiously, he nursed the ship towards the ground, still not sure that the planet would not suddenly disappear from around them and they would be once again in the thick of battle with the alien ships. The experiences of the past half-hour had shattered his nerves, almost sapped his confidence.

They landed on a mile-square field which was bare but for a collection of small buildings at its far end.

'What now?' Willow said.

'We disembark – we got here comparatively safely and we were aided. They'd be unlikely to go to all the trouble they did if they wished us harm. Also I'm curious to find out about the people of "Entropium".' Renark pushed his big frame into a spacesuit and the others followed his example.

'What happened back there?' Talfryn said a trifle shakily.

'I should imagine we experienced some sort of space-time slip. We know nothing of this system to speak of. We must be prepared for anything and everything – we can't even be certain that actions we make here will have the results and implications they would have in normal space-time. We could, for instance, walk forward and discover that we were one step backwards, could jump and find ourselves buried in rock. Be careful, though – I doubt if anything as drastic as that will happen here, particularly since human beings seem to inhabit the world and have built a city here. But we must go warily.'

Chapter Three

THE SCARLET SPACECRAFT was the only other ship on what was obviously a landing field. They wondered where the rest of the fleet had gone. As they cautiously disembarked, they saw that the crew of the scarlet ship were doing the same. Some of the figures were human.

And, for the first time, they were seeing alien and obviously intelligent life forms.

Renark checked his wrist gauge. 'Looks as if we don't need suits,' he said, 'but it's just as well to be careful.'

He was tense as he walked across the charred ground towards the other group. He studied the aliens mingled with the human beings.

There were two sextupeds with four arms each and completely square heads containing a row of tiny eyes and beneath them a small mouth; several hopping creatures similar to kangaroos but obviously reptilian; a long-legged creature who towered over the others with a body proportionately smaller, a round body supporting long, swinging arm-tentacles and a round head.

The leader of the six human beings was young, smiling, fair and dressed in a style which had been out of fashion in the galaxy for two hundred years – a loose blue shirt, baggy trousers tucked into green gaiters, and with mauve pumps on his feet. Over the shirt was a pleated coat fanning out from his waist and dropping to his calves. His weapons included an unfamiliar pistol and a rifle slung over his shoulder. He swaggered.

'Move high, you load,' he said in a peculiar accent. 'How strong goes galaxy – same?'

'It's changed,' replied Renark, recognising in the youth's archaic slang a patois once used by the old CMG – the Criminal Musicians' Guild – which, two hundred years before, had been composed of men outlawed because they refused to play the specific kinds of music deemed 'healthy' by the music censors.

But, two hundred years ago, the Shifter had been unheard of and Migaa not settled. Renark was curious. He could understand that two centuries hadn't passed as far as the young man was concerned, the flow of time being different here. Yet there was something wrong.

'You're after me, aren't you?' the young man said. 'I blew the long note around two-twenty W.W. Three. You?'

'This is now four hundred and fifty-nine years after World War Three on Earth,' Renark said. 'We use a new reckoning, though. How did you get here? Mankind had only just reached the Rim when you were around.'

'Accident, com. We were on the run – chased by Geepee ships – ran straight here. Found strange mixture, man – I inform you – and everyone from future. You're the farthest into the future I've met. Kol Manage is my name. Let's go.'

'Go where?'

'Entropium.' He pointed at the city. 'Come on, it's a long blow.'

The city could be seen about two miles away, scarring the sky-line with a peculiar assortment of massive structures, some horribly ugly. But at least its outline now seemed firm and definite.

'Haven't you got ground transport?' Talfryn asked.

'Sometimes, com – not today. We scrap it all. Too square…'

'Why was that?'

'It palled, you know – we build something different sometime.'

Renark fumed inwardly. This casual attitude was aggravating when he needed clear, definite answers to the questions concerning him.

There was little time to lose. Now they were here he wanted to get started on his investigations. Yet the careless attitude of the Entropites threatened to slow him down, even though they didn't deliberately try to curtail him.

'Who runs the planet?' he asked Kol Manage as the group began to straggle towards the city.

'We all do. I guess you'd call Ragner Olesson boss. That's where we're going now – he wants to see you. He likes to see all newcomers.'

'Can't we get there faster? I'm in a hurry.'

'Well, stop hurrying, man – you've come to the end of the track. Ease up – there's nowhere to hurry to.'

'What do you mean?' Renark's tense mouth was grim.

'What do you think? You didn't like it there – you'll have to like it here. Simple.' And Kol Manage refused to answer any further questions.

They reached the suburbs of the city and were watched incuriously by some of the inhabitants, human and unhuman.

The population and the buildings comprised a disordered rabble which Renark found distasteful.

They walked through dirty streets which didn't seem to lead anywhere and it was nearly dark before they got to a square skyscraper, alive with light in its many windows.

The peculiar apathetic atmosphere of the city was as strong here as anywhere, but Renark hoped that at least some answers to his questions would be forthcoming. The atmosphere, he noted, was similar to Migaa's – only ten times worse.

The youth's companions dispersed but Manage led Renark and the others into the skyscraper and up a couple of flights of grubby stairs. They came to a door and Manage pushed it open.

The four people stayed uncertainly in the entrance to the big chamber, which was an untidy combination of control room and living quarters. Manage walked across it.

Two men looked up coolly at his approach. Both were middle-aged. One was rugged and handsome.

Renark glanced in distaste at the place. Computers and other equipment lined one wall of the room. The floor was littered with carpets of clashing designs, papers, clothing and various objects – a couple of rifles, a flower vase, cups, files and books. Tables, chairs and couches were placed here and there in apparent disorder. The two men sat on a long couch near the largest computer. A door behind them opened onto another room.

'Enter,' said the handsome man casually to the four. 'We watched you come in – you made the quickest start I've ever seen. The rest shouldn't be here for a little while yet.'

'They're probably having trouble with a police patrol,' Count Renark said, entering with a degree of caution.

'I'm Ragner Olesson,' said the big man. He looked hard at Renark, obviously seeing something unfamiliar in the Guide Senser's stern expression – perhaps, erroneously, sensing a rival to his leadership.

'Count Renark von Bek,' said the ex-Warden, 'these are my friends.' He didn't introduce them.

'Well, Count Renark, all you need to know is this. Don't try to change things here. We like it as it is. You can do what you want in Entropium, anything you want at all – but don't interfere with us.'

Renark frowned, feeling himself growing increasingly angry. This wasn't the reception he'd expected, and casualness and disorder of the kind he saw was annoying in his present frame of mind. His whole being was geared to one thing, one object.

He said: 'Are you the boss of Entropium?'

'If you like. But I don't push anyone around as long as they keep to themselves any ideas they've got of taking over or changing things radically. Get it?'

'Now, listen,' said Renark. 'I'm looking for information, that's all. Maybe you can help me.'

The man laughed, then sneered. He got up and swaggered closer to Renark, seeming a trifle agitated, however, as if Renark's statement was unprecedented.

'What kind of information, mister? We've got plenty of space to move around here, so go and look for it somewhere else. I don't like being disturbed. If you try to make troubles you can get off the planet –' he smiled sardonically – 'or get killed. Your choice.'

Controlling himself, Renark said calmly: 'So what's expected of us now?'

'Look, you do what you like – so long as you don't bother anyone. Right now you're bothering me.'

'Aren't you interested in why we're here? You helped us fight off the fleet that attacked us. Why did you do that?'

'You're here like everyone else who comes, because you don't like it where you came from. Right? We sent our fleet to help you because the more of us there are and the more ships we've got, the less chance the Thron – it was their ships that attacked you – have of invading us. Simple.'

'I'm here,' said Renark impatiently, 'to discover the nature of this system – what makes it work. I'm not a criminal on the run and I'm not just a casual explorer. The very future of humanity may well hang on what I discover or fail to discover here. Is that clear?'

Olesson's companion got up. He was an intelligent-looking man with a tired face. His whole attitude was one of weariness and boredom.

'I'm Klein – I used to be a scientist of sorts. You won't find out anything about the Shifter, my friend. There's no line of inquiry you can follow that leads anywhere. Every fact you uncover is a contradiction of anything you've learned previously.'

Renark's voice was savage. 'I'm going to force the truth out of this system, Mr Klein.'

His companions moved uncomfortably and Asquiol's slender right hand rested on the butt of his anti-neutron beamer. They were well aware that they were outnumbered here. They didn't feel Renark's anxiety and were therefore less ready to alienate their hosts.

But Klein smiled slightly, showing no annoyance. 'There have been many who've tried – and all failed. The concept is too alien for us to grasp, don't you understand? It isn't a question of your capacity for reasoning or anything else. Why not just accept the fact that you're safe from the cares of the universe – the multi-verse. Find yourself a niche and settle down. You can be quite comfortable here – nobody expects anything of you.'

'There must be *some* questions you can answer to give me a clue, a starting point?'

'Harry,' Olesson said impatiently, 'forget these bums, will you?

Let them do what they like so long as they stop worrying us. Let them make their "investigations". They won't get anywhere.'

'I'm easy,' Klein said to Renark, ignoring his companion. 'But there's not much I can tell you. What do you want to know?'

'For a start, tell me something about the Shifter as you know it from living on it.'

Klein shrugged and sighed. 'We pick up all kinds of intelligent life forms as we travel. Usually fugitives, sometimes explorers. They've settled on planets – if you can call it settled – that suit them best. Once on a planet, only a fool leaves it.'

'Why?'

'Because if the planets are wild, then space outside is wilder. A trip outside the atmosphere sends anyone quite mad. Why do you think nobody leaves the planets? Only the Thron are insane enough already to do it. You've seen it at its best – when it's been calmer. That's why we had to wait so long before sending out help – not many people dare to risk travelling in space most of the time. It's usually worse near the perimeter, too. You were lucky to get help at all.'

'What's wrong with it?'

'Nobody knows – but, most of the time, space out there is filled with chaos. Things appear and disappear, time becomes meaningless, the mind breaks…'

'But it wasn't too bad while we were coming here.'

'Sure. The Thron had something to do with that, I guess. They seem to know a bit more about controlling whatever it is.'

'Then, if that's so, there must be some means of discovering the real nature of the Shifter.'

'No. I reckon the Thron have just been lucky.' Klein stared with curiosity at Renark. 'What exactly do you want to know – and why?'

'That's my business.'

'You've got a bigger reason than mere curiosity. You said so. You tell me and maybe I'll decide to go on. If not, I don't want to bother. I want to see what you're leading up to.'

'You can tell us now, Renark, surely,' urged Talfryn. The ex-Warden sighed.

'All right. About three years ago I made contact with the crew of an intergalactic spaceship. Though it had come from another galaxy, it wasn't so very different from ours – and the crew was human. This in itself was astonishing. They had no knowledge of our history, just as we had none of theirs. They landed on Golund, a backwater planet under my jurisdiction. I went out to meet them. We learned one another's language and we talked. One of the things they told me was that, in their galaxy, human beings were the only intelligent life form.'

'Just like ours,' Klein nodded.

'And, I suspect, just like any other galaxy in our particular universe. Tell me, Klein, where do the aliens we've seen come from?'

'Different space-time continua. Every STC seems to have only one dominant, intelligent life form. I can't explain it.'

'It must mean something. That's what I suspected, anyway. A phenomenon natural to every STC universe. But what isn't happening, I hope, in every STC, is what is happening in our particular universe.'

'Happening?' Talfryn spoke.

'The visitors from the other galaxy came to warn us. Their news was so terrible that I had to keep it to myself. To have released it would have been to start galaxy-wide panic.'

'What the hell is happening?' Even Olesson became interested.

'The end of the universe,' Renark said.

'*What!*' Talfryn gasped.

'The end of the universe – so far as humanity's concerned, at any rate.'

'And the Gee-Council don't know?' Asquiol said. 'You didn't tell them – why?'

'Because I was counting on the Shifter to offer a clue that might save us.'

'Not just the end of a galaxy,' Klein said softly, 'but an entire universe. *Our* universe. How do you know, Renark?'

'The visitors gave me proof – my own space-sensing ability did the rest. I'm convinced. The universe has ceased to expand.'

'That's a problem?' Olesson said.

'Oh, yes – because, not only has it ceased expanding, it is now contracting. All matter is falling back to its source. All the galaxies are rapidly drawing together – and at a far greater speed than they expanded. And the speed increases as all matter is drawn back to the hub of our universe! Soon all the galaxies will exist as a single mote of matter in the vastness of space. Then even that mote may vanish, leaving – vacuum. So far this inward movement is restricted to the galaxies, but, soon, when they all come together, it will involve the stars, the planets – everything.'

'This is theory,' Klein spoke softly.

'Fact,' said Renark. 'My visitors' experiments are conclusive. They have tested the theory in their laboratories and found that when the matter has contracted as much as it can and it forms a pellet of astounding density it just disappears. They believe that when it reaches the final stage it enters other dimensions as a photon, possibly in some greater universe – the one encompassing the multiverse, itself, perhaps.'

'So it disappears – like the Shifter?'

'That's right.'

'I still don't know why you came here,' Klein said. 'Because it's safe? We *are* safe, aren't we?'

'I came here,' said Renark, more calmly now, 'in the hope of discovering a means of travelling into another universe.'

'You think because the Shifter travels through the multiverse that you can find out how it works and build some kind of machine that will do the same – is that it?' Klein seemed interested, even enthusiastic.

'That's it. If I can discover the Shifter's secret, I may be able to return to our universe. As a Guide Senser I could probably find it – and warn them of what's happening and offer them a means of escaping into a universe which isn't undergoing this change.

Olesson put in: 'Whatever happens, we're all right, eh?'

Renark nodded. 'Yes. But that doesn't appeal much to me.'

The others didn't reply. Although horrified, they also seemed relieved.

Renark sensed this. 'You're still with me?' he said to his friends.

'We've nothing to lose,' Talfryn said uncomfortably.

'Nothing,' agreed Asquiol.

The equipment beside them squealed. Olesson moved ponderously towards it, tuned in the receiver, got sound and a picture. 'Yes.'

The face on the screen said: 'More visitors, Ragnar – a big load from Migaa are coming in now.'

'The usual routine,' said Olesson, shutting off the receiver.

Chapter Four

RENARK AND HIS companions watched the screens as the shoals of craft from Migaa entered the Shifter's area of space.

Then the Thron ships came slashing upwards from their planet – like sharks. There was an insane, inexplicable anger in their ferocity.

From other directions a large, motley force of Entropium warships helped the Migaan craft dispose of the outnumbered Thron vessels. The fight was much shorter than Renark's.

'They're just in time,' commented Olesson, watching the screen. 'The system's due to begin transition again pretty soon. Better wave your universe goodbye, Renark. You won't be seeing it again for some time if at all.' He grinned callously.

Ignoring the big man, Renark turned to his friends.

'We'll have to split up. There must be people here who aren't just criminals – people who've made some attempt to explore or analyse the system. They can help us. Move about the city – ask questions.'

There was a peculiar note in Klein's voice. 'Go to see Mary the Maze, Renark. I can't guarantee she'll help, but she'll serve as a warning to you. She was an anthropologist, I hear. She explored as much of the Shifter as she was able. But go and see where her curiosity got her, Renark.'

'Where is she?'

'I'm not sure – but everyone knows her on Northside. You'll find her soon enough if you ask.'

'Okay, I will.' He said to the others: 'You take other parts of the city. Don't ignore any piece of information, speculation or rumour – it could all be useful. We've got to work fast!'

'But fast,' sneered Olesson as they left.

Walking out of the untidy building, they saw the bright arrows of fire searing down on the landing field two miles away. They split up.

Renark had chosen the worst possible time to look for anyone.

As he went from hotel to hotel, from bar to bar on the north side of Entropium, the men and women from Migaa began to pour exuberantly in.

They got drunk quickly and the whole city came alive and excited. Not only human beings celebrated the new 'shipment's' arrival. Aliens of many kinds joined in with their own forms of merrymaking.

Once, a creature like a giant cross between a slug and a caterpillar addressed him in high-pitched Terran, but he ignored it and moved on, searching, asking questions, getting incoherent or facetious replies.

And then the nightmare really began.

Quite suddenly Renark felt nausea flood through him, felt his vision blur and sent out a mind-probe which took in the whole of the system and part of the galaxy beyond it. His mind just refused to accept some of the information it received – he couldn't take it in.

The galaxy seemed distant, and yet retained the same point in space in relation to the Shifter.

Then the whole planet seemed suddenly engulfed by a weird, greyish mist. The darkness gave way to it.

For an instant, Renark thought he saw the buildings of the city begin to fade again. He felt weightless and had to cling to the side of a house. The house seemed solid enough, but its components moved beneath his hands and his own body seemed diffused, lacking its normal density. As his mind swirled, he returned it to the comforting reality of the galaxy, as he habitually did in times of stress. But the galaxy was no longer real.

It seemed ghostly, he was losing touch with it. He very nearly panicked, but controlled himself desperately.

Then he understood what was happening.

They were leaving the galaxy – leaving the universe Renark loved, that he was prepared to die for. He had an unreasoning sense of betrayal – as if the galaxy were leaving him rather than the reverse. He breathed heavily. He felt like a drowning man and sought for something to grab – physically and mentally. But there was nothing. Nothing constant. Nothing that did not change as he sensed or saw it.

The grey city seemed to tilt at an angle and he even felt himself sliding. He staggered on down the crazily angled street, his hands before him as if to ward off the maddening horror of all nature gone wrong.

The only thing he could cling to was abstract – something that could become disastrous reality – his reason for coming here. So he fought to remember that.

The trans-dimensional shift had begun. That was obvious.

Realisation had come to the newcomers in Entropium almost simultaneously. There were pockets of silence in a hundred taverns throughout the city.

Renark forced himself to keep moving. Movement was something – movement proved he still had some control over his body if not over the insane environment he had entered. But, as the realisation came, his legs slowed without his noticing. He had trained himself never to regret anything resulting from his conscious actions, but now he had to fight the emotion rising within him. The emotion came with the understanding that his chance of returning to his own universe before the Shifter's orbit brought it back again was low.

He could not afford to relax now until his mission was ended, could not afford to risk following up a wrong line of investigation, could not afford to think of anything but his ultimate reason for coming here.

The ground rose up like a tidal wave and as suddenly subsided again.

He pressed on. His intensity of thought was savage. He tore at his own mind, trying to force every extraneous thought, every piece of unnecessary information, out of it, to make himself into a calculating, acting machine with one object – to wrench the Shifter's secret from the chaotic turmoil of the trans-dimensional system.

He forgot the emotion momentarily engendered by the shift.

Light suddenly faded, bloomed again, faded. The buildings seemed to shimmer like a mirage, the very axis of the planet seeming to tilt once more, and Renark fell flat, clutching at ground which crawled beneath his hands.

He heard confused sounds of fright.

He looked up and, through the ghostly shapes that billowed ahead of him, saw the doorway of a tavern. He staggered up and moved towards it. Finally, he was inside, looking at the people there.

The newcomers were patently terrified, but the old residents seemed to be taking the planet's disordered behaviour with equanimity. They were evidently used to it. This must happen every time the system shifted into a new section of the multiverse.

Hoarsely, he said: 'Where do I find Mary the Maze?'

He repeated the question until a swarthy man looked up from his girl and his drink and said: 'Rupert House – two blocks that way.' He pointed with his thumb.

The planet was still doing crazy things. It still flickered with alternate night and day; the ground seemed alive, liquid, crawling. But Renark pushed on through the nightmare until he saw the sign saying Rupert House.

He opened a door that made his hand itch, and went inside. 'Mary the Maze?' he said thickly to the first man he saw.

The man, sharp-faced, small, dressed in black, said: 'Who wants her?'

'Renark wants her – where is she?'

The man stayed silent.

Renark grasped him. 'Where's Mary the Maze?'

'Let go – she's upstairs where she always is – room Red Seven.'

Renark, his head thumping, half-blind with the strain which the Shifter's transition was putting on his mind and metabolism, forced himself up several escalators and found the room he wanted.

He knocked. Then he opened the door.

Mary the Maze was a miserable sight. Beautiful, blank –

debased, in her mumbling insanity, to a travesty of ideal humanity.

Renark saw immediately that she had obviously been a highly intelligent woman. She was still physically beautiful, with a lean, clean face, large brown eyes, wide mouth, long black hair and full breasts. She had on only a dirty skirt and her fingers wandered across an intricate keyboard of the kind once used on the over-complicated sentient spaceships, popular a hundred years before, until scrapped for their tendency to have nervous breakdowns in emergencies. But there was only a keyboard – it was not connected to anything.

Renark's savage mood faded as he came softly into the little room, looked at its walls of bare plaster, the pilot's couch ripped from some ship and evidently used as a bed by the madwoman.

'Mary?' he said to the muttering wreck. 'Mary?'

She stared at him and the look in her eyes repelled him.

'Adam? Ah, no. Come in, Castor, but leave Pollux outside. Or is it Ruben Kave, Hero of Space, come to visit me?' Her mouth broadened, the lips curving upwards. She made a vague, graceful gesture with her hand. 'Do sit down,' she said. 'Are you Corum yet?'

There was nowhere to sit. He remained standing, disturbed, nonplussed.

'I'm Renark,' he said. 'I want information. It's important – can you help me?'

'Help…?' The voice was at first detached. Her fingers moved constantly over the keyboard. 'Help…?' Her face twisted. Then she screamed. '*Help!*'

He took a step forward.

The hands moved more swiftly, agitatedly over the board.

'*Help!*' She began to emit a kind of soft scream.

'Mary,' he said urgently. He could not touch the smooth shoulders. He leaned over the drooling woman. 'It's all right. They say you've explored the Shifter – is that true?'

'True? What's true, what's false?'

'What was it like, Mary? What did this to you?'

A groan, masculine and desperate, came from the woman. She stood up and walked unsteadily towards the couch, lay down on it, gripping the sides.

'What's the Shifter, Mary? What is it?' His face felt tight, as tight as his rigidly controlled emotions.

'Chaos...' she mumbled, 'madness – super-sanity – warmth. Oh, warmth... But I couldn't take it, no human being could – there's no anchor, nothing to recognise, nothing to cling to. It's a whirlpool of possibilities crowding around you, tossing you in all directions, tearing at you. I'm falling, I'm flying, I'm expanding, I'm contracting, I'm singing, I'm dumb – my body's gone, I can't reach it!'

Her eyes stared. Suddenly she looked at him with some sort of intelligence. 'Renark you said your name was?'

'Yes.' He was steeling himself to do something he didn't want to do.

'I saw you once, perhaps – there. Here. There.' She dropped her head back and lay on the couch mumbling.

He sensed the chaos of the Shifter brawling about in the back of his mind. He thought he knew how it could have turned her mad – felt some sympathy with what she was talking about.

He gave all his attention to her, using his sensing ability to sort her out into her composite atoms, concentrated on her sensory nerves and her brain structure in an effort to get some clue to the effect which the Shifter had had on her.

But there was little physically wrong, although it was obvious that the quantity of adrenaline flooding her system was abnormally high and that this, perhaps, was the reason for her almost constant movement.

But her mind wasn't open to Renark. He was not a telepath and was almost glad at that moment that he couldn't see into her wrenched-apart mind. Neither was he telekinetic, but nonetheless he hated even this form of intrusion as he studied her muscle responses, her nervous system, in an effort to find some clue how to pull her together long enough to get some answers to his questions.

He felt her move.

'Asquiol!' she said. 'Isn't that a name – something to do with you? Aren't you dead?'

How could she possibly know of Asquiol?

'Yes. Asquiol's the name of my friend. But I'm alive...'

He half-cursed the introduction of this new element of mystery in an already difficult situation. 'What about Asquiol?'

But there was no response from the madwoman, who had now resumed her vacant staring at the ceiling.

He tried another tack. 'Mary – where did you go? What did you discover?'

'The ragged planet,' she muttered. 'I go there – went there – last – the Lattice Planet. Stay away.'

Now he wanted to shake the information out of her but he had to coax.

'Why?' he said more gently. 'Why, Mary?'

'Doesn't travel with the Shifter – not all of it, some of it – exist in other dimensions, travelling independently? The Hole is there – the dwellers lurk in the Hole. They know everything – they mean no harm, but they are dangerous. They know the truth, and the truth is too much!'

'What truth?'

'I forget – I couldn't hold it. They told it to me. It wasn't fair.' She stared at him again and once more intelligence was in her eyes. 'Don't believe in justice, Renark – don't for an instant take its existence for granted. It doesn't exist. You learn that in the *gaps*, you can make it – but it breaks down in the real universe. You find that in the *gaps*.'

'Gaps? What are they?' He wondered at the peculiar accent she put on the word.

'The ragged planet's *gaps*.' She sighed and fidgeted on the couch. 'That's where I finally forgot – where every theory, every scrap of information gathered on the other planets was meaningless. And I forgot – but it did me no good. I was curious... I'm not now, but I want rest, peace, and I can't have it. It goes on. They know, though – they know, and their hate has kept them sane...'

'Who are "they", Mary?'

'The Thron – the horrible Thron. And the Shaarn know, too, but they are weak – they couldn't help me. The beasts. Don't let them push you into the… untime… the unspace. Their weapons are cruel. They do not kill. You grow lost.'

'Thank you, Mary,' Renark said, at a loss to help her. 'I will go to Thron.'

She rose from the couch, screaming: 'I said not, spiral, magenta, irri-bird, night. Not, sight of a droan – *not*: Oh, no…'

She began sobbing and Renark left the room.

He walked down the corridor, brooding, dissatisfied with the little he had learned, but now he had a definite plan of action. He must go to Thron and discover the truth of Mary's statement.

Whatever happened, the Thron would be of more help – assuming they could be encouraged to help – than the decadent inhabitants of Entropium, who refused to know anything. Though he could half-sympathise with anyone who didn't wonder or question. The boiling chaos of the Shifter as it moved through the dimensions of the multiverse was enough to disturb anyone.

He walked out of the hotel and found, to his relief, that the planet seemed to have quietened down and was presumably in normal space again, but in an alien universe.

As he walked swiftly towards the building, he allowed his mind to put out tendrils and was relieved when he sensed, beyond the insane perimeter of the Shifter, the solid, ordered planets and suns of a wide, spiral galaxy like his own in general components, although here and there he came across organic and chemical formations which he did not recognise.

When he got back to the control room in the skyscraper, Klein said: 'Half the new Migaa-load are dead. As usual, they panicked and caused trouble while we were in transit, so we cleaned them up. The rest are settling down or running back to the launching pads… How did you get on with Mary?'

'She said that the Thron knew about the Shifter's nature – or that's what I believe she said.'

Asquiol and Willow, both pale, walked in. He nodded to them.

'Were the Thron the race who initially attacked us?' he asked Klein.

Far away he heard ships blasting off. Klein cursed. 'They were warned. That's another lot on their way to death.'

'What do you mean?'

'Every time there are newcomers who try to use the Shifter as a transport from their own universe to another, we warn them that once they're here they're stuck. But they try. Maybe one or two make it – I don't know. But I think not. Something stops you leaving the Shifter once you're here.'

'It's impossible to get off?' Willow said worriedly.

Renark glanced at Willow. It was funny, he thought, how crisis took different people in different ways. Willow sounded as if she was going to break down. Asquiol evidently hadn't noticed it. He was curious to see how Talfryn would look and act when he came back.

Klein was talking. 'That's right, honey. It's harder to get out than in. You don't exist *entirely* in the space-time matrix of the universe which the Shifter is currently in. We kind of overflow into other dimensions. So when you try to leave, you hit the dimensions at a slight angle and – *whoof!* you break apart. Some of you goes one way, some of you goes another. No, you can't get out.'

'Renark – you have more problems,' Asquiol said, fiddling with his gloves.

'And more coming, from what I've learned,' Renark said tiredly. 'What did *you* find out?'

'Not much of anything definite. The eleven planets are called a variety of names by a variety of human and non-human people. There are a million theories about the Shifter's nature, mainly based on folklore and superstition. They say the Thron were here first and might be native to the system. This could explain some of their resentment of alien ships entering.'

'Anything else?'

'There's some race called, colloquially, the "jellysmellies", who are supposed to know the history of the multiverse. There's a planet called Ragged Ruth which is supposed to be the epitome of Hell in this hellish system.'

'That seems to confirm what Mary told me,' he nodded.

Talfryn came in. His body was loose, worn out. He sat down on the couch.

Renark paused for a moment. 'There are questions which we've *got* to answer. And we can't take our time getting those answers.

'Why does the Shifter follow this orbit? *How* does it do it? If we can discover the principle, there may be a chance of adapting it to build ships to evacuate our galaxy. The logic – if that's the word – is abhorrent to us, but it must be mastered. Are all the universes contracting at the same time, I wonder?'

He asked this last question almost hesitantly, bringing it into the open for the first time.

'If so, there is virtually no chance of evacuation. On the other hand, what we discover may enable us to...'

Klein laughed: 'To stop a universe in its natural course of decay or reorganisation? No, Renark!'

'Yes, Klein – if that has to be done!'

'What the hell are we all talking about?' Talfryn said tiredly from the couch. 'We're only three men – against the natural universe. Not to mention the unnatural universe – this terrible place.'

He shook his head. 'Frankly, the little information I've picked up makes me feel helpless, useless, ineffectual in the face of what's happening. I feel ready to give up, not to fight against something that is, judging by all the facts, an immense and inescapable movement of the forces of nature which must logically result in the end of the human race – of all organic life both in our universe, and in others. The human race has had its day – we might as well face it. If you can answer that, Renark, I'd be grateful...'

Suddenly, Renark didn't want Talfryn with him any more. 'I doubt if I could give you an answer which would satisfy you,' he said sadly. 'You're fatalistic. And a fatalist, if you'll forgive me, is also a misanthropist.

'The quality which humanity has, unlike any other form of life in our universe, is its power to control nature. It is the mark of *Homo sapiens* that he has, for millennia, refused to let his environment control him to any real extent. He has adapted to it, adapted it, conquered it. This imminent disaster facing the race is on a larger scale – but the rule still applies. In this case we may be forced to leave our environment and start to work adapting to, and controlling, a new one. If we can do that, we will have proved for ever our right and our reason for existence!'

Talfryn, taken aback by the force of Renark's reply, couldn't answer. He shook his head again and remained broodingly silent.

Renark had sensed the man's weakness as a mechanic senses that a piece of equipment, driven beyond its inherent endurance, is due to fail. So he said: 'You'd better stay here.'

Talfryn nodded. 'I've failed you, Renark. But, honestly, it's too big – far too big. Some of us can be optimistic for just so long. But facts must be faced.'

'Facts can be altered,' Renark said, turning away.

'You're giving up?' Asquiol blinked. 'Why?'

'I'm a creature of circumstance,' said Talfryn with a bitter half-smile. He got up and left the room.

Asquiol turned to Renark. 'Why has he done that? Is there something I don't know about?'

'Let's hope so,' Renark said quietly.

He watched his friend who, disturbed and disorientated, turned to look for a long moment at Willow.

Her eyes began to fill with tears.

'I couldn't face it,' she said. 'Not any more – not after what we just went through…'

'You've stopped loving me, is that it?'

'Oh, no, Asquiol – I'll always love you. You… you could stay here with me.'

Asquiol looked sharply at Renark.

'We go to Thron,' said Renark. 'If you wish to come.'

'Look after yourself, Willow,' said Asquiol. 'I may return – who knows?' And he walked away from her.

He and Renark left the room, left the building and the city and made for the pads, for their black ship, bound for horror and perhaps death.

'He was a fool,' said Willow calmly to Klein. 'There are many who refuse their responsibilities. Fooling themselves they search for a "higher ideal". He was a fool.'

'What are responsibilities?' said Klein laconically. 'He knows. Responsibility, my dear, is another word for self-interest. For survival.'

She looked at Klein uncomprehendingly.

'I wish he had stayed,' she said.

Chapter Five

RENARK SPOKE THE ship's master-command bringing the whole complicated vessel to life.

He could not be satisfied with thoughts and theories now. He wanted decisive and constant action – dynamic action which would bring him to a source that would answer the questions crowding his mind.

As he charted his course to Thron, he remembered something and turned to Asquiol sitting moodily in the gunnery seat, staring at his instruments.

'Did you ever know of Mary the Maze before you came here?' he asked.

Silently Asquiol shook his head.

Renark shrugged. He felt badly for his friend, but couldn't afford to let his personal emotions influence his chosen course of action.

From what he had gathered, fewer laws than ever applied in the interplanetary space of the Shifter than on the planets themselves. Therefore he was going to have difficulty in simply navigating the comparatively small area of space between them and Thron.

He said without turning, 'Once in space I must not be disturbed, and am relying on you to perform all necessary functions other than the actual piloting of the spaceship. I have to anchor my mind to Thron, and must steer the ship through altering dimensions as well as space and time. Therefore, in the event of attack you must be ready, must meet it as best you can. But I will not be able to afford to know. Do you understand?'

'Let's get started, for God's sake,' Asquiol said impatiently.

'And don't be too ready with those anti-neutron cannon,' Renark said as he pressed the take-off button.

The ship throbbed spacewards.

And then they hit horror!

61

Chaos.

It had no business to exist. It defied every instinctively accepted law that Renark knew.

Turmoil.

It was fantastically beautiful. But it had to be ignored, mastered or destroyed, because it was *wrong*!

Agony.

The ship coursed through myriad, multi-dimensional currents that swirled and whirled and howled about it, that rent the sanity of the two brave men who battered at it, cursed it and, in controlling themselves, managed somehow to stave off the worst effects.

Terror.

They had no business to exist here. They knew it, but they refused to compromise. They made the disorder of the tiny universe bend to their courage, to their strength and their wills, creating a pocket of order in the screaming wrongness of unchained creation.

Temptation.

They had nothing but their pitiful knowledge that they were human beings – intelligent, reasoning beings capable of transcending the limits which the universe had striven to set upon them. They *refused*; they fought, they used their minds as they had never used them, found reserves of reason where none had previously been.

And, at last, because they were forced to, they used every resource of the human mind which had lain dormant since man had created 'human nature' as an excuse to let his animal nature order his life.

Now they rejected this and Renark steered the ship through the malevolent currents of the unnatural area of space and howled his challenge to it. And the three words '*I am human!*' became his mental war-cry as he used his skill to control the metal vessel plunging on the random spacial and temporal currents – forcing its way through blazing horror towards the angry world of Thron!

All about him, Renark was aware of other dimensions which seemed to lie in wait for his ship, to trap it, to stop it from ever reaching its goal. But he avoided them and concentrated all his powers on keeping a course for Thron.

For hours the two men fought against insanity, fought the craziness that had turned Mary the Maze into an idiot.

Then, at last, Thron appeared on the V. Weak, trembling but exuberant, Renark coasted the spaceship into Thron's atmosphere and, although the brooding planet offered new dangers of a more tangible kind, it was with relief and hope that he arrived there.

They could not speak to one another just then. But both were conscious of the welding companionship which had come about during their journey.

They had been fused together, these two men, by mutually shared horror and victory.

Breathing deeply, Renark dropped the ship down and began a cautious reconnaissance of the planet.

Apart from one domed city at the Northern Pole, it appeared deserted. There were cities, certainly, but uninhabited. They picked up no signals, their scanners observed no obvious signs of life. Where were the ferocious Thron? Surely not all at the small city on the Northern Pole?

'The hell with it,' Renark said. 'Let's go right in and see what happens. I've staked everything so far on one throw, and haven't, as yet, lost by it. Are you willing?'

'I thought *I* was supposed to be reckless.' Asquiol smiled. 'Good. We can land in that big square we saw in the largest city.'

Renark nodded agreement, adjusted the controls of the ship and flew in over the big city. He brought it flaming down on the hard, rocky substance of the city square.

They landed to find only silence.

'Shall we disembark?' Asquiol asked.

'Yes. There's a locker over there, beside you. Open it, will you?'

Asquiol swung the casing back and raised his eyebrows. There was a small armoury of handguns in the locker. Renark had never been known to carry or use any weapon designed to kill.

'Give me the anti-neutron beamer you see there,' Renark said.

Asquiol didn't question Renark but took the holstered gun from its place and handed it over. Renark looked at it strangely.

'Desperate measures,' he said softly. 'I have little sympathy at the moment with the Thron, although they may have justifiable reasons for their seemingly unreasoning belligerence. But our mission transcends my moral code, much as I hate to admit such a thing possible, and our lives are, as far as the human race is concerned, important.'

'Let's go,' said Asquiol.

Renark sighed. They suited up and took the elevator to the airlock.

Although bizarre and obviously created by alien intelligence, Renark and Asquiol could work out the function of most of the buildings and machines they observed as they padded through the deserted streets of the apparently deserted city.

But they couldn't explain why the city was deserted or where the inhabitants had gone. Obviously they had not been gone for any length of time, for there were no signs of erosion or encroaching nature.

With his mind, Renark quested around, searching the buildings for life, but he could only sense peculiar disturbances in the temporal and spacial layers spreading out beyond the Shifter continuum.

Life hovered out there like a ghost, sometimes apparently close, sometimes further away. It was disturbing.

They toured the city and were just returning to the square where the ship rested when something happened.

'God, I feel sick...' Asquiol screwed up his eyes.

Renark felt the same. He had momentary double vision. He saw faint shadows flickering at the edge of the structures about them, shadows of the same shape, size and appearance as the more solid buildings and machines. These shadows seemed to merge with the material structures – and all at once the city was alive, inhabited.

The place was suddenly full of doglike, six-legged beings using four legs for motion and two as hands.

The Thron!

Shocked, they pulled their pistols from their holsters and

backed towards the ship as the Thron saw the humans in their midst.

All was consternation.

Thron soldiers levelled weirdly curled tubes at the two men and fired. The humans were flung to the ground as their suit-screens absorbed or repelled the worst of the charges.

'Shoot back or we've had it!' Renark yelled.

They raised themselves on their bellies, aiming their own dreadful weapons.

Beams of dancing anti-matter spread towards the Thron troops, met them, made contact and seethed into their bodies.

Those bodies imploded, crushing inwards and turning to min-uscule specks of shattered matter before vanishing entirely. The backlash shivered against the humans' protective suits. And the beams waltzed on, fading slightly as they progressed, entered one group after another, destroying wherever they touched, whether organic or inanimate matter, until their power faded. Only a few Thron were left in the immediate area.

'They don't seem ready to talk,' Asquiol said sardonically over the suit radio. 'What now, Renark?'

'Back to the ship, for the meantime.'

Inside the control cabin their communications equipment was making all sorts of noises. Asquiol attempted to tune it in and eventually succeeded in getting a regular series of high-frequency signals which he could not quite interpret as being coded signals or actual speech. He brought the pitch down lower and realised with astonishment that he was listening to stilted Terran. Renark was busy keeping the scanners trained on the Thron, who were coming out into the open around the square again. But he listened.

'*Beware the Thron... Beware the Thron... Beware the Thron...*'

Whether it was a warning or a threat, he couldn't tell. Asquiol said, careful to adjust his outgoing signal to the frequency involved: 'Who are you? I am receiving you.'

'We are enemies of the Thron. We are the Shaarn, whose ancestors consigned the Thron to this existence. But they have machines which you are not equipped against – forces which will hurl you out of this system altogether and into limbo. Take off immediately and head for the Northern Pole. We saw you pass over us but have not, until now, been able to discover your means of communication and the form it takes. We apologise.'

'How can we trust them?' Asquiol asked.

'The frying pan or the fire – it makes no difference,' Renark replied. 'I'm lifting off. Tell them we're coming.'

Asquiol relayed the message.

'You must hurry,' the Shaarn spokesman said, 'for we are small and have few defensive devices against the Thron. You must reach our city before they do, since we will have but a short time to spare to let you in and close our barrier again.'

'Have it ready – we're coming,' said Asquiol.

The ship soared upwards again, levelled off and headed at high speed for the polar region.

They made it in under a minute. They saw the dome flicker and fade, entered its confines as it closed over them again, and came down gently on a small landing field within the city. It was more a town, with few buildings taller than three storeys, encompassing a small area compared with the expanse of the Thron cities. Overhead they observed the Thron ships come rushing over the polar city and were half blinded by the bolts of energy which sprayed the force-dome above them.

They stayed where they were and waited to be contacted.

Eventually the communications equipment spoke: 'I am pleased that we were successful. There is no point in waiting until the Thron have expended their rage. The force-shield will absorb their most ferocious attacks. We are sending out a vehicle for your assistance. Please take it to the city when you are ready to do so.'

A few moments later a small air carriage, open-topped and made of thin, golden metal, floated up to the ship and hovered by its airlock.

'Well, let's see how friendly the Shaarn really are!' said Renark. They descended to the airlock, passed through it and entered the little air boat which spun on its axis and returned to the city at a more leisurely speed.

Renark felt fairly confident, from what Mary the Maze had said, that these people would be friendly.

They entered the city proper and the air boat cruised downwards, landing gently outside the entrance to a small, unornamented, unpretentious building.

Two figures came out. They were doglike, having six appendages. Asquiol gasped and instinctively reached for his pistol in an unthinking response. Then he saw that these creatures, so like the Thron, were unarmed, and he calmed himself.

The Shaarn, like the Thron, were extremely pleasing to the human eye – perhaps because they resembled friendly dogs.

With peaceful gestures, the two figures beckoned Renark and Asquiol to leave the air boat. When they did so they passed through a series of simply furnished rooms containing no recognisable equipment, and out into a courtyard which, like the city, was covered with an iridescent force-dome.

Here was a laser transceiver not unlike their own. One of the Shaarn went up to it and spoke into the transmitter. It took them several moments to tune into the humans' suit wavelengths and, for an instant, before they adjusted their own controls, they were blasted with the high-pitched noises they had heard before.

Then the Shaarn spokesman said: 'We regret, sincerely, that our welcome could not have extended to the whole planet, but as you will have realised, we control little of it. I am Naro Nuis and this is my wife Zeni Ouis. You are von Bek and Asquiol of Pompeii, I believe.'

'That's so, but how did you know?' Count Renark replied.

'We were forced – and you must forgive us – to intrude on your minds in order to discover the means to build the communications equipment. We are telepaths, I am afraid…'

'Then why the need for the laser?'

'We had no idea how you would take telepathic interference in your minds, and it is against our code to intrude except in the direst emergencies.'

'I should have thought that's just what we were in,' Asquiol said somewhat rudely.

'I see,' said Renark. 'Well, as far as I am concerned, telepathic communication would be preferable. We have telepaths among our own race.'

'So be it,' Naro Nuis said.

'You have obviously some important reason for braving the dangers of Thron,' said a voice in Renark's skull, 'but we avoided investigating it. Perhaps we can help?'

'Thank you,' Count Renark said. 'Firstly, I am curious to learn why the Thron are so belligerent; secondly, whether it is true that your race was the first to come to this system. Much hangs on what I learn from you.' He told the Shaarn how his race faced annihilation.

The alien appeared to deliberate. At length he 'pathed:

'Would you object if we intruded still further on your minds for a while by means of a telepathic link? By this method you will see something of the history of the Shaarn and will discover how this system originally took this somewhat unusual orbit through the multi-dimensional universe.'

'What do you say, Renark?' Asquiol's voice came over the suit-phone.

'I think the suggestion is excellent.'

They were led into a semi-darkened room where food and drink were served to them. They felt relaxed for the first time in ages.

'This place is simply to aid your receptivity to what we are about to do.'

'And what is that?'

'We are going to reconstruct for you the history of the war between the Shaarn and the Thron. The history began many millennia ago, when our ancestors were completing their explorations of our own space-time galaxy...'

At Naro Nuis's request they blanked their minds, and the history began...

Chapter Six

THEY WERE THE golden children of the galaxy. The Shaarn – the searchers, the wanderers, the enquirers. They were the magnificent bringers of gifts, bestowers of wisdom, dealers of justice. In their great star-travelling ships they brought the concept of mercy and law to the planets of their galaxy and formed order out of chaos, cut justice from the stuff of chance.

The Shaarn hurled their ships inwards to the Hub, outwards towards the Rim.

Proud, wise and merciful, self-confident and self-critical, they spread their seed to inhabit planets in many different systems. The laughing darlings of an ancient culture, they poured outwards, always searching.

The Shaarn ships sang and hurtled through the bewildering regions of chaos-space, avoiding war, recognising privacy, but bringing their wisdom and knowledge to anyone requesting it. They had come, also, to accept that all intelligent races took roughly the same form as themselves.

The mighty Shaarn were cynics and idealists, innocent and ancient – and their ships coursed further towards the worlds of the Rim.

The starship, *Vondel*, captained by Roas Rui, burst into normal space half a light year from a binary star the Shaarn called Yito. Around Yito circled eleven worlds, each following a wider orbit than the next – eleven mysteries which Roas Rui and her crew of scientists and sorcerers regarded with excitement and curiosity. Eleven balls of chemicals and vegetation, organic and inorganic life. Would they find intelligence? New concepts, new knowledge? Roas Rui hoped that they would.

The Shaarn, in their early days of space travel, had known fear when encountering foreign cultures, but those times were gone.

In their power and their confidence, they were unable to conceive of a race greater than their own, a technology more highly developed. On some worlds near the Rim they had come across traces of a star-roving people; but the traces were incredibly ancient and pointed to a long-dead race – their ancestors, perhaps – who had travelled the stars and then degenerated. Thus, it was not with fear that Roas Rui regarded the fourth world nearest Yito when her ship, its reactor idling, went into orbit around it.

Roas Rui reared herself effortlessly onto her four hind limbs in order to see better the purple-clouded world which now filled the viewing-screen. Her shaggy, doglike head craned towards the screen and her mouth curved downwards in an expression of pure pleasure. She turned her head and showed her long, slim teeth to emphasise her delight.

'It's a huge planet, Medwov Dei,' she released to her lieutenant who stood by the screen control board, manoeuvring dials in order to bring the world into closer perspective.

Medwov Dei thought, without moving his head, 'The gravity is almost identical to that of Shaarn.'

Rui thought, 'Woui Nas was right in his hunch again. He always picks the planet which most closely approximates Shaarn in gravity and atmosphere. He's one of the best sorcerers we have in the Division.'

Medwov made a clicking sound with his mouth to indicate agreement. He was very big, the largest member of the crew and every inch of five feet high. He was dedicated to the Exploratory Division, even more than the other members. With regard to his work, he was a fanatic, probably due to the fact that, because of his immense size, he had little success with the female Shaarn. At least he, personally, blamed his height, but it was well known that, as a young cadet, he had once killed a domestic beast in anger. Naturally, this had led to his near-ostracism and had precluded his ever rising above the rank of lieutenant. Medwov inhaled wetly and continued to work at the control panel, deliberately blocking his mind to any but the most urgent thoughts which might emanate from his commander.

Almost childishly, Roas Rui laughed the high-pitched whine of the Shaarn. Her excitement mounted as she directed her two pilots to prepare for descent onto the planet's surface.

'Prepare defence screens.' She sent out the traditional commands as a matter of course. Some of her orders were obeyed by the control operators before she even thought of them. 'Switch to gravity-resisters.' Machines moaned delicately throughout the huge bulk of the starship. 'Descend to two thousand feet.'

The *Vondel* plunged through the atmosphere of the new planet and hovered two thousand feet above its surface. Now the screens showed a vast landscape of forest land composed predominantly of waving indigo fronds which stretched like a sea in all directions, broken occasionally by clumps of taller vegetation coloured in varying shades of blue. It was beautiful. Roas Rui's long body shook with emotion as she beheld it. To the Shaarn all new planets were beautiful.

'Begin testing,' she said.

The computers began their intricate job of classifying all the components of the planet. At the same time, the sorcerers began to put themselves swiftly into trance-state, seeking to discover intelligent life of any kind, whether natural or supernatural, and also its attitude or potential attitude to the Exploratory Division.

The findings of computers and sorcerers were relayed instantly to Roas Rui, herself now in semi-trance. Both parts of her brain received the information and assembled it into an ever-increasing, detailed picture of the newly discovered planet.

Woui Nas:

I have found a mind. Bewildered. Uncertain. Passive. More minds. As before. New! Mind. High intelligence. Anger. Controlled. Urge to destroy very strong: directed at (possible) Rulers or Representatives. New! Mind. Low I.Q. Misery. Bewildered. Passive. New! Something bad. Very bad. Evil here, but am finding resistance to probes.

Pause...

Power. Evil. Great resistance to probes. Am prepared to fight or retreat. Require orders!

Pause...

Repeat. Require orders!

Roas Rui beamed a message to the controllers to continue recording the data and concentrated all attention on making a full link with Woui Nas, who had 'pathed the urgent request.

'I am with you now, Woui Nas. Can you bring me in?'

'Unprecedented reaction, captain. Please absorb.'

Roas Rui could sense the frightened amazement of Woui Nas as she submerged herself in the other's mind and allowed the old sorcerer to guide her outwards towards the source of the emanations. Almost instantaneously, she felt the aura of disgusting malevolence, coupled with an intelligence more powerful than her own. Roas Rui was one of the most intelligent members of her race – her capacity for absorbing and relating knowledge was tremendous – but she had found more than her match in the mind which now sensed the presence of her own.

Roas Rui, under the direction of Woui Nas, probed further into the mind which she had contacted. She probed while her senses shrieked with danger and urged her to retreat.

Suddenly her brain throbbed as a thought came savagely from the contacted entity: *'Get out! We intend to destroy you, intruders.'*

There was no attempt to ask questions of the explorers. No tinge of curiosity. An order – and a statement.

Roas Rui and Woui Nas retreated from the malevolence and separated minds.

'What now?' Woui Nas asked from his cabin, a quarter of a mile away from the control room where Roas Rui sat shaking.

'Incredible,' the captain said. 'Quite unprecedented, as you remarked. There is a force here to equal the Shaarn – even to better it. But the *evil!*'

'I must admit that, as we neared the planet, I sensed it,' Woui Nas informed the captain. 'But it was difficult then to define it. These entities are capable of blocking off our most powerful probes.'

'Our ancestors would have been far more careful when making a new planetfall,' Roas Rui said grimly. 'We are becoming too complacent, Brother Sorcerer.'

'*Were*,' Woui Nas remarked dryly. 'Perhaps this is the kind of shock our people need.'

'Possibly,' Roas Rui agreed. 'But now we are in danger of turning our immediate peril into a philosophical problem. Since this contact is unprecedented, and since the regulations state categorically that we should obey any culture which demands that we leave its environs, I would suggest to you that a group makes contact immediately with Headquarters on Shaarn and asks for instructions.'

'And meanwhile?' Woui Nas enquired.

'I do not wish to be destroyed. And neither, I think, do any other members of the ship's complement.' She beamed a quick order to her pilots. 'We are returning to Shaarn. This is an emergency.' She knew that her pilots would need no further orders.

Swiftly, the *Vondel* climbed into deep space and merged into chaos-space.

So the initial contact between the Shaarn and the Thron was made.

After millennia of ignorance of each other's existence, the exploratory team which had come to a Thron-dominated world brought the two mighty cultures into contact at last. It was inevitable.

And the war between Shaarn and Thron was also inevitable.

It was not a war like most wars. It did not hinge on economics. It only partially hinged on conflicting ideologies. It was simply that the Thron refused to tolerate the presence in the galaxy of another intelligent race, physically like themselves and almost as powerful.

They intended to destroy the Shaarn. To obliterate completely all traces of their civilisation. The Thron had not concentrated so much on the building of starships, but it did not take them long to build ships which almost equalled those of the Shaarn.

Thron controlled an empire comprising twenty-six systems. The Thron themselves were comparatively few in number – but they had total dominance over their subject planets.

The Federation of Shaarn comprised some fifty systems and three hundred planets upon which intelligent races, like themselves, existed. When Shaarn informed them of the impending war, one hundred and sixty-two of those planets elected to join with the Shaarn. The rest claimed neutrality.

The war progressed. It was vicious and dreadful. And a month after it had begun the first planet was destroyed by the Thron – a neutral planet. And all life was destroyed with the planet.

Realising the danger was great, but unable to consider an alternative to continuing the struggle, the Shaarn directed their scientists to invent a way of stopping the war so that no more destruction of life should take place.

The scientists devised a means of removing the Thron from the galaxy, even from the very universe – a means, if it worked as they hoped, of forever exiling that malevolent and evil people.

They discovered the continuum-warp device which, they believed, would be capable of hurling the eleven Thron home worlds out of their continuum and into another. This would efficiently halt the Thron's insensate aims of ruling the galaxy.

So a squadron of ships, each armed with the device, reached the Thron home system of Yito and directed their beams onto the planets and their sun.

At first they succeeded only in shifting the planets through space, altering the position around the binary, resulting in the equidistant position they now occupied. The Thron retaliated and the Shaarn hurled the Thron warships effectively into another space-time continuum. Returning their attention to the system, they blasted it with warp rays time after time and, quite suddenly, it was gone – vanished from the Shaarn's space-time into another. The war was over.

But, as it happened, the Shaarn had not been entirely successful in their plan since the system kept right on travelling through the dimensions, eventually establishing an orbit which it still followed. Not only this, but most of the Shaarn ships were caught up in the vortex they had created and were drawn, by means of the force they had themselves released, after the Shifter.

They attempted, desperately, to return to their own space-time but, for some reason, it was now blocked, not only to them but to the Shifter itself. The system could never pass through the Shaarn's space-time again.

The Thron, demoralised and bewildered, did not offer a threat of immediate counter-attack for they were busily consolidating on their fortress world, abandoning their slaves to any fate that came.

The Shaarn were able to land their ships, establishing a small, well-protected city at the Northern Pole of a planet they called Glanii. Here they remained for ages, vainly attempting to devise a means of returning to their own system.

Later the Thron, too, came to Glanii, where they could be nearer their hated enemies.

The Thron eventually learned what had happened to them and also began work on the problem. They invented a machine which could fling them and all their artefacts through the multi-dimensional space-time streams to their home continuum and exact vengeance on the Shaarn. So far they had not been entirely unsuccessful.

This explained why Renark and Asquiol had found the planet apparently deserted of Thron, who at the time of their arrival had been attempting another jump through the dimensions.

The war between the Thron and the representatives of the Shaarn had become a stalemate, both races concentrating most of their energies on attempts to return to their home continuum. So it had been for millennia, with the Thron, resenting further encroachments on their sundered territory, attempting to destroy any newcomers who came, like vultures, opportunistically to the Shifter System.

And that, to the date of Renark's coming, was briefly the history of the Sundered Worlds...

Count Renark was in a calmer frame of mind when the experience was over. At last he was no longer working in the dark – he had definite, conclusive facts to relate to his questions and was confident that the Shaarn would supply him with further useful information.

Naro Nuis telepathed discreetly: 'I hope the history was of some use to you, Renark von Bek.'

'Of great use – but I gather you are unable to supply me with any detailed information of the dimension-warping device.'

'Unfortunately, that is so. From what we can gather, the continua-warp, operating as it did by means of certain laws discovered in the Shaarn continuum, will not work in the same way from outside the continuum. I believe this was deliberately done by our scientists in order that the Thron would never be able to return.'

'I'm surprised that by this time you haven't joined forces with the Thron, since you seem to have a common aim.'

'Not so. In fact, this is our main point of contention these days. The Thron are determined to regain our original universe, whereas that is the last thing we want. We will be pleased to halt the progress of the Shifter in *any* continuum but our own, and this would destroy, for ever, their chance to continue the war.' The alien sighed – a surprisingly human sound. 'It may be that the Shifting mechanism is an irreversible process. In that case our efforts are hopeless. But we do not think so.'

Renark was bitterly disappointed. If the beings who engendered the Shift no longer understood how it operated, this was logically the end of the trail. But he would not admit to himself that there was nothing more he could do. That was unthinkable.

He rose to his feet, his mind working intensely, busily forming the recent knowledge into the kind of pattern best suited to his present needs. Well, there was time yet. He had to be optimistic – there was no turning back. He refused to accept any factors other than those he could use objectively. Somewhere in this system...

They left the chamber and made for the ship. On the way, Renark noticed signs of animated work in a large, low-slung building with open, hangar-type doors. It struck him as out of tune with the millennia-long deadlock of which he had just learned.

He remarked on this to Naro Nuis. The alien immediately responded with interest.

'That is the result of a long period of research. We are now building equipment with which we hope to halt the Shifter System.'

Renark stared in amazement. '*What*? After the story of gloom you have just told us?'

'I told you our experiments continued,' Naro Nuis replied, puzzled. 'Soon we will begin ferrying the equipment into space, to take it as near to the suns as possible.'

'And yet you still claim to have no knowledge of the Shift principle!' Renark's excitement was mounting at the thought that the creature had been lying.

'That is so,' Naro Nuis told him. 'We have despaired of ever discovering the principle behind the phenomenon. But, with any luck, we think we might bring it to a stop, even though we don't understand it.' He added: 'This is the culmination of a very long series of experiments. *Very* long. If we succeed, we shall not need to know. The problem will have vanished.'

Renark's sudden hope dissipated. 'And what are your chances of succeeding?'

Naro Nuis paused before answering. 'The expedition is fraught with dangers. Our long absence from space has lost us some of our skills in interplanetary flight.'

'What of the Thron? Do they know of your plans?'

'They have some inkling, of course. They will try to stop us. There will be a great battle.'

Renark continued the walk to his ship. 'When do you plan to lift this equipment off?'

'In half a revolution of the planet.'

He stopped abruptly. 'Then I must ask one favour.'

'What is that?'

'Delay your experiment. Give me time to find out what I must know.'

'We cannot.'

There was no arguing with the Shaarn. His tone was uncompromising. He explained: 'How can we be sure that you will have even a chance of success in your endeavour? Every moment we delay means that our chances of stopping the Shifter and holding off the Thron are lessened.'

'But the future of my entire race depends upon me!'

'Does it? Have you not taken it upon yourself presumptuously to save your fellows? Perhaps the process you described is natural – perhaps the members of your race will accept that they are to perish along with their universe. As for us, there is no need to delay and we must act quickly. The Thron – when they are not attempting to jump through the dimensions – patrol the planet in their ships. As soon as we begin ferrying the equipment there will be a battle. We will have to work speedily and hold off the Thron at the same time.'

'I see,' Renark said bitterly.

Later, Asquiol said: 'But what if you did stop the Shifter? Supposing you stopped it in a universe like the one we have just left? You would be destroyed along with the rest.'

'That is true – but the chances of that happening are not very great. We must risk it.'

'Then you will not wait?'

'No,' Naro Nuis said again, regretfully. 'Your hopes of success are slim. Ours are better. You must understand our position. We have been trying to stop the Shifter for thousands of years. Would you call a halt to your progress on behalf of a race you never heard of – which, according to only two of its members, was in some kind of danger?'

'I might,' Renark said.

'Not after thousands of years,' said Asquiol. 'Not that long.'

Naro Nuis's thoughts came gently. 'You are welcome to stay with us if you wish.'

'Thanks,' Renark said harshly, 'but we don't have much time.'

'I think your efforts will be wasted,' the Shaarn 'pathed, 'but since you are so anxious to find help you might go to the world of the Ekiversh.'

'Ekiversh?'

'The Ekiversh are intelligent metazoa who have a fully developed race memory. They gave us some help in building the machine with which we intend to stop the Shifter. They have lived so long that their knowledge is very great. They are good-natured, friendly and, because of their structure and type, live on the only planet in the system which is not in some way torn by strife. The Thron could learn something from the Ekiversh but, in their arrogance, they would not deign to do so. We have not often visited them, for whenever we leave our city the wrath of the Thron is turned upon us. But we have made telepathic communication when certain favourable laws have applied, for short periods, in the system.'

'Can you point out their planet on my chart?'

'With pleasure.

Naro Nuis accompanied them aboard their ship, looking around him with pleasure and curiosity. 'A bizarre craft,' he said.

'Not by our standards.' Renark produced the chart.

The alien bent over it, studying the figures marked there. At last he pointed. 'There.'

'Thanks,' said Renark.

'Let's get started, shall we?' Asquiol drummed his fingers.

'The Thron will be awaiting you when you leave here,' Naro Nuis said. 'Are you sure you want to risk it?'

'What else could we do?' Renark was close to anger.

The alien turned away from him.

Asquiol shouted at Naro Nuis: 'Haven't you any idea what you will do if you stop the Shifter? You could strand us here with no means of saving our people – no means of going back, even if we did find the information we need. You *can't* begin your experiments yet!'

'We must.'

Renark put his hand on Asquiol's arm. 'We must get to Ekiversh as soon as possible and see what we can learn before the Shaarn succeed in stopping the Shifter in orbit.'

'Then I had better leave,' Naro Nuis said sadly.

With mixed emotions, Renark said goodbye to the alien, thanking him for his help.

In the control seat Renark tensed. Asquiol fidgeted in his own seat by the gunnery panel.

Suddenly the force-dome over the city flickered, flashed bright orange and boiled backwards, leaving a gap. Renark's finger smashed down on the firing switch. The ship trembled, screamed and lifted.

Then they were through the gap in the screen, whining up through the clouds towards the madness of the Shifter's space.

Thron ships spotted them instantly and came flashing in their direction.

Asquiol didn't wait for Renark's order this time. As they sped into deep space, he fired.

The Thron ships flickered away from the cold, searing stream of anti-neutrons which Asquiol, in his desperation, had dared again to employ, and which their instruments told them meant instant disruption. Even so, some vessels were caught for an instant in the periphery of the deadly flow, and must have suffered for it. Anti-neutrons, possessing no electrical charge, could not be stopped by any energy screen.

Asquiol could almost see the Thron licking their wounds.

He had hoped that this first exchange would frighten the attackers badly enough to give Renark time to make a clean get-away. But the Thron had the advantage of being able to manoeuvre in Shifter space. Renark gritted his teeth as he piled on power and plunged into the billowy *twistiness* which this region presented to his mind. It was almost like piloting a boat through mad, storm-tossed seas.

But they were seas that intruded into the mind.

The Thron came after them, and Asquiol saw them somersault preparatory to firing. He hesitated, reluctant to use his weapon a second time. Then great slams of force hit them.

The ship skidded and bucked. 'Don't pussyfoot, Asquiol,' Renark roared uncharacteristically. 'Let them have it!'

Asquiol clung to the firing arm of the anti-neutron gun. Blindly, he turned up the density to maximum and sprayed space. Phantasmal green flares showed, on the screen before him, where he scored hits.

Renark closed his eyes and concentrated hard on the piloting.

The collapse of atomic structures on a large scale was not a pleasant experience for a Space Senser.

After that, the surviving Thron ships withdrew. There was silence in the cabin of Renark's ship for some time.

A few hours later Renark made a quick mental exploration. He found what he'd expected. The Shaarn had begun the first stages of the experiment. There was evidence of fierce fighting near the Thron planet, and somewhere sunward a sizeable installation was being set up.

He probed further. The Shaarn would not be unmolested for long. A large fleet was assembled an hour's journey away, and would soon no doubt do much to impede the progress of the Shaarn's labours. In spite of the friendliness shown him by his hosts, Renark began to regret the Thron warships destroyed by Asquiol.

Soon, Renark felt, he would be gaining a complete picture of the workings of the multiverse. There were other things he wished to know and he had a feeling that if he lived he would know them soon.

Once again they were experiencing the chaotic and bewildering currents of outer space. But this time there was little emotional reaction, for their self-confidence was strong.

But Renark still had to fight to keep the ship on course in the stormy, apparently lawless and random flowings of time and space, skimming the ship over them like a stone over water, through myriad sterechronia, through a thousand million twists of the spacial flow, to come finally to Ekiversh...

Chapter Seven

IMMEDIATELY THEY LANDED on the peaceful oxygen planet, tiny, polite threads of thought touched their minds, asked questions.

Responding to the delicacy of the impressions, Renark and Asquiol made it clear that they wished to contact the Ekiversh as the Shaarn had suggested. They remained in the spaceship, pleased to see the light green chlorophyll-bearing plants which were not unlike Earth's.

At last there appeared outside the ship what at first appeared to be a heaving mass of semi-transparent jelly. Disgusted, Renark was repelled by the sight and Asquiol said: 'The jellysmellies. Remember I told you they were some sort of legend on Entropium? Metazoa – *ugh*!'

A voice in Asquiol's head said humbly: 'We are deeply sorry that our physical appearance should not appeal. Perhaps this will be a better form.'

Then the whole mass reared up and slowly transformed itself into the shape of a giant man – a giant man composed of hundreds of gelatinous metazoa.

Renark could not decide which form was least unattractive, but he blocked the idea out of his mind and said instead: 'We have come to converse with you on matters of philosophy and practical importance to us and our race. May we leave our ship? It would be good to breathe real air again.'

But the metazoan giant replied regretfully: 'It would be unwise, for though we absorb oxygen as you do, the waste gases we exhale are unpleasing to your sense of smell.'

'The "jellysmellies",' Renark said to Asquiol. 'That explains their name.

'We were informed that you are equipped with race memory,

that in effect you are immortal,' Renark thought tentatively at the glutinous giant.

'That is so. Our great experience, as you may know, was to have witnessed, in the early days of our race, the Dance of a Galaxy.'

'Forgive me, but I don't understand the implications of that,' Renark said. 'Could you perhaps explain what you mean?'

'It was believed,' said the metazoa, 'that those whom we call the Doomed Folk had passed away in a distant galaxy in our original universe, and that galaxy – which had known great strife – was quiet again in readiness for the Great Turn which would be the beginning of a new cycle in its long life. We and other watchers in nearby galaxies saw it shift like a smoky monster, saw it curl and writhe and its suns and planets pour in ordered patterns around the Hub and out around the Rim, re-forming their ranks in preparation.

'The Dance of the Stars was a sight to destroy all but the noblest of watchers, for the weaving patterns depicted the Two Truths Which Bear the Third, so that while the galaxy re-formed itself to begin a fresh cycle through its particular Time and Space, it also cleansed its sister galaxies of petty spirits and those who thought ignoble thoughts.

'For millions of years, the Dance of the Galaxy progressed – ordered creation, a sight so pleasing to intelligent beings. It gave us much in the way of sensory experiences and also enabled us to develop our philosophy. Please do not ask us to explain it further, for the sight of a galaxy dancing can be defined in no terms possessed by either of us.

'When at last the Dance was over, the Hub began to spin, setting the pattern for the new Cycle. And slowly, from the Hub outwards to the Rim, the suns and planets began to turn again in a course that would be unchanged for aeons.

'So it began, and so – after time had passed – did its denizens begin to hammer out its marvellous history.

'They came, at length, to our galaxy and, because they were impatient of the philosophical conclusions we had drawn about the nature of the multiverse, set about destroying our ancient race. A few of us fled here, since we abhor violence.'

'You witnessed a galaxy reorder itself by its own volition!' Renark sensed at last that his most important question was close to being answered.

'Not, we feel, by its own volition. Our logic has led us, inescapably, to believe that there is a greater force at work – one which created the multiverse for its own purposes. This is not a metaphysical conclusion – we are materialists. But the facts are such that they point to the existence of beings who are, in the true sense, supernatural.'

'And the multiverse – what of that? Does it consist of an infinite number of layers, or...?'

'The multiverse is finite. Vast as it is, it has limitations. And beyond those limitations exist – other realities, perhaps.'

Renark was silent. All his life he had accepted the concept of infinity, but even his rapidly developing mind could not quite contain the new concept hovering at the edge of his consciousness.

'We believe,' said the metazoa gently, 'that life as we know it is in an undeveloped, crude state – that you and we represent perhaps the first stage in the creation of entities designed, at length, to transcend the limitations of the multiverse. It has been our function, all of us, to have created some sort of order out of original chaos. There is no such thing, even now, as cause and effect – there is still only cause and coincidence; coincidence and effect. This, of course, is obvious to any intelligence. There is no such thing as free will. There is only limited choice. We are limited not only by our environment, but by our psychological condition, by our physical needs – everywhere we turn we are limited. The Ekiversh believe that, though this is true, we can conceive *of* a condition in which this is not so – and perhaps, in time, create that condition.'

'I agree.' Renark nodded. 'It is possible to overcome all restrictions if the will is strong enough.'

'That may be so. You have certainly come through more than any other entity – and it has been your spirit which has been the only thing to keep your mind and body co-ordinated for so long. But, if you wish to continue your quest for as far as you can go in a finite universe, you have the worst experience to come.'

'What do you mean?'

'You must go to the Lattice Planet. There you will meet the dwellers in the Abyss of Reality. Perhaps you have heard of the place as the Hole.'

Yes, Renark had heard the name. He remembered where. Mary had told him about it.

'What exactly is this planet?'

'It does not move through the multiverse in the same way as the rest of the planets in this system, yet in a sense it exists in *all* of them. Pieces of it move in different dimensions, all shifting independently. Sometimes the planet may be fairly complete on random occasions. At other times the planet is full of... *gaps*... where parts of it have ceased to exist according to the dimensional laws operating in whichever continuum the Shifter is in. It is believed that there exists somewhere in this planet a gateway through to a mythical race called the Originators.

'Since you have nowhere else to go, we would suggest that you risk a visit to this planet and attempt to find the gateway, if it exists.'

'Yes, we shall try,' said Renark softly. Then another thought came to him. 'Why isn't this planet, Ekiversh, subject to the same chaotic conditions existing elsewhere?' he asked.

'That is because, before we fled our home universe, we prepared for the conditions which we expected to meet, and we used our skill and knowledge to create a very special organism.'

The glutinous giant seemed to heave its shining body before the next thought came.

'We call it a conservator. The conservator is simply an object, but an object of a peculiar kind which can only exist under a certain set of laws. In order to maintain its own existence, it conserves these laws for a distance around it. These laws, of course, are those under which we exist and under which you, for the most part, exist also. With a conservator in your ship, you will not experience your earlier difficulties in traversing interplanetary space and, also, you will be less likely to lose your way on the Lattice Planet which, incidentally, you know of as Roth, or Ragged Ruth.'

'I am grateful,' Renark said. 'The conservator will be of great assistance.' Then another thought occurred to him. 'You are aware of my reason for coming here – because the universe where I belong is contracting. Could not a number of these conservators be built in order to stop the course which my universe is taking?'

'Impossible. Your universe is not contravening any natural laws. The laws which apply to it are bringing about this change. You must discover why this is happening – for everything has a purpose – and discover what part your race is to play in this reorganisation.'

'Very well,' said Renark humbly.

Several of the metazoa detached themselves from the main body and disappeared in the direction of a line of hills, travelling rapidly. 'We go to fetch a conservator,' the pseudo-giant told him.

Renark used the wait to explore his own state of mind. Strangely, without any great strain, he could now accept the enormity of the realisation which had been dawning on him ever since he first came to the Shifter. And he knew now, unquestioningly, that his whole journey, his trials and endeavours, had had, from the beginning, a definite *purpose* – there was logic in the multiverse. The Ekiversh had convinced him. And that purpose, he thought with dawning clarity, transcended his original one – transcended it and yet was part of it!

But there was much more, he felt, to undergo before this new need in him would be consummated. For now he was to undergo the worst part of the journey – to the planet that had sent Mary the Maze insane. Roth – Ragged Ruth – the Lattice Planet.

The metazoa returned bearing a small globe of a dull ochre colouring. This they placed on the ground, near the airlock of the spaceship.

'We shall leave you now,' the metazoa telepathed, 'but let us wish you knowledge. You, Renark and Asquiol, are the messengers for the multiverse – you must represent us all if you succeed in reaching the Originators – presuming they exist. You go further towards reality than any other intelligent beings, apart from the dwellers of the Hole, have done before…'

Asquiol got into a suit and went outside to collect the conservator. Renark watched him, his gaze unblinking, his thoughts distant, as he returned and placed the globe on the chart desk beside Renark.

Automatically, Renark prepared himself for take-off, thanked the metazoa and pressed the drive control.

Then they were plunging upwards, cutting a pathway of law through the tumbling insanity of interplanetary space.

But this time there was no need to fight it. The conservator acted just as the Ekiversh had predicted, setting up a field all about itself where its own laws operated. Relieved, they had time to talk.

Asquiol had been taken aback by all the events and information he had received. He said: 'Renark, I'm still bewildered. Why exactly are we going to Roth?'

Renark's mood was detached, his voice sounding far away even to his own ears. 'To save the human race. I am realising now that the means of salvation are of a subtler kind than I previously suspected. That is all.'

'But surely we have lost sight of the original purpose for this mission? More – we are living in a fantasy world. This talk of reality is nonsense!'

Renark was not prepared to argue, only to explain. 'The time has come for the dismantling of fantasies. That is already happening to our universe. Now that we have this one chance of survival we must finally rid ourselves of fantasies and seize that chance!

'For centuries our race has built on false assumptions. If you build a fantasy based on a false assumption and continue to build on such a fantasy, your whole existence becomes a lie which you implant in others who are too lazy or too busy to question its truth.

'In this manner you threaten the very existence of reality, because, by refusing to obey its laws, those laws engulf and destroy you. The human race has for too long been manufacturing convenient fantasies and calling them laws. For ages this was so. Take war, for instance. Politicians *assume* that something is true, *assume* that strife is inevitable, and by building on such false assumptions, lo and behold, they create further wars which they have, ostensibly, sought to prevent.

'We have, until now, accepted too many fantasies as being truths, too many truths as fantasies. And we have one last chance to discover the real nature of our existence. I am prepared to take it!'

'And I.' Asquiol spoke softly, but with conviction. He paused and then added with a faint half-smile: 'Though you must forgive me if I still do not fully comprehend your argument.'

'You'll understand it soon enough if things go right.' Renark smiled broadly. Roth now loomed huge on the V.

With a deliberate lack of reverence, Asquiol commented: 'It looks like a great maggoty cheese, doesn't it?'

In the places seeming like glowing sores, they could see right through the planet. In other places there were *gaps* which jarred the eyes, numbed the mind.

Although they could see vaguely the circular outline, the planet was gashed as though some monstrous worm had chewed at it like a caterpillar on a leaf.

Refusing to let the sight overawe him – though it threatened to – Renark brought his skill as a Guide Senser to bear. Deliberately, yet warily, he probed the mass of the weird planet. Where the *gaps* were, he sensed occasionally the existence of parts of the planet which should, by all the laws he knew, be in the same space-time. But they were not – they existed *outside* in many other levels of the multiverse.

He continued to probe and at last found what he was searching for – sentient life. A warmth filled him momentarily.

Had he found the dwellers? These beings appeared not wholly solid, seemed to exist on *all* layers of the multiverse!

Could it be possible? he wondered. Did these beings exist on all planes and thus experience the full knowledge of reality, unlike the denizens who only saw their own particular universe and only experienced a fraction of the multiverse?

Though he could conceive the possibility, his mind could not imagine what these beings might be like, or what they saw. Perhaps he would find out?

He understood now why Mary the Maze played insanely with her lifeless keyboard on Entropium.

Another thought came to him and he felt about with his mind and learned, with a sinking regret, that the Shaarn had succeeded in beating back the Thron. He could not tell definitely, but it seemed that the Shifter's motion through the multiversal levels was slowing down.

Hastily he re-located the dwellers. There were not many and they were on a part of the planet he felt he could find – a part not having its whole existence in the area now occupied by the Shifter, but probably visible to the human eye. With the aid of the conservator he felt fairly certain of finding the mysterious Hole.

Speed was important, but so was caution. He did not wish to suffer an ironical end – perishing now that he was so close to his goal.

He brought the ship down over a *gap* in order to test the conservator's powers.

They were extremely strong. As he came closer, the planet seemed to form itself under him as the missing piece shifted into place like a section of a jigsaw puzzle. It worked.

Now Renark lifted the ship away again and saw the piece fade back, wrenched into its previous continuum. He could not afford to land his ship on such a dangerous location. So he moved on and came down slowly on a surface which, he hoped, would remain in this continuum until he was ready to return.

If he did return, he told himself. The ominous activity near the binary was increasing – perhaps, already, the Shifter had stopped!

Asquiol was silent. He clutched the conservator to him as he followed Renark out of the ship's airlock.

The planet seemed a formless mass of swirling gases and they received a distinct sense of weightlessness for a moment as they placed their feet on its unnatural surface.

Dominated by the dreamlike insecurity of the planet, striking, first, patches of weightlessness, and later patches where their feet seemed entrenched in dragging mud, they moved warily on, Renark in the lead.

Though it was dark, the planet seemed to possess its own luminous aura, so that they could see a fair distance around them. But there were places where, somehow, their vision could not penetrate – yet they could see beyond these places! Even when they walked on rocky ground, it seemed impermanent.

As they moved, the area immediately around them would sometimes alter as the conservator exerted its strange power. But, as if to compensate for this, new *gaps* continued to form elsewhere.

Struggling to keep his objective clear, Renark felt ahead with his mind, awed by the remarkable fluxions taking place constantly.

The planet was perpetually *shifting*. It was impossible to tell which part of it would be in existence even for a few moments at a time. Sundered matter, as chaotic as the unformed stuff of the multiverse at the dawn of creation, wrenched, spread and flung itself about as if in agony.

But, remorselessly, Renark pushed onward, filled with a sense of purpose which dominated his whole being.

Stumbling on, drunk by their visions of chaos, they did not lose their objective for a moment.

Sometimes near, sometimes distant, the Hole became their lodestar, beckoning them with a promise of truth – or destruction!

Chapter Eight

A T LAST, AFTER more than a weary day, they stood above the Hole, and as rock unformed itself and became gas, Renark said hollowly:

'They are in there. This is where we'll find them, but I do not know what they are.'

Though their tiredness made them inactive, Count Renark felt that he had never been more conscious, more receptive to what he saw. But his reception was passive. He could only look at the shifting, shining, dark and myriad-coloured Hole as it throbbed with power and energy.

They stared down at it, filled with knowledge and emotion.

After several hours' silence, Asquiol spoke. 'What now?'

'This is the gateway of which we learned on Thron and Ekiversh,' said Renark. 'I can do nothing now but descend into it in the hope of achieving our aim.' Now the human race seemed remote, a fantasy, unreal – and yet important. More important than it had ever been before.

He moved towards the very brink of the Hole and lowered himself into its pulsing embrace.

Asquiol paused for a moment behind him and then followed. They ceased to climb down, for they were now floating, going neither up nor down, nor in any definite direction, but yet floating – somewhere. The conservator had ceased to work – unless it still worked and, in some way, these laws applied more rigorously to it than any it had previously conserved.

Again they were on solid ground, on a small island in an ocean. They stepped forward and knew they were in the heart of a blazing sun; stepped back and were in the middle of a bleak mountain range. From the tops of the mountains an entity looked down and welcomed them.

They moved towards it and were suddenly in an artificial chamber which seemed, at first, to have dead, black walls. Then they realised they were looking out into a void – emptiness.

To their left a being appeared.

It seemed to be constantly fading and reappearing. Like a badly tuned V-set, Renark thought, desperately looking for something to cling to. He felt cut off entirely from anything he knew.

The being began to speak. It was not Terran he spoke. He conversed in a combination of sonic and thought waves which struck responses in Renark's mind and body. He realised that these entities may have once been like himself, but had lost the power of direct speech when they gained the power to dwell on all levels of the multiverse.

He found he could communicate with the entity by modulating his own speech and thinking as far as possible in pictures.

'*You wish* (complicated geometric patterns) *help...?*'

'Yes (picture of universe contracting)...'

'*You from* (picture of a pregnant woman which changed quickly to a womb – an embryo, not quite human, appeared in it)...?'

Renark deliberated the meaning of this, but did not take long to realise what the entity was trying to say. Already he had half realised the significance.

Logic, based on the evidence he had seen and heard in the rest of the Shifter, was leading Renark towards an inescapable conclusion.

'Yes,' he said.

'*You must wait.*'

'For what?'

'(Picture of a vast universe, multi-planed, turning about a central point) *Until* (picture of the Shifter moving through time, space and other dimensions towards the Hub)...'

Renark realised what the picture meant. It could only mean one thing. He had only been shown it briefly, yet he understood clearly.

He had been shown the centre of the universe, the original place through which all the universal radii passed, from which all things had come. There were no alternate universes at the centre. When the Shifter passed through the centre – what...?

But what if the Shaarn succeeded in stopping the system's progress before it reached the Hub? He had to dismiss the idea. If the Shifter stopped too soon there would be no need for further speculation. No need for anything.

'What will happen there (misty picture of the multiverse)?' he asked.

'Truth. *You must wait here until* (Hub with Shifter) *then go* (the binary star – the Shifter's star)...'

He had to wait in limbo until the Shifter reached the Hub and then they must journey towards – no, *into* – the sun!

He transmitted a horrified picture of himself and Asquiol burning.

The being said: '*No*,' and disappeared again.

When it reappeared, Renark said: 'Why?'

'*You are expected.*' The being faded, then vanished.

Since time did not exist here they couldn't tell how long they had waited. There were none of the usual bodily indications that time was passing.

Quite simply, they were in limbo.

Every so often the being, or one like it, would reappear. Sometimes he would impart information regarding the Shifter's slow progress, sometimes he would just be there. Once a number of his kind appeared but vanished immediately.

Then, finally, the dweller appeared and a picture of the Shifter entering the area of the Multiversal Centre manifested itself in Renark's mind.

With relief and a bounding sense of anticipation, he prepared to experience – *Truth*.

Soon, whether he lived or died, remained sane or went insane, he would know. He and Asquiol would be the first of their race to *know*.

And this, they both realised, was all that mattered.

Then they went outwards towards the flaring, agonisingly brilliant suns.

They felt they had no physical form as they had known it, and yet could sense the stuff of their bodies clinging about them.

They poured their massless bodies into the fiery heat, the heart of the star, and eventually came to the Place of the Originators – not their natural habitat, but a compromise between Renark's and theirs.

They saw, without using their eyes, the Originators.

They could hear the Originators communicating, but there was no sound. All was colour, light and formlessness. Yet everything had a quality of bright existence, true reality.

'You are here,' said the Originators musingly, as one. 'We have been awaiting you and grown somewhat impatient. Your rate of development was not what we had hoped.'

On behalf of his race, in the knowledge of what the Originators meant, Renark said: 'I am sorry.'

'You were always a race to progress only when danger threatened.'

'Do we still exist?' Renark asked.

'Yes.

'For how long?' Asquiol spoke for the first time.

The Originators did not answer his question directly. Instead, they said: 'You wish us to make changes. We expected this. That is why we speeded up the metamorphosis of your universe. You understand that although your universe is contracting, it will still exist as individual galaxies, suns and planets, matter of most kinds in different formations?'

'But the human race – what of that?'

'We should have let it die. Intelligent organic life cannot undergo the strains of the change. If you had not come to us, we should have let it die – regretfully. But our judgement was correct. We let you know of the coming catastrophe and you used all your resources of will and judgement to come here as we hoped you would.'

There was a pause, and then the Originators continued: 'Like all other races in the multiverse, yours is capable of existing on all levels. Not just one. But, because of these links you have with the rest of the levels, you would have perished, being not fully natural to just one level. None of the intelligent forms could survive such a catastrophe. We were responsible for placing them all in their present environment. Each plane of the multiverse serves as a separate seeding bed for a multitude of races, one of which may survive and succeed us. Your plane serves, in your terms, as a womb. You are our children – our hope. But if you fail to overcome the special limitations we set upon you, you, like us, shall die. But you shall die... still-born.

'Then what is to become of us?'

'We made the changes in your universe in order to accelerate your rate of development, so that representatives of your race would find a way to us. To the greatest extent you have succeeded, but you must return rapidly and inform your race of their need to develop more rapidly. We shall afford you the means, this time, of evacuating your universe. But we are growing old, and you, of all the intelligent races in the multiverse, are needed to take our place. You cannot do that until you are ready. Either you succeed in achieving your birthright, or, like us, perish in chaos and agony.

'You have proved to us that we were justified in selecting you. You *can* overcome the boundaries we set around you. But hurry, we beg you – hurry...'

'What will happen if we succeed?'

'You will experience a stage of metamorphosis. Soon you will no longer need a universe of the kind you know now. Things are coming to an end. You have the choice of life – more than life – or death!'

Renark accepted this. It was all he could do. 'And us – what is our function now?'

'To perform what you set out to do.'

There was a long, long pause.

Womb-warmth filled the two men and time stopped for them as the Originators exuded sympathy and understanding. But glowing like hard reality beneath this, Renark sensed – his own oblivion? His own death? Something lay there in the future. Something ominous was in store for him.

'You are right, Renark,' said the Originators.

'I can't be right or wrong. I have no idea what my fate is.'

'But you sense, perhaps, our foreknowledge of your termination as a physical entity – perhaps your end as a conscious entity. It is hard to tell. Your spirit is a great one, Renark – a mighty spirit that is too great for the flesh that chains it. It must be allowed to spread, to permeate the multiverse!'

'So be it,' Renark said slowly.

Asquiol could neither understand nor believe what the Originators were saying. His form – golden, flashing red – bounced and flared before Renark as he said: 'Are you to die, Renark?'

'No! No!' Renark's voice roared like a tower of flame. He addressed his friend. 'When I am gone you must lead our race. You must direct them towards their destiny – or perish with them. Do you understand?'

'I accept what you say, but without understanding. This experience is driving us to madness!'

The cool tones of the Originators swept inwards like flowing ice to catch their attention and silence them. 'Not yet, not yet. You must both retain something of your old forms and your old convictions. Your part is not played out yet. Now that you understand the nature of the multiverse, it will not be difficult to supply you with material means for escaping your shrinking universe. We will give you knowledge of a machine to produce a warp effect and enable your people to travel to another, safer universe where they will undergo further tests. Our plans have not fully worked themselves out yet. There are others of your race involved – and you must meet and react and harden one another before you can fulfil the destiny we offer you. You, Asquiol, will be entrusted with this part of the mission.'

'Renark is the strongest,' Asquiol said quietly.

'Therefore Renark's spirit must be sacrificed as a gift to the rest of you. This is necessary.'

'How shall we accomplish this exodus to a new universe?' Renark asked hollowly.

'We will help. We shall instil in your fellow creatures a trust in the word of you both. It will necessarily be a temporary thing. Once you have left your universe, our workings must be of a subtler sort, and only the efforts of certain individuals will save you.'

'We shall be on our own?' Asquiol questioned.

'Virtually, yes.'

'What shall we find in this new universe?'

'We do not know, for it is likely that your jump will be a random one into *any* of the other multiversal planes. We cannot guarantee you a friendly reception. There are forces opposed to our purpose – meaner intellects who strive to prevent the evolution of our being.'

'Our being?' Asquiol's shape flickered and re-formed.

'Yours – ours – everyone's. We, the Originators, are intelligent optimists, since we see a purpose, of sorts, to existence. But there are pessimists in the universe. They prey upon us, seek to destroy us, since they themselves have given up hope of ever breaking the bonds which chain them to the half-real state in which they exist. They have their unknowing supporters among your own segment of the total race.'

'I understand.'

With those two words they became whole men. They saw, at last, the real universe – the myriad-planed universe comprising many, many dimensions so that there was no empty space at all, but a crowded, rich existence through which they had previously moved unknowing.

With an effort of his titanic will, Renark said urgently: 'One thing. What *is* your purpose? What is our ultimate purpose?'

'To exist,' was the simple reply. 'You cannot have, as yet, real knowledge of what that means. Existence is the beginning and the end. Whatever significance you choose to put upon it is irrelevant. If we were to die before you were ready to take our place, then all our creations would die. The multiverse would die. Chaos would flood over everything and what to us would seem a formless, mindless, fluctuating shroud would mark our passing.'

'We do not want that,' said Asquiol and Renark together.

'Neither do we. That is why you are here. Now – the information you will need.'

Their minds, it seemed, were taken by a gentle hand and sent along a certain course of logic until, at length, they had complete understanding of the principle involved in building dimension-travelling spaceships.

In what was, for them, normal space-time, it would have been virtually impossible to have formulated the principle in all its aspects. But now, dwelling in the whole multiverse, the logic seemed simple. They were confident that they could impart the information to their own race.

'Are you satisfied?' the Originators asked.

'Perfectly,' Renark said. 'We must hurry now, and return to our own universe. The exodus must begin as soon as possible.'

'Farewell, Renark. It is unlikely that when we meet again you will remember us. Farewell, Asquiol. When *we* meet again let us hope that you have succeeded in this matter.'

'Let us hope so,' Asquiol said gravely.

Then their beings were spreading backwards and streaming through the multiverse towards the ship which still lay on Roth.

Chapter Nine

THE TRAVELLER STOPPED at the sagging filling station, the last human artefact before the long, grey road began again.

A huge, shapeless haversack bulged on his stooping back, but he walked along effortlessly, smiling in the depths of his lean, black face, his hair and beard wild about him.

Kaal Yinsen whistled to himself and took the road north. It was several centuries since the Earth had been populated by more than the few thousand people living here now, and this was the way he liked it. Kaal Yinsen had never had a dream in his life, and when this one came it came with force.

The road faded, the whole surface of the planet reared up, whirled and bellowed. Suddenly he knew he must head south again. This he did and was joined, on the way, by hundreds of families going in the same direction.

Bossan Glinqvist, Elected of Orion, sat in an office which was part of an isolated metal city, hanging in space close to the heart of the galaxy. He picked up the file on Drenner Macneer and began to leaf through it, not sure that his duties as Moderator in the Galactic Council were sufficiently satisfying to make him live a third of his adult life in so unnatural an environment. Macneer's case was a difficult one, requiring all Glinqvist's concentration and intelligence to judge.

The man had instigated a breach-of-code suit against the Council – accusing it of failing to represent the interests of a minority group of traders who, because of a change in a tariff agreement between Lanring and Balesorn in the Clive System, had lost their initiative to survive by labour and were currently living off the citizens' grant on a remote outworld. It was a serious matter. Glinqvist looked up, frowning, and experienced a powerful hallucination.

Soon afterwards he was giving orders for the city to be set in motion – an unprecedented order – and directed towards the Kassim System.

These were but two examples of what was happening to every intelligent denizen of the galaxy.

Every human being, adult or child, was filled with the same compulsion to journey towards certain central planets where they gathered – and waited patiently.

On Earth, the few inhabitants of the planet felt that the very ground would give beneath the weight of so many newcomers. Normally, they would have been resentful of the appearance of outsiders on the recently healed globe, but now, with them, they waited.

And at last they were rewarded.

They saw its vague outlines in the sky. On PV screens all over the planet they watched it land on a tendril of fire. A spaceship – a Police Cruiser. It was scarred and battered. It looked old and scarcely spaceworthy.

There was silence everywhere as they watched the airlock open and two figures emerge.

Millions of pairs of eyes winced and failed to focus properly upon the figures. They strained to see *all* the figures, but it was impossible. The men who came out of the ship were like ghostly chameleons, their hazy bodies shifting with colour and energy and light.

The watchers seemed to see many images overlaid on the two they recognised as men, images which seemed to stretch out into other dimensions beyond their powers to see or to imagine.

These visitors were like angels. Their set faces glowed with knowledge; the matter of their bodies was iridescent; their words, when they began to speak, throbbed in tempo with the pulse of the planet so that it was as if they heard an earthquake speak, or an ocean or a volcano, or even the sun itself giving voice!

Yet they understood that these messengers were human. But humans so altered that it was almost impossible to regard them as such.

They listened in awe to the words and, in part at least, they understood what they must do.

Renark and Asquiol delivered the ultimate message. They told of the threat inherent in the contracting universe. They told how this had come about and why. And then they told how the destruction of the race could be avoided.

They spoke clearly, in careful terms, looking out at their listeners from the depths of their faraway minds. No longer existing wholly in any one plane of the multiverse, they needed to concentrate in order to keep this single level in complete focus.

The myriad dimensions of the multiverse coursed in ever-changing beauty as they spoke. But this experience they could not as yet convey, for it was beyond speech. And the stuff of their bodies changed with the multiverse in scintillating harmony so that the watchers could not always see them as men. But, nonetheless, they listened.

They listened and learned that the multiverse contained many levels and that their universe was but one level – a fragment of the great whole. That it was finite, yet beyond the power of their minds to comprehend. They learned that this structure had been created by beings called the Originators. They learned that the Originators, sensing they would die, had created this multiverse as a seeding ground for a race to take their place. They learned that they, the embryonic children of the Originators, were to be given their last chance to take over. They were given a choice: Understand and overcome the pseudo-real boundaries of time and space as they understood them, therefore claiming their birthright – or perish!

Then Renark and Asquiol left the planet Earth, passing on to another and then another to impart their news.

Wherever they passed they left behind them awed silence, and each human being that heard them was left with a feeling of *completeness* such as he knew he had been searching for all his life.

Then the two multifaceted messengers called technicians and scientists and philosophers to them and told these men what they must do.

Soon after, the vehicles, which had been fitted with the Inter-continua-Travelling device, swarmed in the depths of space beyond the Rim, ready to carry the human race into another universe.

At the head of the tremendous space-caravan the small, battered Police Cruiser lay. In it, Renark and Asquiol took their final leave of one another.

Outside the cruiser, a small space car awaited Renark.

The two beings looked at one another's shifting forms, stared about them to absorb the pulsating sight of the total multiverse, clasped hands, but said nothing. It was preordained that this must happen.

Sorrowfully, Asquiol watched his friend board the space car and vanish back towards the Hub of the galaxy.

Now he had to make ready the giant fleet. The Galactic Council had sworn him full powers of leadership until such a time as he would no longer be needed. The efficient administration which had run the galaxy for many years was admirably suited to organising the vast fleet and they took Asquiol's orders and translated them into action.

'At precisely 1800 hours General Time, each ship will engage its I.T. drive.' Asquiol's lonely voice echoed across the void through which the fleet drifted.

Somewhere, out of sight of Asquiol or the human race, a small figure halted its space-car, climbed into a suit, clambered from the car and hung in space as it drifted away.

Now they could observe the galaxies rushing down upon one another. They came together and joined in one blazing symphony of light as the human race plunged through the dimensions to the safety of another universe where another intelligent life form waited to receive it – perhaps in friendship, perhaps in resentment.

Then the contraction was swifter, sudden.

Only Renark remained behind. Why, the race would never know – and even Renark was uncertain of his reasons. He only knew there had to be a sacrifice. Was it the ancient creed of his savage ancestors, translated into the terms of the Originators? Or did his action have some greater meaning? There would be no answer. There could be none.

Faster and faster, the universe contracted until all of it existed in an area that seemed little larger than Renark's hand. Still it shrank, as Renark watched it now as if from a distance. Then it vanished from his sight, though he could still sense it, was still aware of its rapidly decreasing size.

He knew that there was a point to which a thing can be reduced before it ceases to exist, and finally that point was reached. Now there was a gap, a real flaw in the fabric of the multiverse itself. His universe, the galaxy, the Earth, were no longer there – possibly absorbed into a larger universe beyond even Renark's marvellous senses. Perhaps, in this greater universe, his universe existed as a photon somewhere. Only Renark was left, his shifting, shimmering body moving in a void, the stuff of it beginning to dissipate and disappear.

'God!' he said as everything vanished.

His voice echoed and ached through the deserted gulf and Renark lived that moment for ever.

Book Two

The Blood Red Game

Chapter Ten

IN HIS DEEP sorrow, Asquiol was resolved to carry on Renark's work and bring to finality the Originators' plans for the human race.

The fleet was dropping, dropping, dropping through layer after layer of the multiverse in a barely controlled escape dive.

Soon he must give the order to slow down and halt on one level. He had no idea which to choose. Though he was aware of the multiverse, his vision, unlike Renark's, could not extend beyond its previous limits. He had no inkling of what to expect in the universe in which they would finally stop.

In the great multiverse they were merely a scattering of seeds – seeds that must survive many elements if they were to grow.

Finite, yet containing the chaotic stuff of infinity, the multiverse wheeled in its gigantic movement through space.

To those who could observe it from beyond its boundaries – the Originators – it appeared as a solid construction, dense and huge. Yet within it there were many things, many intelligences who did not realise that they dwelt in the multiverse, since each layer was separated from another by dimensions. Dimensions that were like leaves between the layers.

Here and there the mighty structure was flawed – by fragments which moved *through* the dimensions, through the leaves, passing many universes; by a vacuum existing where one small part had vanished. But, on the whole, the universes remained unknown, one to another. They did not realise that they were part of a composite structure of fantastic complexity. They did not realise their purpose or the purpose for which the multiverse had been created.

Only the chosen knew – and of them only a few understood.

So, fleeing from their newly non-existent galaxy, the human

race began its great exodus into a new space-time continuum – pierced the walls of the dimension-barrier and came, at last, into another universe.

By this action, humanity also entered a new period of its history.

But Asquiol of Pompeii was no longer an individual. He had become many individuals and was therefore complete. Now there was no better leader for the human fleet; no better mentor to guide it. For Asquiol existed in a multitude of dimensions, his vision extended beyond the limitations of his fellows, and saw all that humanity could one day become – if they could make the effort.

Asquiol of Pompeii, captain of destiny, destroyer of boundaries, becalmed in detachment, opened his eyes from a sad reverie and observed the fleet he led.

His screen showed him the vast caravan of vessels. There were space-liners and battleships, launches and factory ships, ships of all kinds and for all purposes, containing all the machinery of a complex society on the move. There were ships of many designs, some ornate, some plain, containing one part in common – the I.T. drive.

Asquiol deliberately ceased to wonder why Renark had elected to stay behind in the dying universe. But he still wished it had not happened. He missed the confidence which had come to him from Renark's presence, from Renark's will and spirit. But Renark and his will were in the past now. Asquiol had to find strength only from within himself – or perish.

And if he perished, ceased to be what he was, then the danger of the race itself perishing would be heightened considerably. Therefore, he reasoned, his survival and the survival of the race were linked.

Twenty-four hours of relative time had not passed since the fleet left the home universe. He decided that the next universe, irrespective of what it was, should be the one to remain in. Quickly he gave the order. 'De-activate I.T. drive at 1800 hours.'

At 1800 hours exactly, the fleet ceased to fall through the dimensions and found itself entering the fringes of a strange galaxy, not knowing what they might encounter or what danger might exist here.

On board the administration ships, men worked on data which was pouring in.

They charted the galaxy; they learned that, in construction, it was scarcely different from their own. Asquiol wasn't surprised – each layer of the multiverse differed only slightly from the next.

Guide Sensers investigated the nearer suns and planets, while telepaths explored the widespread systems for signs of intelligent life. If they discovered such life they would then have to assess, if possible, its attitude towards the refugee-invaders now entering the confines of its galaxy. This was a new technique, one which Asquiol had learned from the Shaarn.

Flanking the fleet were the great battlewagons of the Galactic Police, now entrusted with the guardianship of the mighty cara-van as it plunged at fantastic speed through the scattering of suns that was the Rim of the spiral galaxy.

Hazy lights filled space for several miles in all directions, the ships of the fleet swimming darkly through it. Beyond the fleet was the sharper darkness and beyond that the faint sparks of the stars. The light emanated from the ships like a swirling, intangible neb-ula, moving constantly towards a destination it might never reach.

But Asquiol saw more than this, for Asquiol saw the multiverse.

It required, in fact, a certain effort now to devote his attention to only one plane, no matter how vast. As soon as he relaxed his attention, he felt the absolute pleasure of dwelling on all the planes simultaneously, of seeing around him all that there was in the area of the multiverse he now occupied.

It was like existing in a place where the very air was jewelled and faceted, glistening and alive with myriad colours, flashing, scintillating, swirling and beautiful.

This was a richer thing, the multiverse as a whole. In it Asquiol could see his own fleet and the faraway stars, but the space between everything was crammed full. The multiverse was packed thick with life and matter. There was not an inch which did not possess something of interest. Vacuum was, in a sense, that which separated one layer from another. When all the layers were experienced as a whole, there was no wasted vacuum, no dark nothingness. Here was everything at once, all possibilities, all experience.

He was suddenly forced to pull himself back from this individual experience. The special alarm over his laser-screen was shrilling urgently.

A face appeared on the screen. It was pouched and puffy, heavily jowled like that of a bloodhound.

'Mordan.' Asquiol addressed the Galactic Councillor who was captain-in-chief of Police.

'Asquiol.' Even now Asquiol's power was virtually absolute, Mordan couldn't bring himself to call him 'prince', for the Galactic Council had not agreed to restore the now meaningless title. Mordan spoke heavily: 'Our Guide Sensers and Mind Sensers have come up with important information. We have located and contacted an intelligent species who appear to have noticed our entry into this space-time. They are evidently a star-travelling race.'

'How have they reacted to our entry?'

'We aren't sure – the Sensers are finding it difficult to adjust to their minds...'

'Naturally, it will take time to understand a non-human species. Let me know if you have any further news.'

Mordan had been screwing up his eyes while looking at Asquiol's image. There appeared to be several images, in fact, each containing a different combination of colours, overlapping one another. It was as if Asquiol looked out at Mordan through a series of tinted, opaque masks covering his body and interleaving on either side. The image that Mordan took to be the original lay slightly to one side of the multiple image and, for him, in better focus than the rest. He evidently could not equate this image with what he remembered – the cynical, moody, vital young man whom he had divested of title and power a few years before. Now he saw a lean, saturnine man, the face of a fallen archangel, stern with the weight of leadership, the eyes sharp yet staring into a distance containing little that Mordan felt he could observe.

With his usual feeling of relief, Mordan switched out and relayed Asquiol's message to the Senser team.

As he waited for further news, Asquiol didn't exert his mind by trying to contact the new species directly.

That would come later. He decided to allow the Sensers time to assemble as much general data as possible before he turned his full attention to the problem.

He kept in mind the Originators' warning that certain intelligences were quite likely to receive the human race with insensate hostility, but he hoped the universe they were in contained life that would welcome them and allow them to settle where they could. If the intelligences were hostile, the fleet was equipped to fight – and, in the last resort, run. He had already ordered the lifting of the ban on the anti-neutron cannon, and this devastating armament was virtually invincible. As far as he knew there was no known screen that could withstand it. The fleet was already alerted for battle. There was nothing to do at the moment but wait and see.

He returned his thoughts to problems of a different nature.

Landing on and settling new planets within this galaxy would only be a minor problem compared with the task of taking over from the Originators.

He thought of his race as a chicken in an egg. Within the shell it was alive, but aware of nothing beyond the shell. With the act of breaking through the barrier of dimensions separating its universe from others, it had broken from its enclosing and stifling shell to some awareness of the multiverse and the exact nature of things.

But a hatched chicken, thought Asquiol, may believe the breaking of the shell to be the ultimate action of its life – until the shell shattered and the whole world was visible in all its complexity. Then it discovered the farmyard and the countryside with all their many dangers. It discovered that it was only a chick and must learn and act to survive if it was to grow to adulthood.

And what, Asquiol considered ironically, was the eventual fate of the average chicken? He wondered how many other races had got this far in the ages of the multiverse's existence. Only one would survive, and now it had to be the human race, for if it did not attain its birthright before the Originators died, then none would take its place. The multiverse would return to the chaos from which the Originators had formed it.

Quasi-death and the stuff of death would engulf the cosmos. The tides of chance would roll over all existing things, and the multiverse, bereft of guidance and control, would collapse into its original components. All sentience, as the Originators and their creations understood it, would perish!

It was this knowledge that enabled him to keep his objective in the forefront. The race must not perish; it must survive and progress, must achieve the marvellous birthright that was its promised destiny. The race must replace the Originators while there was still a little time.

Was there sufficient time?

Asquiol didn't know. He had no way of knowing when the Originators would die. He had, in this case, to attempt to pack centuries of evolution into the shortest possible period. Whether, immediate danger averted, the race would allow him to continue with his mission he did not know. Now that the weird influence of the Originators had been removed, mankind could throw away its birthright, and consequently the life of all ordered creation, by one ill-judged or fear-inspired decision.

Even now there were elements in the fleet who questioned his leadership, questioned his vision and his motives. It was easy to understand this suspicious impulse which was at once man's salvation and doom. Without it he ceased to reason; with it he often ceased to act. To *use* the impulse objectively was the answer, Asquiol knew. But how?

Without the usual warning, Mordan's face appeared on the laser. He stared into emptiness since he preferred not to have to see Asquiol's disturbing image.

'These intelligences are obviously preparing to attack us,' he said urgently.

So the worst had happened. In which case the threat must be met. 'What preparations are you making?' Asquiol said in a level voice.

'I have alerted our battle force and all essential craft are now protected by energy screens – administration ships, farm ships, factory ships. These I intend to reassemble at the centre of our formation since they are necessary for survival.

'Around these I will put all residential ships. The third section comprises all fighting craft, including privately owned vessels with worthwhile armament. The operation is working fairly smoothly, though there are a few recalcitrants I'm having difficulty with. We are forming totally to enclose your ship so that you are properly protected.'

Asquiol drew a deep breath and said slowly: 'Thank you, Mordan. That sounds most efficient.' To Mordan, his voice seemed to produce – like his image – intrinsic, faraway echoes that carried past Mordan and beyond him. 'How do you intend to deal with these recalcitrants?'

'I have conferred with the other members of the Galactic Council and we have come to a decision – subject to your approval.'

'That decision is?'

'We will have to use more direct powers of action – make emergency laws only to be declared null and void after the danger has passed.'

'The example of history should deter you from such a decision. Powers of dictatorship, which you give me and yourselves, once assumed are liable to last beyond the circumstances for which they were devised. We have not employed coercion, force, or anything like it, for two centuries!'

'Asquiol – there is no time for debate!'

Asquiol made up his mind immediately. Survival, for the moment, was of primary importance. 'Very well. Take on these powers – force the recalcitrants to obey our orders, but be sure not to abuse the powers or we will find ourselves weakened rather than strengthened.'

'This we know. Thank you.'

Asquiol watched, his mood brooding and disquieted, as the fleet re-deployed into a great oval shape with his own battered ship in the centre, the nut in an inordinately thick shell.

Chapter Eleven

ADAM ROFFREY WAS a loner, a rebel without a cause, a hater of state and organisation.

He morosely watched the ships re-forming about him, but remained where he was, refusing to answer the signal on his screen. His large head, made larger by the thick, black beard and hair covering it, had a dogged, insolent set. He was refusing to budge and knew he was within his rights.

The flexible laws of the galaxy had been bent by him many times, for the rights of the citizen were varied and complex. He could not be forced to take part in a war; without his permission the authorities could not even contact him. Therefore, he sat tight, ignoring the urgent signal.

When Councillor Mordan's bloodhound face appeared, unauthorised, on the laser-screen, Roffrey disguised his shock and smiled sardonically. He said lightly, as he always said things, whatever the gravity of the statement: 'It's a lost cause, Mordan. We can't hope to win. We must be fantastically outnumbered. Asquiol's forcing the race to commit suicide. Are we voting?'

'No,' said Mordan, 'we're not. For the duration of the emergency all citizens' rights are liable to be waived if necessary. You have no choice but to comply with the decision of Asquiol and the Galactic Council. Asquiol knows what's best.'

'He doesn't know what's best for me. I'm the only lost cause I've ever backed, and that's the way it's staying!'

Councillor Mordan regarded the black-bearded giant grinning out of the PV screen and he frowned. 'Nobody leaves the fleet, Roffrey. For one thing, it's too dangerous, and for another, we've got to keep it tight and organised if we're to survive!'

He said the last words to a blank screen. He whirled round in his control chair and shouted to a passing captain. 'Alert the perimeter guard. A ship may try to leave. Stop it!'

'How, Councillor Mordan?'

'Force – if there is no other alternative,' said Mordan, shocking the captain, who had never received such an order in his whole career.

Adam Roffrey had been antisocial all his life.

His living had been made on the fringes of the law. He wasn't going to give in to the demands of society now. The chips were down for the fleet – that was his guess – and he had no reason for sticking around. He objected to the discipline required to fight complicated space-battles; he objected to the odds against the human race winning the battles; he objected to the fact that he was being personally involved. Personal involvement was not in his line.

So he broke the energy seals on his anti-neutron cannon and prepared to blast out. As he moved away from the rest of the fleet, several Geepee gunboats, alerted by Mordan, flitted towards him from nadir-north-west.

He rubbed his hairy chin, scratched his forehead and reached out a hairy hand to his drive control. At full power he retreated, away from the oncoming ships, away from the fleet, into the unknown space of the unknown universe.

He was prepared to take such chances to avoid curtailment of his personal liberty.

But his ship, a peculiar vessel, at first sight an impossible old hulk, a space launch got up to look like a merchantman and fitted like a battlewagon, could not hope to outdistance the Geepee craft in the long run. Already they were beginning to catch up.

Humming to himself, he debated his best course of action.

There was one sure method of evading immediate danger as well as the alien threat already visible as a huge fleet of spherical vessels, seen on his screens, approached the fleet from the depths of space.

But to take that way out, although he had considered it much earlier in another context, could be highly dangerous.

The odds were that, if he committed himself to it, he would never see another human being again.

The necessity to make a decision was increasing.

His ship, like all those in the great cosmic caravan, was fitted with the I.T. drive enabling him to travel through the dimensions. He had already taken the trouble to learn all he could about multi-dimensional space and certain things existing in it. He knew, suddenly, where he was going.

The idea had been in the back of his mind for years. Now he would be forced to go.

The Geepee ships were getting closer, their warning blaring on his communicator. He pressed a key on his chart-viewer, keeping a wary eye on the oncoming ships.

Though the Geepees were nearer, the two embattled fleets were far behind. He saw faint splashes of coloured light on his screen. He was tense and was surprised to note that he had a feeling half of relief, half of guilt that he had missed the battle. He wasn't a coward, but now he had something to do.

A quick glance at the slide of equations on the viewer and his hand was reaching for the crudely constructed controls of the I.T. drive. He pulled a lever, adjusted the controls, and quite suddenly the Geepee ships seemed to fade away. And fading into the place where they had been was a backdrop of great blazing suns that made his eyes ache.

Once again he experienced the unique sensation of falling through the layers of the multiverse.

Rapidly, as he operated the I.T. drive, the suns faded to be replaced by cold vacuum, which was replaced by an agitation of gases heaving about in an unformed state, scarlet and grey. He was phasing quickly through the layers, through universe after universe with only a slight feeling of nausea in his stomach and a fierce determination to reach his destination.

The Geepee ships hadn't followed him.

They had probably decided that their first priority was to aid the human fleet.

He travelled through space as well as time and the separating dimensions, and he was heading back in the direction where, in his home universe, the edge of the galaxy had been. He had all the bearings he needed and, as he moved on one level, he moved through others at reckless speed.

He knew where he was going – but whether he would make it was a question he couldn't answer.

Asquiol of Pompeii watched the battle on his screens with a feeling akin to helplessness. Mordan was conducting the war, needing only basic orders from him.

Am I doing as much as I could? he wondered. *Am I not accepting too complacently what I have discovered?*

It was easy for him to dominate the fleet, for his mind had become at once flexible and strong and his physical presence overawed his fellows. There was a part of him, too, which was not at ease, as if he were a jigsaw complete but for the last piece, and the section that would complete him was just – tantalisingly – out of reach.

Somewhere in the multiverse he felt the piece existed – perhaps another intelligence that he could share his thoughts and experiences with. He was almost certain it was out there, yet what it was and how he would find it he did not know. Without it, his picture of himself was incomplete. He felt that he functioned but could not progress. Had the Originators deliberately done this to him? Or had they made a mistake?

At first he had thought it was the loss of Renark which gave him the sense of incompleteness. But Renark's loss was still there, inside him, kept out of mind as much as possible. No, this was another lack. A lack of what, though?

He bent closer to observe the battle.

The fleet's formation was lost as yet another wave of attackers pounced out of space, their weapons lances of bright energy.

They were not impervious to anti-neutron cannon, but the two forces were fairly matched as far as technology went. There were more of the aliens and they had the double advantage of being in home territory and defending it. This was what primarily worried Asquiol.

MICHAEL MOORCOCK

But he could do nothing decisive at the moment. He would have to wait.

Again, while Mordan sweated to withstand and retaliate against this fresh attack, Asquiol let his mind and being drop through the layers of the multiverse and contact the alien commanders. If they would not accept peace terms, he strove to arrange a truce.

To his surprise, this suggestion seemed acceptable to them.

There *was* an alternative to open war – one which they would be delighted to negotiate.

That was?

The Game, they said. Play the Game with us – winner takes all.

After he had got some inkling of the Game's nature, Asquiol deliberated momentarily. There were pros and cons...

Finally, he agreed and was soon watching the enemy ships retreating away into the void.

With some trepidation, he informed Mordan of his decision and awaited its outcome.

This new development in their struggle with the aliens disturbed Mordan. War he could understand. This, at first, he could not. All psychologists, psychiatrists, physiologists and kindred professionals had been ordered to the huge factory ship which engineers were already converting.

From now on, according to Asquiol, the battle was to be fought from this single ship – and it had no armaments!

Asquiol was unapproachable as he conferred with the alien commanders in his own peculiar way. Every so often he would break off to issue strange orders.

Something about a game. Yet what kind of game, wondered Mordan, required experts in psychology as its players? What was the complicated electronic equipment that technicians were installing in the great converted hold of the factory ship?

'This is our only chance of winning,' Asquiol had told him. 'A slim one – but if we learn how to play it properly, we have a chance.'

Mordan sighed. At least the truce had allowed them time to

118

regroup and assess damage. The damage had been great. Two thirds of the fleet had been destroyed. Farm ships and factory ships were working at full capacity to supply the rest of the fleet with necessities. But tight rationing had been introduced. The race was subsisting on survival rations. The initial joy of escape was replaced by gloomy desperation.

Adam Roffrey could see his destination.

He slammed the I.T. activator to the 'off' position and coasted towards the looming system ahead.

It hung in empty space, the outlines of its planets hazy, following a random progression around a magnificent binary sun.

The legendary system rose larger on his V-screen. The unnatural collection of worlds came closer.

The epic story of Count Renark and Prince Asquiol on their quest to the Sundered Worlds was common lore among the human race. But the story – or, at least, part of it – had had a special significance for Roffrey.

Renark and Asquiol had left two members of their party behind – Willow Kovacs and Paul Talfryn.

Roffrey knew their names. But dominant in his skull was another name – a woman's, the woman he had come to find.

If he did not find her this time, he told himself, then he would have to accept that she was dead. Then he would have to accept his own death also.

Such was the intensity of his obsession.

As he neared the Sundered Worlds he regarded them with curiosity. They had changed. The planets were spaced normally – not equidistantly, as he had thought. And, as far as he could tell, the system had stopped shifting.

Now he remembered part of the story which would fast become a myth among those who had fled their own galaxy. A doglike race called the Shaarn had attempted to stop the system's course through the dimensions.

Evidently they'd succeeded.

His maps aided him to find Entropium and he cruised into the

Shifter's area warily, for he knew enough to expect two kinds of danger – the Thron and the lawless nature of the Shifter itself.

Yet, wary as he was, it was impossible to observe either chaos or enemy as he swept down over Entropium, scanning the planet for the only city that had ever been built there.

He didn't find the city, either.

He found, instead, a place where a city had been. Now it was jagged rubble. He landed his ship on a scattered wasteland of twisted steel and smashed concrete.

Scanning the surrounding ruins, he saw shadowy shapes scuttling through the dark craters and between the shattered buildings. His experience told him nothing about the cause of this catastrophe.

At length, sick at heart, he climbed into space armour, strapped an anti-neutron pistol to his side, descended to the airlock and placed his booted feet on the planet's surface.

A bolt of energy flashed from a crater and spread itself over his force-screen. He staggered back to lean against one of his ship's landing fins, lugging the pistol from its holster.

He did not fire immediately for, like everyone else, he had a certain fear of the destructive effects of the a-n gun.

He saw an alien figure – a dazzling white skin like melted plastic covering a squat skeleton, long legs and short arms, but no head that he could see – appear over the edge of the crater, a long metal tube cradled in its arms and pointing at him.

He fired.

The thing's wailing shriek resounded in his helmet. It absorbed the buzzing stream of anti-neutrons, collapsed, melted and vanished.

'Over here!'

Roffrey turned to see a human figure, all rags and filth, waving to him. He ran towards it.

In a crater which had been turned into a crude fortress by the piles of wreckage surrounding its perimeter, Roffrey found a handful of wretches, the remnants of the human population of Entropium.

The man who had waved had a fleshless head and huge eyes. Dirty, scab-covered skin was drawn tight over his skull. He fingered his emaciated body and eyed Roffrey warily. He said: 'We're starving here. Have you got any supplies?'

'What happened?' Roffrey said, feeling sick.

There was desolation everywhere. These human beings had evidently banded together for protection against similar bands of aliens. Evidently, also, only the fittest survived.

The ragged man pointed at the rubble behind him. 'This? We don't know. It just hit us...'

'Why didn't you leave here?'

'No ships. Most of them were destroyed.'

Roffrey grimaced and said: 'Keep me covered while I return to my ship. I'll be back.'

A short time later he came stumbling back over the rubble with a box in his hands, his boots slipping and sliding on the uneven ground. They clustered around him greedily as he handed out vitapacks.

Something terrible had happened to the planet – perhaps to the whole system. He had to know what – and why.

Now a woman separated herself from the group squatting over their food. The man with the fleshless head followed her.

She said to Roffrey: 'You must be from the home galaxy. How did you get here? – Did they... find how the Shifter worked?'

'You mean Renark and Asquiol?'

Roffrey looked hard at the woman, but he didn't know her. He noted that she had obviously been beautiful, probably still was under the filth and rags. 'They got through. They discovered more than they bargained for here – but they got through. Our whole universe doesn't exist any more. But the race – or the part which left – is still going. Maybe it's wiped out by now. I don't know.'

The man with the fleshless head put his arm around the woman. They looked like a pair of animated skeletons and the man's action enhanced the bizarre effect.

'He didn't want you then and he won't now,' he said to her.

Roffrey saw tension between them, but couldn't understand why.

She said: 'Shut up, Paul. Are Renark and Asquiol safe?'

Roffrey shook his head. 'Renark's dead. Asquiol's okay – he's leading the fleet. The Council gave him complete leadership during the emergency.' Roffrey felt he could name both of them now. He pointed at the man. 'Are you Paul Talfryn?'

Talfryn nodded. He cocked his head towards the woman. She dropped her eyes. 'This is Willow Kovacs – my wife. We sort of got married... Asquiol's mentioned us, eh? I suppose he sent you back for us?'

'No.'

Willow Kovacs shuddered. Roffrey reflected that she didn't appear to like Talfryn very much; there was a kind of apathetic hatred in her eyes. Probably she regarded Talfryn merely as a protector, if that. But it was no business of his.

'What happened to the rest of the human population?' Roffrey said, concentrating on his own affairs and trying to ignore the sickening feeling of disgust at the sight of such degeneration. 'Were they all killed?'

'Did you see anything when you came through the ruins?' Talfryn asked. 'Little, scuttling animal shapes, maybe?'

Roffrey had seen them. They had been repulsive, though he didn't know why.

Talfryn said: 'All those little creatures were intelligent once. For some reason, the Shifter stopped shifting. There was a long period of absolute madness before she seemed to settle down again. This happened – that happened.

'When the trouble started, the actual forms of human beings and aliens changed, devolving into these. Somebody said it was metabolic pressures combined with time-slips induced by the stop, but I didn't understand it. I'm a scientist – an astro-geographer. Unlicensed, you know...' He seemed to sink into an attitude of detachment and then looked up suddenly. 'The city just crumbled. It was horrifying. A lot of people went mad. I suppose Asquiol told you...'

'I've never met Asquiol,' Roffrey broke in. 'All my information is second-hand. I came particularly to find another person. A woman – she helped Renark with information. Mary the Maze – a madwoman. Know her?'

Talfryn pointed upwards to the streaked sky.

'Dead?' said Roffrey.

'Gone,' Talfryn said. 'When the city started breaking apart, she took one of the only ships and just spun off into space. She probably killed herself. She was like a zombie, and quite crazy. It was as if some outside pressure moved her. I heard she wanted to get to Roth. That was a crazy thing to want to do, in itself! She took one of the best ships, damn her. A nice one – Mark Seven Hauser.'

'She was heading for Roth? Isn't that the really strange planet?'

'As I said, she was crazy to go there. If she *did* get there.'

'You think there'd be a chance of her still being alive if she made it?'

'Maybe. Asquiol and Renark obviously survived.'

'Thanks for the information.' Roffrey turned away.

'Hey!' The skeleton suddenly became animated. 'You're not leaving us here! Take us with you – take us back to the fleet, for God's sake!'

Roffrey said: 'I'm not going back to the fleet. I'm going to Roth.'

'Then take us with you – anywhere's better than here!' Willow's voice was shrill and urgent.

Roffrey paused, deliberating. Then he said: 'Okay.'

As they neared the ship, something small and scaly scuttled across their path. It was like nothing Roffrey had seen before and he felt he never wanted to see it again. Entropium, when it flourished, had contained the seeds of corruption – and now corruption was dominant, a physical manifestation of a mental disease. It was an unhealthy place, with intelligent species scrabbling and fighting like animals to survive. It was rotten with the sickness that came from a state of mind as much as anything.

He was glad to reach the ship.

As Willow and Talfryn climbed into the airlock, he glanced back at the ruins. His face was rather grim. He helped them aboard and closed the lock.

Now he turned his thoughts to Mary the Maze.

Chapter Twelve

ROFFREY DEBATED HIS next move, sitting hunched at the controls while he checked the astrochart before him. It didn't tally with the Shifter as it now was, but it would do. He could recognise descriptions of planets even though they had changed their location.

Willow and Talfryn were cleaning up. They were both beginning to look better. The ship itself was hardly tidy. It was not even very clean and there was a smell of the workshop about it – of oil, burnt rubber, dirty plastic and old leather. Roffrey liked it that way.

He scowled then. He *didn't* like company. *I'm getting soft*, he told himself.

Now he was going to Roth he began to feel nervous at what he might find there.

Talfryn said: 'We're ready!'

He activated the ship's normal drive and lifted off. He was tempted to burn the city to rubble as he passed, but he didn't. He got into space with a feeling of relief, heading in a series of flickering hops used for short journeys towards Roth, now hanging the farthest away from the parent binary, as if deliberately set apart from the rest of the system.

Roth, more than any other planet in the Shifter, defied the very logic of the cosmos and existed contrary to all laws. Roth – nicknamed Ragged Ruth, he remembered – still contained the impossible *gaps*. There, two men had become super-sane. But Mary, poor Mary who had helped them – she had found only madness there.

Had she gone back to try and lay the ghost that was her insanity? Or had her motives been induced by madness? Perhaps he would find out.

The planet was big now. The screens showed nothing but the

monstrous globe with its speckled aura, its shifting light-mist, its black blotches and, worst of all, the *gaps*. The *gaps* which were not so much seen as unseen. Something should be there but human eyes couldn't see it.

Roffrey flung the ship down through Roth's erratically tugging gravisphere, swinging towards the unwelcoming surface which throbbed below like a sea of molten lava, changing and shifting. The seas of hell.

There seemed to be no consistent gravity. His instruments kept registering different findings. He fought to keep the descent as smooth as possible, concentrating on the operation, while Willow and Talfryn gasped and muttered, horrified by the vision.

He frowned, wondering what was familiar about the disturbing world. Then he remembered that the one time he had seen Renark and Asquiol they had possessed a similar quality, impossible to pin down, but as if their bodies had existed on different levels only just invisible to the human eye.

Yet this place was ominous. The men's images had been beautiful.

Ominous!

The word seethed around in his brain. Then, for one brief second, he passed through a warmth, a pleasure, a delight so exquisite yet so short-lived that it was as if he had lived and died in a moment.

He couldn't understand it. He had no time to try as the ship rocked in response to the weirdly unbalanced tug of Roth's gravity. Lasers scanned the unstable landscape as he navigated with desperate skill, gliding low over the flame-mist boiling on the surface, trying without success to peer into the *gaps*, all his instruments operating on full power but few giving him any sensible readings.

Had Mary tried, perhaps like Renark, to find the Originators? Had something driven her back to the world that had turned her mad?

Then he spotted a ship on his screens, a ship surrounded by achingly disturbing light-mist. It was the Mark Seven Hauser. Mary's ship. And his energraph told him that the drive was active.

That meant it had only recently landed or else was about to take off. He had to land fast!

He made planetfall in a hurry, cursing the sudden grip of gravity for which he only just succeeded in compensating as he brought his ship close to the other vessel. His gauntleted fingers stabbed at keys and he got into immediate contact with the Hauser on a tight PV beam.

'Anyone aboard?'

There was no reply.

Both Willow and Talfryn were peering at the screen now, bending over his shoulder.

'This ship seems to have arrived only recently,' he said.

It meant nothing to them and he realised that it meant little to him, either. He was pinning his hopes on too thin a circumstance.

He operated the V, scanning as best he could the surrounding territory. Strange images jumped upon the screen, fading as rapidly as they approached. Harsh, craggy, crazy Roth, with its sickness of rock and the horror of the misty, intangible, unnatural *gaps*.

That men could survive here was astounding. Yet evidently they could. Asquiol and Mary had been living evidence. But it was easy to see how they went mad, hard to understand how they kept sane. It was a gaping, raw, boiling, dreadful world, exuding, it seemed, stark malevolence and baleful anger in its constant and turbulent motion.

Mary could easily have disappeared into one of the *gaps* or perished in some nameless way. His lips tightened as he left the screen and opened the spacesuit locker.

'If I need help I'll call you on my suit-phone,' he said as he picked up his discarded helmet. 'If you need them – suits are here.' He went to the airlock's elevator. 'I'll keep my suit-phone receiver on. If you see anything – any trace of Mary – let me know. Have the scanners working full-time.

'You're a fool to go out there!' Talfryn said heavily.

'You're a non-participant in this,' Roffrey said savagely as he clamped his faceplate. 'Don't interfere. If it's obvious that I'm dead, you've got the ship to do what you like with. I've got to see what's in the Hauser.'

Now he was in the outer lock. Then he was lowering his body from the ship into a pool of yellow liquid that suddenly changed to shiny rock as he stepped onto it. Something slid and itched beneath his feet.

His lips were dry, the skin of his face seemed cracked and brittle. His eyes kept focusing and unfocusing. But the most disturbing thing of all was the silence. All his instincts told him that the ghastly changes taking place on the surface should make *noise*. But they didn't. This heightened the dreamlike quality of his motion over the shifting surface.

In a moment, his own ship could no longer be seen and he reached the Hauser, noting that the lock was wide open. Both locks were open when he got inside. Gas of some kind swirled through the ship. He went into the cabin and found traces of the pilot having been there recently. There were some figures scribbled on a pad beside the chart-viewer. The equations were incomprehensible – but they were in Mary's writing!

A quick search through the ship told him nothing more. Hastily he pulled himself through the cabin door and down the airlock shaft until he was again on the surface. He peered with difficulty through the shifting flame-mist. It was thoroughly unnerving. But he forced himself through it, blindly searching for a madwoman who could have gone anywhere.

Then two figures emerged out of the mist and, just as suddenly, merged back into it.

He was sure he recognised one of them. He called after them. They didn't reply. He began to follow but lost sight of them.

Then a piercing shout blasted into his suit-phone. '*Asquiol! Oh, Asquiol!*'

He whirled around. It was the voice of Willow Kovacs. Was Asquiol looking for him? Had the fleet been defeated? If so, why had the two men ignored his shout?

'*Asquiol! Come back! It's me, Willow!*'

But Roffrey wanted to find Mary the Maze; he wasn't interested in Asquiol. He began to run, plunging through hallucinations, through shapes that formed silently around him as if to engulf him, through turquoise tunnels, up mauve mountains. In places, gravity was low and he bounded along; in others it became almost impossible to drag his bulk.

Now he entered another low-gravity patch and bounded with bone-jarring suddenness into a heavy one. Painfully he lifted his booted feet, barely able to support his heavy body.

Then a voice – perhaps through his suit-phone, perhaps not. He recognised the voice. His heart leapt.

'It's warm, warm, warm... Where now? Here... but... Let me go back... Let me...'

It was Mary's voice.

For a moment he didn't respond to the shock. His mouth was dry, his features petrified. His body froze as he strained to hear the voice again. 'Mary – where are you?'

It was as if he were experiencing an awful dream where menace threatened but he was unable to escape, where every step seemed to take every ounce of energy and every scrap of time he possessed.

Again he croaked: 'Mary!'

But it was not for some minutes that he heard the reply: *'Keep moving! Don't stop. Don't stop!'*

He didn't know whether the words were addressed to him or not, but he thought it best to obey them.

He began to sway and fall down, but he kept moving. It was as if the whole planet were above him and he was like Atlas, slowly crumpling beneath its weight.

He screamed.

Then Willow's voice blasted through: *'Asquiol! Asquiol!'*

What was happening? It was all too confusing. He couldn't grasp... He felt faint. He looked up and saw several small figures scurrying across a planet he held in his hands. Then he was growing, growing, growing... scale upon scale...

Again he screamed. A hollow, echoing roar in his ears.

His heart beat a frantic rhythm against his rib cage until his ears became filled with the noise. He panted and struggled, crawling up over the curved surface of the planet, hanging on to it as if by his fingernails.

He was a great giant, larger than the tiny planet – but at the same time he was a flea, crawling through syrup and cotton-wool.

He laughed then in his madness.

He laughed and stopped abruptly, grasping for the threads of sanity and pulling them together. He was standing in a light-gravity patch and things suddenly looked as normal as they could on Roth.

He glanced through a rent in the mist and saw Mary standing there. He ran towards her.

'Mary!'

'*Asquiol!*'

The woman was Willow Kovacs in a suit – Mary's old suit. He made as if to strike her down, but the look of disappointment on her face stopped him. He pushed past her, changed his mind, came back.

'Willow – Mary's here, I know…' Suddenly he realised the possible truth. 'My God, of course. Time's so twisted and warped we could be seeing anything that's happened at any time in the past – or the future!'

Another figure came stumbling out of the light-mist. It was Talfryn.

'I couldn't contact you from the ship. There's a woman there. She…'

'It's an illusion, man. Get back to the ship!'

'You come with me. It's no illusion. She entered the ship herself!'

'Lead the way back,' Roffrey said. Willow remained where she was, refusing to budge. At length they had to lift her, squirming, and carry her back. The ship was only three yards away.

The woman wore a spacesuit. She was lying on the floor of the cabin. Roffrey bent over her, lifting the faceplate.

'Mary.' he said, softly. 'Mary – thank God!'

The eyes opened, the big soft eyes that had once held intelligence.

For a short time intelligence was there – a look of incredible awareness. Then it faded and she formed her lips to say something, but they twisted downwards into an idiot grin and she subsided into a blank-eyed daze.

He got up wearily, his body bowed. He made a gesture with his left hand. 'Willow, help her out of the suit. We'll get her into a bunk.'

Willow looked at him with hatred: 'Asquiol's out there... You stopped me.'

Talfryn said: 'Even if he was he wouldn't want you. You keep pining for him, wishing you'd followed him earlier. Now it's too late. It's no good, Willow, you've lost him for ever!'

'Once he sees me he'll take me back. He loved me!'

Roffrey said impatiently to Talfryn: 'You'd better help me, then.'

Talfryn nodded. They began getting Mary out of the suit.

'Willow,' said Roffrey as they worked, 'Asquiol wasn't there – not now. You saw something that probably happened months ago. The other man was Renark – and Renark's dead? You understand?'

'I saw him. He heard me call him!'

'Maybe. I don't know. Don't worry, Willow. We're going back to the fleet if we can – if it still exists. You'll see him then.'

Talfryn wrenched off a piece of space-armour from Mary's body with a savage movement. His teeth were clenched but he said nothing.

'You're going back to the fleet? But you said...' Willow was disconcerted. Roffrey noted a peculiar look, a mixture of eagerness and introspection.

'Mary needs treatment. The only place she'll get it is back there. So that's where I'm going. That should suit you.'

'It does,' she said. 'Yes, it does.'

He went over to the ports and closed their shutters so they couldn't see Roth's surface. It felt a little safer.

Talfryn said suddenly: 'I get it, Willow. You've made it plain. I won't be bothering you from now on.'

'You'd better not.' She turned on Roffrey. 'And that goes for you, too, for any man.'

'Don't worry,' he grinned. 'You're not my type.' Roffrey smiled then at Mary, who sat drooling and crooning in her bunk. He winked at her. 'You're my type, Mary,' he said genially.

'That's cruel,' Willow said sharply.

'That's my wife.' Roffrey smiled, and then Willow saw at least a trace of what the smiling eyes and grin hid.

She turned away.

'Let's get going,' said Roffrey briskly. Now that he had made up his mind, he wanted to waste no time returning to the fleet.

He couldn't guess how long Mary had been on Roth. Maybe only a few minutes of real time. Maybe a hundred years of Roth's time. He did not let himself dwell on this, just as he refused to consider the extent of her mental derangement. The psychiatrists in the fleet might soon be supplying him with all the information they possibly could. He was prepared to wait and see.

He went over to her. She shrank away from him, muttering and crooning, her big eyes wider than ever. Very gently he made her lie down in the bunk and strapped her into its safety harness. It pained him that she didn't recognise him, but he was still smiling and humming a little tune to himself as he climbed into the pilot's seat, heaved back a lever, adjusted a couple of dials, flipped a series of switches and soon the drone of the drive was drowning his own humming.

Then, in a flicker, they were off into deep space and heading away from the Sundered Worlds into the depths of matterless void. It was such an easy lift-off, Roffrey felt, that it was almost as if a friendly hand had given them a push from behind...

It was with a sense of inevitability that he began the descent through the dimension layers, heading back to the space-time in which he'd left the fleet of mankind.

Meanwhile, human brains were jarred and jumbled as they strove to master the Game. Minds broke. Nerves snapped. But, while scarcely understanding what it was about, Mordan forced his team to continue, convinced that humanity's chance of survival depended on winning...

Whistling sounds were the first impressions Roffrey received as he phased the ship out of the Shifter's space-time and into the next level.

Space around them suddenly became bright with black-and-yellow stars, the not-quite-familiar whirl of a spiral galaxy soaring outwards in a wild sprawl of suns. The whistling was replaced by a dreadful moaning which pervaded the ship and made speech impossible.

Roffrey was intent on the new instruments. The little experience he had of the Intercontinua-Travelling device had shown him that the ship could easily slip back through the space-time layers and become totally lost.

The instruments hadn't been designed for wide travelling of this kind and Roffrey knew it, but each separate universe in the multiverse had its particular co-ordinates, and the instruments, crude as they were, could differentiate between them. On the main V-screen Roffrey had a chart which would recognise the universe into which the human race had fled. But the journey could be dangerous, perhaps impossible.

And then the noise increased to become painful, no longer a monotone but a pulsating, nerve-racking whine. Roffrey phased into the next layer.

The galaxy ahead was a seething inferno of unformed matter, hazy, bright, full of archetypal colour – reds, whites, blacks, yellows – pouring about in slow disorder. This was a universe in a state of either birth or dissolution.

There was near-silence as Roffrey phased out of this continuum and into the next. His whistling, which he had been doing all the while, was light and cheerful. Then he heard Mary's groans and he stopped.

Now they were in the centre of a galaxy.

Massed stars lay in all directions. He stared at them in wonder, noticing how, with every phase, the matter, filling the space around them, seemed to change its position as well as its nature.

Then the stars were gone and he was passing through a turbulent mass of dark gas forming into horrible, half-recognisable shapes which sickened him so that he could no longer look but had to concentrate on his instruments.

What he read there depressed and shocked him!

He was off course.

He chewed at his moustache, debating what to do. He didn't mention it to the others. The co-ordinates corresponded to those on the chart above the screen.

As far as the ship's instruments were concerned, they were in the space-time occupied by Asquiol and the fleet!

Yet it was totally different from what he remembered. Gas swirled in it and he could not see the stars of the galaxy.

Had the fleet been completely wiped out?

There was no other explanation.

Then he cursed. The black gas suddenly became alive, a roaring and monstrous beast, many-tendrilled, dark blue, flame-eyed, malevolent. Willow and Talfryn gasped behind him as they saw it loom on the screen. Mary began shrieking, the sounds filled the cabin. The ship was heading straight towards the monster. But how could something like this exist in the near-vacuum of space?

Roffrey didn't have time for theories. He broke the energy seals of his anti-neutron cannon as an acrid smell filled the cabin and the beast rapidly changed from deep blue to startling yellow.

The guns swung on the beast and Roffrey stabbed the firing buttons, then backed the ship away savagely.

The ship shuddered as the guns sent a deadly stream of anti-neutrons towards the monster. Meanwhile, the beast seemed, impossibly, to be absorbing the beams and new heads had grown on its shoulders – disgusting, half-human faces gibbering and yelling, and they could *hear* the cries! Roffrey felt and tasted bile in his throat.

Talfryn was now bending over him, staring at the screen. 'What is it?' he shouted above Mary's screams.

'How the hell should I know?' Roffrey said viciously. He righted the ship's backward velocity, stabbed the cannon buttons again. He heaved his big body round in the control seat and said: 'Make yourself useful, Talfryn. See if the co-ordinates on that chart tally absolutely with those on this screen.'

The monster lurched through the dark mist towards the little launch, its heads drooling and grinning. There wasn't time to wonder what it was, how it existed.

Roffrey aimed at its main head. He began to depress the firing button.

Then it had gone.

There were a few wisps of gas in the dark, sharp space of the galaxy Roffrey immediately recognised.

They were in the right galaxy!

But now a new danger threatened. Replacing the monster was a squadron of fast, spherical vessels – those he had glimpsed just before leaving the fleet. Were they the victors, cleaning up the last of the race? They were passing on the zenith-south flank of Roffrey's battered launch. He trailed the ship round on a tight swing so that he was now directly facing the oncoming alien ships.

The launch was responding well, but the cabin shook and rattled as he stood his vessel on a column of boiling black fire and glided away from the round ships, having shot a tremendous burst towards them. Something was disturbing him. He found it hard to concentrate properly. Talfryn was obviously having the same trouble. A quick look behind him showed Mary's gaping mouth as she screamed and screamed.

Talfryn clung instinctively to the hand-grip and shouted: 'The co-ordinates tally perfectly.'

'That's news?' Roffrey said lightly.

Willow had joined Mary and was attempting to comfort her. Mary was rigid, staring ahead of her with fixed, glazed eyes. It was as if she could see something that was invisible to the others. Her screams rang on, a horrible ululation in the confined cabin.

Willow peered through the bad light at the two men half-silhouetted up ahead, the one in the control seat, the other standing over him, their dark clothes picked out against the spluttering brightness of the screens and instruments, their faces in shadow, their hands white on the controls.

The lighting was very dim as all power sources were drained to provide the ship with maximum power.

She looked out of the nearest port. Space was blank – suddenly colourless. She looked back at the men and her vision was engulfed by a horrible disharmony of colour and noise, sense impressions of all kinds – obscene, primeval, terrible – throwing her mind into disorder so that she found it almost impossible to differentiate between her five senses.

Then, when she had completely lost her ability to tell whether she was smelling or hearing a colour, her head was filled with a single impression that combined as one thing to her sense: smell, sight, touch, sound and taste were all there, but the combination produced a unified sense that all were blood red.

She thought she was dead.

Roffrey shouted and the sound hung alone for a moment before he saw it merge into the blood red disharmony. He felt madness approach and then recede – approach and recede, like a horrible tide, for with each sweep it came a little closer. His body vibrated with the tension, sending out clouds of blood red trailers through the cabin which he saw – no, he heard it, as the note of a muted trumpet. It horrified him, for now something else was creeping through, something coming up from his oldest memories, something of which he hadn't even been aware.

He was immersed in self-loathing, self-pity, suddenly knowing what a debased thing he was…

But there was something – he didn't know what – aiding him in spite of his confusion, aiding him to cling to his personal being, to sweat out the tumble of disordered impressions and terrible thoughts, and to hit back.

He hit back!

Mary was still quivering in Willow's arms – taut, tense, no longer screaming.

The waves began to peter out.

Willow struck, too. Struck back at whatever it was that was doing this to them.

The waves faded and, slowly, their senses were restored to normal.

Suddenly Mary's body relaxed. She had passed out. Talfryn was slumped on the floor and Roffrey was hunched in the control seat, growling.

He peered through the rapidly fading pulsations and saw with satisfaction that the anti-neutrons had done their job, though he hadn't been able to direct them properly, nor had he been fully conscious of directing them.

Some of the ships were making off, others were warped lumps of metal spinning aimlessly in the void. He began whistling to himself as he adjusted the controls. The whistling died as he said: 'You all right back there?'

Willow said: 'What do you think, superman? Mary and Paul have passed out. Mary took it worse than any of us – she seemed to bear the brunt of it. What was it, do you think?'

'I don't know. Maybe we'll get our answers soon.'

'Why?'

'I've sighted our fleet!'

'Thank God,' said Willow, and she began to tremble. She dared not anticipate her reunion with Asquiol.

Roffrey headed for the fleet – going back as fast as he'd left.

Chapter Thirteen

THE FLEET HAD been badly depleted since he left it. It was still big – a sprawling collection of ships, stretching mile upon mile in all directions and resembling nothing so much as a vast scrapyard, guarded by the cruising Geepee battlewagons.

In the centre of the fleet, a little distance from Asquiol's battered cruiser (easily recognised by its slightly out-of-focus outline) was a huge factory ship with the letter 'G' emblazoned on its side. This puzzled Roffrey.

Then the Geepee patrol contacted him.

To his astonishment, he had the pleasure of being received almost cordially. They began to guide him into a position fairly close to the factory ship with the G on its side.

While Roffrey was getting his ship into line, a man in the loose, unmilitary garb which was identical save for rank insignia with all other Geepee uniforms, appeared on the PV screen, his stern, bloodhound face puzzled. The large band on his left sleeve also bore a letter G.

'Hello, Mordan,' Roffrey said with cheerful defiance.

Willow wondered at the vitality and control which Roffrey must possess in order to seem suddenly so relaxed and untroubled.

Mordan smiled ironically. 'Good morning. So you decided to return and help us after all. Where have you been?'

'I've been on a mercy trip rescuing survivors from the Shifter,' Roffrey said virtuously.

'I don't believe you,' Mordan said candidly. 'But I don't care – you've just done something nobody thought was possible. As soon as we assemble our data I'll be getting in touch with you again. We need all the help we can get in this business – even yours. We're up against it, Roffrey. We're damn near finished.' He broke off as if to pull himself together. 'Now, if you *are* carrying extra passengers, you'd better register them with the appropriate authorities.' He switched out.

'What did all that mean?' said Talfryn.

'I don't know,' Roffrey said, 'but we may find out soon. Mordan obviously knows something. The fleet's evidently suffered from attacks such as we experienced. Yet there is more order now. The battle, or whatever it is, seems to have taken a different course.'

Willow Kovacs cradled Mary Roffrey's head in her arm and gently wiped a trickle of saliva from the madwoman's mouth. Her own heart was beating swiftly and her stomach seemed contracted, her arms and legs weak. She was very frightened now at the prospect of reunion with Asquiol.

Roffrey locked the ship's controls and came aft, staring down at the two women with a light smile on his sensuous, bearded mouth. He began stripping off his suit and the overalls beneath, revealing a plain quilted jacket of maroon plastileather and grubby white trousers tucked into soft leather knee-boots. 'How's Mary?'

'I don't know,' Willow said. 'She's obviously not sane... Yet there's a different quality about her insanity. Something I can't pin down.'

'A doctor maybe will help,' Roffrey said. He patted Willow's shoulder. 'Contact the admin ship will you, Talfryn? Send out a general call till you can get it.'

'Okay,' Talfryn said.

Worst of all, Roffrey thought as he stared down at his wife, had been the all-pervading red – blood red. It had been unmistakeable as blood. Why had it affected him so badly? What had it done to Mary?

He scratched the back of his neck. He hadn't slept since he left the fleet. He was full of stimulants, but he felt the need for some natural sleep. Maybe later.

When Talfryn had contacted the Registration Ship, which had as its job the classification of all members of the fleet so that it would be easier to administer the survivors if they at last made planetfall, they were told that an official would be sent over in a short while.

Roffrey said: 'We need a psychiatrist of some sort, quickly. Can you help?'

'Try a hospital ship – though it's unlikely you'll be lucky.'

He tried a hospital ship. The doctor in charge wasn't helpful.

'No, I'm afraid you won't get a psychiatrist for your wife. If you need medical treatment we'll put her on our list. We're over-worked. It's impossible to deal with all the casualties...'

'But you've got to help her!' Roffrey bellowed.

The doctor didn't argue. He just switched out.

Roffrey, bewildered by this, swung round in his chair. Willow and Talfryn were discussing the earlier conflict with the alien ships.

'They must be hard pushed,' Roffrey cursed. 'But I'm going to get help for Mary.'

'What about those hallucinations we had back there?' Talfryn said. 'What caused them?'

'It's my guess we were experiencing the force of one of their weapons,' Roffrey replied. 'Maybe what happened to us on Roth made us more susceptible to hallucination.'

'A weapon – yes, it could be.'

The communicator buzzed. Talfryn went to it.

'Registration,' said a jaunty voice. 'Mind if I come aboard?'

He was a pale and perky midget with genial eyes and a very neat appearance. His gig clamped against Roffrey's airlock and he came bustling through with a case of papers under his arm.

'You would be Captain Adam Roffrey,' he lisped, staring up at the black-bearded giant.

Roffrey stared down at him, half in wonder. 'I would be.'

'Good. And you embarked with the rest of the human race roughly two weeks ago – relative time, that is. I don't know how long it was in *your* time, since it is not always possible to leave and return from one dimension to another and keep the time flow the same – kindly remember that.'

'I'll try,' said Roffrey, wondering if there was a question there.

'And these three are...?'

'Miss Willow Kovacs, formerly of Migaa...'

The midget scribbled in his notebook, looking prim at the mention of the planet Migaa. It had possessed something of a reputation in the home galaxy.

Willow gave the rest of her data. Talfryn gave his.

'And the other lady?' the little official asked.

'My wife – Doctor Mary Roffrey, born on Earth, née Ishenko; anthropologist; disappeared from Golund on the Rim in 457 Galactic General Time, reappeared from Shifter System a short while ago. The Geepees will have all her details prior to her disappearance. I gave them to the police when she disappeared. As usual, they did nothing.'

The midget frowned, then darted a look at Mary. 'State of health?'

'Insane,' said Roffrey, quietly.

'Curable or otherwise?'

'Curable!' said Roffrey. The word was cold as flint.

The tiny official completed his notes, thanked them all and was about to leave when Roffrey said:

'Just a minute. Could you fill me in on what's happened to the fleet since I left?'

'As long as we keep it brief, I'd be pleased to. Remember, I'm a busy little man!' He giggled.

'Just before we got here we had a tussle with some alien ships, experienced hallucinations, and so on. Do you know what that was?'

'No wonder the lady is insane! For untrained people to withstand the pressure, it's amazing! Wait till I tell my colleagues! You're heroes! You survived a wild round!'

'Bully for us. What happened?'

'Well, I'm only a petty official – they don't come much pettier than me – but from what I've *gathered*, you had a "wild round". That is,' he explained quickly, 'anyone straying beyond the confines of the fleet is attacked by the aliens and has to play a wild round, as we call it – one that isn't scheduled to be played by the Gamblers. We're not really supposed to do that.'

'But what *is* this Game?'

'I'm not sure. Ordinary people don't play the Game – only the

Gamblers in the Game Ship. That's the one with the big "G" on it. It isn't the sort of game I'd like to play. We call it the Blood Red Game because of the habit they have of confusing our senses so that everything seems to be the colour of blood. Psychologists and the like play it and they are called Gamblers...'

'How often is it played?'

'All the time, really. No wonder I'm a bundle of nerves. We all are. Citizens' rights have been waived, food supplies reduced... We're having a pause just at the moment, but it won't last long. Probably they're recovering from your little victory.'

'Who'd know details about this Game?'

'Asquiol, of course, but it's almost impossible to see him. The nearest people ever get is to his airlock, and then only rarely. You might try Mordan, though he's not too approachable, either. Mr High and Mighty – he's worse than Asquiol in some ways.'

'Mordan seems interested enough to tell us already,' Roffrey nodded. 'But I've got to speak to Asquiol on another matter, so I might as well try to combine them. Thanks.'

'A pleasure,' the midget enthused.

When he had gone, Roffrey went to the communicator and tried to contact Asquiol's ship. He had to get by nearly a dozen officials before he made contact.

'Adam Roffrey here, just in from the Shifter. Can I come to your ship?'

He received a curt acceptance. There had been no picture.

'Will you take me with you?' Willow asked. 'He'll be surprised. I've been waiting a long, long time for this. He predicted we might meet again, and he was right.'

'Of course,' Roffrey agreed. He looked at Talfryn. 'He was a friend of yours, too. Want to come?'

Talfryn shook his head. 'I'll stay here and try to find out a bit more about what's going on here.' He took a long, almost theatrical look at Willow and then turned away. 'See you.'

Roffrey said: 'Just as you like.' He went to the medical chest and took out a hypodermic and a bottle of sedative, filled the hypo and pumped the stuff into Mary's arm.

Then he and Willow left his launch and, by means of personal power units, made their way to Asquiol's ship.

The airlock was open, ready for them, and it closed behind them as they entered. The inner lock, however, did not open.

Instead, they saw the light of an internal viewer blink on as they waited and they heard a brooding voice – a polite, faraway voice that seemed to carry peculiar echoes which their ears could not quite catch.

'Asquiol speaking. How may I help you?'

Willow, masked in her spacesuit, remained silent.

'I'm Adam Roffrey, just in from the Shifter System with three passengers.'

'Yes?' Asquiol's acknowledgement bore no trace of interest.

'One of them is my wife – you know her as Mary the Maze. She helped Renark in the Shifter.' Roffrey paused. 'She sent you to Roth.'

'I am grateful to her, though we didn't meet.'

'I've tried to contact a psychiatrist in the fleet. I haven't succeeded.' Roffrey kept his voice level. 'I don't know where they all are, but my wife's condition is desperate. Can you help?'

'They are all playing the Game. I am sorry. Grateful as I am to your wife, the first priority is to the race. We cannot release a psychiatrist.'

Roffrey was shocked. He had expected some response at least. 'Not even to give me advice how to help her?'

'No. You must do what you can for her yourself. Perhaps a medical man will be able to give you certain kinds of help.'

Roffrey turned disgustedly back towards the outer lock. He stopped as Asquiol's voice came again: 'I suggest you contact Mordan as soon as you can.'

The voice cut off.

Willow spoke. She felt as if she had died and the word was the last she would ever utter.

'Asquiol!'

At length, they returned to Roffrey's ship.

Mary was sleeping peacefully under the sedative but Talfryn

had disappeared. They did not bother to wonder where he had gone. They sat by Mary's bunk, both of them depressed, their thoughts turned inward.

'He's changed,' Willow said flatly.

Roffrey grunted.

'He doesn't sound human any longer,' she said. 'There's no way of appealing to him. He doesn't seem to care about the approval of the rest of us. His loyalty to these mysterious creatures he contacted seems greater than his loyalty to his friends – or the rest of mankind, for that matter.'

Roffrey stared down at Mary. 'He doesn't care about anything except this "mission" he has. Everything is being sacrificed and subordinated to that one aim. I don't even know how valid it is. If I did I might be able to argue with him!'

'Perhaps Paul could talk to him. I got scared. I meant to tell him who I was. I might be able to later.'

'Save it. I'll see what Mordan wants with me first.'

Roffrey moved over to his control panel and operated the screen. 'Mordan?'

'Mordan here.' The Gee-Councillor's face appeared on the screen. He seemed disconcerted when he saw Roffrey.

'I was just going to contact you. You and Talfryn have been enlisted as Gamblers – subject to preliminary tests.'

'What the hell, Mordan? I'm not interested. Tell Talfryn about it. I've got a sick wife to think about.'

'Talfryn's already here.' Mordan's face was serious. 'This is important – though it may not look like it to you. There's a war to the death on and we're up against it. I'm directly responsible to Asquiol for enlisting any men I think will help us win. You've given us a great deal of trouble already. I'm empowered to kill anyone liable to disrupt our security. Come over to the Game Ship – and come fast! If you refuse we'll bring you over forcibly. Clear?'

Roffrey switched out without answering.

Defiantly, he waited by Mary's bed. She was beginning to show signs of improving, physically, but how her mind would be when she came out of the drugged sleep he didn't know.

Later, two Geepees demanded entry. Their launch was clamped fast against his. They threatened to hole his ship and enter that way if they had to. He opened the airlocks and let them in.

'What can one extra hand do?' he said.

One of them replied: 'Any man who can hold off an enemy attack virtually single-handed is needed in the Game Ship. That's all we know.'

'But I didn't...' Roffrey stopped himself. He was losing his grip.

The Geepee said with false patience: 'You may not have realised it, Captain Roffrey, but you did something a while ago that was impossible. You held out under the combined attack, mental and physical, of ten enemy ships. Most people couldn't have taken an attack from even one!'

The other Geepee drawled: 'That means something. Look at it this way. We're damn near beaten now. We took a hell of a lambasting during the initial alien attacks. We're the last survivors of the human race and we've got to stay together, work for the common good. That's the only way you'll look after your wife in the long run. Don't you see that?'

Roffrey was still not convinced. He was a stubborn man. There was an atavistic impulse in him which had always kept him away from the herd, and outside the law, relying entirely on his own initiative and wits. But he was also an intelligent man so he nodded slightly and said: 'Very well – I'll speak to Mordan anyway.' Then he turned to Willow. 'Willow, if Mary shows any sign of getting worse, let me know.'

'Of course, Adam.'

'You'll stay with her – make sure she's all right?'

She looked into his face. 'Naturally. But when she's under the sedative there's something else I've got to do.'

'Yes. I understand.'

He shrugged at the Geepees, who turned and led him through the airlock.

Chapter Fourteen

THE GAME SHIP was bigger than an old battlewagon, even more functional-looking, a little barer of comforts. Yet it did not seem prepared for battle. There was an atmosphere of hushed silence aboard and their boots clanged loudly along the corridor which led to Mordan's cabin.

A sign on the door read: *Deputy Game Master Mordan. Strictly Private.* The letters were heavy black on the white door.

The Geepee accompanying Roffrey knocked on the door.

'Enter!'

They went through into a cabin cluttered with instruments.

There were some Roffrey recognised: an encephalograph, an optigraph-projector – machines for measuring the power of the brain, equipment for testing visualising capacity, for measuring I.Q. potential, and so on.

Talfryn was sitting in a comfortable chair on the other side of Mordan's desk. Both men had their hands clenched before them – Talfryn's in his lap, Mordan's stretched out across the empty desk.

'Sit down, Roffrey,' said Mordan. He made no reference to Roffrey's defiance of orders. He seemed perfectly controlled. Perhaps over-controlled, thought Roffrey. For a moment he sympathised – wasn't that his own condition?

He sat down as the Geepee guard left. 'Okay,' he said curtly. 'Get on with it.'

'I've been explaining to Talfryn how important you both are to this project,' Mordan said crisply. 'Are you prepared to go along with us on the first stage of our tests?'

'Yes.' He was almost responding to the decisive mood.

'Good. We've got to find out exactly what qualities you possessed which made defeat of that alien fleet possible. There is a chance, of course, that you were lucky, or that being unprepared

145

for the sense-impression attack on you and having no understanding of its origin, you were psychologically better prepared to meet the attack. We'll know the answers later. Let me recap on recent events first.'

Mordan spoke rapidly: 'As you know, we entered this universe several weeks ago and encountered its inhabitants shortly after entry. These people are non-human, as might be expected, and regard us as invaders. That's fair enough, since we should think the same in their position. But they made no attempt to assess our potential strength, to parley or order us away. They attacked. We have no idea even what they look like, these aliens. You saw how quickly they had mobilised an attack on our fleet, well before we had a chance to talk and tell them why we are here.'

'What happened after the first battle – the one I saw?'

'There were several others. We lost a lot of ships of all kinds. Finally, Asquiol contacted them by his own methods, and intimated that we were quite prepared to settle on planets unsuitable for them and live in friendly co-operation with them. But they wouldn't accept this. However, they came up with an alternative to open warfare.' He sighed and waved his hand to indicate the massed equipment.

'We did not reckon with the predominant society existing here. It is based on a Code of Behaviour which we find, in parts, very difficult to grasp.

'In our terms it means that the status of a particular individual or group is decided by its ability to play a warlike game which has been played in this galaxy for centuries. We call it the Blood Red Game, since one of their prime "weapons" is the ability to addle our sense-impressions so that we get a total sensory experience of the colour red. You already know this, I believe.'

Roffrey agreed. 'But what, apart from confusing us, is it meant to do? And how does it work?'

'We believe that the aliens have come to rely, when disputes break out among themselves, on more subtle weapons than energy-cannon or anything similar. If we wished, we might continue to use our familiar weapons to fight them, as we did at first. But we should have only a slight chance of winning. Their weapons make you better than dead, in their view. They turn you insane. If you were dead you'd be out of the way. But since you're alive but useless as a fighter, you drain our resources and slow us down in many ways. But that's only part of it. There are rigid, complicated rules which we are having to learn as we go along.'

'What are the stakes?' Roffrey asked.

'If we win so many rounds of the Game without relying on our ordinary armaments, the aliens will concede us the right to rule, as absolute monarchs, their galaxy! Big stakes, Captain Roffrey. We lose our lives, they lose their power.'

'They must be confident of winning.'

'Not according to Asquiol. The fact that they *are* winning at the moment is obvious, but their love of playing this Game is so ingrained that they welcome any new variety. You see, both sides have got to do more than simply play the Game, they have the added difficulty of not understanding the opponent's capabilities, susceptibilities, psychology and so forth. In that, we're even. In other things, such as experience of playing the Game, they have the advantage.'

'Where do we come into this?'

'We're hoping that you are the aces we need in order to win. Your ship was the only human ship which has ever succeeded in beating the fantastic odds. Somehow, you have something we need to beat the aliens!'

'And you don't know what it is?'

'Right.'

'Do we possess it jointly – or does only one of us possess this protective "shield-attack" quality, whatever it is?'

'We're going to find that out, Captain Roffrey. That's why we're testing you both. Although you were actually at the controls of your ship, Talfryn, I understand, was beside you.'

Talfryn spoke slowly: 'What we have to seek, I gather, is a *moral* advantage over the aliens. It is not a question of numbers but prestige. If we win, we gain sufficient status for them to accept our dominance. If we lose... what?'

'If we lose, we'll be beyond caring. Our supplies are so short we can't risk phasing into a new universe at this late stage.' Mordan turned his attention back to Roffrey. 'Do you see that, captain? Your wife is only one of a few victims of insanity in the fleet at the moment. But if we don't win the Game, we'll all be mad – or dead.'

Roffrey understood the logic. But he was still suspicious of it.

'Let's get these tests over with,' he said. 'Then maybe we'll know where we're going. I'll make up my mind afterwards.'

Mordan tightened his lips, nodding a trifle. 'As you like,' he said. He spoke towards his desk. 'Ask the testing team to come here.'

Two men and a woman entered Mordan's cluttered cabin.

Mordan stood up to introduce them. 'This is Professor Selinsky,' he said.

The tallest of the group detached himself and walked over to Roffrey and Talfryn. He stretched out his fat hand and smiled warmly. 'Glad you're here. It looks as if you and your friend may be able to help us out of our present difficulties.' He shook hands with them and said: 'These are my assistants. Doctor Zung –' a small, gloomy man of Mongolian appearance – 'and Doctor Mann –' a young, blonde-headed woman who looked like an adventure-fiction heroine.

'I've heard of you, professor,' said Talfryn. 'You used to hold the Chair of Psychedelics at Earth.'

'That's right,' Selinsky nodded. Then he said: 'We'll give you an ordinary test with the electro-encephalograph first. Then we'll put you to sleep and see if we can get at the subconscious. You're prepared to accept all our tests, I presume.' He looked at Mordan who made no reply.

Roffrey said: 'Yes. As long as it doesn't involve brainwashing.'

Selinsky said sternly: 'This is the fifth century, you know – not the fifth century pre-war.

'I thought Asquiol's and Mordan's motto had become "Needs Must When The Devil Drives",' Roffrey said as he sat in the seat which Doctor Zung had prepared for him.

But the reference made no impression on Mordan who had probably never heard it. Roffrey was given to obscure quotations – it was all part of his atavistic outlook. Mary had once accused him of being deliberately obscure in his references, of reading old books merely in order to pick up unfamiliar quotations to fling at people he despised or disliked. He had agreed. Part of her attraction, he had added, was that she, at least, knew what he was talking about.

A small, glass-alloy helmet was now being fitted over his scalp. He hated such devices. He hated it all. As soon as this is over, he promised himself, I'll show them what independence really means.

Such thoughts and emotions gave the scientists some interesting, if hardly usable, findings.

Professor Selinsky appeared calm as he checked over the material so far gained from the sleeping men. 'All this will require careful analysis, of course,' he said. Then he shrugged his shoulders.

'What have you found out?' Mordan said.

'Frankly, I can't find any clue at first sight as to what they've got that people we're using haven't already got. They're both intelligent – Roffrey quite superlatively so, but there's only a grain of something out of the ordinary. Naturally, this quality would be subtle – we expected that – but Roffrey isn't the only loner in the human race and he isn't the only one with a high I.Q.' He sighed.

'But their memories for sensory-experiences are very good,' Doctor Mann said eagerly. 'In any event they will help swell the Gambling strength.'

'A poor second,' said Zung disgustedly as he uncoupled electrodes and neatly placed his personal equipment in its cases. 'I'll agree that we need all the Gamblers we can recruit – but these men were going to give us the answer to the problem of defeating the aliens. That's what we hoped, didn't we, professor?'

Selinsky said: 'This project is wearing us all down, Zung. There's not a scrap of reason for your defeatist tone. We have a lot of work to do before we can analyse our findings. Meanwhile –' he turned to Mordan who had been sitting in his chair with a look of studied indifference on his seamed, bloodhound's face – 'I suggest we put these men on our regular strength. No need to waste them while we study their results. Let them be trained.'

'You're sure they'll work all right with the rest?' Mordan said, getting up.

'Why shouldn't they?' Selinsky pointed his thumb towards the door. 'You know what the atmosphere in there's like, with O'Hara and everything... None of them are what you would call "normal". Our Gamblers are all neurotics these days, by definition. Normal people couldn't stand the strain – normal people couldn't hit back. We count on unusual physiological and psychological patterns to play the Game.'

'I trust Talfryn,' Mordan said, 'he's much more susceptible to persuasion. But Roffrey's a born troublemaker. I know – I've dealt with him more than once.'

'Give him something important to handle, in that case.' Selinsky swung the arm of the optigraph away from Roffrey's chair. The man stirred but didn't wake. 'He's the kind who needs to be kept active – who needs to feel that every action he makes is personally inspired.'

'There never was such a thing,' said Mordan, walking over and staring down at his old enemy.

'Then don't tell him.' Selinsky smiled faintly. 'It's egocentricity of that order which has pushed humanity up the scale. Renark and Asquiol were the same – they may sometimes have the wrong information, but they get better results than we do.'

'Of a kind,' Mordan agreed reluctantly.

'It's the kind we need right now,' Selinsky told him as he and his assistants bustled out of the cabin. 'We'll send a couple of attendants to take care of them.'

'You'll need the whole damn police force to take care of Roffrey once he starts getting stubborn,' Mordan said fatalistically. He liked Roffrey, but he knew Roffrey didn't like him. He'd come to the somewhat comforting conclusion that Roffrey didn't really like anyone – apart from his wife. It was a great pity that he'd found her, Mordan reflected.

Selinsky and his assistants pored over their findings. Mann, although a good and clever scientist, was beginning to tire of the routine work. As they paused for coffee, she said to Selinsky: 'Something occurred to me, professor, which may mean nothing, but it's worth throwing out for discussion, I think.'

Selinsky, who disapproved of Mann's weakness for theorising while on the job, said impatiently: 'What is?'

'Well, in the history we got from records, both Talfryn and Roffrey were on that planet they call Roth – in the Sundered Worlds – the Lattice Planet. Parts of it exist in different continua, rather like Asquiol is supposed to do. Could this planet have exerted some kind of influence on them? Or perhaps if they stood the test of staying sane on Roth – it turned Roffrey's wife mad, remember – they are therefore better fitted for fighting the aliens?'

Selinsky drained his coffee cup and ran a finger across his wet lips. 'There may be something there,' he said. 'Look, I'll tell you what. Work something out properly, in your spare time, and show me your ideas in a report.'

'Spare time!' Mann said explosively, though she was pleased at Selinsky's encouragement – a rare thing in itself.

'Well, you can't sleep *all* of those six hours,' said Zung quietly, grinning to himself as he went back to his work.

Willow Kovacs felt more resigned now. Roffrey had been away too long for there to be much chance of his coming back soon. She filled the hypo and gave Mary another sedative, but she didn't, after all, take one herself. In this calmer frame of mind her thoughts had again turned to Asquiol. She must contact him, she felt. At least she would have a clearer idea of how to act after she had seen him – whatever happened.

She experienced some difficulty in getting Roffrey's communications equipment to work, but finally she contacted Mordan.

The Gee-Councillor's sagging face appeared on the screen. He was hunched over his desk apparently doing nothing. He looked incredibly tired. Willow decided he must be keeping himself awake with stimulants.

He gave her a nod of recognition and said: 'Kovacs, if you're worried about Roffrey and Talfryn, there's no need. They have been recruited as Gamblers and will no doubt be getting in touch with you during a rest period.'

'Thanks,' she said, 'but there was something else.'

'How important is it, Kovacs? You understand that I'm very…'

'I wish to contact Asquiol directly.'

'That's impossible now. And, anyway, you wouldn't find it desirable if you realised what he looks like. What do you want to say to him?'

'I can't deal through someone else – it's a purely personal matter.'

'Personal? I remember – you had some emotional relationship…'

'We were very close on Migaa and on the Shifter worlds. I'm sure he would want to see me.' She didn't sound as if she particularly believed her own words.

'Next time I report to him I'll pass your message on. That's all I can do, I'm afraid.' Mordan stared curiously at her but said nothing more.

'Will he contact me if he gets your message?'

'If he wants to that's exactly what he will do. I'll tell him what you've said – I promise.'

The screen shimmered and was empty again. Willow turned it off and walked slowly back to where Mary was sleeping.

'What's going to happen to you in all this?' she said.

There was in Willow a large capacity for sympathy with those in distress. Even now, with troubles of her own which she hadn't counted on before she'd reached the fleet, she could turn her attention to Mary.

But what had at first been a detached emotion of sympathy, such as she could feel towards anyone in an unpleasant predicament, was fast running into a less healthy feeling. She was beginning to sense a kinship with Mary. They were both very lonely women – the one lacking any contact with her fellows, trapped inside her disturbed and jumbled mind, veering between near-sanity and complete madness; the other with a growing conviction that, in her moment of need, she had been deserted – not only by Asquiol, but by Talfryn and Roffrey too.

She sat by the screen, waiting for Asquiol to contact her. She sat stiffly. The cabin was silent, as silent as the space through which the fleet moved. She shared with the rest of humanity a demoralised, disillusioned sense of loss, of unknowing, of confusion. And as in the rest of them, these feelings were crystallising into fear.

Only the certain knowledge that loss of control at this time would bring utter destruction of mind or body allowed them to keep going.

Kept active by drugs, sent to sleep by sedatives, driven by the uncompromising will of Asquiol and his tool Mordan, the Gamblers prepared for another round of the Game.

Chapter Fifteen

THEY WERE SEATED in threes, each group before a large PV which mirrored the scene on the huge screen over their heads. The chamber was dark, illuminated solely by light from instruments and screens. Below the small screens were even smaller ones, in two rows of six. Mordan, who had brought Talfryn and Roffrey into the chamber, explained in a soft voice what purpose they served.

Roffrey looked about him.

Three sections of the circular chamber were occupied with the screens and seated before them each had its trio of operators – pale, thin men and women, for the most part, living off nervous energy and drugs. They had glass-alloy caps, similar to those he had worn while taking the tests. No-one looked up as he entered.

'The screen above us is, as you can see, merely a wide-angle viewer which enables us to scan the space immediately around the fleet,' Mordan was saying. 'Each group of operators – Gamblers, we call them – is delegated a certain area of this space to watch for signs of alien expedition. So far as we can gather, it is part of their code to come close – within firing range – to our fleet before beginning the round. Apart from that, we are given no warning that a fresh round is about to commence. That's why we keep constant watch. Presumably among themselves the aliens have subtler ways of beginning, but this seems to be their compromise.

'When an alien expedition comes into view the team sighting it alerts the rest and they all concentrate on that area. The smaller rows of screens record the effect which we beam towards the aliens. They record hallucinatory impulses, and these are broken down into sections governed by the different senses, brainwaves of varying frequencies, emotional-impulses such as fear, anger and so on, which we are capable of simulating. We have, of course, projectors, magnifiers and broadcasting equipment which is capable of responding to the commands of the Gamblers. But primarily, in the last resort, everything depends on the imagination, quick reactions, intelligence and ability to simulate emotions, thoughts and so on, which each individual Gambler possesses.'

'I see.' Roffrey nodded. In spite of himself, he was interested. 'What happens then?'

'Just as many of our emotions and impulses are unfamiliar and incommunicable to the aliens, the same applies to them. Presumably half the impressions and mental impulses we have flung at us do not have the effect the aliens desire, or would get in their own kind. But we have the same difficulty.

'These men have been playing the Game long enough to recognise whether the effects they send are effective or not, and can guard against those effects which are most dangerous to us. Winning the Game, at this stage, anyway, depends largely upon the extent to which we can assimilate and analyse what works and what doesn't work. This also, of course, applies to the aliens. You, for instance, had the hallucination of a monster beast which shocked not only your instincts, triggering fear, panic, and so on, but shocked your logical qualities since you knew that it was impossible for such a beast to exist in the vacuum of space.'

Roffrey and Talfryn agreed.

'This sort of effect is what the aliens are relying on – although in the general run of things these days they have learned to be much more subtle, working directly on the subconscious as they did to a large extent on you, after the beast-image didn't get the result they wanted. Therefore our psychologists and other researchers are gathering together every scrap of information which each round gives us, trying to get a clear picture of what effects will have the most devastating results on the aliens' subconscious. Here, as I mentioned, we are fairly well matched – our minds are as alien to them as theirs are to us.

'The prime object in playing the Blood Red Game, therefore, is to find the exact impulse necessary to destroy the qualities which we term self-respect, strength of character, intrinsic confidence, and so on.'

Mordan exhaled heavily. 'The number of losses we've had can be assessed when I tell you that we've got two hundred men and women alone who are curled up into foetal balls in the wards of our hospital ships.'

Talfryn shuddered. 'It sounds revolting.'

'Forget that,' Mordan said curtly. 'You'll lose all sense of moral values after you've been playing the Game for a short time. The aliens are helping us to do what philosophers and mystics have been preaching for centuries. Remember it? *Know thyself*, eh?'

He shook his head, staring grimly around the chamber where the grey-faced Gamblers watched the screens concentratedly.

'You'll get to know yourself here, all right. And I'm sure you won't like what you learn.'

'Easier on the brooder, the introvert,' Roffrey said.

'How deep can one man go in probing his innermost impulses before he pulls back – out of self-protection if nothing else?' Mordan said sharply. 'Not far in comparison to what the aliens can do to you. But you'll find out.'

'You're giving an attractive picture,' Roffrey said.

'Damn you, Roffrey – I'll talk to you after your first round. This may, now I come to think of it, do you an awful lot of good!'

They were joined by a third individual. He had obviously been a Gambler for some time. They were beginning to recognise the type. He was tall, thin and nervous.

'Fiodor O'Hara,' he said, not bothering to shake hands. They introduced themselves in the same curt manner.

'You will be in my charge until you become familiar with the Game,' O'Hara said. 'You will obey every order I give you. Try not to resist me. The sooner you are trained, the sooner you will be able to play the Game without any direction. I believe you are what they call an individualist, Roffrey. Well, you will have to conform here until you have mastered the Game – then your individualism will doubtless be of great use, since we depend on such qualities.

'Most of the people here are trained in some branch of psychology, but there are a few like yourselves – laymen – who have a sufficiently high I.Q. to be receptive, almost instinctively, to the needs of the Game. I wish you luck.

'You will find it a great strain to keep your ego free and functional – that is really all you have to learn to do as a beginner. You will carry out defensive strategy, as it were, until you are adept enough to begin attacking the enemy. Remember, both of you, physical strength and daring mean absolutely nothing in this war. And you lose not your life, but your sanity – at first anyway.'

Roffrey scratched the back of his neck. 'For God's sake, let's get started,' he said, impatiently.

'Don't fret,' Mordan said as he left them. 'You'll soon know when another round begins.'

O'Hara took them to a row of empty seats. There were three seats, the usual screen and the miniature screens beneath it. Immediately in front of them were small sets of controls which were evidently used to operate the sense-projectors and other equipment.

'We have a short vocabulary which we shall use later for communication while the Game is in progress,' O'Hara said, settling the skull-cap on his head. 'Switch sound, for instance, means that if, at a certain moment, you are concentrating on taste sensations, I have decided that sounds would be more efficient against the enemy. If I say, "Switch taste", it means that you send taste impressions. That is simple – you understand?'

They showed their assent. Then they settled themselves to await their first – and perhaps last – round of the Blood Red Game.

The morality of what they were doing – invading this universe and attempting to wrest dominance of it from the native race – had bothered Asquiol little.

'Rights?' he had said to Mordan when the Councillor had relayed the doubts of some of the members of the fleet. 'What rights have they? What rights have we? Because they exist here doesn't mean that they have any special *right* to exist here. Let them, or us, *establish* our rights. Let us see who wins the Game.'

Asquiol had more on his mind than a squabble over property, dangerous as that squabble could be for the race.

This was humanity's last chance of attaining its birthright – something which Asquiol had almost attained in his ability to perceive simultaneously the entire multiverse – to take over from the Originators.

Somehow he had to teach his race to tap its own potential. Here, those Gamblers who might survive would be of use.

The race had to begin on the next stage of its evolution, yet the transition would have to be so sudden it would be a violent revolution.

And there was the personal matter of his *incompleteness*: the torturing frustration of knowing the missing piece that would make him whole was so close – he could sense it – as to be almost within his grasp. But what was it?

Dwelling in thought, Asquiol was grave.

Even he could not predict the eventual outcome if they won the Game. More able to encompass the scope of events than the rest of the race, in some ways he was as much in a temporal vacuum as they were – quite unable to relate past experience with present, or the present with whatever the future was likely to be.

He existed in all the many dimensions of the multiverse. Yet he, in common with all others, was bound by the dimension of Time. He had cast off the chains of Space but was tied, as perhaps all denizens of the multiverse would always be, by the imperturbable prowl of Time, which brooked no halt, which condoned no tampering with its movement, whether to slow it or to speed it.

Time, the changer, could not be changed. Space, perhaps, the material environment, could be conquered. Time, never. It held the secret of the First Cause – a secret not known even to the Originators who had built the great, finite multiverse as a seeding bed – a womb – for their successors. But should the human race survive the birth pangs and succeed the Originators, Asquiol felt that it would not present a key to the secret.

Perhaps, in many generations – each generation measured as a stage in humanity's evolution – it would be found. But would the solution to the puzzle be welcomed? Not by his race – but maybe its great-grandchildren would be capable of accepting and retaining such knowledge. For once they replaced the Originators they would have the task of creating *their* successors. And so it would continue, perhaps *ad infinitum* – to what greater purpose?

He stopped this reverie abruptly. In this respect he was a pragmatist. He could not concern himself with such pointless speculation.

There was a lull in the Game. The coming of Roffrey's ship and its defeat of the aliens had evidently nonplussed them for a while. But Roffrey, so far, had not experienced the real struggle which was between trained minds capable of performing the most savage outrage there could be – destroying the id, the ego, the very qualities that set man above other beasts.

For a moment he wondered about Talfryn, but stopped the train of thoughts since it led to another question troubling him.

Asquiol allowed his concentration to cease for a moment as he enjoyed the rich nourishment that experience of dwelling on all planes of the multiverse gave him. He thought: *I am like a child in a womb, save that I know I am in the womb. Yet I am a child with a part missing, I sense it. What is it? What will complete me? It is as if the part would not only complete me, but complete itself at the same time.*

As was happening increasingly, he was interrupted by a sharp signal from the communicator.

He leaned forward in his chair, the strange shadows and curious half-seen images dancing about him. As he moved, the area of space between him and the communicator seemed to spray apart, flow and move spasmodically like water disturbed by the intrusion of an alien body. This happened whenever he moved, although he himself was only aware of his passing his arm through many objects which exerted a very faint pressure upon his limbs.

He could not only see the multiverse, he could also feel it, smell it, taste it. Yet this was little help in dealing with the aliens, for he found it almost as difficult as the rest of his race to understand the actual psychology of the non-human attackers.

The communicator came to life.

'Yes?' he said.

Again, Mordan had not turned on his own receiver, so that whereas Asquiol could see him, he need not subject himself to the eye-straining sight of Asquiol's scintillating body.

'A few messages,' Mordan went through them quickly. 'Hospital ship OP8 has disappeared. We heard that the I.T. field was becoming erratic. They were repairing it when they just... faded out of space. Any instructions?'

'I saw that happen. They're safe enough where they are. No instructions. If they're lucky they'll be able to rejoin the fleet if they can adjust their field.'

'Roffrey and Talfryn, the two men who succeeded in withstanding the B.R. effect so successfully, have been subjected to all Professor Selinsky's tests and he is studying the results now. In the meantime they are being taught how to play the Game.'

'What else?' Asquiol observed Mordan's worried expression.

'There were two others on Roffrey's ship. One of them was the madwoman – Mary Roffrey. The other calls herself Willow Kovacs. I have already forwarded this information, you remember.'

'Yes. Is that all?'

'Kovacs asked me to pass a message on to you. She says that you were personally acquainted on Migaa and later in the Shifter. She would like it if you could spare the time to get in touch with her. The ship is on 050 L metres for tight contact.'

'Thank you.'

Asquiol switched out and sat back in his seat. There was in him still some part of the strong emotion he had felt for Willow. But he had had to rid himself of it twice. Once when she had declined to follow him to Roth, once after he met the Originators. His impression of her was, by now, a little vague – so much had happened.

He had had to dispense with many valuable emotions when he assumed control of the fleet. This was out of no spirit of ambition or will to dominate, simply that his position demanded maximum control of his mind. Therefore, emotions had to be sacrificed where they could not directly contribute to what he was doing. He had become, in so far as ordinary human relationships were included, a very lonely man. His perception of the multiverse had more than compensated for the breaks in human contact he had been forced to make, but he rather wished that he had not had to make those breaks.

Normally, he never acted on impulse, yet now he found himself turning his communicator dial to the wavelength 050 L metres. When it was done he waited. He felt almost nervous.

Willow saw her screen leap into life and she quickly adjusted her own controls with the information indicated above the screen. She acted hurriedly, excitedly, and then the sight she saw froze her for a moment.

After that, her movements were slower as she stared fascinatedly at the screen. 'Asquiol?' she said in a faltering voice.

'Hello, Willow.'

The man still bore the familiar facial characteristics of the Asquiol who had once raged through the galaxy spreading chaos and laughter in his wake.

She remembered the insouciant, moody youth she had loved. But this… this Satan incarnate sitting in its chair like some fallen archangel – this golden sight bore no relation to him as she remembered him.

'Asquiol?'

'I'm deeply sorry,' he said, and smiled at her with a melancholy look for an archangel to wear.

Her face reflected the peculiar dancing effect which the image on the screen produced. She stepped back from it and stood with her shoulders drooping. And now she had only the memory of love.

'I should have taken my chance,' she said.

'There was only one, I'm afraid. If I'd known, I perhaps could have convinced you to come with us. As it was I didn't want to endanger your life.'

'I understand,' she said. 'Tough for me, eh?'

He didn't reply. Instead he was glancing behind him.

'I'll have to switch out – our opponents are starting another round of the Game. Goodbye, Willow. Perhaps, if we win, you and I can have another talk.'

But she was silent as the golden, brilliant image faded from the screen.

Chapter Sixteen

O'HARA TURNED TO his companions.

'This is your trial,' he said. 'Get ready.'

There was a faint humming sensation in the huge, circular chamber.

O'Hara had adjusted his screen so that he could now see the alien ships swimming through space towards them. Only a few miles from the fleet they came to a stop and remained, in relation to the fleet, in a fixed position.

Roffrey suddenly found himself thinking of his childhood, his mother, what he had thought of his father and how he had envied his brother. Why should he suddenly decide to...? Hastily he pulled himself out of this reverie, feeling slightly nauseated by a random thought that had begun to creep into his conscious mind. This was akin to what he'd experienced earlier, but not so intense.

'Careful, Roffrey – it's beginning,' said O'Hara.

And it was only a mild beginning.

Whatever the aliens had learned of the human subconscious, they used. How they had gained such a store of information, Roffrey would never know – though the human psychiatrists had a similar store of 'weapons' to turn back against their enemies.

Every dark thought, every unhealthy whim, every loathsome desire that they had ever experienced was dredged up by the alien machines and shoved before their conscious minds.

The trick, as O'Hara had said, was to forget values of good and evil, right and wrong, and to accept these impressions for what they were – desires and thoughts shared by everyone to some degree.

But Roffrey found it hard going.

And this was not all. The alien means of triggering these thoughts was spectacular and mind-smashing in its clever intensity.

He found it difficult to define what was sight or smell, taste or sound. And pervading it all, in the aching background of everything, was the swirling, whirling, chattering, shrieking, odorous, clammy, painful colour – the Blood Red sense.

It was as if his mind had exploded. As if it were gouting its contents, awash with blood and the agony of naked thoughts, unclothed by prejudice and self-deception. There was no comfort in this world he had suddenly entered – no release, no rest or hope of salvation. The alien sensory-projectors were forcing him further and further into his own mind, jumbling what was there when it did not suit their purpose to show it to him as it really was. All his conscious thoughts and senses were scrambled and jellied and altered. All his subconscious feelings were paraded before him and he was forced to look.

In the back of his mind was a small spark of sanity repeating over and over again: 'Keep sane – keep sane – hang on – it doesn't matter – it's all right.' And at times he heard his own voice blended with dozens of others as he howled like a dog and cried like a child.

Yet in spite of all this that was flung against him and the rest, in spite of the loathing he began to feel for himself and his fellows, there was still the spark which kept him sane.

It was at this spark that the aliens aimed their main concentration, just as the more experienced Gamblers in the human ranks aimed to destroy the little sparks of sanity alive in their opponents.

Never in the history of the human race had such dreadful battles been fought. This was more like a war between depraved demons than between material creatures.

It was all Roffrey could do to keep that spark alive as he sweated and struggled against the columns of sound, the vast, booming waves of smells, in the groaning movement of colour.

And as if in keeping with this battleground, the Blood Red mingling of senses swam and ran and convulsed and heaved themselves through his racked being, hurled themselves along his neural tracts, hacked past his cortical cells, mauled his synapses and shook body and brain into a formless, useless jelly of garbled receptions.

Blood Red! There was nothing now save the Blood Red shrilling of a pervading, icy, stinking taste and a washed-out feeling of absolute self-loathing that crept in everywhere, in every cranny and corner of his mind and person so that he wanted nothing more than to shake it aside, to escape from it.

But it trapped him – the Blood Red trap from which he could only escape by retreating back down the corridors of his experience, to huddle comfortingly in the womb of...

The spark flared and sanity returned completely for a moment. He saw the sweating, concentrated faces of the other operators. He saw Talfryn's face writhing and heard the man groaning, saw O'Hara's thin hand on his shoulder and grunted an acknowledgement. He glanced at the tiny screen which was fluttering with dancing graphs and pulsating light.

Then he was reaching for the small control panel before him, and his bearded face bore a twisted half-smile as he shouted: '*Cats!*

'*And they crawl along your spines with their claws gripping your nerves.*

'*Tides of mud, oozing. Drown, creatures, drown!*'

The words themselves were of little effect, but they were not meant to be – they were triggering off emotions and impressions in his own mind.

He was attacking now! Using the very emotions and impressions which the aliens had released. And he had grasped some understanding of how they could react to these things, for there had been in their attack several impressions which had meant nothing to him, translated into his own terms. These he flung back with a will and his own screens began to leap to the horrid rhythms of his savagely working mind.

First he sent the Blood Red impressions back, since these were obviously a preliminary attack which formed the basis of the Game. He didn't understand why this should be, but he was learning quickly. And one of the things he had learned was that reason played little part while the Game was on. That instinct had to be turned into a fighting tool. Later the experts could analyse results.

But then he felt the hysteria leave him and there was silence in the chamber.

'Stop! Roffrey – stop! It's over – they won. Christ! We haven't got a hope now!'

'Won? I haven't finished...'

'Look –'

Several of the Gamblers were sprawled on the floor, mewling and drooling insanely. Others were curled into tight foetal balls. Attendants rushed in to tend to them.

'We've lost seven. That means the aliens won. We got perhaps five. Not bad. You nearly had your opponent, Roffrey, but they've pulled back now. You'll probably get another chance. For a first-timer you did exceptionally well.'

Talfryn was insensible when they turned their attention to him.

O'Hara appeared unconcerned. 'He's lucky – it looks as if he's only blacked out. I think he's tough enough to take another round or two now he's got used to the Game.'

'It was – filthy...' Roffrey said. His whole body was tight with strain, his nerves were bunched, his head ached terribly, his heart pumped wildly. He even found it hard to focus on O'Hara.

Seeing his trouble, O'Hara took a hypodermic from a case in his pocket and gave Roffrey an injection before he could protest.

Roffrey began to feel better. He still felt tired, but his body started to relax and the headache was less intense.

'So that's the Blood Red Game,' he said after a moment.

'That's it,' said O'Hara.

Selinsky studied the papers Mann had prepared for him.

'You may well have something here,' he said. 'It is possible that the Shifter exerts a particular influence on the human mind that equips that mind for withstanding the attacks of the aliens.'

He looked up and spoke to Zung, who was fiddling with some equipment in one corner of the room.

'You say that Roffrey stood up particularly well in his first round?'

'Yes,' the little Mongolian nodded. '*And* he resumed the attack without direction. That's rare.'

'He's valuable enough without having any special characteristics,' Selinsky agreed.

'What do you think of my suggestions?' Mann said, almost impatiently, wanting to get back to her own line of inquiry.

'Interesting,' Selinsky said, 'but still nothing very definite to go on. I think we might ask to see Roffrey and Talfryn and find out what we can about their experiences in the Shifter.'

'Shall I ask them to come here?' Zung suggested.

'Yes, will you?' Selinsky frowned as he studied Mann's notes.

Mary was emerging from the turmoil of her ruined brain. Half afraid, for the knowledge of her insanity preyed always on her sane mind, she was reassembling her reason.

Suddenly there was no more confusion. She lay there, eyes seeing nothing at all – no sights of disordered creation, no threatening creatures, no danger. All she heard was the slight scuffling sound of somebody moving about near her.

Very carefully, she thought back.

It was hard to distil a sense of time out of the chaos of memory. It had been as if she had spent most of her life in a whirlpool, performing such meaningless actions as piloting a ship, opening airlocks, making equations that flowed away from her and disappeared.

There had been periods when the turmoil of the whirlpool had abated – sane periods where she had hovered on the brink of insanity but never quite succumbed. There had been the first arrival at the Shifter, looking for the knowledge she had found on Golund. There had been a landing on Entropium, and then a chaotic journey among the planets through chaos-space that contained no perceivable laws, only a turbulent inconsistency; landing, finding nothing, keeping a hold on her sanity which kept threatening to crack; and finally to Roth where her mind had gone completely. Aware of warmth. Then away from Roth in a manner she could never remember, back to Entropium; a man who asked her questions – Count Renark – and the horror of half-sanity finally smashed by the cataclysm that had turned Entropium into rubble; the dash for the Hauser, crashing on a peaceful planet – Ekiversh, perhaps? – and resting, resting – then on to Roth... chaos... warmth... chaos...

Why?

What had kept pulling her back to Roth, so that every time she returned her sanity had given out a little more? Yet the last time there had been something extra – a turning point, as if she had gone full circle, on the road *back* to sanity. She had met entities there, things of formless light that had spoken to her. No, that was probably an hallucination...

With a healthy sigh she opened her eyes. Willow Kovacs stood over her. Mary recognised the woman who had comforted her and smiled.

'Where's my husband?' she said quietly, and composed her features.

'Feel better now?' Willow said. The smile she gave in reply was sorrowful, but Mary saw it was not her that Willow pitied.

'Much. Is Adam...?'

'He's been recruited to play this Game.' Briefly Willow explained all she knew. 'He should be getting in touch soon.'

Mary nodded. She felt rested, at peace. The horror of her madness was a faint memory which she pushed further and further back. Never again, she thought. That was it – I'm all right now. That was the last time. She felt herself drifting into a deeper, more natural sleep.

Roffrey and Talfryn entered Selinsky's lab. Roffrey, huge and powerful, his black beard seeming to bristle with vitality, said: 'More tests, professor?'

'No, captain. We wish merely to question you on one or two points which have cropped up. To tell you the truth, neither of you appears to possess any strong trait which can account for your besting so many opponents. We have discovered that the reason you were able to beat those ships with such apparent ease was that *every* one of their Gamblers was beaten – put out of action by some force so powerful that it crossed space without any sending equipment to aid it. Their receivers turned the emanations into a force which destroyed their minds completely. But you possess no qualities of sufficient strength which could account for this. It is as if you needed an... amplifier of some kind. Can you explain that?'

Roffrey shook his head.

But Talfryn was frowning and said nothing. He appeared thoughtful. 'What about Mary?' he said slowly.

'Yes, that may be it!' Zung looked up from his notes.

'No, it isn't,' Roffrey said grimly.

Talfryn broke in: 'She's the one. Your wife, Roffrey. She was absolutely crazy on Entropium. She travelled between the Shifter's planets when space was wild and chaotic. She must have had a tremendous reserve of control somewhere in her if she could stand what she did. She could have picked up all kinds of strange impressions that worked on her brain. She did, in fact. She's our amplifier!'

'Well, what about it?' Roffrey turned round and looked at the three scientists standing there eagerly, like vultures who had spotted a dying traveller.

Selinsky sighed. 'I think we're right,' he said.

Mary stared out at the hazy light of the fleet dropping through darkness towards the far-off stars gleaming like lights at the end of a long, long tunnel.

'Adam Roffrey,' she said aloud, and wondered what she would feel when she saw him.

'How did you get to the Shifter?' Willow asked from where she sat.

'I ran away from Adam. I got tired of his restless life, his constant hatred of civilisation and ordered society. I even tired of his conversation and his jokes.

'Yet I loved him. Still do. I'm an anthropologist by profession, and took advantage of Adam's trips to the remote outworlds to keep my hand in. One time, we landed on Golund – the planet with signs of having been visited by a race from another galaxy. I hunted around the planet but got no more than the scant information available. So I left Adam and went to the Shifter when it materialised in our space-time, hoping to find some clues there. I searched the Shifter System, I searched it and clung to my sanity by a thread. But Roth was the last straw, Roth finished me.'

She turned back to look at Willow, smiling. 'But now I feel saner than I've ever done – and I'm thinking of settling down if I can. What do you think of that, Willow?' Her eyes were serious.

'I think you're nuts,' Willow said tactlessly. 'Don't sell out for the easy life. Look at me...'

'It's been hard, though,' said Mary, staring at the floor. 'Far too hard, Willow.'

'I know,' she said.

The communicator whistled. Mary went to it, operated the control.

It was Roffrey.

'Hello, Adam,' she said. Her throat felt constricted. She put her hand to it.

'Thank God,' he said, his weary face impassive.

She knew she still loved him. That alone was comforting.

'You got a doctor, then?' he said.

'No,' she said smiling. 'Don't ask me how – just accept that I'm sane. Something happened – the fight with the aliens, something on Roth, maybe just Willow's nursing. I don't know. I feel a new woman.'

His face softened as he relaxed. He grinned at her. 'I can't wait,' he said. 'Can you and Willow come over to the Game Ship right away? That's why I contacted you – before I knew.'

'Certainly,' she said. 'But why?'

'The people here think that all four of us, as a sort of team, managed to beat off the alien sense-impression attack. They want to give you a few routine tests along with Willow. Okay?'

'Fine,' she said. 'Send over a launch to collect us and we'll be with you.'

She thought she saw him frown just before he switched out.

Much later, Selinsky screwed up his tired face and pushed his hand over it. He shook his head briskly as if to clear it, staring at the two women who, under sedatives, lay asleep in the testing chairs.

'There's certainly something there,' he said, rolling a small light-tube between his palms. 'Why couldn't we have tested all four of you together? A stupid oversight.' He glanced at the chronometer on his right index finger.

'I've no idea why, but Asquiol is to broadcast to the entire fleet in a little while. About the Game, I think. I hope the news is good – we could do with some.'

Roffrey was ill at ease, brooding, paying scant attention to the scientist. He stared down at Mary and he suddenly felt weak, ineffectual, as if he no longer played a part in her life, and could hardly control his own. An unusual feeling – connected, perhaps, with the shape that events seemed to be taking…

Now she remembered. As she slept, physically, her mind was alert. She remembered landing on Roth, of stumbling over the surface, of falling down an abyss that took her upwards; of the strange, warm things that had entered her brain… She remembered all this because she could sense something similar quite close to her. She reached out to try and contact it, but failed – only just failed. She felt like a climber on a cliff face who was reaching for the hand of the climber just above, the fingers stretching out carefully, desperately, but not quite touching.

There was somebody out there – somebody like her – but somehow more like her than she was! That was the impression she got. Who or what was it? Was it a person, such as she defined the word, or something else? Her original…?

Adam? No, it wasn't Adam. She realised she had spoken his name aloud.

'I'm here,' he said, smiling down at her. She felt his big hand grasping her firmly, encouragingly.

'Adam… there's something… I don't know…'

Selinsky appeared beside her husband. 'How are you feeling?' he asked.

'Fine, physically. But I'm puzzled.' She sat up in the chair, dangling her legs, trying to touch the floor. 'What did you find out?'

'Quite a bit,' he said. 'And we'll be needing you. Are you willing to take a big risk and help us play the Game?'

Mary wondered why her husband was so quiet.

Chapter Seventeen

THIS TIME, ASQUIOL realised, he would have to visit the Game Ship personally, for the time he had feared had come.

The aliens had virtually won the Blood Red Game.

Jewelled, the multiverse spread around him, awash with life, rich with pulsating energy, but it could not compensate for his mood of near-despair. Coupled with the empty ache within him, the ache for the missing piece which seemed so close, it threatened to control him.

He still could not trace the source, but it was there. Something, like him but not so developed, was in touch with him, with the multiverse. He began to put mental feelers into the multiverse, searching.

But then his conscience made him withdraw from this and concentrate once more on the immediate problem. As had happened on past occasions, he had been in communication with the alien leaders. This time they had found it hard to disguise their jubilation, for the Game had taken firm shape.

They were winning. Even with the setback they had received from Roffrey's ship, their score had mounted enormously.

Asquiol still found it difficult to comprehend their method of scoring, but he trusted them. It was unthinkable for them to cheat.

His way of communicating with them was the way he and Renark had learned from the Originators. It wasn't telepathy. It relied on no exact human sense, but involved the use of waves of energy which only one in complete awareness of the multiverse might sense and harness. It did not involve words, but used pictures and symbols. It had been by analysis of some of these symbols which Asquiol had passed on to them that the psychiatrists had managed to devise 'weapons' for use against the aliens.

Asquiol still had no idea of what the aliens called themselves and did not even have a clear impression of their physical appearance. But their messages were easy enough to interpret and the fact remained that the human race had reached a crisis point.

Only one more round of the Game would decide the issue!

Then, if the human race refused to accept the decision and began open war again, Asquiol knew they were doomed, for their fleet was too depleted to stand any chance at all.

News received recently did not alter this certainty. A number of farm ships had broken down, others had been lost completely or been destroyed in their early physical encounters with the aliens. Less than two thousand ships of all kinds remained in the fleet – a vast enough caravan by any ordinary standards, but nearly a quarter of a million ships had originally left the home universe.

It was in a mood bordering on hopelessness that he stretched out a scintillating arm and put his communicator onto a general broadcast wavelength to inform the race of what he had learned. It was rare for him to do this, since direct contact with members of his race was becoming increasingly less attractive. He began: 'Asquiol here. Please listen attentively to my message. I have recently been in contact with our attackers and they have informed me that, as far as they are concerned, the game is virtually won. They are confident they will be the victors. This means our position is very nearly hopeless.

'We have, at most, enough supplies to last us for a month. Unless we make planetfall on some habitable world soon, you will all be dead.

'The only way in which we can survive is to win, decisively, the last round of the Game. The aliens already have a considerable advantage over us and feel that they can, in the next round, sufficiently increase this to ensure victory.

'Our Gamblers are weary and we have no more recruits. We have drained our talent as we have drained our resources. Our scientists are still working to devise a new way of beating the aliens, but I must tell you that time is running very short. Those among you not directly involved in playing the Blood Red Game had best make what plans you can, bearing in mind what I have said.

'To the Gamblers and all those attached to the Game Ship I can only ask for greater effort, knowing you have worked at full capacity for many days. Remember what we can win. *Everything*! Remember what we stand to lose. *Everything*!'

Asquiol sat back, his message still unfinished. He breathed in the exotic scents of the multiverse, saw the hull of his ship a stark outline against an overpoweringly beautiful background of living chaos; sensed, again, that peculiar feeling of kinship with another entity. Where was it? In this universe – or another?

Then he continued: 'I myself will not be directly affected by the outcome, as many of you have guessed. But this is not to say I am unaffected by my trust – to lead the race to safety in the first instance, and to something more in the second. There are those among you who ask what became of my companion Renark, our original leader. You wonder why he stayed behind in the contracting universe. My answer is vague, for neither of us got a clear idea from the Originators why this had to be. It is probably that the stuff of his great spirit was spread amongst us, to give all of us extra vitality – the vitality that we need. It may also have been that he sensed his rôle finished and mine only to have begun. Perhaps that is an arrogant thing to say.

'Renark was a brave man and a visionary. He was confident that our race, by its own efforts, could avoid, destroy or survive all danger. He was a believer in human will conquering all obstacles – physical, intellectual and metaphysical. In this, perhaps, he was naïve. But without that idealism and naïveté, our race could not have survived.

'However, what saved us from one form of peril may not be able to save us from another. Different problems require different solutions. Will alone is not now sufficient to win the Blood Red Game. It must be remembered that the circumstances of our present predicament are much more complex than when Renark and I went on our quest.

'We must be totally ruthless, now. We must be strong and courageous. But we must also be devious, cautious and sacrifice any idealism which made us embark on this voyage. Sacrifice is for survival – and the survival of a greater ideal.'

Asquiol wondered whether to continue. But he decided he had said sufficient for the moment.

Again he sat back, allowing himself to experience full unity with the multiverse.

'Where are you...?' he said, half-aloud. 'Who are you?'

The need was tangible in him – disconcerting, distracting his attention from the matter he must give all his mind to.

He had already been in contact with the Game Ship and now waited impatiently for the signal which would tell him a vessel was ready to take him there.

He rose and paced the cluttered cabin, the light shivering and breaking apart into rays of shining blue, gold and silver; shadows quivered around him and at times there seemed to be several ghostly Asquiols in the cabin.

At length the launch clamped against the side of his ship and he passed through his airlock and into the cramped cabin of the launch. Quickly it cruised over to the Game Ship and eased sideways into a receiving bay. The great outer doors closed down swiftly and Asquiol stepped out to be greeted by Mordan.

'Perhaps,' he said, 'with your aid, Asquiol...'

But Asquiol shook his iridescent head. 'I have little special power,' he said. 'I can only hope that my aid will help the Gamblers to hang on a little longer.'

'There is something else. Selinsky wants to see you. It appears that all four of those people who came in from the Shifter have some kind of group-power...'

They were striding along the corridors, their boots clanging on metal.

Asquiol said, 'I'll speak to Selinsky now.'

He stopped as Mordan paused beside a door. 'This is Selinsky's lab.'

'Is he in?'

Mordan turned a stud and entered. Selinsky looked up, blinking as Asquiol followed Mordan in.

'An honour...' he said, half-cynically.

'Mordan tells me, professor, that you are on to some new development?'

'Yes, that's so. The woman – Mary Roffrey. She's not only sane now, she's... what? Super-sane! Something was done to her mind on Roth. The whole nature of it altered. It is very different from anyone else's – except, perhaps...'

'Mine?' Asquiol felt excitement creeping through him. 'Is she, then, like me – as you see me?'

Selinsky shook his head. 'She seems perfectly normal – until you analyse her brain structure. She's what we need, all right.'

Asquiol was beginning to see the pattern now. Was this woman the missing piece in his existence? Had the Originators done something to her brain in order to form her into what she potentially was – a weapon? He could only guess.

Selinsky said: 'She wasn't a product of the alien attack at all. She was a product of more than just a series of madness-inducing hallucinations on Roth. Something or somebody had actually tampered with her brain. It's the most delicately balanced thing I've ever seen!'

'What do you mean?' Asquiol asked.

'One way – utter madness; the other way – unguessable sanity.' Selinsky frowned. 'I'd hate to be in her position. We've got her doing a quick training course with O'Hara at the moment. But playing the Game could ruin her mind for good, tip the balance once and for all.'

'You mean she'd be irredeemably insane?'

'Yes.

Asquiol pondered. 'We must use her,' he said finally. 'Too much is at stake.'

'Her husband is against the idea, but she seems to be taking it all right.'

'He's the troublemaker – Roffrey,' Mordan interposed.

'Will he give trouble in this business?'

'He seems resigned,' Selinsky said. 'A strange mood for him. Playing the Game seems to have wrought a change in him. Not surprising...'

'I must see her,' Asquiol said with finality, turning to leave the laboratory.

They began the long walk down the corridor to the Game Chamber.

Now Asquiol wanted to see Mary Roffrey – wanted to see her desperately. As he strode along, his mind worked quickly.

Ever since he and Renark had gone to the Shifter, their paths had crossed indirectly. He had never met her – yet she had been the person to supply Renark with a lot of important information without which they might never have reached the Originators. What was she? Some puppet of the Originators which they were using to aid the race? Or was she something more than a puppet?

She must be the missing factor in his own existence. Yet obviously she had no direct contact with the multiverse. She had the power to strike devastatingly back at the aliens – and he had no comparable power. There were things that linked them, yet there were qualities that separated them also. It was as if they both represented certain abilities which humanity was capable of possessing. She had something *he* didn't have – he had something *she* didn't have. How similar were they?

This, perhaps, he would find out in a moment.

He went over in his mind the information he had. Mary's mind had been primarily responsible for disorientating the aliens in a wild round of the Game. At that stage she had acted as a conductor for the rest. All of them having been on Roth, they were probably that much more capable of fighting the aliens than anyone else in the fleet. Therefore they would use the other three as well as Mary.

But uppermost in his mind was what Selinsky had just told him. Mary's mind could improve – or snap irreparably under the stress of this last round.

He knew what he would have to do now. But it was a heavy weight. As he contemplated it, the light around him seemed to fade, become colder and less frenetic in its movement. Sadness, such as he had never thought to experience again, filled him, and he fought it unsuccessfully.

He might, in essence, have to murder a woman – and cut himself off from the power she possessed. The power that was part of him as well as of her.

It was getting late – too late for anything but immediate action. The time of the last round was approaching.

They reached the door of the Game Chamber...

Chapter Eighteen

IN THE MAIN chamber, Mary was seated beside Willow and listening to the briefing. The other Gamblers were readying themselves for the last round. They were ill at ease and weary. Many of them did not look up even when Asquiol came in, flinging the door of the chamber open and striding quickly across the great room. The light flowed about the many facets of his body and streamed away behind him.

Mary turned round and saw him. 'You!' she said.

A look of puzzlement crossed Asquiol's face. 'We've met?' he said. 'I don't remember.'

'I saw you with Renark several times – on Roth.'

'But we left Roth ages ago!'

'I know – but Roth is a strange planet. Time is non-existent there. Anyway, it wasn't only that.'

'Then how else did you recognise me?'

'I've sensed you've been here all the time. Even before we reached the fleet, I think.'

'But obviously you do not exist, as I do, in the entire multiverse. What could the link be, I wonder?' Then he smiled. 'Perhaps our mutual friends the Originators could tell us.'

'Probably it's simpler than that,' Mary replied. The sense of empathy with Asquiol was like nothing she had ever experienced before. 'Because we have seen them and gained from the contact, we recognise it in each other.'

'Very likely.' He nodded, then suddenly noticed that Willow was staring at him, her eyes full of tears. He took control of himself and said briskly: 'Well, we had better get ready. I'm going to be in control of this project. You, Mary, will work under my direction using – as power, as it were – the other three, Roffrey, Talfryn and Willow. It's quite simple – a sort of gestalt link.'

She looked at the others, who had crossed the room from where Selinsky and his team were working on a mechanism. 'Did you hear that?' Adam had the look of a dumb beast in pain as he stared at her for a moment before dropping his eyes.

'We heard it,' he said. 'All of it.'

She glanced at Asquiol as if seeking his advice, but he couldn't help her. Both of them were now in a similar position – Mary with Roffrey and Asquiol with Willow.

The time was nearing, Mary felt, when she would have to sever her ties with her husband.

The time had passed, Asquiol reflected, when he and Willow could have been united by the common bond which he and Mary possessed.

As they looked at one another, they seemed to convey this without need of speech.

O'Hara interrupted them: 'Get ready, everyone! Remember, we need an overwhelming win in the round that is to follow. This round will be the last we have to play. Winning it must be decisive!'

The five people, Asquiol and Mary in the lead, went towards the specially prepared panel.

Selinsky and his team finished their work and stepped aside.

The five composed themselves to play.

Both Willow and Adam Roffrey had to force themselves to concentrate, but both were motivated by a different fear. Willow feared that Mary would become extra-sane through her ordeal. Roffrey feared she would become insane, while he hated the alternative which would break their relationship before it ever had a chance to resume.

Asquiol was his rival now, Roffrey saw. Yet Asquiol hardly knew it himself.

Only Talfryn was not afraid of the possible results. Either way, he felt, he stood to win – so long as Mary was effective in helping the Gamblers win the Game.

Asquiol bent close to Mary and whispered: 'Remember I am in the closest possible touch with you, and you with me. However near you feel you are coming to insanity, don't panic. I'll keep you on the right course.'

She smiled at him. 'Thanks.'

The tension rose as they waited.

It was so delicate, the first probe. As delicate as a slicing scalpel.

O'Hara shouted: 'Don't wait for them. Attack! Attack!'

In contact with Mary now, Asquiol began to dredge up Mary's memories from the deepest recesses of her subconscious, doing to her what only a totally evil man might do.

Yet, even as she slipped into the giddy, sickening whirlpool of insanity, it was obvious to her that Asquiol was not evil. There was no malice in him at all. It was taking fantastic control for him to force himself to continue. But he did continue. He worked at her mind, slashing at it, tearing at it, working it apart in order to remould it, and he did it in the full knowledge that he might, in the final analysis, be committing a dreadful crime.

Beside him, the trio sweated, feeding power to Mary that was channelled by Asquiol and directed by him at the alien attackers.

'There they are, Mary – you see them!'

Mary turned glazed eyes towards the screen. Yes, she saw them.

It was suddenly like horrible darkness then, roiling through her. Red-hot needles forced themselves into the grey mass of her brain. It was like being a tightened banjo string. Tighter and tighter until she must surely snap. She couldn't... She couldn't...

She laughed. It was a huge joke against her. They were all laughing at her.

She sobbed and mewled and lashed back at the pouring stream of demons and hobgoblins that came prancing and tumbling down the long corridors of her mind. They sniggered and simpered and fingered her brains and her body and pulled her nerves about, enjoying their sport, caressing the parts of her they captured.

She lashed back as the whole scene became pervaded with the Blood Red sense that had always been there. She knew it. She was familiar with it and she hated it more than anything else.

Gone were emotions – gone self-pity, gone love – gone yearning and jealousy and impotent sadness. The trio linked and locked and lent their strength to Mary. Everything that she felt, they felt. Everything she saw and did, they saw and did. And at times, also, so close were the five blended, they saw something of what Asquiol saw and it lent them strength to pass on to Mary.

On and on they went, driving at the aliens, hating them and sending back impression after impression from the multiple brain.

To the alien players of the Game, it was as if they had suddenly been attacked by an atomic cannon in a war that had previously been fought with swords. They reeled beneath the weight of the attack. They reeled, they marvelled and, in their strange way, they admired. But they fought back even harder, playing, after the initial shock, coolly and efficiently.

Roffrey broke contact at the sound of a voice outside. It was O'Hara shouting: 'We're winning; they were right. Somehow she has the key to the whole mastery of the Game. She does something with her mind that reflects back to them exactly the thing most loathsome to them. There's a twist there somewhere that no human experience could have made. She's doing it!'

Roffrey stared at him for a moment as if in panic, and then returned his attention to the Game. For a moment, O'Hara watched him before he returned his own attention. Their gains were slowly mounting – and Mary's inspiration seemed to be encouraging the rest of the Gamblers to give their best.

'This is our finest hour,' O'Hara said thickly. 'Our finest hour.'

And as he passed her he saw Mary's twisted and distorted face with the sweat and saliva all over it, wreathed in the same flickering images that surrounded Asquiol's intent face.

Now she knew she was winning. *Now* she could see they were reeling back. *Now* she felt victory within her reach. Although the madness was frenzied and all-consuming, there was behind it all the confidence that Asquiol's presence gave her, and she kept sending, though her mind and body ached with searing agony.

Then, quite suddenly, she blacked out, hearing a voice call from a long way off: '*Mary! Mary!*'

Asquiol, knowing that he had aided her to reach this state, could hardly bear to continue. But he had to. He put a hand to her sweat-wet hair and dragged the head back to stare into the vacant eyes.

'Mary – you *can* send them away. You *can*!' He began to communicate with her. He forced her attention to the screens.

She threshed in her chair. For a second she stared at him. To his relief he saw sanity there.

'*Asquiol,*' she said, '*what is it we were?*'

'*We can be the same, Mary – now!*'

And then she was bellowing in his face, her laughter seeming a physical weight battering around his head so that he wanted to fling up his hands to ward it off, to run and escape, to hide from what he had created. But again he forced control on himself and pushed her face towards the screens.

Roffrey, pain-drunk, glared at him, but did nothing.

Finally, she was roaring and tearing. Asquiol couldn't make contact with her. One of her hands flailed out, the nails slashing his face. Roffrey saw the blood come and was half-astonished. He had forgotten that Asquiol was in many ways as mortal as himself. Somehow it made the feelings in him worse.

Asquiol fought to control this rage, turn it against the aliens. He battled to resume empathetic contact with Mary.

She stirred, her name formed and curled and buzzed through the darkness. She reached out for it.

Elsewhere, many of the Gamblers had already succumbed to the force of the alien impressions. Tidal waves of garbled sense-impressions were being flung against them and even the strongest were finding it hard to resist, to keep the spark of sanity alive and to retaliate.

Asquiol used the communicating-sense that allowed him to contact the aliens and 'converse' with them. He did this to Mary. He shoved impressions and pictures into her mind, things taken from his own memory. And so real did they become, in such close empathy was he with the woman, that he felt his own sanity slipping away. But he was the controlling part of the team – he had to keep aware. He held on for as long as he could, then straightened his back, gasping.

Those watching saw the light surrounding him skip erratically and dim suddenly. Then it became brighter, like a flaring explosion.

And then the light appeared to make contact with Mary. The same thing appeared to happen to her body. Her image split and became many images...

Asquiol! ASQUIOL! ASQUIOL!

Hello, Mary.

What is it?

Rebirth. You're whole now.

Is it over?

By no means!

Where are we, Asquiol?

On the Ship.

But it's...

Different, I know. Look!

She saw, through facet after facet, her husband, the girl and the other man. They were staring at her in astonishment. Angled, opaque images surrounded every space they did not occupy.

'Adam,' she said, 'I'm sorry.'

'It's all right, Mary. I'm not. Good luck – like I said.' Roffrey was actually smiling.

A new image swam into focus – O'Hara gesticulating.

'I don't know what's happened to the woman and I don't care. Get your attention back to the Game, or it's lost!'

She turned, and the horrifying impressions came back, but it was as if they were pressed through a filter which took away their effect on her mind.

Carefully, she searched her being. She felt Asquiol beside her, felt the warmth of his encouragement. She lashed back, with deliberate and savage fury, searching out weaknesses, using them, splitting the alien minds to shreds. Asquiol guided her – she could feel it. Talfryn, Willow and Adam supplied power and extra impressions which she took and warped and sent out.

More of the Gamblers were dropping out and attendants were kept busy clearing them from the chamber. There were only five complete teams left.

But it was victory. Mary and Asquiol could feel it as they worked together – oblivious of everything else – to defeat the aliens. They felt at that moment as if they knew everything about their opponents, to such an extent that they were even in danger of giving up out of sympathy.

They fought on, riding a tide of conquest. Soon the entire alien complement was finished. They retreated back and stared around them.

'Asquiol – what happened?'

Asquiol and Mary saw Willow looking up at them. They smiled at her and said: *'This was the Originators' plan, Willow. They obviously did not allow sufficiently for human weakness – but they did not count on the strength of the human spirit, perhaps. Please don't suffer, Willow. You have done more today for humanity than you could ever have done for any single person.'*

They turned to regard the others. *'You too, Roffrey – and you, Talfryn. Without you it is unlikely that we could have defeated the alien intelligences. Everything has suddenly become a clear pattern. There was, perhaps, a purpose for Willow and Talfryn when they stayed behind. There was a purpose, also, for Roffrey when he took it into his head to visit the Shifter. We nearly threw away our chance.'*

'What exactly has happened?' Mordan interrupted. 'Have you become one entity?'

'No.' Asquiol spoke with a slight effort. 'Existing on the multiversal level, we are capable of linking minds to form a more powerful single unity. That was how we finally defeated our opponents.

'Obviously this was part of the Originators' plan. But they never do anything for us directly. At best, they merely put certain aids in our path. If we can make use of them – assuming we realise what they are – so much to the good. If we can't, we suffer. We were near complete defeat there. If we had not got some hint of Mary's abilities when we did, the plan would have come to nothing. As it was, we were lucky.'

Mary said: 'I must have been watched by the Originators right from the start – even before I met you.'

Asquiol continued: 'The Originators make things especially difficult for people they think are... material for the new, multiversal race. Simply, only the fittest survive.'

Mordan said obsequiously, yet hastily: 'But the aliens... can we not discover what our peace terms are? We must hurry... the farm ships...'

'Of course,' Asquiol nodded. 'Mary and I will return to my ship and contact them from there.'

Mary and Asquiol moved towards the exit, gave one last glance at the three others, and left.

'What the hell have you got to smile about, Roffrey?' Talfryn said accusingly.

Roffrey felt at peace. Maybe it was the mood induced by weariness, but he didn't think so. There was no more pain in him, no more jealousy, no more hatred. He moved over to the big blank screen and stared up at it. The place suddenly brightened as assistants switched on the central lights and began clearing up the mess the Gamblers had left...

'I give up.' Talfryn shook his head, perplexed.

'That's the trouble,' Willow said. 'So many of us do, don't we?'

Epilogue

ASQUIOL OF POMPEII took Mary the Maze back to his ship. They felt more at ease there, since the ship was better suited to their own metabolic state.

Here, with Asquiol acting again as a guide for Mary, they pooled their resources together and contemplated the radiant multiverse around them.

Then they put out a tendril of multiversal thought-matter along the familiar layers, seeking the alien minds.

Then they were in contact!

When the alien leaders came to the ship, Mary gasped and said in normal speech: 'God! They're beautiful.'

They were beautiful, with delicate bones and translucent skins, great, golden eyes and graceful movements. Yet there was a look of decadence. Like depraved, wise children.

'The Originators warned me to beware of races they called pessimists,' Asquiol said, 'races who had despaired of ever attaining full awareness of the multiverse, who had so completely lost the urge to transcend their limitations that the tiny core of *being* had, over millennia, been almost completely eroded. Doubtless these are of that kind.'

By use of their unique method, they once again conversed with the aliens and were astonished by the mood of total defeat, the unquestioning acceptance of the winners' rights to dictate any terms they wished.

They had lost their urge to transcend physical confines and in so doing had lost pride – real pride, also.

Absolute defeat – lost spirit – utter hopelessness – concede all rights you wish to take...

This mood was sufficient to add almost the last pressure on the victors' already weary minds. A great pity welled up in them as they communicated their terms to the conquered.

Accept terms – any terms acceptable – we have no status – you have all status – we are nothing but your tools to use…

So conditioned were the aliens to the code applying to the Game they had played for centuries, perhaps millennia, that they could let this unknown opponent do as it liked. They were conditioned to obeying the victor. They could not question the victor's right. Their shame was so intense that they threatened to die of it – yet there was no trace of bitterness, no trace of resentment or lingering pride…

Asquiol and Mary resolved to help them, if they could.

The aliens left.

Would they ever see them again? As the spherical ship moved away, Asquiol and Mary sent out a polite impression that congratulated them on their ingenuity and courage, but it met with no response. They were beaten – no praise could alter that. They gave them positions of planets suitable for human occupation – they were totally unsuited for themselves, anyway – and then they fled.

They did not go to nurse grudges, for they had none. They did not plot retaliation, for such a thing was inconceivable. They went to hide – to reappear only if their conquerors demanded it.

They were a strange people whose artificial code had obviously completely superseded natural instincts.

As the alien ship disappeared, Asquiol and Mary broke their contact with the leaders.

'I'd better inform Mordan. He'll be delighted, anyway.' Asquiol operated the V. He told the Gee-Councillor of his meeting.

'I'll start the fleet moving towards some habitable planets right away. Give me an hour.' Mordan smiled tiredly. 'We did it, Asquiol. I must admit I was close to accepting defeat.'

'We all were,' Asquiol smiled. 'How are the other three?'

'They've gone back to Roffrey's ship. I think they're okay. Roffrey and the girl seem quite happy, strangely. Do you want me to keep tabs on them?'

'No.' Asquiol shook his head, and as he did so the light broke and re-formed around it, the images scattering and merging. Asquiol stared at Mordan's weary face for a moment. The Councillor shifted uncomfortably beneath the fixed stare.

'I could do with some natural sleep,' he said at last, 'but I've got to get the fleet moving first. Is there anything else?'

'Nothing,' said Asquiol, and switched out.

There was a subdued mood of victory about the re-formed fleet as he and Mary watched it from one of the ports.

'There's a lot more to do, Mary,' he said. 'This is really only the beginning. I once compared the human race to a chick smashing out of its shell. The comparison still applies. We've broken the shell. We've survived our first period in the multiverse – but will we survive the second and the third? Is there a huge, cosmic farmer with an axe somewhere thinking of serving us up for dinner when we're plump enough?'

She smiled. 'You're worn out. So am I. Give yourself time to think properly. It's the reaction – you're depressed. That kind of emotion can harm a lot of the work we still have to do.'

He looked at her in surprise. He was still unused to having company that he could appreciate, someone who could understand what he felt and saw.

'Where are we going?' he said. 'We need to plan carefully. The degraded condition of the fleet can't be allowed to continue once we make planetfall. Galactic Law will have to be firmly re-established. Men like Mordan, who have been more than useful in the past because of their pragmatic virtues which would have been hindered by possession of the kind of vision we need now, will have to be taken out of positions of power. We've become a grim race lately – out of necessity. If we let matters slide, Mary, the race could easily degenerate back into something worse than its pre-exodus state. If that happened, our destiny might be out of reach for good. There isn't much time. The Originators made that clear when Renark and I first met them.'

He sighed.

'With me to help you,' she said, 'the hard work will be easier.

I know it's going to be hard, but there are two of us now. You noticed how Adam and Willow were beginning to respond back in the Game Ship? There must be dozens like them in the fleet, potentially capable of joining us. Soon, perhaps in only a few generations, there will be a race of people like us, until there are enough to take the place of Originators.'

'Not that many,' Asquiol said. 'Most people are happy as they are. Who can blame them? It will be an uphill climb.'

'That's the best way to climb hills.' She smiled. 'And remember – keep your impression of those aliens we saw firmly in your mind. We have an example now of how we could degenerate. Perhaps it was fated that we should meet that race. It will serve as a reminder – and a warning. And with a reminder like that, we are not likely to fail.'

Around them, as they sat in contemplation, the multiverse flowed, thick and solid, so full. And this could be the heritage of their race.

He laughed lightly. 'There's a scene in *Henry the Fourth* where Falstaff learns that Prince Hal, his old drinking companion, is now king. He gathers his friends about him and tells them good times have come, for he is "Fortune's Steward", and the king will honour them and allow them to behave as they like with impunity. But, instead, King Henry banishes Falstaff for a buffoon and troublemaker. Falstaff realises then that instead of becoming better, things are going to be worse. I sometimes wonder if, perhaps, I'm not "Fortune's Steward" – leading the whole race towards a promise I can't keep…'

Mary's multifaceted face smiled encouragingly. 'There are still the Originators. But even without them humanity has always had to act without being able to foresee the outcome of its actions – ever since we began the long climb upwards. We're stumblers; we have to convince ourselves of the results we will achieve without ever knowing if we can succeed. But we quite often do succeed. We have a long way to go, Asquiol, before we shall ever be able to know for certain the outcome of our actions. Meanwhile, we keep going. We have to keep trying to cut justice from the stuff of chaos.'

'We're probably the most optimistic race in the multiverse!' said Asquiol, embracing her.

They laughed together. And the spirit of Renark, which had permeated humanity to give it a unified strength, seemed to share their joy.

The multiverse shifted, swirled and leapt, forever changing and delighting them with its chaos, its colour, its variety. All possibilities existed there.

All promise, all faith, all hope.

The Winds of Limbo

For Judy Merril

Chapter One

IT WAS A vast cavern. Part of it was natural, part of it had been hollowed out by the machines of men. Some parts were deep in dancing shadow and others were brilliantly illuminated by a great blazing mass – a roaring, crackling miniature replica of the sun itself, that hung, constantly quivering and erupting, near the high roof.

Beneath this blazing orb a tall column rose up as if to meet it, and arms akimbo upon a platform at the top stood a gross figure, clad in ragged harlequin costume. A soft, floppy, conical hat was jammed over his lank, yellow hair; his fat-rounded face was painted white, his eyes and mouth adorned with smears of red, yellow and black, and on the ragged red jerkin stretched taut upon his great belly was a vivid yellow sunburst.

Below this gross harlequin the dense crowd surrounding the column ceased its movement as he raised an orange hand that seemed to shoot from his torn sleeve like fingers of flame.

He laughed. It was as if the sun had voiced unearthly humour.

'Speak to us!' the crowd pleaded. 'Fireclown! Speak to us!'

He ceased his laughing and looked down at them with a peculiar expression moving behind the paint. At length he bellowed:

'I am the Fireclown!'

'Speak to us!'

'I am the Fireclown, equipped for your salvation. I am the gift bearer, alive with the Fire of Life, from which the Earth itself was formed! I am the Earth's brother...'

A woman in a padded dress representing the body of a lion cried shrilly: 'And what are we?'

'You are maggots feeding off your mother. When you mate it is like corpses coupling. When you laugh it is the sound of the winds of limbo!'

'Why? Why?' shouted a young man with a lean, mean face and a pointed chin that could pierce a throat. He leapt exuberantly while his eyes glinted and looked.

'You have shunned the natural life and worshipped the artificial. But you are not lost – not yet!'

'What shall we do?' sobbed a government official, sweating in the purple jacket and purple pantaloons of his rank, caught by the ritual enough to fidget and forget to stay in the shadows. His cry was echoed by the crowd.

'*What shall we do?*'

'Follow me! I will reinstate you as Children of the Sun and Brothers of the Earth. Spurn me – and you perish in your artificiality, renounced by Nature on whom you have turned your proud backs.'

And again the clown broke into a laugh. He breathed heavily and roared his insane and enigmatic humour at the cavern roof. Flames from the suspended miniature sun leapt, stretched and shot out, as if to kiss the Fireclown's acolytes who laughed and shouted, surging about him, applauding him.

The Fireclown looked down as he laughed, drinking in their adoration.

In a shadow cast by the dais, detached from the milling crowd, a gaunt negro stood as if petrified, his eyelids painted in checks of red and white, his mouth coloured green. He wore an extravagant yellow cut-away coat and scarlet tights. He looked up at the Fireclown and there were tears of hunger in his eyes. The negro's name was Junnar.

The faces of the crowd were lashed and slashed by the leaping fire, some eyes dull, some bright, some eyes blind and some hot, overloaded with heat.

Many of the figures wore masks moulded in plastic to caricature their own faces – long noses, no noses, slit eyes, cow eyes, lipless mouths, gaping mouths. Some were painted in gaudy colours, others were naked and some wore padded clothes representing animals or plants.

Here they gathered around the dais. Many hundreds of them,

loving the man who capered like a jester above them, lashing them with his wriggling rhetoric, laughing, laughing. Scientists, pickpockets, spacemen, explorers, musicians, confidence tricksters, blackmailers, poets, doctors, whores, murderers, clerks, perverts, government officials, spies, policemen, social workers, beggars, actors, politicians, riff-raff.

Here they all were. And they shouted. And as they shouted the gross Fool capered yet more wildly and the flame responded frenetically to his dancing and his own wordless cries.

'The Fireclown!' they sobbed.

'The Fireclown!' they bellowed.

'The Fireclown! The Fireclown!' they howled and laughed.

'The Fireclown!' He giggled and he danced like a madman's puppet upon his dais and sang his mirth.

All this, in the lowest level of the multistoreyed labyrinth that was the City of Switzerland.

With a great effort the negro Junnar turned his eyes away from the Fireclown, stumbled backwards, wrenched his body round and ran for one of the black exits, bent on leaving before he was completely trapped by the Fireclown's spell.

Behind him, the sound of the maddened crowd diminished as he ran along fusty, ill-smelling corridors until he could no longer hear it. Then he began to walk up ramps and stairs until he came to an escalator. He stepped onto the escalator and let himself be taken up to the top, a hundred feet from the bottom. This corridor was also deserted, but better lighted and cleaner than those he had left. He looked up and found a sign at an intersection:

NINTH LEVEL (Mechanics) Hogarth Lane – Leading to Divebomber Street and Orangeblossom Road (Elevators to Forty Levels)

He made for Orangeblossom Road, an old residential corridor but very sparsely inhabited these days, found the elevators at the end, pressed a button and waited impatiently for five minutes before one arrived. He entered it and rose non-stop to the forty-ninth level. Outside he crossed the bright, bustling corridor and got into a crowded lift bound for the sixty-fifth – the topmost – level.

The liveried operator recognised him and said deferentially: 'Any tips for when the next election's going to be held, Mr Junnar?'

Junnar, abstracted, tried to smile politely. He shook his head. 'Tomorrow, if the RLMs had their way,' he said. 'But we're not worried. People have faith in the Solrefs.' He frowned. He had caught himself using a party slogan again. Apparently the operator hadn't noticed, but Junnar thought he saw a hint of irony in the man's eyes. He ignored it, frowned again, this time for a different reason. Obviously people were *losing* faith in the Solar Referendum Party. A sign of the times, he thought.

At length the elevator reached the sixty-fifth level and the operator called out conscientiously: 'Sixty-five. Please show appointment cards as you go through the barrier.'

The people began to shuffle out, some towards transport that would take them right across the vast plateau of the Top Level, some towards the distant buildings comprising the Seat of Government, various Ministries and the private accommodations of important statesmen, politicians and civil servants.

Built with the money of frightened businessmen during the war scares of the 1970s, the city had grown upwards and outwards so that it now covered almost two thirds of what was once the country of Switzerland – one vast building. A warren with mountains embedded in it, it had begun as a warren of super-shelters *below* the mountains. The war scares had died down, but the city had remained along with the businessmen and, when the World Government was formed in 2005, it seemed the natural place for the capital. In 2031, in a bid to get full rights of citizenship for outworld settlers, the Solar Referendum Party had been formed. Four years later it had risen to power. Its first act had been to declare that henceforth they were a Solar Government running the affairs of the Federation of Solar Planets.

But since then more than sixty years had passed. The Solrefs had lost much of their original dynamism, having become the most powerfully conservative party in the Solar House.

The official at the barrier knew Junnar and waved him through.

Sun poured in through the glass-alloy dome far above his head and the artificially scented air was refreshing after the untainted stuff of the middle levels and the impure air of the lowest.

He walked across the turf-covered plaza, listening to the splashing fountains that at intervals glinted among beds of exotic flowers. He was struck by the contrast between the hot excitement, the smell of sweat and the surge of bodies he had just left, and this cool, well-controlled expanse, artificially maintained yet as beautiful as anything nature could produce.

But he did not pause to savour the view. His pace was hurried compared with the movement of the few other people who sauntered with dignity along the paths. At a distance, the tall white, blue and silver buildings of the ambiguously named Private Level reflected the sun and enhanced the atmosphere of calm and assurance of the Top.

Junnar crossed the plaza and walked up a clean, gravelled path towards the wide stone arch that opened onto a shady court. Around this court many windows looked down upon the cool pool in its centre. Goldfish glinted in the pool. At the archway, a porter left his lodge and planted himself on the path until Junnar reached him. He was a sour-faced man, dressed in a dark grey blouse and pantaloons; he looked at Junnar with vague disapproval as the flamboyant negro stopped and produced his pass, sighing: 'Here you are, Drew. You're very conscientious today.'

'My job is to check all passes, sir.'

Junnar smiled at him. 'You don't recognise me, is that it.'

'I recognise you very well, sir, but it would be more than my job's worth to...'

'Let me in without checking my pass,' Junnar finished for him. 'You're an annoying man, Drew.'

The porter didn't reply. He was not afraid of incurring Junnar's disapproval since he had a strong union that would be only too ready to take up cudgels on his behalf if he was fired without adequate grounds.

So temporarily disorientated was Junnar that he allowed this tiny conflict to carry him further, and as he went into the court he shrugged and said: 'It's better to have friends than enemies, though, Drew...' Immediately he felt foolish.

He took out a pack of proprietary brand marijuanas and lit one as he went through a glass-panelled door into the quiet, deserted hall of the building. The hall was lined with mirrors. He stood staring at himself in one of them, drawing deeply on the sweet smoke, collecting his thoughts and pulling himself together. This was the third time he had attended one of the Fireclown's 'audiences' and each time the clown's magnetism had drawn him closer and the atmosphere of the great cavern had affected him more profoundly. He didn't want his employer to notice that.

After a moment's contemplation Junnar went to the central glass panel which was on the right and withdrew a small oblong box from his pocket. He put it close to his mouth.

'Junnar,' he said.

The panel slid back to reveal a black, empty shaft. There was a peculiar dancing quality about the blackness. Junnar stepped into it and, instantaneously, was opening the inner door of a cabinet. He walked out and the door closed behind him. He was in a corridor lighted by windows that stretched from floor to ceiling and showed in the distance the thick band of summer cloud far below.

Immediately opposite him was a great door of red-tinted chrome. It now opened silently.

In the big, beautiful room, two men awaited him. One was young, one was old; both showed physical similarities, both appeared impatient.

Junnar entered the room and dropped his cigarette into a disposal column.

'Good afternoon, sir,' he said to the old man, and nodded to the young man. 'Good afternoon, Mr Powys.'

The old man spoke, his voice rich and resonant. 'Well Junnar, what's happening down there now?'

Chapter Two

ALAN POWYS FINGERED the case of papers under his arm, studying his grandfather and the painted negro as they confronted one another. They made a strange pair.

Minister Simon Powys was tall and heavy without much obvious fat, but his face was as grim and disturbing as an Easter Island god's. The leonine set of his head was further enhanced by the flowing mane of white hair which reached almost to his shoulders, hanging straight as if carved. He wore the standard purple suit of a high-ranking cabinet minister – he was Minister for Space Transport, an important office – pleated jacket, padded pantaloons, red stockings and white pumps. His white shirt was open at the neck to reveal old but firm flesh, and on his breast was a golden star, symbol of his rank.

Junnar was sighing and spreading his hands. 'If you, Minister Powys, want to stop him you should act now. His power increases daily. People are flocking to him. He *seems* harmless, in so far as he doesn't appear to have any great political ambitions, but his power could be used to threaten society's stability.'

'Could be? I'm sure it *will* be.' Minister Powys spoke heavily. 'But can we convince parliament of the danger? There's the irony.'

'Probably not.' Alan Powys spoke distantly, conscious of an outsider's presence. He thought he glimpsed, momentarily, a strange expression on the negro's face.

'Helen and that mob of rabble-rousers she calls a political party are only too pleased to encourage him,' Minister Powys grumbled. 'Not to mention certain members of the government who seem as fascinated by him as schoolgirls on their first dates.' He straightened his shoulders which were beginning to stoop with old age. 'There must be some way of showing them their mistake.'

Alan Powys chose not to argue with his grandfather in Junnar's presence. Personally, however, he thought the old man over-emphasised the Fireclown's importance. Perhaps Junnar sensed this, for he said softly:

'The Fireclown has a certain ability to attract and hold interest. The most unlikely people seem to have come under his spell. His magnetism is intense and almost irresistible. Have you been to one of his "audiences", Mr Powys?'

Alan shook his head.

'Then go to one – before you judge. Believe me, he has *something*. He's more than a crank.'

Alan wondered why the normally self-possessed and taciturn negro should choose to speak in this way. Perhaps one day he *would* attend a meeting. He certainly was curious.

'Who is he, anyway?' Alan asked as his grandfather paced towards the window comprising the outer wall of the room.

'No-one knows,' Junnar said. 'His origins, like his theories, are obscure. He will not tell anyone his real name. There are no records of his fingerprints at Identity Centre; he seems demented, but no mental hospital has heard of him. Perhaps, as he says, he came down from the sun to save the world?'

'Don't be facetious, Junnar.' Minister Powys pursed his lips, paused, then took a long breath and said: 'Who was down there today?'

'Vernitz, Chief of the China Police – he is in the city on a vacation and to attend the Police Conference next Sixday. Martha Gheld, Professor of Electrobiology at Tel Aviv. All the Persian representatives currently elected to parliament...'

'Including Isfahan?' Minister Powys was too well bred to shout, but there was astonishment in his voice. Isfahan was the leader of the Solref faction in the Solar House.

'Including all the Persian Solrefs, I'm afraid.' Junnar nodded. 'Not to mention a number of Dutch, Swedish and Mexican party members.'

'We had advised our members not to take part in the Fireclown's farcical "audiences"!'

'Doubtless they were all there on fact-finding missions,' Alan interrupted, a faint gleam in his eyes.

'Doubtless,' Powys said grimly, choosing to ignore his grandson's irony.

'Your niece was there, too,' Junnar said quietly.

'That *doesn't* surprise me. The woman's a fool. To think that she could be the next President!'

Alan knew that his cousin, Helen Curtis, leader of the Radical Liberal Movement, and his grandfather were both planning to run for President in the forthcoming Presidential elections. One of them was sure to win.

'All right, Junnar.' Simon Powys dismissed his secretary. The negro went out through a side door opening on an inner passage leading to his own office.

When the door had closed, Alan said: 'I think you place too much importance on this character, Grandfather. He's harmless enough. Perhaps he could threaten society – but it's doubtful if he would. You seem to have an obsession about him. No-one else, in politics at least, seems so concerned. If the situation became serious people would soon leave him or act against him. Why not wait and see?'

'No. I seem to have an obsession, do I? Well, it may be that I'm the only man not blinded to what this Fireclown represents. I have already drafted a Bill which, if it gets passed, could easily put a stop to the fool's posturing.'

Alan laid his briefcase on the desk and sat down in one of the deep armchairs. 'But will it? Surely it isn't wise at this stage to back what could easily be an unpopular motion. The Fireclown is an attractive figure to most people – and as yet harmless. If you were to oppose him openly it might cost you votes in the Presidential election. You could lose it!'

Alan felt he had scored a point. He knew how important winning was to the old man. Since the formation of the Solar Referendum Party, a Powys of every generation had held the Presidential chair for at least one term of his life – a Powys had in fact formed the first Solref cabinet. Yet it was likely that Powys would not be voted in, for public opinion was gradually going against the Solrefs and tending to favour the more vociferous and dynamic RLM, which had grown rapidly in strength under Helen Curtis's fiery leadership. Throughout his life Simon Powys had aimed at the Presidency, and this would be his last chance to gain it.

'I have never sacrificed principles for mere vote-catching!' Simon Powys said scornfully. 'It is unworthy of a Powys to suggest it, Alan. Your mother would have been horrified if she had heard such a remark coming from her own son. Though you have the look of a Powys, the blood, whoever gave it you, is not Powys blood!'

For a second before he controlled himself, Alan felt pain at this remark. This was the first time his grandfather had referred to his obscure origins – he had been illegitimate, his mother dying soon after he was born. Though, in his grim way, Simon Powys had assured his grandson's education and position, he had always been withdrawn from Alan, caring for him but not encouraging friendship or love. His wife had died five years earlier and she and Alan had been close. When Eleanor Powys died Simon had begun to see a little more of Alan, but had always remained slightly distant. However, this remark about his bastardy was the first spoken in anger. Obviously the matter of the Presidency was weighing on his mind.

Alan ignored the elder Powys's reference and smiled.

'City Administration – if I may return to the original topic – isn't worried by the Fireclown. He inhabits the disused lower levels and gives us no trouble, doesn't threaten to come upstairs at all. Leave him alone, Grandfather – at least until after the election.'

Minister Simon went to the picture window and stared out into the twilight, his erect body silhouetted against the distant mountains.

'The Fireclown is a tangible threat, Alan. He has admitted that he is bent on the destruction of our whole society, on the rejection of all its principles of progress and democracy. With his babbling of fire-worship and nature-worship, the Fireclown threatens to throw us all back to disorganised and retrogressive savagery!'

'Grandfather – the man isn't that powerful! You place too much importance on him!'

Simon Powys shook his head, his heavy hands clasping behind him.

'I say I do not!'

'Then you are wrong!' Alan said angrily, half-aware that his anger was not so much inspired by the old man's righteousness as by his earlier, wounding remark.

Simon Powys remained with his back to Alan, silent.

At least his grandfather's solid reputation for integrity and sticking to what he thought was well earned, Alan reflected. But that reputation might not save him if the Fireclown became a political issue in the elections.

His own view, shared with a great many people, was that the Fireclown's mysterious appearance a year ago was welcome as an agent to relieve the comparative monotony of running the smoothly ordered City of Switzerland.

'Goodbye, Grandfather,' he said, picking up his briefcase. 'I'm going home. I've got a lot of work to get through this evening.'

Simon Powys turned – a considered and majestic movement.

'You may like to know that I have approached the City Council on this matter, suggesting that they completely seal off the lower levels. I hope they will adopt my suggestion. City Administration, of course, would be responsible for carrying it out. As Assistant Director, you would probably be in charge of the project.'

'If the City Council have any sense they'll ignore your suggestion. They have no evidence of law-breaking on the Fireclown's part. They can take no legal steps against him. All he has done, so far as I can see, is to address a public meeting – and that isn't a crime in this democracy you've been boasting of. To make it one would invalidate your whole argument. Don't you agree?'

'One short step back could save us from a long slide down,' Minister Powys said curtly as Alan left the room.

Entering the elevator that would take him home to the sixty-fourth level, Alan decided that he could have misjudged his grandfather over the matter of the Fireclown. He had heard a great deal about him and his 'audiences' and, emotionally, was attracted by the romantic character of the man. But he had argued the Fireclown's case too strongly without really knowing it at first hand.

He left the elevator and crossed to the middle of the corridor, taking the fastway belt towards his flat. As he neared it, he crossed to the slowway with instinctive practice, produced a small box from his pocket and spoke his name into it. The door of the flat opened in the wall.

In the passage his manservant took his briefcase and carried it into the study. 'We were expecting you home earlier, sir. Madeleine apologises, but she feels the polter may be overdone.'

'My fault, Stefanos.' He was not particularly fond of synthetic poultry, anyway.

'And Miss Curtis is waiting for you in the living room. I told her you hadn't dined…'

'That's all right.' Outwardly decisive, he was inwardly confused. He even felt a slight trembling in his legs and cursed himself for an uncontrolled buffoon. He had only once seen Helen, briefly, since their affair had ended, at a party.

He entered the austere living room.

'Good evening, Helen. How are you?'

They did not shake hands.

'Hello, Alan.'

He could not guess why she was here but he did not particularly want to know. He was afraid he might get involved emotionally with her again.

He sat down. She seated herself opposite him in the other padded, armless chair. She was made up – which was unusual. Her lips were a light green and she had on some sort of ultra-white powder. Her eyebrows and eyelids were red. Her taste, he thought, had never been all it might. She had an almost triangular face; short, black hair and a small nose so that she looked rather like a cat – save for the make-up which made her look like a corpse.

'I hear you attended the Fireclown's "audience" today?' he said casually.

'Where did you hear that? Bush telegraph? Have you been at a cocktail party?'

'No.' He smiled half-heartedly. 'But spies are everywhere these days.'

'You've been to see Uncle Simon, then? Is he planning to use the information against me in the election?'

'I don't think so – no.'

She was evidently nervous. Her voice was shaking slightly. Probably his own was, too. They had been very close – in love, even – and the break, when it had finally come, had been made in anger. He had not been alone with her since.

'What do you think your chances are of winning it?'

She smiled. 'Good.'

'Yes, they seem to be.'

'Will you be pleased?'

She knew very well that he wouldn't be. Her political ambitions had been the main reasons for their parting. Unlike all the rest of his family, including remote cousins, he had no interest in politics. Maybe, he thought with a return of his earlier bitterness, Simon Powys had been right about his blood being inherited from his unknown father. He shook his head, shrugging slightly, smiling vaguely.

'I – I don't know,' he lied. Of course he would be disappointed if she won. He hated the political side of her character. Whereas he had nothing against women in politics – it would have been atavistic and unrealistic if he had an objection – he felt that her talents lay elsewhere. Perhaps in the painting she no longer had time for? She had been, potentially, a very fine painter.

'It's time the Solar System had a shake-up,' she said. 'The Solrefs have been in for too long.'

'Probably,' he said non-committally. Then, desperate to get it over: 'Why are you here, Helen?'

'I wanted some help.'

'What kind of help? Personal…?'

'No, of course not. Don't worry. When you said it was over I believed you. I've still got the mark on my shoulder.'

This had been on his conscience and her reference to it hurt him. He had struck her on her shoulder, not really intending the blow to be hard, but it had been.

'I'm sorry about that...' he said stumblingly. 'I didn't mean...'

'I know. I shouldn't have brought it up.' She smiled and said quickly: 'Actually, I want some information, Alan. I know that you're politically uncommitted, so I'm sure you won't mind giving it to me.'

'But I don't have any *secrets*, Helen. I'm not in that position – I'm only a civil servant, you know that.'

'It's not really a secret. All I want is some – what d'you call it? – advance information.'

'About what?'

'I heard a rumour that the City Council plan to close off the lower levels. Is that true?'

'I really couldn't say, Helen.' News was travelling fast. Obviously an indiscreet councillor had mentioned Simon Powys's letter to someone and this had been the start of the rumour. On the other hand, his grandfather, when he told him of it, had understood that he would keep the old man's confidence. He could say nothing – though the truth would put paid to the rumour.

'But you're in City Administration. You must know. You'd be responsible for the project, wouldn't you?'

'If such a project were to be carried out, yes. But I have been told nothing either by the City Council or my director. I should ignore the rumour. Anyway, why should it bother you?'

'Because if it's true it would be interesting to know which councillors backed the motion, and who egged them on. The only man with sufficient power and a great enough obsession is your grandfather – my uncle, Simon Powys!'

'How many Solar Referendum councillors are in the Council?' he asked vaguely. He was smelling her perfume now. He remembered it with a sad nostalgia. This was becoming too much to bear.

'There are five Solrefs, three RLMs, one independent Socialist and one Crespignite who slipped in somewhere on the pensioners' vote. Giving, if you *are* so ignorant of simple politics, a majority to the Solrefs and virtual control of the Council, since the Crespignite is bound to vote with them on nearly every issue.'

'So you want to tell the people that this hypothetical closing down of the lower levels is a Solref plot – a blow to their liberty.'

'My very words,' she said with a kind of triumphant complacency.

He got up. 'And you expect me to help you – to betray confidence, not to mention giving my own grandfather's opponents extra ammunition – and let you know what the City Council decides before it is made public? You're becoming foolish, Helen. Politics must be addling your brains!'

'But it means nothing to you, anyway. You're not interested in politics!'

'That's so. One of the reasons I'm not interested is because of the crookedness that seems to get into the best of people – people who think any means to win elections are fair! I'm not naïve, Helen. I'm from the same family as you. I grew up knowing politics. That's why I stay out of it!'

'Surely you don't support this victimisation of the Fireclown, Alan? He is a simple, spontaneous...'

'I'm not interested in hearing a list of the Fireclown's virtues. And whether I support any "victimisation", as you call it, is of no importance. As a matter of fact, I'm attracted to the Fireclown and consider him no danger at all. But it seems to me that both you and Grandfather are using this man for your own political ends, and I'll have no part of it!' He paused, considering what he had said, then added: 'Finally, there has been no "victimisation", and there isn't likely to be!'

'That's what you think. I support the Fireclown for good reasons. His ambitions and the ambitions of the RLM are linked. He wants to bring sanity and real life back to this machine-ridden world. We want real values back again!'

'Oh, God!' He shook his head impatiently. 'Helen, I've got a great deal of work to do before I go to bed tonight.'

'Very well. I have, too. If you reconsider...'

'Even if there was a plot to *arrest* the Fireclown I wouldn't tell you so that you could use it for political fuel, Helen.' He suddenly found himself moving towards her, gripping her arm. 'Listen. Why get involved with this? You've got a good chance of winning the election without indulging in dealings of this sort. Wait until you're President, then you can make the Fireclown into a Solar Trust if you like!'

'You can't understand,' she said grimly, shaking herself free of his hand. 'You don't realise that you have to be comparatively ruthless when you know what you're aiming for is *right*.'

'Then I'm glad you know what's right,' he said pityingly. 'I'm bloody glad you know. It's more than I do.'

She left in silence and he went back to his chair, slumping down heavily and feeling, with morose pleasure, that he had scored.

The mood didn't last long. By the time Stefanos came in to tell him his meal was waiting for him he had sunk into a brooding, unconstructive melancholy. Brusquely he told his manservant to eat the meal himself and then go out for the rest of the evening.

'Thank you, sir,' Stefanos said wonderingly, chewing his ridged underlip as he left the room.

In this mood in which his confrontation of his ex-mistress had left him, Alan felt incapable of work. The work was of little real importance anyway, routine stuff which he had hoped to clear up before he took his vacation in a fortnight's time. He decided to go to bed, hoping that a good ten hours' sleep would help him forget Helen.

He had reached the point where he felt he must see the mysterious figure for himself, since so many matters seemed to be revolving around him all of a sudden.

He walked into the darkened hall and ordered the light on. The light responded to his voice and flooded the flat. The tiny escalator leading upstairs began to move, too, and he stepped on it, letting it carry him to the landing.

He went into his bedroom. It was as sparsely furnished as the rest of the flat – a bed, mellowlamp for reading, a small shelf of books, a wing on the headboard of the bed for anything he cared to put there, and a concealed wardrobe. The air was fresh from the ventilators, also hidden.

He took off his scarlet jacket and pants, told the wardrobe to open, told the cleaning chute to open and dropped them in. He selected a single-piece sleeping suit and moved moodily to sit on the edge of the bed.

Then he got up and went back to the wardrobe, removed an ordinary suit of street garments and put them on.

Rapidly, feeling that he should have taken something with him – a weapon or a notebook or an alarm signaller which would contact the police wherever he was – he left the flat and took the fastway towards the elevators.

He was going to the lower levels. He was going to find the Fireclown.

Chapter Three

H E WAS UNREASONINGLY annoyed that the liveried operator should recognise him and stare at him curiously as he was taken down to the forty-ninth level. In the back of his mind he was thrilling to the experience, unremembered since boyhood, of exploration. He had chosen nondescript clothes so that he might move about incognito.

He was alone in the unmanned elevator as it dropped swiftly to the ninth level, causing him the added excitement of being alone and virtually helpless against danger.

He stepped boldly into the ill-lit corridor named – incongruously – Orangeblossom Road, and then advanced cautiously until he saw a sign which read: *Escalators (down) five levels.*

He rode the escalators into the chilly depths of the City of Switzerland, feeling as if he were descending into some frozen hell and at the same time making a mental note that if people were, indeed, inhabiting the lower levels, then City Administration should, out of humanity, do something about the heating arrangements.

He wished he had some warmer clothing, but that would have meant applying to Garment Centre, since he rarely went outside save on vacation, and then all necessary apparel was supplied.

But as he advanced deeper he became aware of a growing warmth and a thick, unpleasant smell that he gradually recognised as being, predominantly, the smell of human perspiration. In spite of his revulsion he sniffed it curiously.

As he walked slowly down the ramp leading to the notorious first level, reputed to be the haunt of undesirables well before the Fireclown first made his appearance, he saw with a slight shock that the light was dancing and had an unusual quality about it. As he drew closer his excitement increased. Naked flame! The light came from a great, burning torch which also gave off uncontrolled heat!

He approached it as close as he dared and stared at it, marvelling. He had seen recordings of the phenomenon, but this was the first time... He withdrew hastily as the heat produced sweat from his forehead, walking along a corridor that reminded him, with its dancing, naked light, of the fairyland of his childhood fantasies. On reflection, he decided it was more like the ogre's castle, but so delighted was he by this wholly new experience that he forgot caution for a while. It only returned as he rounded another corner and saw that the roof was actually composed of living rock, so moist that it dripped condensed water!

Alan Powys was not an unsophisticated young man, yet this was so remote from his everyday experience that he could not immediately absorb it on any intellectual level.

From ahead came sounds – the sounds of excited human voices. He had expected a vast conclave of some description, but he heard only a few people, and they were conversing. Occasionally, as he drew nearer, he heard a reverberating laugh which seemed to him so full of delighted and profound humour that he wished he knew the joke so that he could join in. If this was the Fireclown's famous laughter, then it did not strike him as at all insane.

Still, he told himself, keeping in the shadows, there were many forms of madness.

A cave came into view on his right. He hugged the left-hand wall and inched forward, his heart pounding.

The cave appeared to turn at a right angle so that he could only see the light coming from it, but now he could make out fragments of words and phrases. At intervals there came a spluttering eruption of green light and each time he was caught in the flare.

'... shape it into something we can control...'

'... no good, it's only a hint of what we might...'

'... your eyeshield back. I'm going to...'

A hissing eruption and a tongue of green flame seemed to turn the bend in the cave and come flickering like an angry cobra towards Alan. He gasped and stepped back as the roaring laughter followed the eruption. Had he been seen?

No. The conversation was continuing, the pitch of the voices now high with excitement.

He crossed the corridor swiftly and stood in the mouth of the cave, straining his ears to make out what they were talking about.

Then he felt a delicate touch on his arm and heard a whispering voice say: 'I'm afraid you can't go in there. Private, you know.'

He turned slowly and was horrified at the apparition that still touched his arm. He withdrew, nauseated.

The horrible figure laughed softly. 'Serves you right. They could keep me just to stop people nosing around!'

'I didn't know you had any kind of secrecy,' Alan babbled. 'I really do apologise if...'

'We welcome visitors, but we prefer to invite them. You don't mind?' The skinless man nodded towards the corridor. Alan backed into it, forcing himself to ignore the bile in his throat, forcing himself to look at the creature without obvious revulsion – but it was difficult.

Flesh, veins and sinews shone on his body as if the whole outer covering had been peeled off. How could he move? How could he appear so calm?

'My skin's synthetic – but transparent. Something in it takes the place of pigment. They haven't worked out a way of giving the stuff pigmentation yet – I was lucky enough to be the guinea pig. I could use cosmetics, but I don't. My name's Corso. I'm the Fireclown's trusty henchman and deal with anyone interested in coming to his audiences. You arrived at the wrong time. We had one this afternoon.'

Obviously Corso was used to random explorers, particularly those curious about the Fireclown. Deciding to play his part in the rôle Corso had mistakenly given him, Alan looked down at the floor.

'Oh, I'm sorry. When's the next one?'

'Day after tomorrow.'

'I can come then?'

'Very welcome.'

Alan turned to retrace his way.

'See you then,' said the skinless man.

When Alan turned the corner of the corridor he had to lean against the wall for some moments before he could continue. Too many unexpected shocks this evening, he told himself.

As he began to recover his composure his curiosity started to operate again. What was going on? From what he had seen and heard, the Fireclown and a group of his friends were conducting some sort of laboratory experiment – and Corso, the skinless man, had been left on guard to turn pryers away.

Well, everyone had a right to their privacy. But his curiosity came close to overwhelming him. He began to return towards the cave when a soft voice that he recognised said:

'It wouldn't be wise. If you went back a second time Corso would know you were no innocent would-be initiate.'

'Junnar!' he hissed. 'What are you doing here?'

But he heard only a faint scuffling and received no reply.

Perhaps, however, the negro's advice was good. There was no point in making anyone suspicious since he would, if discovered, be excluded from any future chance of seeing the Fireclown.

He began to return towards the ramp. What on earth had Junnar been doing in the lower levels? Was he there on his own business or on Simon Powys's? Perhaps the negro would tell him tomorrow, if he could find an excuse for leaving the C.A. building and visiting his grandfather's apartment.

Vaguely irritated that he had seen so little of the Fireclown's domain and nothing at all of the Fireclown himself, he finally arrived on the sixty-fourth level, took the fastway to his flat and went to bed with something of his earlier sullen mood eliminated.

The day after tomorrow he would definitely attend the Fireclown's 'audience'.

Very deliberately, the next morning, Alan concentrated his thoughts entirely on his job. By the time he arrived at his office in

City Administration on North Top, he had turned his thoughts to the matter of elevator installation which the City Council had decided was necessary to speed up pedestrian flow between levels.

His Assistant Directorship was well earned, but he had to admit that having it was partly due to his family connections and the education which his grandfather had insisted on him having. But he was a hard and conscientious worker who got on well with his staff, and the director seemed pleased with him. He had been doing the job for two years since he had left university.

He spent the morning catching up on lost time until just before lunch when Carson, the director, called him into his office.

Carson was a thin man with an unsavoury appearance. He was much respected by those working under him. His chin, however, always looked as if he needed a shave and his swarthy face always appeared to need a wash. But this wasn't his fault. After a little time in his company the first impression of his unsavouriness vanished swiftly.

Carson said mildly: 'Sit down, Alan. I wonder if you could leave the elevator matter for a while and turn it over to Sevlin to get on with. Something else has cropped up.'

Powys sat down and watched Carson leaf through the papers on his desk. The director finally selected one and handed it to him.

It was headed *Low Level Project*, and a glance told Alan it was the proposed plan to seal off the lower levels from the upper ones.

So Helen had been right in her thinking. Simon Powys did hold sufficient sway with the City Council to have his 'suggestions' put into action.

Carson was staring at his own right thumb. He did not look up. 'It will involve temporarily re-routing pedestrian traffic, of course, though to save trouble we could work at night. It would be worth paying the men double overtime to get it done as quickly as possible.'

'With a minimum of fuss?' Alan said with an edge to his voice.

'Exactly.'

'The Council hasn't announced this publicly, I presume?'

'There's no need to – no-one lives in the lower levels any more. There will be emergency doors constructed, naturally, but these will be kept locked. It shouldn't bother anyone...'

'Except the Fireclown!' Alan was so furious that he found difficulty in controlling himself.

'Ah, yes. The Fireclown. I expect he'll find somewhere else to go. Probably he'll leave the city altogether. I suspect he's no real right to live there in the first place.'

'But the vids, the RLM – and therefore the main weight of public opinion – all regard the Fireclown in a favourable way. He has a good part of the world on his side. This isn't political dynamite – it's a political megabang!'

'Quite.' Carson nodded, still regarding his thumb. 'But we aren't concerned with politics, are we, Alan? This is just another job for us – a simple one. Let's get it over with.'

Alan took the papers Carson handed him and got up. The director was right, but he could not help feeling personally involved.

'I'll get started after lunch,' he promised. He went back to his office, put the papers in his confidential drawer, went to the roof of the C.A. building and took a cab across the spacious artificial countryside of the Top towards his grandfather's apartment, which lay close to the Solar House at South Top.

But when he got there he found only Junnar and another of his cousins – Helen's brother, Denholm Curtis.

Curtis dressed with challenging bad taste. His clothes were a deliberate attack, a weapon which he flaunted. They proclaimed him an iconoclast impatient of any accepted dogma whether reasonable or not. Above the striped and polka-dotted trappings draping his lean body was a firm, sensitive head – the heavy Powys head with calm eyes, hopeful, seeming to be aware of detail and yet disdainful of it. Curtis's eyes were fixed on the future.

'Hello, Denholm, how are you?' He and his cousin shook hands.

'Fine – and you?'

'Not bad. And how's the Thirty Five Group? Still bent on gingering up the mother party?'

Curtis led the radical wing of the Solref party. His group was small but vociferous and carried a certain amount of weight in the Solar House. Yet, though he stuck to the traditional party of the Powys family, he would have been much more at home in his sister's movement. But his interest was in changing the party to change the policy rather than splitting away from it and forming a fresh one.

Curtis hadn't replied to Alan's question. He glanced at the big wall clock just as his grandfather came hurrying in through the side door.

'Grandfather.' Alan stepped quickly forward but old Simon Powys shook his head.

'Sorry, Alan. I have to get to the Solar House immediately. Coming, Denholm?'

Curtis nodded and the two of them left the room almost at a run.

Something was in the air, Alan guessed, and it wasn't the closing down of the lower levels. This seemed much more important.

'What's going on, Junnar?'

The negro looked slightly embarrassed as their eyes met, but he spoke coolly.

'They're calling on old Benjosef to resign.'

Benjosef, a dedicated member of the Solrefs, was Solar President. His two terms of office had been popular but not particularly enlightened. He had not had much public support over the last year, partly because he was slow to agree on a policy of expansion and colonisation involving Mars and Ganymede.

'On what issue?'

'The planets. Ganymede and Mars are ready for settlers. There are businessmen willing to invest in them, ships ready to take them – but Benjosef is reluctant to pursue a policy of expansion because *he* says we haven't a sufficiently good organisation for controlling it yet. He wants to wait another ten years to build up such an organisation, but everyone else is impatient to get started. You know the story...'

'I know it,' Alan agreed.

The projects to make the two planets inhabitable and fertile had been started over a hundred years previously and it had been hard enough holding private enterprise and would-be settlers back before they were ready. Benjosef had been foolish to take a stand on the issue, but he had done what he thought was right and his conviction now seemed likely to topple him.

'What are his chances of staying in power for the rest of his term?' Alan asked curiously.

'Bad. Minister Powys and the majority of Solrefs have to stand by him, of course, but Mr Curtis and his group have sided with the RLMs. The other parties are fairly equally divided between both sides, but Mr Curtis's support should give the vote against the President.'

Once again Alan was glad he had decided to have no part of politics. Even his just and stern old grandfather was going to behave like a hypocrite, giving a vote of confidence for Benjosef while encouraging Curtis to vote against him.

He decided that there wasn't much he could do, since everyone would be at the Solar House, including, of course, Helen. The current session ended in a fortnight and the next President would have to be elected during the recession. Probably, he thought ironically, both the main runners had their machines all geared for action.

'You'll be kept pretty busy from now on, I should think,' he said to Junnar. The negro nodded, and Alan continued: 'What were you doing in the lower levels last night?'

'Keeping an eye on the Fireclown,' Junnar said shortly.

'For Grandfather?'

'Yes, of course.'

'Why is he so malevolent toward the Fireclown? He seems harmless to me. Has Grandfather any special knowledge that the public doesn't have?' Alan was only partly interested in what he himself was saying. The other half of his mind was wondering about the elections – and Helen.

Junnar shook his head. 'I don't think so. It's a question of your point of view. Minister Powys sees the Fireclown as a threat to society and its progress. Others simply see him as a romantic figure who wants a return to a simpler life. That's why he's such a popular cause with so many people. We all wish life were simpler – we're suckers for the kind of simple answer to our problems that a man like the Fireclown supplies.'

'Simple answers, sure enough,' Alan nodded, 'but hardly realistic.'

'Who knows?' Junnar said tersely.

'Is Grandfather going to use the Fireclown as a platform?'

'I expect so. It will be taken for granted that whoever wins will encourage the expansion bill. So the other main dispute will be the Fireclown.'

'But it's out of all proportion. Why should the Fireclown become a major issue?'

Junnar smiled cynically. 'Probably because the politicians want him to be.'

That answer satisfied Alan and he added:

'Hitler, as I remember, used the Jews. Before him, Nero used the Christians. Minority groups are always useful – they turn people's attention away from real issues which the politicians have no control over. So Miss Curtis and Minister Powys are using the Fireclown, is that it? One in support, one against. People will take an interest in a battle over such a colourful figure and forget to question other policies. It sounds almost unbelievable, yet it happens. History proves that. What does Grandfather plan to do about the Fireclown if he gets to power?'

'Maybe nothing,' Junnar said. 'Maybe nothing at all – once he's in power.' Then he smiled brightly. 'No, it's not fair. After all, I am Simon Powys's private secretary. He really is deeply concerned about what the Fireclown represents rather than the man himself.'

The apparent return of loyalty in Junnar brought an awakening echo in Alan. He nodded.

'Perhaps we don't do either of them justice. I was forgetting they are both Powyses with a strong sense of family honour.'

Junnar coughed. 'I think I'd better go over to the Solar House myself. Can I arrange an appointment for you to see your grandfather?'

'No, don't bother.'

'Are you going to the Fireclown's audience tomorrow?'

'Probably.'

'I may see you there.'

'Yes,' said Alan. He glanced at his watch and noted that he would arrive back to his office late. He and Junnar walked into the corridor and went their separate ways.

Alan sighed as he studied the Low Level project. Basically it was a simple job to organise the sealing off of all entrances, stopping elevators and escalators and cutting off light and heating where they existed. Ten levels were to be shut down, involving the moving of less than a thousand people to accommodation higher up. The residents of levels nine and ten would welcome the change, he knew. They, at least, could be relied upon to support the operation.

No, it wasn't the project itself but the way the media would treat it, what Helen Curtis would say about it. It was going to cause City Administration and the City Council as much trouble as if they told the populace they had decided to torture and kill all pet dogs in the city. And this move would have worldwide repercussions – the Fireclown had been the subject of innumerable popular features treating him in a sympathetic manner.

Already he was convinced that his grandfather had committed political suicide by this move. But, for the moment, he wasn't worried so much about that as about the trouble he and the director would come in for.

He, in particular, would be slandered – the grandson of the man who wanted to victimise the innocent Fireclown. He would be talked of as a puppet in the hands of the old man. Doubtless he would even be shouted at in the public corridors.

He contacted City Works, waited for the manager to be located.

Tristran B'Ula was, like Junnar, a Zimbabwean from what had

once been Rhodesia. The State of Zimbabwe had grown to great power in the African Federation and many of the Solar System's best administrators came from there.

'Good afternoon, Tristran.' Alan was on friendly terms with the manager. 'New project I'd like to have a word with you about.'

B'Ula pretended to groan. 'Is it important? All my available manpower is taken up at the moment.'

'The City Council wants us to give this priority. It's also highly confidential. Is there anyone else in the room with you?'

B'Ula turned, looked behind him and said: 'Would you mind leaving the room for a minute or two, Miss Nagib?'

His pretty Egyptian secretary crossed the screen.

'Okay, Alan. What is it?'

'The City Council wants us to seal off ten levels – numbers one to ten, to be precise. Concrete in the entrances, lighting, heat and water supply cut off, elevators and escalators to stop operation.'

It took B'Ula a moment to absorb all this. His face showed incredulity. 'But that's where the Fireclown is! What are we expected to do? Wall him up – entomb him?'

'Of course not. All residents will be moved before the project goes ahead. I'd thought of housing them in those spare corridors in Section Six of the Fifteenth Level and Sections Twelve and Thirteen of the Seventeenth Level. They'll need to be checked to make sure they're perfectly habitable. The Chemical Research Institute were going to take them over since they're getting a bit cramped, but they'll have to...'

'Just a minute, Alan. What's going to happen to the Fireclown?'

'Presumably, he'll take the alternative accommodation we're offering to everyone else,' Alan said grimly.

'You know he wouldn't do that!'

'I don't know the Fireclown.'

'Well, I'm having no part of it,' B'Ula said rebelliously, then he switched out.

Completely taken aback, Alan sat at his desk breathing heavily. This, he decided, was only a hint of how the news would be received by the public. His colleague had always struck him as a solid, practical man who did his job well – a good civil servant, like himself. If Tristran B'Ula could be so affected by the news as to risk his position by refusing to obey the City Council, then how would others take it?

The word *Riot* popped into Alan's head. There had been no public disorder in a hundred years!

This was even bigger than he'd expected.

Another thing – B'Ula felt so strongly about it that he wasn't likely to keep the project secret. Someone had to convince the Zimbabwean that the closing off of the levels was not a threat against the Fireclown. Reluctantly, he would have to tell Carson of his little scene with the manager.

Slowly he got up from his desk. Slowly he walked into Carson's office.

Chapter Four

B ENJOSEF HAD RESIGNED.
   After a meeting in the Solar House lasting well into the night as Benjosef tried to put his arguments to the Solar representatives, the old President had been shouted down.

Denholm Curtis had asked for a vote of no confidence in Benjosef. The ballot had been secret, and though Simon Powys had seemed to support Benjosef it had been a masterly deception. He had managed to convey the image of a strong man standing beside his leader out of nothing but loyalty. In spite of favouring – or appearing to favour – Benjosef's cautious policies, Simon Powys had risen in public esteem. Doubtless the heavy Solref vote would be his in the election. Alan was sure that his grandfather had actually voted against Benjosef. Principles the old man might have – and plenty of them – but they seemed at that moment to carry little weight against Simon Powys's actions. This strange duality which seemed to come upon even the best politicians was not new to Alan, yet it constantly shocked him.

At 0200 Benjosef, baffled by what he considered mad recklessness on the part of the Solar House, reluctantly resigned as President, his term of office, which should have continued for another eighteen months, to finish with the current session.

Alan read and saw all this as he breakfasted, glancing from screen to screen and constructing all the details of the dramatic, and in some ways tragic, session. He rather sympathised with Benjosef. Perhaps he was old and wise, perhaps he was just old. Simon Powys was only five years younger, but he possessed a forceful vitality that belied his age. Alan observed, judiciously, that Helen Curtis had not actually demanded the President's resignation, though other members of her party had been vociferous in attacking him. It would not have been diplomatic or polite for a would-be President to ask the current head to step down.

He sighed and finished his coffee – a new brand from which the caffeine had been removed and replaced by a stimulant described as 'less harmful'. The strange thing was it tasted better, though he would have liked to have denied this.

So now the fight was between his grandfather and his cousin. Would Simon Powys see the light of day at last and ignore the Fireclown issue? As yet, of course, it had not really become an issue. It would take a political battle to make it one. Or would he plug on? Alan had a sad feeling that he would – particularly if Helen drew the Fireclown into her platform.

When he got to the office Carson was looking pale and even less savoury than usual. People were not chosen as directors of City Administration for their looks; but at this moment Alan rather wished they had a smiling, pleasant-faced he-man who could cozen the public into realising the truth of the situation.

'What did B'Ula have to say, sir?' Alan asked.

'I was unable to contact him, Alan. I tried the Works but he must have left immediately he switched out on you. I tried his private number but his wife said he had not come back. When I tried again later he still wasn't there.'

'What was he doing, I wonder?'

'I can tell you. He was broadcasting the news everywhere. Not only broadcasting but elaborating it. You can imagine what he said.'

'I can imagine what would be said by some. But B'Ula…'

'I've just had Chairman Fou on the line. He says the Council is most disturbed, thinks we should have been able to judge B'Ula better. I pointed out, somewhat obscurely, that they appointed B'Ula. But it seems we're the scapegoats – from the public's point of view and evidently from the Council's.'

'The news this morning was so full of "stormy scenes in the Solar House" that they probably haven't got round to us yet,' Alan said with mock cheerfulness. 'But doubtless we'll be getting it in an hour or two.'

'I expect so. Well, we've still got work to do. I'm going over to Works myself, to see what the men think of the project. If they oppose it as strongly as B'Ula we're going to have trouble with the unions before long.'

'What will we do if that happens?'

'Brick up the bloody levels ourselves, I suppose.' Carson swore.

'Black labour!' Alan said, shocked. 'We'd have a system-wide strike on our hands then!' It was true.

'I'm hoping the City Council will realise the implications and back down gracefully.' Carson walked towards the door. 'But they didn't seem as if they were going to, judging by Chairman Fou's tone. Goodbye, Alan. Better stick to something routine until I find out what's happening.'

When Alan buzzed for his filing clerk his secretary came in.

He raised an eyebrow. 'Where's Levy?'

'He didn't come in this morning, Mr Powys.'

'Is he sick?'

'I don't think so. I heard a rumour he'd asked for his back-pay from the cashiers and said something about resigning.'

'I see. Then will you bring me the Pedestrian Transport file? Number PV12, I think it is.'

As he ploughed through the monotonous work, Alan learned from his secretary that about a quarter of the staff in the C.A. building had not turned up for work that morning. That represented over three hundred people. Where were they all? It was evident why they had left.

The whole business was growing into a monster. If three hundred people from one building alone could feel so strongly about the Fireclown, how many millions were there supporting him?

To Alan it was incredible. He knew, intuitively, that so many people could not be roused merely because of the proposed closing down of ten virtually unused levels – or, for that matter, give up their jobs in support of the Fireclown. It must be that the Fireclown represented something, some need in modern mankind which, perhaps, the sociologists would know about. He decided not to ask a sociologist and risk being plied with so many explanatory theories that his mind would be still further confused.

But what was this tenuous zeitgeist?

Perhaps the world would be in flames before he ever found out. Perhaps, whatever happened, no-one would ever really know. He decided he was being too melodramatic. On the other hand, he was extremely disturbed. He had a liking for peace and quiet – one of the reasons why he had rejected the idea of entering politics – and the world's mood was distinctly unpeaceful.

Facing facts, he realised that this was not a localised outbreak, that it would have to grow in magnitude before it died down or was controlled. What had his grandfather started? Nothing, really of course. His move had merely served to bring it out into the open, whatever it was.

But the people's hysteria was increasing, becoming evident everywhere. An hysteria that had not entered the human race since the war scares two centuries earlier. It seemed to have blown up overnight, though perhaps he had seen its beginnings in the worship of the Fireclown, the demand for Benjosef's resignation and other, smaller, incidents that he had not recognised for what they were.

The morning dragged. In the back of his mind something else nagged him until he realised that this was the night when the Fireclown was to hold his 'audience'. He felt slightly perturbed at attending it now that public anger seemed to be building to such a pitch, but he had said he would go, promised himself that he would go – and he would.

Carson came back just as Alan's secretary brought him some lunch.

'Any luck?' Alan said, offering his boss a slice of bread impregnated with beef extract. Carson refused it with an irritable wave of his hand, apologising for his brusque gesture with a slight smile.

'None. Most of the workmen didn't turn up this morning, anyway. The union leaders deny influencing them, but someone has...'

'B'Ula?'

'Yes. He spoke to a public meeting last night, attended by most of the men who work for him. Told them that this victimisation of the simple Fireclown was a threat also to *their* liberty. The usual stuff. And once the news got round, he wasn't the only one talking and rabble-rousing. At least a dozen others have used the same theme in speeches to incredibly big crowds. They didn't have to do much convincing, either. The crowds were already on their side.'

'It's all happened so suddenly.' Alan repeated his earlier thoughts aloud. 'You wouldn't think a thing like this could grow so fast. People aren't even bothering to speak to their political representatives or beam the City Council.'

'That's what's so peculiar. We might have expected angry letters demanding that we call a halt to the project – and if we'd had enough of them we should have had to. That's democracy, after all. I'd really thought the idea of law and order had finally sunk into the human race. Looks as if I was wrong.'

'Disproves the Fireclown's cant about "artificial living" producing "artificial" men and ideas. The public's chock-a-block with human nature this morning. They seem as hysterical and as bloodthirsty as they ever were.'

'Mass neurosis and all that.' Carson stared at his thumb, inspecting the nail. It was dirty. However much he cleaned them his nails always seemed to get dirty a few moments afterwards.

By mid-afternoon, Carson and Alan were staring in blank incredulity at one another. At least two hundred more people had not come back after lunch. It was useless to attempt continuing work.

Another disturbing point was that they had been unable to contact the City Council. The beam had been jammed continuously. Obviously *some* people had decided to ask the City Council about the matter.

'I think we'd better go quietly to our homes,' Carson said with a worried attempt at jocularity. 'I'll keep a skeleton staff on and give the rest the afternoon off. I might as well, they'll probably be walking out soon, anyway.'

Glad of this for his own reasons, Alan agreed.

He returned to his flat and changed into the nondescript suit he had worn earlier. He had had some trouble getting there, for the corridors were packed. Angry and excited conversations were going on all over the place. Ordered discipline had given way to disorganised hysteria and it rather frightened him to see ordinary human beings behaving in a manner which, to him, was a rejection of their better selves.

Outside in the jostling corridor he was carried by the crowd to the elevators and had to wait for nearly a quarter of an hour as the mob's impatience grew. There just weren't enough elevators to take them all at once.

Down, down, down the levels. Into level nine and they milled down the escalators and ramps, Alan unable to go back now even if he had wanted to.

The smoke from the torches of the first level, the smell of sweat, the atmosphere of tension, the ululating roar of the crowd all attacked his senses and threatened to drug his brain as the crowd entered a huge cavern which, he knew, had once been part of an underground airstrip during the years when the city had first been planned.

And at last he saw the Fireclown, standing upon the tall column that served him as a dais, seeming to balance his huge bulk precariously on the platform.

There above him, Alan saw the spluttering mass of the artificial sun. He remembered having heard of it. The Fireclown had made it – or had it made – and somehow controlled it.

'What's this? What's this?' The Fireclown was shouting. 'Why so many? Has the whole world suddenly seen the error of its ways?'

There were affirmative shouts from all around him as the crowd answered, somewhat presumptuously, for the rest of the planet's millions.

The Fireclown laughed, his gross bulk wobbling on the dais.

Thousands upon thousands of people were packing into the cavern, threatening to crush those already at the centre. Alan found himself borne towards the dais as the Fireclown's reverberating laugh swept over them.

'No more!' the Fireclown cried suddenly. 'Corso – tell them

they can't come in... Tell them to come back later. We'll be suffocated!'

The Fireclown seemed baffled by the crowd's size – bewildered, perhaps, by his own power.

Yet was it his own power? Alan wondered. Was not the mob identifying the Fireclown with something else, some deep-rooted need in them which was finding expression through the clown?

But it was immaterial to speculate. The fact remained that the Fireclown had become the mob's symbol and its leader. Whatever he told them they would do – unless, perhaps, he told them to do nothing at all.

The mob was beginning to chant:

'Fireclown! Fireclown! Fireclown! Speak to us!'

'How shall the world end?' he cried.

'In fire! In fire!'

'How shall it be born again?'

'In fire!'

'And the fire shall be the fire of man's spirit!' the Fireclown roared. 'The fire in his brain and his belly. Too long has the world lived on artificial nourishment. The nourishment of processed food, the nourishment of words that have no relation to reality, the nourishment of ideas that exist in a vacuum. We are losing our birthright! Our heritage faces extinction!'

He paused as the mob moved like a mighty, restless tide. Then he continued:

'I am your phoenix, awash with the flames of life! I am your salvation! You see flames above.' He raised an orange painted hand to the spluttering orb near the ceiling of the cavern. 'You see flames around you.' He indicated the torches. 'But these fires only represent the real flames, the unseen flames which exist within you, and the Mother of Life which sweeps the heavens above you – the sun!'

'The sun!' the mob shrieked.

'Yes, the sun! Billions of years ago our planet was formed from the stuff of the sun. The sun nurtured life, and it finally nurtured the life of our earliest ancestors. It has nurtured us since. But does modern man honour his mother?'

'No! No!'

'No! Our ancestors worshipped the sun for millennia! Why? Because they recognised it as the Mother of Life. Without the sun man could never have been born on Earth! The Earth itself could not have been formed!'

Some of the mob, obviously old hands at this, shouted: 'Fire is Life!'

'Yes,' the Fireclown roared. 'Fire is Life. And how many of you here have ever seen the sun? How many of you have ever been warmed directly by its rays? How many of you have ever seen a naked flame?'

A wordless bellow greeted each question.

Alan had to fight the infectious hysteria of the crowd. Though it was true that many of the city's populace had never been out-side, they had led better and fuller lives within the walls. And there was nothing forbidding them to take a vacation beyond the city. It was a kind of agoraphobia, not the State, which held them back. They had, at any rate, reaped the benefits of the sun in less direct ways – from the great solar batteries which supplied power to the city.

As if he anticipated these unspoken thoughts, the Fireclown carried on:

'We are misusing the sun. We are perverting the stuff of life and changing it to the stuff of death! We use the sun to power our machines and keep us alive in plastic, metal and concrete coffins. We use the sun to push our spaceships to the planets – planets where we are forced to live in wholly artificial conditions, or plan-ets which we warp and change from what they naturally are into planets that copy Earth. That is wrong! Who are we to change the natural order? We are playing literally with fire – and that fire will soon turn and shrivel us!'

'Yes! Yes!'

In an effort to remain out of the Fireclown's spell, Alan encour-aged himself to feel dubiously towards the logic of what he was saying. He continued in that vein for some time, drumming the words into the ready ears of the mob, again and again.

The Fireclown's argument wasn't new. It had been said, in milder ways, by philosophers and politicians of a certain bent for centuries – possibly since the birth of the industrial revolution. But, for all this, the argument wasn't necessarily right. It came back to the question of whether it was better for man to be an unenlightened savage in the caves, or whether he should use the reasoning powers and the powers of invention which were his in order to gain knowledge.

Feeling as if he had hit upon an inkling of the trouble, Alan realised that the Fireclown and those, like his grandfather, who opposed him were both only supporting *opinions*. Any forthcoming dispute was likely to be a battle between ignorance of one sort and ignorance of another.

Yet the fact remained – trouble was brewing. Big trouble unless something could be done about it.

'All religions have seen the sun as a representation of God...' the Fireclown was saying now.

Perhaps he was sincere, Alan thought; perhaps he was innocent of personal ambition, unaware of the furore he was likely to create, thoughtless of the conflict that was likely to ensue.

And yet Alan was attracted to the Fireclown. He *liked* him and took a delight in the man's vitality and spontaneity. It was merely unfortunate that he should have come at a time when public neurosis had reached such a peak.

Now a voice was shouting something about the City Council. Fragmented phrases reached Alan about the closing of the levels, an attack against the Fireclown, a threat to free speech. It was marvellous how they accepted the principles of democracy and rejected them at the same time by talk of mob action!

Marvellous – and deeply frightening. He turned to see if he could get back and out. He could not. The mob pressed closer, packed itself tighter. A horrifying vision of thousands of mouthing faces surrounded him. He panicked momentarily and then suppressed his panic. It could not help him. Little could.

The Fireclown's voice bellowed for silence, swore at the mob, reviled it. Abashed, the crowd quieted.

'You see! You see! This is what you do. So the City Council is to close off the levels. Perhaps it is because of me, perhaps it isn't! But does it matter?'

Certain elements shouted that it did matter.

'What kind of threat am I to the City Council? What threat am I to anyone? I tell you – *none*!'

Alan was mystified by these words, just as the mob was.

'None! I want no part of your demonstrations, your petty fears and puny conflicts! I do not expect action from you. I do not want action. I want you only to become aware! You can change your physical environment, certainly. But first you must change your mental attitude. Study the words you are using today. Study them and you will find them meaningless. You have emotions – you have words. But the words you have do not describe your emotions. Try to think of words that will! Then you will be strong. Then you will have no need for your stupid, overvaunted so-called "intelligence". Then you will have no need to march against the Council Building!'

Alan himself sought for words to describe the Fireclown's state at that moment. What had been said had impressed him in spite of his decision to observe as objectively as possible. They meant nothing much, really. They had been said before. But they *hinted* at something – gave him a clue…

Noble bewilderment. The elephant attacked by small boys. And yet concerned for them. Alan was impressed by what he felt to be the Fireclown's intrinsic innocence. But such an innocence, it could topple the world!

Placards now began to appear in the crowd:

NO TO BURYING THE FIRECLOWN!
HANDS OFF THE LOWER LEVELS!
COUNCIL CAN'T QUENCH THE FIRE OF MAN!

Amused by the ludicrous messages, Alan made out others. SONS OF THE SUN REJECT COUNCIL PLAN! was, perhaps, the best.

MICHAEL MOORCOCK

His mind began to skip, taking in first a fragmented scene – faces, placards, turbulent movement, a woman's ecstatic face; then a clipping of sound, a sudden idea that he could easily follow the Fireclown if he could hear the man convince him in cooler, more intellectual phrases; the flaring gash of light that quickly bubbled from the tiny sun and then seemed to be drawn back into it.

'Fools!' The Fireclown was shouting, incredulity and anger mixed on his painted face.

It seemed to Alan that the paint had been stripped away and, for the first time, he became aware of the *man* who stood there. An individual, complex and enigmatic.

But the glimpse did not last, for he felt the pressure from behind decreasing.

At least half the mob had turned away and were surging towards the cavern's exit.

And the Fireclown? Alan looked up. The Fireclown was appealing to them to stay, but his words were drowned by the babble of hysteria.

Now Alan was borne back with the crowd, was forced to turn and move with it or risk being trampled. He looked up at the dais and saw that the fat body of the Fireclown had developed a slump that hardly seemed in keeping with his earlier vitality.

As the mob boiled up to the third level, Alan saw Helen Curtis only a few yards ahead of him and to his left. He kept her in sight and managed, gradually, to inch through the stabbing elbows and hard shoulders.

On the ninth level he was just able to get into the same elevator with her. He shouted over the heads of the others:

'Helen! What the hell are you doing here?'

He saw a placard, FIRECLOWN FIRST VICTIM OF DICTATORSHIP, bob up and down and realised she was holding it.

'Do you think this will win you votes?' he demanded.

She made no reply but smiled at him. 'I'm glad to see you came. Are you with us?'

'No, I'm not. And I don't think the Fireclown is either! He doesn't want you to fight for his "rights" – I'm sure he's perfectly able to look after himself!'

'It's the principle!'

'Rubbish!'

The doors of the giant elevator slid up and they crossed the corridor to the row of elevators opposite. The liveried attendants attempted to hold the crowd away but were pushed back into their own elevators by the force of the rush. He managed to catch up with her and stood with his body tight against her side, unable to shift his position.

'This sort of thing may win you immediate popularity with the rabble, but what are the responsible voters going to think?'

'I'm fighting for what I think right,' she said defiantly, grimly.

'You're fighting...' He shook his head. 'Look, when we reach sixty-five make your way home. Speak for the Fireclown in the Solar House if you must, but don't make a fool of yourself. When this hysteria dies down you'll look ridiculous.'

'So you think this is going to die down?' she said sweetly.

The doors opened, the elevators disgorged their contents and they were on the move again, streaming across the quiet gardens towards the distant Civic Buildings.

It was night. The sky beyond the dome was dark. The crowd exhibited a moment's nervous calm, its pace slowed and then, as Helen shouted: 'There! That's where they are!' and flung her hand theatrically towards the Council Building, they moved on again, spreading out and running.

Vid-people were waiting for them, taking shots as they surged past.

Helen began to run awkwardly, her placard waving in her hands.

Let her go, Alan thought, old emotions returning to heighten his confusion. He turned back.

No! She mustn't do it! He hated her political ambitions, but they meant much to her. She could throw everything away with this ill-considered action of hers.

Or would she? Perhaps the day of ordered government was already over.

'Helen!' He ran after her, tripped and fell heavily on a bed of trampled blue roses, got up. 'Helen!'

He couldn't see her. Ahead of the crowd lights were going on in the Civic Buildings. Fortuitously, and perhaps happily for the City Council – all of whom had private apartments in the Council Building – the headquarters of the City Police were only a block away. And that building was lit up also.

He hoped the police would use restraint in dealing with the crowd.

When he finally saw Helen again she was leading the van of the mob who now chanted the unoriginal phrase: 'We want the Council!'

Unarmed policemen in their blue smocks and broad belts began to muscle their way through the crowd. Vid cameras tracked them.

Alan grasped Helen's arm, trying to make himself heard above the chant. 'Helen! For God's sake, get out – you're liable to be arrested. The police are here!'

'So what?' Her face was flushed, her eyes overbright, her voice high.

He reached up and tore the placard from her hands, flinging it to the ground. 'I don't want to see you ruined!'

She stood there, her body taut with anger, staring into his face. 'You always were jealous of my political success!'

'Can't you see what's happening to you? If you must play follow-my-leader, do it in a more orderly way. You could be President soon.'

'And I still will be. Go away!'

He shook her shoulders. 'Open your eyes! Open your eyes!'

'Oh, don't be so melodramatic. Leave me alone. My eyes are wide open!'

But he could see she had softened slightly, perhaps simply because of the interest he was taking in her.

Then a voice blared: 'Go back to your homes! If you have any complaints, lodge them in the proper manner. The Council provide facilities for hearing complaints. This demonstration will get you nowhere! The police are authorised to stop anyone attempting to enter the Council Building!'

Helen listened until the broadcast finished. Then she shouted: 'Don't let them put you off! They'll do nothing until they see we mean business.'

Two hundred years of peace had taught Helen Curtis nothing about peaceful demonstration.

It was such a small issue, Alan told himself bewilderedly, such a small issue that could have been settled by a hundred angry letters instead of a mob of thousands.

The crowd was attempting to press past the police barrier.

Finally the barrier broke and fights between the police and the demonstrators broke out. Several times Alan saw a policeman lose his temper and strike a demonstrator.

He was disgusted and perturbed, but there was nothing he could do.

Wearily, he walked away from the scene. For the time being all emotion had been driven from him.

Chapter Five

MISERABLY, UNSURE OF his direction, Alan let his feet carry him aimlessly.

He was sure that the riot marked some important change in the course of Earth's history, but knew with equal certainty that it would be twenty years before he could look back and judge why it had happened.

Helen, I love you, he thought, *Helen, I love you.* But it was no good. They were completely separated now. He had picked an old scab. He should have left it well alone.

He looked up and found that he was approaching the building which housed his grandfather's apartment. He realised at the same time that he needed someone to talk to. There had been no-one since he and Helen had parted. The stern old man would probably refuse to listen and would almost certainly refuse to give him any advice or help, but there was nothing else for it.

He did not have a sonarkey for the matterlift, so he climbed the stairs very slowly and went to the main door of the big apartment.

A servant answered and showed him in.

Simon Powys was sitting in his lounge intently watching the vid relaying scenes of the riots outside. He turned his great head and Alan saw that his brooding eyes held a hint of triumph.

'So the Fireclown was uninterested in power, was he?' Simon Powys smiled slightly and pointed at the set. 'Then what's that, Alan!'

'A riot,' Alan said hollowly. 'But though it's in the name of the Fireclown he didn't encourage it.'

'That seems unlikely. You were mixed up in it for a while, weren't you? I saw you on that –' he pointed again at the screen. 'And Helen, too, is taking an active part.'

'Very active.' Alan kept his tone dry.

'You disapprove?'

'I tried to stop her.'

'So you've changed your opinion of the Fireclown. You realise I was right. If I had my way, every one of those rioters would be flung into prison – and the Fireclown exiled from the planet!'

Slightly shocked by the savagery of his grandfather's last remark, Alan remained silent. Together they watched the vid. The police seemed to be coping, though their numbers had had to be increased.

'I haven't changed my opinion, Grandfather,' he said quietly. 'Not really, anyway.'

His grandfather also paused before replying: 'I wish you knew what I knew – then you'd fight the Fireclown as strongly as I'm attempting to. The man's a criminal. Perhaps he's more than that. Perhaps this is the last night we'll be able to sit comfortably and watch the V.'

'We both seemed to underestimate the Fireclown's popularity,' Alan mused. 'Are you going to continue your campaign against him?'

'Of course.'

'I should have thought you would spend your time better trying to find out *why* the public is attracted to him?'

'The Fireclown's a menace...'

'*Why?*' Alan said grimly.

'Because he threatens the stability of society. We've had equilibrium for two hundred years...'

'*Why* does he threaten the stability of society?'

Simon Powys turned round in his chair. 'Are you trying to be impertinent, Alan?'

'I'm trying to tell you that the Fireclown himself means nothing. The public is in this mood for another, a deeper, reason. I was down there in the cavern on the first level. I saw the Fireclown try to stop them from doing this but they wouldn't listen to him. *Why?*'

But the old man stubbornly refused to get drawn into an argument. And Alan felt a hollow sense of frustration. His urge to try to clarify his thoughts by means of conversation was unbearably strong. He tried again:

'Grandfather!'

'Yes?'

'The Fireclown pleaded with the crowd not to make this demonstration. I saw him. But the crowd wasn't interested in what he said. They're using him, just as you and Helen are using him for your own reasons. There is something deeper going on. Can't you see that?'

Again the old man looked up at him. 'Very well. The Fireclown symbolises something – something wrong in our society, is that it? If that's the case we cannot strike at the general, we must strike at the particular, because that is what is tangible. I am striking at the Fireclown.'

Alan wasn't satisfied. His grandfather's words were reasonable, yet he suspected that no thought or sensibility lay behind them. His answer had been too pat.

'I intend to do everything possible to bring the Fireclown's activities to a halt,' Simon Powys continued. 'The public may be too blind to see what is happening to them, what dangerous power the clown wields over them, but I will make them see. I will make them see!'

Alan shrugged. It seemed to him that the blind were accusing the blind.

'Politicians!' he said, suddenly angry. 'What hollow individuals they are!'

Suddenly, his grandfather rose in his chair and got up, his back to the vid, his face taut with suppressed emotion.

'By God, I brought you up as a Powys in spite of your mother's shaming me. I recognised you. I refused to take the easy way out and pay some woman to call you her own. You received the name of Powys and the benefits of that name. And this is how you reward me, by coming to my own house and insulting me! I fostered a bastard – and now that bastard reverts to type! You have never understood the responsibilities and the need to serve which marks our family. We are not power-seekers, we aren't meddlers in the affairs of others! We are dedicated to furthering civilisation and humanity throughout the Solar System! What do you understand of that, Alan whatever-your-name-is?'

'I think it most noble,' Alan sneered, trying to hold back the tears of pain and anger in his eyes. His body trembled as it had done when, as an adolescent, he had been told the story of his birth. 'Most noble, Grandfather, all you and the Powys clan have done for me! But you could not keep my mother alive with your high sentiments! You would not let her marry the man who fathered me! I know that much from Grandmother. Some rough spaceman, wasn't it? Could you kill him by shame, the way you killed my mother?'

'Your mother killed herself. I did everything for her...'

'And judged her for everything!'

'No...' The old man's face softened.

'I've always given you the benefit of every doubt, Grandfather. I've always respected you. But in this business of the Fireclown I've seen that you can be unreasoningly dogmatic, that perhaps what I've heard about you was true! Your attack on me was unfair – just as your attack on the Fireclown is unfair!'

'If you knew, Alan. If you knew just what...' The old man straightened his back. 'I apologise for what I said to you. I'm tired – busy day – not thinking properly. I'll see you tomorrow, perhaps.'

Alan nodded wordlessly and left, moved to an emotion towards his grandfather which, he decided, could only be love. Love? After what they had both said? It seemed to him that everything was turning upside down. The chaos of the mob, the chaos of his own moods, the chaos of his private life – all seemed to point towards something. Some cure, perhaps, for his own and the world's pain?

On the roof of the building he looked around for a car which would carry him above the riot below to North Top, where he could probably use one of the small private elevators. Above the dome the sky was clear and the moon rode the sky in a casual arc. Near the edge of the roof he saw Junnar.

The Zimbabwean was also watching the distant rioters.

'You're too late,' he said cheerfully. 'You missed the best of it. They're dispersing now.'

'I was *in* the best of it.' Alan joined him and saw that a much smaller crowd continued to demonstrate, but that most of the people were moving slowly back towards the elevator-cone.

'Did you see any arrests?' Junnar asked.

'No. Did you?'

'The police didn't seem too keen. I think they took a couple in – probably examples.'

'What does all this mean, Junnar? What's happening to the world?'

'I'm not with you?' Junnar stared at Alan in curiosity.

'Nobody is, I guess. I'm sure that these riots are not just the result of the Fireclown's speeches in his cavern. I'm sure they've been brewing for ages. Why are the people so frustrated they have to break out like this suddenly? What do they want? What do they lack? You know as well as I do that mass demonstrations in the past were often nothing to do with the placards they waved and the cant they chanted – it was some universal need crying out for satisfaction, something that has always been in man, however happy and comfortable his world is. What is it this time?'

'I think I know what you mean.' Junnar offered Alan a marijuana but he refused. 'That down there – the Fireclown – the impatience to expand to the new Earth-type planets – the bitter arguments in the Solar House – individual frustration – the "time for a change" leaders in the V-casts. All threatening to topple society from its carefully maintained equilibrium. You mean it's some kind of –' Junnar groped for a word – '*force* that's entered the race, that we should be doing something, changing our direction in some way?'

'I think that's roughly what I mean. I'm finding it hard to put it into words myself.'

'Well, this is perhaps what the Fireclown means when he says we're turning our backs on the natural life. With all our material comfort, perhaps we should look inward at ourselves instead of looking outward at the new colony planets. Well, what do we do about it, Mr Powys?'

'I wish I knew.'

'So do I.' Junnar exhaled the sweet smoke and leaned back against the rail.

'You seem to understand what the Fireclown's getting at. *You* must believe that he's innocent of causing these riots. Can't you tell my grandfather that?'

Junnar's manner changed. 'I didn't say the Fireclown was innocent, Mr Powys. I agree with your grandfather. He's a menace!' He spoke fiercely, almost as fiercely as Simon Powys had done earlier.

Alan sighed. 'Oh, all right. Goodnight, Junnar.'

''Night, Mr Powys.'

As he climbed into an automatic car and set the control, he caught a final glimpse of the negro's sad face staring up at the moon like a dog about to bay.

To Alan, the world seemed suddenly sick. All the people in it seemed equally sick. And it was bad enough today. What would it be like tomorrow? he wondered.

Next morning he breakfasted late, waiting for Carson to call him if he was wanted at the office. All the vids were full of last night's rioting. Not only had the City Council building been attacked but others, taking advantage of the demonstration, had indulged in sheer hooliganism, smashing shop-fronts in the consumer corridors, breaking light globes, and so on. Damage was considerable; arrests had been made, but the Press didn't seem to complain. Instead, they had a better angle to spread:

C.A. MAN GRAPPLES PRESIDENTIAL CANDIDATE!
Alan Powys attacks Fireclown supporters!

A picture showed him wrenching Helen's banner from her grasp. In the story he was described as an angry spokesman for the establishment and Helen as the heroine of the hour, going amongst the people to stand or fall with them. Maybe she had been playing her game better than he had at first thought, he decided.

On the V, a commentator's voice was heard over the noise of the riot:

'Last night, beautiful would-be President, Miss Helen Curtis, led a peaceful party of demonstrators to the City Council building on Top. They were there to protest against the abuse of Council power which, as everyone knows now, was to take the form of a secret closing of ten of the lowest levels of the City of Switzerland. Miss Curtis and her supporters saw this as a deliberate move to stop free speech, an attempt to silence the very popular figure known as the Fireclown, whose harmless talks have given many people so much comfort and pleasure.

'The peaceful demonstration was savagely broken up by large bodies of policemen who forced themselves through the crowd and began making random arrests almost before the people could lodge their protest.

'It is not surprising that some of the less controlled elements among the demonstrators resisted arrest.'

Shot of demonstrator kicking a policeman in the behind.

'Reliable witnesses attest to police brutality towards both men and women.

'In the van of the police bully-boys came Alan Powys, grandson of Miss Curtis's rival in the forthcoming Presidential elections – and Assistant Director of City Administration, who had already begun work on closing off the lower levels.'

Shot of Alan grappling with Helen.

'But even Mr Powys couldn't silence the demands of the crowd!'

Shot of him walking away. He hadn't realised vids were tracking him the whole time.

'And he went back to report his failure to his grandfather, Simon Powys.'

Shot of him entering the apartment building.

The cameras panned back to the riot, and the commentary continued in the same vein. He was horrified by the lies – and helpless against them. What could he do? Deny them? Against an already prejudiced public opinion?

'Obviously someone Up There,' the commentator was saying, 'doesn't like the Fireclown. Perhaps because he's brought a bit of life back into our drab existence.

'This programme decries the totalitarian methods of the City Council and tells these hidden men that it will oppose all their moves to encroach further upon our liberties!'

Fade-out and then fresh shots of a surly-looking individual talking to a V-man.

Reporter: 'This is Mr Lajos, who narrowly escaped wrongful arrest in yesterday's demonstration. Mr Lajos, tell the viewers what happened to you.'

Lajos: 'I was brutally attacked by two policemen.'

Lajos stood staring blankly into the camera and had to be prodded by the reporter.

Reporter: 'Did you sustain injuries, Mr Lajos?'

Lajos: 'I sustained minor injuries, and if I had not been saved in time I would have sustained major injuries about my head and body.'

Lajos's head seemed singularly free from any obvious injuries.

Reporter: 'Did the police give you any reason for their attack?'

Lajos: 'No. I was peacefully demonstrating when I was suddenly set upon. I was forced to defend myself...'

Reporter: 'Of course, of course. Thank you, Mr Lajos.'

Back in the studio, a smiling reporter bent towards the camera.

'It's victory for Miss Curtis and her supporters, folks. The Fireclown won't be bothered by the Council – not so long as we keep vigilant, anyway – for the Council told the people a few minutes ago that...'

The picture faded and Carson's face appeared in its place. That was the one irritation of combining communication and entertainment in the single vidserve.

'Sorry if I butted in, Alan. Have you heard the news?'

'Something about me – or about the Council?'

'The Council – they've backed down. They've decided not to

close off the levels, after all. Maybe now we can get on with some work. Will you come to the office as soon as you can?'

Alan nodded. 'Right away,' he said, and switched out.

As he took the fastway to the elevators, he mused over the manner in which the riot had been reported. He was certain that the police had tried not to use violence. Yet, towards the end, they might have lost their patience. These days the police force required superior intelligence and education to get into it, and modern police weren't the good-for-nothing-else characters of earlier times. Still, it could have been that because one side ignored established law and order, so did the other. Violence tended to breed violence.

Violence, he thought, is a self-generating monster. The more you let it take control, the more it grows.

He didn't know it, but he was in for a taste of it.

Two muscular arms suddenly shot out from each side of him. His face slammed against them and he lost his balance on the fastway, falling backwards and sliding along. Two figures rushed along beside him and yanked him onto the slowway.

'Get up,' one of them said.

Alan got up slowly, dazed and wary.

He stared at the tall, thin-faced man and his fatter, glowering partner. They were dressed in engineers' smocks.

'What did you do that for?' Alan said.

'You're Alan Powys, aren't you?'

'I am. What do you want?'

'You're the man who attacked Helen Curtis yesterday.'

'I did not!'

'You're lying.' The man flicked his hand across Alan's face. It stung. 'We don't like Council hirelings who attack women!'

'I attacked no-one!' Alan prepared, desperately, to defend himself.

The fat man hit him, fairly lightly, in the chest.

On the fastway people were passing, pretending not to notice.

Alan punched the fat man in the face and kicked the thin man's shins.

Neither had expected it. Alan himself was surprised at his own bravery. He had acted instinctively. He was also shocked by his own violence.

Now the pair were pummelling him and he struck back at random. A blow in his stomach winded him, a blow in his face made him dizzy. His own efforts became weaker and he was forced to confine himself to protecting his body as best he could.

Then it was over.

A new voice shouted: 'Stop that!'

Breathing heavily, Alan looked up and saw the slightly ashamed face of Tristran B'Ula.

He noticed, too, that all three were wearing a sun emblem on their clothing – a little metal badge.

The thin-faced man said: 'It's Powys – the man who wanted to close the levels. The one who attacked Miss Curtis last night.'

'Don't be a fool,' B'Ula said angrily. 'He didn't want to close the levels; he was taking orders from the Council. I know him – he isn't likely to have attacked Helen Curtis, either.'

B'Ula came closer.

'Hello, Tristran,' Alan said painfully. 'You've started something, haven't you?'

'Never mind about that. What *were* you doing last night?' As B'Ula approached, the two men stepped back.

'I was arguing with Helen, telling her she was stupid. Just as you're stupid. None of you know what you're doing!'

'You got a lot of Press cuttings this morning. If I were you I'd stay off the public ways.' He turned to the two engineers. 'Get going. You're nothing better than hoodlums. You pay too much attention to what the Press says.'

Alan tried to smile. 'The pot calling the kettle black. You started all this, Tris. You should have thought for a while before you began shouting the news about.'

'You're damned ungrateful,' B'Ula said. 'I just saved you from a nasty beating. I did what I had to – I wasn't going to let the Fire-clown be shoved around.'

'This way, he may get worse,' Alan said.

B'Ula grimaced and walked away with the two engineers. Alan looked around for his briefcase but couldn't find it. He got onto the fastway again and took the elevator to the Top, but when he arrived he didn't go to City Administration. He'd heard two people talking in the elevator. There was going to be a debate in the Solar House on last night's riots.

Careless of what Carson would think when he didn't turn up, Alan took a car towards the majestic Solar House where representatives from all over the Solar System had gathered.

He wanted very badly to see his grandfather and his ex-mistress in action.

Solar House was a vast, circular building with tall, slender towers at intervals around its circumference. Each tower was topped by a gleaming glass-alloy dome. The centre of the circle housed the main hall containing many thousands of places for members. Each nation had, like the City of Switzerland, its own councils and sub-councils, sending a certain number of candidates, depending on its size, to the Solar House.

When Alan squeezed his way into the public gallery the House was almost full. Many representatives must have just arrived back in their constituencies after the debate on the outgoing President's policies only to hear the news of the riot, and returned.

Politics hadn't been nearly so interesting for years, Alan thought.

The debate had already opened.

In the centre of the spiral was a small platform upon which sat the President, Benjosef, looking old and sullen; the Chief Mediator, Morgan Tregarith, in ruby-red robes and metallic Mask of Justice; the Cabinet Ministers, including Simon Powys in full purple. In the narrowest ring of benches surrounding the platform were the leaders of the opposition parties – Helen Curtis in a dark yellow robe, belted at the waist, with fluffs of lace at bodice and sleeves; ancient Baron Rolf de Crespigny, leader of the right-wing reactionary Democratic Socialists; John Holt, thin-lipped in black, leader of the Solar Nationalists; Bela Hakasaki, melancholy-faced Hungarian-Japanese leader of the Divisionists; Luis Jaffe of the

New Royalists, and about a dozen more, all representing varying creeds and opinions, all comparatively weak compared with the Solrefs, RLMs, or even the Demosocs.

Behind the circle comprising the opposition leaders all the other Solar representatives sat, first the minor lights in the Solref Cabinet – Denholm Curtis, Under-Secretary for Hydro-Agriculture, was there – then the members of the RLM shadow cabinet; de Crespigny's shadow cabinet shared a tier with John Holt's; behind them were four smaller groups; behind them again six or seven, until, finally, the rank and file, split into planets and continents and finally individual nations.

There were probably five thousand men and women in the Solar House, and they all listened carefully as Alfred Gupta, Minister for Police Affairs, answered a charge made by Helen Curtis that the police had used violence towards last night's crowd.

'Miss Curtis has accused Chief of Police Sandai of exercising insufficient control over his officers; that the men were allowed to indulge in offensive language towards members of the public, attacked these members in a brutal manner and did not allow them to lodge a protest which they had prepared for the City Council. These are all grave charges – charges which have also appeared in the Press and on our V-screens – and Miss Curtis mentions "proof" of police violence having appeared on those media. If the charges are true, then this is a matter of considerable magnitude. But I suggest that the charges are fabrication, a falsification of what actually happened. I have here a statement from Chief Sandai.' He held up a piece of paper and then proceeded to read from it – a straightforward account of what had actually happened, agreeing that some police officers had been forced to defend themselves against the mob, having been pressed beyond reasonable endurance.

Alan had seen one or two of the policemen attack with very little provocation but he felt, from his own observation of the previous night's trouble, that the chief's statement was fairly accurate, although painting his officers a trifle too white to ring true.

The House itself seemed fairly divided on the question, but

when Helen got up to suggest that the paper contained nothing but lies she was loudly cheered. She went on, in an ironical manner, to accuse the Solar Referendum Government of deliberately provoking the riot by allowing the City Council to close off the levels. Minister for Civil Affairs, Ule Bengtsson, pointed out that it was not the government's policy to meddle in local politics and that if this matter had been discussed in the Solar House in the first place, then it might have been possible to veto the Council. But no such motion, he observed cynically, had been placed before the House.

This was indisputable.

Alan saw that Helen had decided to change her tactics, asking the President point-blank if it was not the Solar Referendum Party's fixed intention to silence and get rid of the Fireclown who, though he represented no political threat, was in his own way revealing the sterility of the government's policies in all aspects of life on Earth and beyond it?

Benjosef remained seated. His expression, as it had always been, was strangely affectionate, like an old patriarch who must sometimes chide his children. He spoke from his chair.

'You have heard Miss Curtis accuse my Government of underhand methods in an attempt to rid ourselves of this man who calls himself the Fireclown. I speak in honesty for myself, and for the majority of my cabinet, when I say we have no interest whatsoever in the Fireclown or his activities so long as they remain within the law. Already –' he glanced at Helen with a half-smile on his face – 'it is doubtful whether his supporters have kept within the law, though I have heard that the Fireclown did not encourage last night's riot.'

Alan, looking down on the old man, felt glad that someone, at least, seemed to be keeping things in fair perspective.

Then, surprisingly, the House was shaken by a tremendous verbal roar and he saw that several thousand representatives had risen to their feet and were, for the second time in forty-eight hours, shouting the President down.

He saw his grandfather glance towards the Chief Mediator. His features hidden behind his mask, the Mediator nodded. Simon Powys got up and raised his hands, shouting to be heard. Very gradually, the noise died down.

'You do not disbelieve President Benjosef, surely?'

'We do!' Helen Curtis's voice was shrill, and it was echoed by hundreds of others.

'You think the government is deliberately seeking to outlaw the Fireclown?'

'We do!' Again Helen Curtis's statement was taken up by many of the others.

'And you also think the Fireclown wanted last night's riot?'

There was a slight pause before Helen Curtis replied:

'It was the only way his friends could help him. Personally, he is an ingenuous man, unaware of the forces working against him in the Solar House and elsewhere!'

'So you think the rioters were justified?'

'We do!'

'Is this democracy?' Simon Powys said quietly. 'Is this what my family and others fought to establish? Is this Law? No – it is anarchy. It is anarchy which the Fireclown has inspired, and you have been caught up in the mood. Why? Because, perhaps, you are too unintelligent, too impatient, to see how mankind may profit from this Law we have created! The Fireclown's babblings are meaningless. He talks of our speech having no meaning and turns sensible individuals into a maddened mob with the choice of a few emotional phrases that say nothing to the mind and everything to the belly! The Fireclown has caught popular fancy. That much is obvious.' He sighed and stared around the House.

'I am speaking personally now. For some time I have been aware of the Fireclown's potential ability to whip up the worst elements in human nature. I have seen him as a very great threat to the Solar nation's stability, to our progress, to our development and to individual liberty. And I note from last night's events that I was right...'

Alan saw in astonishment that his grandfather's level words had calmed the assembly, that they seemed to be having some effect. He had to admit that the old man seemed to be right, as he'd said. Yet, in a way, his words were *too* convincing. It was still a feeling he had – a feeling that no-one in the assembly had as yet discussed anything.

Alan thought that, for them, the Fireclown had ceased to exist. He was witnessing a clash between different ways of thoughts, not a debate about the clown at all. He remembered the old Russian technique of choosing a vague name for their enemies and then using it, specifically, to denounce them – attacking the Albanians instead of the Chinese had been one example. Everyone had known who the real enemies were, but there was never a direct reference to them. Still, that had been a calculated technique, rather a good one for its purpose.

But Alan's angry relatives were now using it unconsciously. They were attacking and defending something they were unable to verbalise but which, perhaps wrongly, they were identifying with the Fireclown.

He looked down at the great assembly and for a moment felt pity, then immediately felt abashed by his own arrogance. Perhaps he misjudged them – perhaps they were not less aware but more hypocritical than he thought.

Helen Curtis was speaking again, staring directly into her uncle's eyes as he remained standing up on the platform.

'I have never doubted Minister Powys's sincerity in his denunciation of the Fireclown. But I do say he is a perfect example of the reactionary and conservative elements in the House who are unable to see a *change* as progress. They see their kind of progress, a progress which is inherent in their policies. I see a different kind. Theirs leads to sterility and decay. Ours, on the other hand, leads to an expansion of man's horizons. We wish to progress in many directions, not just one! That is why I see the Fireclown as a victim of the Solref Government. He offers scope and life and passion to human existence. The Solrefs merely offer safety and material comfort!'

'If Miss Curtis had studied the Solar Referendum manifesto in any detail,' Simon Powys exclaimed, addressing the assembly, 'she would have noted that we are pledged first to forming a strong *basis* upon which future society might work and expand. Evidently, from the mob-worship of this disgusting monster, the Fireclown, we have yet to succeed!'

'You see the Fireclown as a threat! You see him as a monster! You hound this man because, in his naïve and simple manner, he has reawakened mankind's spirit!' Helen spoke directly to Powys, her finger pointing up at him. 'Then you are a hollow man with no conception of the realities!'

'So the Fireclown, Miss Curtis tells me, is a happy innocent, bereft of schemes or ambition, a prophet content only to be heard.' Powys smiled at the assembly. 'I say the Fireclown is a tangible threat and that this madman intends to destroy the world!'

Alan craned forward. His grandfather would not possibly have made so categorical a statement without evidence to back it up.

'Prove it!' Helen Curtis sneered. 'You have gone too far in your hatred – senseless and unfounded hatred – of the Fireclown! Prove it!'

Simon Powys's face took on a sterner expression as he turned to speak to the President.

'I have already alerted the City Police,' he said calmly, 'so there is no immediate danger if they work quickly. There is no question of it – I have been supplied with full proof that the Fireclown is planning to destroy the world by flame. In short, he intends to blow up the planet!'

Chapter Six

ALAN WAS ASTOUNDED. For a moment his mood of cynicism held and he was aware of a cool feeling of disbelief as the House, hushed for a second, began to murmur.

Helen suddenly looked frightened. She stared rapidly around the House then up at Powys, whose stern manner could not disguise his triumph.

'Acting on my information, the police have discovered a cache of plutonium warheads...' he continued.

'Warheads!' someone shouted. 'We haven't got any! They were outlawed in forty-two!'

'Presumably the Fireclown or some of his friends manufactured them. It is well known that several scientists have been aiding him with his peculiar experiments with fire.'

'But he would need fantastic resources!'

Simon Powys spread his hands, aware that his moment of power had come.

'Presumably,' he said, 'the Fireclown has them. I told you all that he was more than a mere irritation. His power is even more extensive than I at first guessed.'

Helen sat down, her face pale. She made no attempt to question Powys's statement. She was baffled, yet as convinced of the truth as everyone else in the House.

The crowd in the public gallery was muttering and shoving to get a closer look at Simon Powys.

The old man's leonine head was raised. Evidently he no longer felt the need for oratory. The House was his.

'If the police discover the warhead cache we shall hear the news in a few moments.' He glanced towards the towering central doorway and sat down.

As the tension built up, Alan felt he could take no more of it.

He was preparing to turn back into the crowd behind him when a uniformed figure appeared at a side door and made his way down the tiers towards the platform.

It was Chief Sandai, his brown-yellow face shiny with sweat. Watched by everyone, he climbed up the few steps of the platform and approached President Benjosef respectfully.

The microphone picked up his voice and relayed it throughout the House:

'Mr President, it is my duty to inform you that, acting upon my own initiative, I have declared a state of emergency in the City of Switzerland. A cache of plutonium warheads equipped with remote-control detonators of a type used for setting off bombs from space has been found hidden on the first level. My men have impounded them and await orders.'

Benjosef glanced at Powys. 'Are you sure you have found all the bombs?' he said.

'No, sir. All we know of are those we found. There could be others. These were stored in a disused war-house cavern.'

'You are certain that there was no oversight when the war-house was cleared of its armaments in the past?'

'Perfectly certain, sir. These are new additions. They were being kept in containers previously used for the same purpose, that is all.'

Benjosef sighed.

'Well, Minister Powys, this is really your department now, isn't it? How did you find out about the bombs?'

'My secretary, Eugene Junnar, first reported his suspicions to me two days ago. Later investigations proved them to be true. As soon as I knew I informed the police.' Powys spoke slowly, savouring his triumph.

Benjosef addressed Chief Sandai. 'And have you any evidence to show who was responsible for this illegal stockpile?'

'Yes, sir. It is almost certain that the man concerned is the individual known as the Fireclown. The chamber was guarded by men known to be in his employ. They at first tried to stop us entering, but offered no physical resistance. One of them has since admitted himself to be a follower of the Fireclown.'

'And the Fireclown?' Powys asked urgently.

Chief Sandai swallowed and wiped his forehead. 'Not in our custody yet, sir.'

Angry impatience passed rapidly across Simon Powys's face before being replaced by a further jutting of the jaw and an expression of resolve. 'You had better find him and his accomplices as soon as you can, Sandai. He may well have other bombs already planted. Have you sealed spaceports and checked all means of exit from the city itself?'

'Naturally, sir.' Sandai seemed aggrieved.

'Then hurry and find him, man. The existence of the world may depend on locating him and arresting him immediately!'

Sandai galloped down the steps and strode hastily from the House.

Alan didn't wait for any further development in the debate. Simon Powys had made his point, illustrated it perfectly and punched it home relentlessly to the assembly. It was practically certain the Presidency was his.

Pushing through the crowded gallery, he left to take an elevator down and an escalator out of the House. The news must already have leaked to the Press for V-people were swarming around Chief Sandai, who was obviously flustered and trying to shove his way past them.

Careless of who saw him and the inference that might be put on his act, Alan began to run across the turf towards the nearest elevator cone.

He was sure that his earlier judgement of the Fireclown could not have been so hopelessly wrong. It was only instinct that drove him, but he was so sure that his instinct was right that he was going back, for the second time, to the labyrinthine first level to look at the evidence for himself.

By the time he got to the lower levels another group of vociferous reporters was already on the scene. Police guards surrounded a stack of square, heavy metal boxes, unmarked, at the bottom of the ramp which led down to the first level.

Taking advantage of the police guards' occupation with the reporters, Alan worked his way round them and entered the tunnel which he had gone down earlier – the one which led to the Fireclown's laboratory.

Two guards stood on each side of the entrance. Alan produced his City Administration card and showed it to the men, who inspected it closely.

'Just want to look round, sergeant,' he said coolly to one of them. 'C.A. would like to know what's going on here so we can take whatever precautions are necessary.'

They let him through and he found himself in a big chamber equipped with all kinds of instruments and devices. He couldn't recognise the purpose of many of them. The place was dark, lit only by an emergency bulb burning near the door. It seemed to have been vacated very rapidly, for there was evidence that an experiment had been taking place and had been hastily abandoned. The door of a cooling chamber was open; broken test tubes crunched beneath his feet; chemicals glinted in the half-light, splashed across floor, benches and equipment. He didn't touch anything but made his way to another door. It was an old-fashioned steel door, nearly a foot thick, but it opened when he pushed. In the room the darkness was complete. He went back to find some means of lighting and finally settled for a portable emergency bulb, picking it up by its handle and gingerly advancing into the next room.

The acrid smell of the spilled chemicals was almost unbearable. His eyes watered. This must have been a storeroom. Most of the chemical jars were still intact, so were the boxes of spare parts, neatly labelled. Yet there was nothing to suggest any warlike purpose for the laboratory. There was little manufacturing equipment. It was certain the place had only been used for research. Yet, of course, it was possible that a small manufacturing plant might have been housed in another section of the first level.

He came out of the storeroom and pushed another door on his left. At first he thought it was locked, but when he pushed again it gave. Whereas the storeroom had smelt of chemicals this one smelt merely damp. It was an office. Files and notebooks were stacked around, although a microfile cabinet had been damaged and its contents removed. He noticed also a small, old-fashioned, closed circuit V-screen and wondered what the cameras were aimed at. He switched it on. The screen flickered and showed part of the corridor outside. He turned the control but each picture showed an uninteresting corridor, a cavern or a room, until he turned once more and the screen brightened to show a well-lighted room.

In it were two men and a woman.

The woman was unknown to Alan. But the men were unmistakeable – the skinless Corso, his red, peeled body even more repulsive in good light, and the Fireclown, his great bulk seeming to undulate as he breathed, his face still painted.

Excitedly, Alan tried to get sound, but there appeared to be no sound control on the set. He had no idea where the trio were, but it was fairly certain that cameras were only trained on parts of the first level. Therefore they must be close by.

The woman came up to the Fireclown and pressed her body against him, her right arm spread up across his back, the fingers of the hand caressing him.

He smiled – somehow an extremely generous gesture considering he was now a hunted man – and gently pushed her away, saying something to her. She did not appear annoyed. Corso was more animated. He obviously felt a need for urgency which the Fireclown did not.

Alan suddenly heard a movement in the first chamber and hastily killed the set.

'Mr Powys, sir?' the sergeant's voice shouted.

'What is it?' he replied, inwardly wishing the man dead.

'Wondered if you were all right, that's the only thing, sir – the smell in here is almost overpowering.'

'I'm fine, sergeant, thanks.' He heard the sergeant return to his post.

Now he noticed a smaller door leading off the room. It had no lock of any sort, just a projection at the top. He reached up to inspect it when the door wouldn't open. It was a small bar of metal apparently operated from both sides, sliding into a socket, he fiddled with it for a while, pulled at it and, at last, the right combination of chances released the mechanism and he pulled the door. Alan had never seen a bolt before.

The emergency bulb lit the place and showed him a narrow, low-roofed passage. A rusted sign hung suspended lopsidedly by one chain; the other had broken. Alan caught hold of it, disliking the touch of grimy rust on his fingers, and made out what it said: *Restricted to all personnel!* He let the sign go and it swung noisily against the wall as he continued along the tunnel. Finally he came to another door, but this one would not open at all. He went past it until he reached the end of the tunnel. This was half-blocked by the fallen bulk of another massive steel door. He pulled himself over it, wondering if anyone had ever come this way since the lower levels, which had primarily been used for storing armaments, battle-machines and military personnel, had been abandoned with the Great Disarmament of 2042.

A noise ahead of him suddenly startled Alan and he automatically switched off the emergency bulb.

Voices sounded, at first indistinct and then clearer as Alan moved cautiously closer.

'We shouldn't have left those machines intact. If some fool fiddles about with them, heaven knows what'll happen.'

'Let them find out.' It was the Fireclown's voice, sounding like a pulse-beat.

'And who'll be blamed?' he heard Corso say tiredly. 'You will. I wish you'd never talked me into this.'

'You agreed with my discoveries, Corso. Have you changed your mind now?'

'I suppose not... *Damn!*' Alan heard someone stumble. A woman giggled and said: 'You're too hasty, Corso. What's the hurry? At present they're combing the corridors they know about. We have plenty of time.'

'Unless they find the boat before we get there,' Corso said querulously. Alan was creeping behind them now, following them as they moved along in the dark.

'I'm only worried about the fuel. Are you sure we've enough fuel, Corso?' The Fireclown spoke. Although this man had been accused of planning to blow up the world, Alan felt a glow as he listened to the rich, warm voice.

'We wouldn't make Luna, certainly, on what we've got. But we've got enough to take us as far as we want to go.'

'Good.'

Alan heard a low whine, a hissing noise, a thump, and then the voices were cut off suddenly. A few yards further on his hand touched metal.

He switched on the emergency bulb and discovered that he had come to a solid wall of steel. This was completely smooth and he could not guess how it opened. He tried for almost an hour to get it to work, but finally, his body feeling hollow with frustration, he gave up and began to make his way back in the direction he had come.

A short time later the ground quivered for a few seconds and he had to stop, thinking insanely that the stockpile of bombs had exploded. When it was over, he thought he could guess what had caused it. The Fireclown had made some reference to a boat – a space-boat. Perhaps that had taken off, though how it was possible so deep underground he couldn't guess.

He was feeling intensely tired. His limbs and his head ached badly and he was incapable either of sustained thought or action. He had to keep stopping every few yards in order to rest, his body trembling with reaction. But reaction to what? To some new nervous or mental shock, or was it the cumulative effect of the past few days? He had been unable to sort out and analyse his emotions earlier, and was even less capable of doing so now.

An acute sense of melancholy possessed him as he stumbled miserably on, at last arriving back at the office. Wearily, he dumped the emergency bulb down in the main chamber, suddenly becoming conscious of a tremendous heat emanating from some source outside. When he reached the entrance the guards had gone. Somewhere in the distance he heard shouts and other noises. As he reached the opening onto the main corridor he saw that it was ablaze with light.

And the light – a weird, green-blue blaze – was coming from the Fireclown's great cavern.

A policeman ran past him and Alan shouted: 'What's happening?'

'Fire!' the policeman continued to run.

Now, pouring like a torrent, the flames were eddying down the corridor, a surging, swiftly moving inferno. There was nothing for the fire to feed on, yet it moved just the same, as if of its own volition.

Fascinated, Alan watched it approach. The heat was soon unbearable and he backed into the chamber.

Only at that moment did it dawn on him that he should have run towards the ramps. He was completely trapped. Also, the laboratory contained inflammable chemicals which would ignite immediately the blaze reached them.

He ran towards the entrance again, stupefied by the heat, and saw that it was too late. The wall of heaving flame had almost reached him.

He still felt no panic. Part of him almost welcomed the flames. But the air was becoming less and less breathable.

He wrenched open doors, looking for another exit. The only possible one seemed to be that which he'd just come back from.

It occurred to him that the Fireclown had been misjudged all round – by everyone except his grandfather who had realised the danger.

The Fireclown had released an inferno on the City of Switzerland. But how? He had never seen or heard of any flames like those which now began to dart around the corridor. He coughed and rubbed the sweat out of his eyes.

At last his brain began to function again. But too late, now, for him to do anything constructive.

Suddenly the entrance was filled with a roaring mass of fire. He retreated from it, hit his back against the corner of a bench, stumbled towards the office. As he slammed the steel door behind him he heard an explosion as the flame touched some of the spilled chemicals.

Air was still flowing in from another source in the small tunnel. He kept the door open.

The other door, sealing off the flames, began to heat and he realised, with fatalistic horror, that when it melted, as it inevitably must, he would die.

He would, he decided, leave the office and head into the tunnel at the last minute. Sitting in the darkness, his confused mind began to clear as the heat rose, and he faced death. A peculiar feeling of calm came upon him and belatedly, he began to think.

The thoughts were not particularly helpful in his present predicament. They told him of no way of escape, but they helped him face the inevitable. He thought he understood, now, the philosophic calm which came to men facing death.

For some days, he realised, he had been moving in a kind of half-dream, grasping out for something that might have been – he hesitated and then let the thought come – love. His emotions had ruled him; he had been their toy, unaware of his motives.

He had always been, to a degree, unstable in this way, perhaps because of his tendency to suppress the unpleasant ideas which sometimes came to him. Having no parents, unloved by his grandfather, his childhood had been spent in a perpetual quest for attention; at school he had been broken of his exhibitionism, and the nature of his job gave him no means of expressing these feelings. Now he sought, perhaps, that needed love in the Fireclown with his constant evoking of parent images. Certainly he had sought it in Helen, so much so that a similar need in her had clashed with his own. And now, spurred on by his grandfather's bitter references to his illegitimacy, he had embarked on a search which had led him to this – death!

He got up, abstractly watching the door slowly turning red-hot.

Had many others, like him, identified the Fireclown with some need to feel *wanted*?

He smiled. It was too pat, really – too cheap. But he had hit upon a clue to the Fireclown's popularity even if he was not yet near to the exact truth.

Looking at it from another angle, he assembled the facts. They

were few and obvious. The Fireclown's own psychological need
had created the creed that he had preached, and it had found an
echo in the hearts of a large percentage of the world's population.
But the creed had not really supplied an answer to their ills, had
only enabled them to find expression.

The door turned to smoky white and he smelt the steel smouldering. A slight glow filled the room and his mouth was dry of
saliva, his body drained of sweat.

The world had reached some kind of crisis point. Perhaps it
was, as the Fireclown had said, because man had removed himself
from his roots and lived an increasingly artificial life.

Yet Alan couldn't completely accept this. An observer from
another star, for instance, might see the rise and fall of man-made
constructions as nothing more than a natural change-process. Did
human beings consider an anthill 'unnatural'? Wasn't the City of
Switzerland itself merely a huge anthill?

He saw with surprise that the door had faded from white- to
red-hot and the heat in the room was decreasing. Immediately
there was some hope. He forgot his reverie and watched the
change intently. Soon the door was only warm to his touch. He
pushed at it but it wouldn't budge. Then he realised that the heat
had expanded the metal. He waited impatiently, giving an experimental push every now and then until, at last, the door gave and
he stepped into the ruined laboratory.

The fire had destroyed much, but now the room swam with
liquid. An occasional spurt from the walls close to the ceiling told
him the source of his salvation. Evidently this old section of the
city had had to protect itself against fire more than any other
part – the old automatic extinguishers had finally functioned and
engulfed the fire.

In the passage outside it was the same. The extinguishers had
not been tested – not even known about – for years but, activated
by the extreme heat, they had finally done the job they had been
designed for.

With relief, he began to run up the pitch-dark corridor, at last
finding his way to the ramp. A small heap of containers was still

there, but there were not so many as he had seen earlier. Had the police managed to take them, or had they been salvaged by the Fireclown? It was, of course, virtually impossible for fire to destroy the P-bombs' shielding, but how many knew that these days? How much panic, Alan wondered, had been the result of the Fireclown's holocaust?

Levels all the way up had been swept by fire. He was forced to push his body on and on, climbing the emergency stairways, avoiding charred corpses and wreckage.

Naked flame had not been used in the city for many years and fire precautions had been lax – there had been no need for them until now.

Alan wondered wryly if the Fireclown's popularity was as great as it had been yesterday.

The first group of men he met were on the fifteenth level. They were forcing open a door in a residential corridor, obviously equipped as a rescue team.

They stared at him, astonished.

'Where did you come from?' one of them asked, rubbing a dirty sleeve over his soot-blackened face.

'I was trapped down below – old fire extinguishers put out the fire.'

'They may have put out the fire that the *initial* fire started,' another said, 'but they wouldn't have worked on the first lot. We tried. Nothing puts it out once it's under way.'

'Then why is it out now?'

'Just thank the stars it *is* out. We don't know why. It suddenly subsided and disappeared between the fifteenth and sixteenth levels. We can only guess that the stuff it's made of doesn't last for ever. We don't know why it burns and we don't know what it burns. To think we trusted the Fireclown and he did this to our homes...'

'You're sure it was the Fireclown?'

'Who else? He had the P-bomb cache, didn't he? It stands to reason he had other weapons, too – flame-weapons he'd made himself.'

Alan passed on.

The semi-melted corridors gave way to untouched corridors full of disturbed people, milling around men organising them into rescue teams. Emergency hospital stations had been set up and doctors were treating shock and burn victims, the lucky survivors. The lowest level had been built to withstand destruction of this kind, but the newer levels had not been. If he had been on the tenth level, or even the ninth where a few families had still lived before the blaze, he wouldn't be alive now.

Though climbing the emergency stairs and ramps was hard going, Alan chose these instead of the overcrowded, fear-filled elevators. On he climbed, grateful for the peace and quiet of the stairs in contrast to the turbulence in the corridors.

He was crossing the corridor of the thirtieth level when he saw that one of the shop-fronts – it was a consumer corridor – bore a gaudy slogan. A FREER LIFE WITH THE RLM it said. The place was the election headquarters of the Radical Liberal Movement. Another poster – a tri-di build-up – showed the smiling face of Helen Curtis. At the top, above the picture, it said *Curtis*, and at the bottom, below the picture, it said *President*. The troublesome *for* had been left out.

He stopped and spoke to the door of the place.

'May I come in?'

The door opened. He walked into a poster-lined passage and into a large room stacked with election literature. Bundles of leaflets and posters, all brightly coloured, were stacked everywhere. There didn't seem to be anyone around.

He picked up a plastipaper poster of Helen. An audiostrip in its lining began to whisper softly: *Curtis for President, Curtis for President, Curtis for President*. He flung it down and as it crumpled the whispering stopped.

'I see that's another vote I've lost,' said Helen's voice behind him.

'I had a feeling I was going to meet you,' he said quietly, still staring at the fallen poster.

'It would be likely, in my own election headquarters. This is only the storeroom. Do you want to see the offices? They're smart.' Her voice, unlike her words, was not a bit cheerful.

'What are you going to do with all this now?' he said, waving a tired arm around the room.

'Use it, of course. What did you expect?'

'I should have thought a campaign wouldn't have been worth your time now.'

'You think because I supported the Fireclown when he was popular I won't have a chance now he's unpopular – is that it?'

'Yes.' He was surprised. Her spirit, it seemed, was still there. She didn't have a chance of winning the elections now. Was she hiding the fact from herself? he wondered.

'Look, Alan,' she said forcefully, 'I could have walked into the Presidency without a fight if this hadn't happened. Now it's going to be a tough fight – and I'm rather glad.'

'You always liked a fight.'

'Certainly – if the opposition's strong enough.'

He smiled. 'Was that levelled at me by any chance? I've heard it said that if a man doesn't love a woman enough she thinks he's strong; if he loves her too much she thinks he's weak. Was the opposition weak, Helen?'

'You're very sensitive today.' Her voice was deliberately cool. 'No, I wasn't levelling anything at you. I was talking about your grandfather's happy turn of luck. Our positions are completely reversed now, aren't they?'

'I don't know how I feel about it,' he said, stopping the tendency to sulk. Helen's retort had stung him. 'I'm not really in support of either of you. I think, on the whole, I favour the RLMs. They could still win the constituency elections, couldn't they, even if you didn't get the Presidency? That would give you a strong voice in the House.'

'If they kept me as leader, Alan.' Her face softened as she admitted a truth which previously she had been hiding from. 'Not everyone who approved of my stand yesterday approves of it today.'

'I hate to say I warned you of it. You should have known better, Helen, than to go around whipping up mobs. People have to trust politicians as well as like them. They want a modern, up-to-date President, certainly – but they also want a respectable one. When the voters sit down and think about it, even if this Fireclown business hadn't taken the turn it has, they'll choose the candidate they can feel confidence in. Fiery politics of your sort only work for short spells, Helen. Even I know that much. Admittedly, after showing yourself as a "Woman of the People" you could have stuck to parliamentary debate to make your points and probably danced home. But now you've identified yourself so strongly with the Fireclown that you haven't a hope of winning. I should give it up.' He looked at her wistfully.

She laughed shortly, striding up and down between the bales of posters. 'I haven't a dog's chance – you're right. But I'll keep on fighting. Lucky old Simon, eh? He's now the man who warned the people of their danger. Who else could they vote for?'

'Don't get bitter, Helen. Why don't you start painting again? You know what you're doing in that field. Really, even I know more about politics than you do. You should never have entered them. There are people who are natural-born politicians, but you're just not one of them. I've asked you this a dozen times previously, but I'd still like to know what makes you go on with it.'

'One of the strongest reasons is because the more people disapprove of my actions, the harder I pursue them. Fair enough?' She turned, staring at him quizzically with her head cocked on one side.

He smiled. 'In a word, you're just plain obstinate. Maybe if I'd encouraged you in your political work you might have been a well-known painter by now – and well rid of all this trouble.'

'Maybe. But it's more than that, Alan.' She spoke softly, levering herself up onto one of the bales. She sat there swinging her legs, looking very beautiful. She no longer wore the make-up she'd had on earlier. 'But I've got myself into this now, and I'm going to stick at it until the end. Sink or swim.'

He told her about his visit to the first level – omitting that he'd heard the Fireclown and his friends leaving – and of his narrow escape.

'I thought I was going to be killed,' he said, 'and I thought of you. I wondered, in fact, if we weren't both searching for the same thing.'

'Searching? I didn't know you were the searching kind, Alan.'

'Until this Fireclown business blew up, I was the hiding kind. I hid a lot from myself. But something Grandfather said must have triggered something else in me.' He paused. 'Was it only three days ago?' he mused wonderingly.

'What did he say?'

'Oh,' Alan answered lightly, 'he made a rather pointed reference to the fact that my ancestry isn't all it might be.'

'That was cruel of him.'

'Maybe it did me good. Maybe it brought something into the open. Anyway, I started getting curious about the Fireclown. Then you visited me and I was even more curious. Perhaps because you associated yourself with the Fireclown's creed, I associated him with you and it led on from there. I went to see the Fireclown the same night, you know.'

'Did you speak to him personally?' She sounded envious.

'No. I never got to see him, actually. But I attended yesterday's "audience". I thought I understood why you supported him. In his own heavy way he made sense of a kind.' He frowned. 'But the same could be said for Grandfather, I suppose. That was a good speech this morning.'

'Yes, it was.' She was staring at him, her mouth slightly open, her breasts moving beneath her lacy bodice more rapidly than usual.

'I'm glad all this has happened,' he continued. 'It's done a lot of good for me, I think.'

'You're glad about the P-bombs being found – about the fire, too?'

'No. I couldn't really believe the Fireclown was guilty until I saw the evidence for myself. And I still don't hate him for what he tried to do – for what he still might try to do, for that matter. I feel sorry for him. In his own way he is the naïve and generous giant you tried to tell me about.'

'That's what I think. You were down there – were you satisfied that the Fireclown was responsible for stockpiling those bombs and starting the fire?'

'The evidence was plain, I'm afraid.'

'It's idiotic,' she said angrily. 'Why should he do a thing like that? A man so full of *love*!'

'Love – or hate, Helen?'

'What do you mean?'

'He professed to love mankind – but he hated mankind's works. He hated what he thought were our faults. Not exactly true love, eh?'

'We'll never know. I wonder if he escaped. I hope he has – so long as he doesn't try any more sabotage.'

For the second time in the last few days Alan found himself concealing something from his ex-mistress. He didn't tell her that he knew the Fireclown had managed a getaway, at least from Earth. Instead, he said: 'Should he escape? After all, he was responsible for the deaths of least a hundred people. The residential corridors on nine and ten all the way up to fifteen were full of corpses. Probably a great many more were roasted in their homes. A nasty death, Helen. I know. I came close to it myself. Should he escape without punishment?'

'A man like the Fireclown is probably not conscious of his crime, Alan. So who's to say?'

'He's intelligent. I don't think he's insane, in any way we can understand. *Warped*, perhaps...?'

'Oh, well, let's stop talking about the Fireclown. There's a worldwide search out for him now. The fact that he vanished seems to prove his guilt, at least for Simon Powys and the public. I've noticed a few remained loyal to the Fireclown for some time after they found out about the bombs. If the fire hadn't started he'd probably still have strong support from people who thought the bombs were planted.'

'You can't plant a stack of P-bombs, Helen. The Fireclown must have made them. He's the only one with the resources.'

'That's what everyone thinks. But a few of us politicians know better, Alan.'

'Nuclear weapons have been banned for years. What are you talking about?'

'Not everyone gave up all their stockpile in the early days of the Great Disarmament, Alan. There were quite a few who hung on to some secret arms piles until they saw how things were going. Of course, when the Solar Government was found to work and the threat of war dwindled away to nothing, they forgot about them or got rid of them.'

'Good God! Nuclear bombs. I'm not superstitious. War's a thing of the past. But it seems dreadful that the weapons should still be around.'

'There are plenty,' she said ironically. 'At least enough to fight a major solar war!'

Chapter Seven

A LAN, LIKE THE rest of his contemporaries, had lived so long in a peaceful world that the concept of war, particularly war fought on a nuclear scale, was horrifying. For nearly a century the world had hovered on the brink of atomic conflict, but time after time governments had just managed to avoid it. With the final outlawing of nuclear weapons in 2042, a great sigh of relief had gone up. The human race had come dangerously close to destroying itself, but at last it could progress without that fear forever pressing on it.

And now Helen's casual reference to a solar war!

'You don't mean that as a serious suggestion, did you?' he asked her.

'Alan, the Solar Cabinet, myself and one or two other party leaders have been aware of the existence of nuclear arms for some time. Simon Powys, in his speech before the House this morning, could not reveal that, because if the news leaked we might well have a fresh panic on our hands. Anyway, it suited his purpose to suggest that the Fireclown manufactured them. The Fireclown might have been able to make his, but he could just as easily have *bought* them.'

'*Bought* –?' Alan gasped. 'Bought them from whom?'

'From one of the men who specialise in such things. Over the years there has been a constant "black market" in nuclear arms. The police have been aware of it and they have been vigilant. Many of those who discovered forgotten caches have been arrested and the weapons destroyed. But some haven't. And these men would welcome physical conflict – preferably on Earth or between Earth and *one* of the other worlds, so that they could get to safety on the unthreatened world. If one side began an attack with nuclear arms, the other would have to defend itself – and the dealers could then get any price that they wanted.'

'But, surely, arms dealing on such a scale is impossible!'

'Not if the cards are played right. And it has been evident to me for some time that someone *is* playing their cards right. If he gets the hand he wants – bang! Suddenly, overnight, without any kind of warning and none of the psychological protection people perhaps had a hundred years ago, we'd be plunged into a war of colossal destruction.'

'I can't believe it!'

'Perhaps it's better. Remember, this is only what the dealers wish for – it might not happen. That's why it's so secret. It might be possible to remove the danger once and for all with none of the public knowing it was there. The RLM shadow cabinet have a plan to prevent the eventuality; Simon Powys has another. I think ours is better. Now you know one of the reasons I'm in politics and why I stay in.'

'I'll accept that,' he said a trifle dubiously. 'Do you think the Fireclown's tied up with any of these dealers?'

'If he's tied up with one, he's probably tied up with them all. Those we haven't caught are the most powerful and have very likely formed themselves into a syndicate. That's what the rumours say, at any rate.'

'I saw no evidence of a plant when I explored the Fireclown's level. So it's probable that he could have bought the P-bombs.'

'There's another angle to it,' Helen said thoughtfully. 'Admittedly I may not have been wholly objective about the Fireclown, but what if the dealers had *planted* the P-bombs on him, knowing that someone would eventually find out?'

'Why should they do that?' Alan bent down and picked up a handbill, his eyes fixed on it. It was another picture of Helen, this time in an heroic pose. Fifty words of text underneath briefly outlined her ideals in purple adjectives.

'The arms dealers want a war – preferably one that wouldn't have too destructive results and wouldn't involve all three habitable planets. First, hint that the Fireclown has a stockpile, supply the evidence to be found, take advantage of the scare – and the possibility of the Fireclown possessing more weapons – then unload a ready-made batch of weapons for "defence" of the Solar Government. That way, you see, there might not be a war at all – but the dealers would profit just the same.'

'That sounds close to the truth – if the dealers did frame the Fireclown, of course. But we have proof that he caused the destruction of fifteen levels. How do you explain that? That fire was impossible to extinguish. He had obviously made it, in the same way he manufactured that weird artificial sun in the cavern.'

'He may have been pushed into it – self-defence.'

'No, I don't think so.'

'There's one way we can get more information,' she said briskly, jumping down off the bale. 'We can go and see Simon Powys. He'd know more about it than anyone.'

'Do you want to do that?'

'I'm curious. More than that, Alan.' She smiled nervously. 'I may be able to wheedle something out of the old patriarch that would be advantageous to me in the election. If I could prove that Fireclown was framed it would help a lot.'

He shook his head, wondering at her incredible optimism. 'All right,' he said. 'Let's go.'

Simon Powys received them with the air of the conquering Roman general receiving the defeated barbarian leaders. All he needed, Alan thought, was a toga and a laurel crown.

He smiled urbanely, greeted them conventionally, offered them drinks, which they accepted.

'Come into the study,' he said to his grandson and niece. He led the way. He had furnished the place with deliberate archaism. There were even a few family portraits – of the best-remembered members of the Powys clan. The first Denholm, Alan and Simon Powys hung there, as well as the two women Presidents of the Solar Government. A proud and slightly sombre-looking group. The bookcases were of mahogany, filled primarily with books on politics, history and philosophy. The novels were of the same type – political novels by Disraeli, Trollope, Koestler, Endelmans and De la Vega. Alan rather envied his grandfather's one-track mind. It made him good at his career.

'To tell you the truth,' Simon Powys said heavily. 'I feel sorry for you both. You were misled, as most people were, and this business must have left you slightly in the air. It hasn't done you much good politically, has it, Helen? A pity – you've got good Powys stuff in you – strong will, impersonal ambition...'

'And an eye to the main chance.' She smiled. 'Though you'll probably say, Uncle Simon, that I lack self-discipline and could do with a spot more common sense. You'd probably be right about the self-discipline. I lost out on that one – I think I'm finished now, don't you?'

Alan admired her guile.

Simon Powys nodded regretfully. He probably did regret his niece's political demise, just as he obviously regretted Alan's never having shown an interest in politics. 'Still, you were rather foolish, y'know.'

'I know,' she said contritely.

He turned to Alan. 'And you, my boy? I suppose you understand why I was so adamant earlier?'

'Yes, Grandfather.'

The old man seemed to warm to both of them. 'I shall be President, no doubt, when the next session begins. It was really my last opportunity to take such high responsibility – family tradition demands a Powys of every generation to serve at least one term. I was hoping that you, Alan, would follow on, but I suppose the task will fall to Helen's son and Denholm's. I wish my daughter...' He cleared his throat, seemingly moved to strong emotion, although Alan thought the last line had been a bit stagey. It was probably for his benefit. He wondered why he should have felt such momentary love for his grandfather at their earlier interview.

'What made you suspicious of the Fireclown in the first place?' Helen said, in the manner of a whodunit character preparing the detective for his denouement.

'Instinct, I suppose. Could have told you there was something fishy about him the first time I heard of him. Made Junnar go down and have a look the first opportunity he could. There was also another business which I can't really talk about…'

'He knows about the illegal stockpiles, Uncle,' Helen said forthrightly.

'Really? A bit unwise to spread it around, isn't it?'

'I'm not in the habit of betraying confidences, Grandfather,' Alan said tritely, with a hard look at Helen.

'No. I suppose it's all right. But presumably Helen has impressed you with the need for secrecy?'

'Of course,' Helen said.

'Well, I had a feeling he'd been connected with the dealers. They're the only group of criminals powerful enough to hide a man and help him change his identity. I guessed that he had probably come from their hideout, though this was all conjecture, you understand. The police investigated him and could find nothing to indicate it, though they agreed with me.'

'So, in fact, unless it can be established that the P-bombs are part of the old stock, there is nothing to connect him with the dealers?' Helen said, trying hard not to show her disappointment.

'I have already been in touch with the laboratory analysing the bombs. They tell me they *are* old stock – you would have discovered that soon, anyway, at the next Committee meeting. Obviously we can't tell the public that.'

'Obviously,' said Helen, 'though it might have strengthened my own case in the House slightly.'

'Not to any important degree.'

'What's this committee?' Alan asked curiously.

'We call it the One Hundred Committee, after a slightly less effective British anti-nuclear group which existed in the middle of the twentieth century. Actually there are only ten of us. The Committee is pledged to locating every single nuclear weapon left over from the old days and seeing the offenders punished where possible. We work, of course, in close collaboration with the highly secret ARP – the Arms Removal Police. Our work has been going on for years. Helen is the secretary and I am the chairman. Other important politicians comprise the remaining eight.'

'Very worthy,' said Alan. 'Are you effective?'

'We have been in the past, though our job is becoming more difficult since the dealers work together, pooling their resources. They would welcome an opportunity to sell what they have – perhaps Helen has already told you.'

'Yes, she has. But it occurred to me that you could offer to buy the dealers out now. Surely it would be better to pay their price and have the arms without waiting for a crisis to decide you?'

'That's our main bone of contention,' Helen put in. 'Uncle doesn't agree with buying them now. I want to do that.'

'The fantastic price these brigands would demand would beggar the Solar nation,' Simon Powys said gruffly to his grandson. 'We must do it in secret and justify the expenditure at the same time. It would be impossible. I feel they'll overstep the mark at some stage, then we'll catch them.'

'The expenditure's worth it!' Helen said. 'We could recuperate from poverty, but survival in a nuclear war…!'

'If we caught the Fireclown, then,' Alan said slowly, 'it might give us a lead to the arms dealers.'

'Possibly,' Powys agreed, 'though he might not admit to it. Secondly, he might not even know who the dealers are. They are naturally extremely cautious. However, they are certainly going to take advantage of the trouble the Fireclown has caused. The man must be caught – and destroyed before he makes any more trouble!'

'Grandfather!' Alan was shocked. The death penalty had been abolished for more than a hundred years.

'I'm sorry – I'm extremely sorry, Helen. You must forgive an old man's tongue. These concepts were not quite so disgusting when I was a young man. Certainly we must imprison or exile the Fireclown.'

Alan nodded.

'It's funny,' he said, 'that the Fireclown should preach a return to nature; that, in fact, science leads to mankind's destruction, and yet he should be planning that same destruction – or at very least is a tool of those who would welcome it.'

'Life,' said the old man with the air of a philosopher, 'is full of that sort of paradox.'

Chapter Eight

'I'LL SEE YOU home,' Alan said lightly as they left the apartment.

'That would be nice,' she said.

They walked slowly through the gardens, repaired and beautiful again. The starlight was augmented by soft beams from the roof structure which had the appearance of many tiny moons shining down, each one casting a single, exquisite beam. The Top had been well designed. To live here was the ambition of every young man and woman. It gave people, thought those at the Top, something to aim for.

'If only I could speak to the Fireclown personally,' Helen said wistfully. 'Then at least I'd be able to form a better idea of what he's really like.'

Alan preferred to say nothing.

They reached the door of her apartment on the sixty-third level and went in. Familiar smells greeted him, smells which he always associated with Helen – fresh, slightly scented, of soap and oils. It was strange, he reflected, that women's apartments always seemed to smell better than men's. Maybe it was an obvious thought. He noticed he was breathing a little more quickly, slightly more shallowly.

Neither recognised by outward expression the thought that was in their minds, yet each was aware of the other's emotions. Alan was slightly fearful, for he remembered the conflict between them as well as their old happiness and realised that Helen probably did, too.

'Would you like a nightcap?' she invited.

'I'd prefer coffee, if you've got it.' Unconsciously, he had given her her opportunity. He was torn now, half-afraid of what seemed likely to happen.

She came over to him as he sat down in a comfortable chair beside a small shelf of book-tapes.

She leaned down and stroked his face lightly.

'You look dreadfully tired, Alan.'

'I've had a hard day.' He smiled. He took her hand and kissed it.

'I'll go and get the coffee,' she said.

When she came back she had changed into a pair of chaste pyjamas and a robe of thick, dark blue material. She had a tray of coffee – real coffee from the smell. She put it down on a table and drew up a chair so that the table was between them.

Helen, he thought, *Oh, Helen, I love you*. They were staring at each other, both wondering, perhaps, if this reunion would take on the same pattern as their previous affair.

'We're wiser now,' she said softly, handing him his coffee. 'It's a Powys trait – we learn by our mistakes.'

'There are always different mistakes to be made,' he warned her. It was the last attempt to retreat from the situation and allow her to do the same, as gracefully as possible.

'That's experience,' she said, and the fears were forgotten. Now they looked at one another as if they were new friends.

When they made love that night it was entirely different from anything either had ever before experienced. They treated one another delicately, yet passionately, as if a return to their earlier, less self-conscious love would plunge them back into the turmoil of four months before.

In the morning Alan's arm was aching painfully from having cradled her head all night. He raised her head gently and propped himself on his elbow, tracing the softness of her shoulder with his fingers. She opened her eyes and seemed to be looking at him like a respectful stranger. Presumably there was a similar expression in his own face, for he felt he shared her emotion. He kissed her lightly on the lips and pushed back the bedclothes, swinging himself out of the narrow bed.

He sat slightly hunched on the edge, studying his head and torso reflected in the mirror opposite.

'I've got an idea where the Fireclown is,' he said suddenly.

She was half-asleep and didn't seem to hear him.

He didn't repeat himself then but went into the kitchen to make coffee. He was feeling rather tired now and his legs shook a little as the machine came alive and produced two beakers of hot coffee. He transferred the coffee into cups and took them back.

She was sitting up.

'What did you say about the Fireclown? You know where he is?'

'No, but we might be able to guess.' He told her about over-hearing the trio in the passage.

'Why didn't you tell me about this yesterday?'

'That was yesterday,' he said simply. She understood and nodded.

'They took off in a small space-boat. I've thought about it since and I think there must be a launching ramp leading through the rock to somewhere outside the city. Those old bombs had to be launched from somewhere.'

'That sounds logical. You say he remarked that they didn't have enough fuel to make Luna. They may have made a transcontinental flight.'

'Unlikely. You can't land even a small rocket without at least a few people observing it. I've got a feeling they're orbiting – maybe waiting for someone to pick them up.'

'Or they may have gone to St Rene's?'

'Why should they do that?' The Monastery of St Rene Lafayette was the home of a group of monks who practised a form of scientific mysticism. Little was known about the Order and it was thought that the monks were harmless. The monastery was, in fact, an abandoned space-station which the monks had taken over. The world had decided they were quaintly mad and had all but forgotten them.

'Well,' Helen said, sipping her coffee, 'it's just a connection that my mind made. I associated one "crank" with a group of others, I suppose.'

'Unless they *were* orbiting, it's the only place they could have gone,' Alan agreed. 'I wonder how we could find out.'

'By going there, perhaps.'

'We'd need a boat. We haven't got one.'

'My brother has. A nice job – one of the latest Paolos.'

'Would he let us take it?'

'We don't need to ask. I often use it. I have a pilot's licence, the audiolocks respond to my voice, the ground staff at the port know me – we'd have a good chance of getting away with it.'

'And going to our deaths, maybe. The Fireclown appears to be more ruthless than we thought, remember?'

'But are the monks? They are bound to give sanctuary to those they term "unclears", I believe.'

'It's worth a try.' He got up. 'I'm going to have a bath. Is my green suit still here?'

'Yes.'

'Good.' He glanced at the chronom on the wall. 'It's still early. If we leave now we could...' He turned to her. 'Where is your brother's ship?'

'Hamburg – she's a sea-lander.'

'A fast cab could get us there in an hour. You'd better get up and get ready.' He grinned at her as she sprang out of bed.

Hamburg Spaceport was surrounded by a pleasant garden-city with a population of less than two millions. In contrast to the capital city of Switzerland, its buildings were single- or double-storeyed. Beyond the spaceport buildings water glinted in the summer sun, beneath a pale and cloudless blue sky. As the cab spiralled down towards the landing roof a huge bulbous ship suddenly erupted from the waves, water boiling to steam as it lumbered upwards.

Helen pointed: 'The *Titan*, bound for Mars and Ganymede, probably carrying one of the last seed consignments they need.'

By the time the cab brought them down on the roof the ship had disappeared. From his lodge, the only building on the roof, an official in a brown velvet cut-away and baggy, cerise pantaloons came sauntering towards them. He was a firm-faced man with a smile.

'Good morning, Miss Curtis. Sorry to hear about yesterday,' he said. 'Many people's faith in the Fireclown seems to have been misplaced.'

'Yes, indeed,' said Helen, forcing a smile in response to his. 'I'm planning to make a pleasure trip until the fuss dies down. Is the *Solar Bird* ready?'

'I expect so. She was being checked in the locks, I believe. She should be okay now. Do you want to go straight down?'

'Yes, please.'

He took them into his lodge, a neat office with a big window overlooking the sea which was still heaving and steaming after the *Titan*'s take-off. A small elevator cage was set in one wall. The man opened the gate for them, glancing at Alan in a speculative way. Alan returned his stare blandly and followed Helen into the elevator. It began to hiss downward.

A man in coveralls let them out, a plum, red-faced man with a mechanics' badge on his sleeve.

'Good morning, Miss Helen. Nice to see you.'

'Good morning, Freddie. This is Mr Powys – Freddie Weinschenk.'

They shook hands and Weinschenk led them along an artificially lit corridor. Alan had never been in Hamburg before, but he knew the general design of a modern spaceport. They were now below ground level, he guessed, heading along a tunnel which led under the seabed.

Finally, Freddie ordered a door to open and they were in a dark, cool chamber with metal walls. From one wall, the back half of a small space-yacht projected, seeming, at first, to be stuck on the wall until Alan realised that the other half lay outside and that they were actually in a pressure chamber.

'Thanks, Freddie.' Helen went up to the airlock and spoke to it. It began to slide open; then slowly the four doors all opened and they went into the cramped cabin of the ship. Freddie shouted from outside:

'If you're leaving immediately, miss, I'll start the chamber up.'

'Thanks, Freddie. See you when we get back.'

Helen went to the control panel and touched a stud. The airlocks closed behind them. She switched on the exterior viewer so they could see the chamber. Freddie had left and Alan saw that the

room was swiftly being flooded. Soon it was full and the wall surrounding the ship began to expand away from the ship itself and
he saw the ramp extending outwards into open sea.

'We'll make a soft take-off,' Helen said, strapping herself in the
pilot's couch. Alan got into the other couch. 'We don't want anyone to think we're in a hurry,' she added.

'The softer the better,' he smiled. 'I've only been into space
once and I didn't much care for the trip. She was an old chemical
ship and I was certain she was going to break down every inch of
the journey.'

'You'll see a lot of difference in the *Solar Bird*.' She activated the
drive. 'It's unlikely they could improve a nuclear ship any further.
They'll have to start thinking of some new type of engine now, I suppose, just as the old type starts getting familiar and comfortable.'

The control panel was alive now, its instruments measuring
and informing.

Alan felt a double pounding beat for a second or so, and then
the ship was speeding up the ramp, leaving it, plunging up through
water and then was in daylight, racing into the sky.

She switched on the chart-viewer, selected the area of space
she wanted. It showed her the position of the space-station monastery and gave her all the information she needed.

'I hope our hunch is right,' she said and turned round to see
that Alan had blacked out.

There had been no reason for this at all, since the mounting
pressure outside was completely countered by the ship's internal
mechanisms. It was probably some kind of reflex, she decided.

'I'm a fool,' he said when he was awake again. '*Did* anything happen, or was it just my imagination?'

'Just imagination, I'm afraid. But you needed the sleep, anyway.'

'Where are we?'

'In orbit. We should be getting pretty close to the station in a
little while. For the time being I'm going to pretend we're in
trouble – that way we'll lull any suspicions the monks might have
if they *are* harbouring the Fireclown.'

Soon the wheel of the big station came in sight, the sun bright on its metal. There were two ships they could see hugged in its receiving bays, a big one and a little one. The big one was of unfamiliar design. They could see its title etched on its hull from where they were. *Pi-meson*.

'Funny name for a ship,' Alan commented.

'The monks – if it *is* their ship – have got funny ideas.' She reached out to press a red stud. 'That's the mayday signal. With any luck they should get it.'

In a moment their screen flickered and a face appeared on it – a thin man, lean-nosed and thin-lipped.

'Would it be impertinent to deduce that you are in trouble?' he said.

'It wouldn't be, no,' Helen replied. 'Can you help us?'

'Who knows? Can you manoeuvre your ship so that we can grapple, or shall we send out help?'

'The steering seems to be all right,' she said. 'I'll come in.'

She coasted the ship until they were near one of the empty bays and the station's magnegraps pulled them into the bay.

When, finally, they climbed from their ship into the unpleasant air of the monastery they were greeted by the thin-faced monk. He was dressed in a blue habit that did nothing for his already pale face. His hair was short but he had no tonsure. His eyes and cheeks were sunken but, in his own way, he looked healthy enough. He held out a skeletal hand with incredibly long fingers.

'I am Auditor Kurt,' he said as Alan shook hands. 'It is good that we can be of service to you. Please come this way.'

He took them into a small, barely furnished room and offered them tea, which they accepted.

'What exactly is wrong with your ship?' he asked politely.

'I'm not sure. I'm not familiar with the type – it's new. I could not get the landing jets to work when I tested them preparatory to re-entering the atmosphere. It's just as well I did test them.' She had personally jammed the jet control. It could be fixed easily.

'You were lucky to be so close.' The monk nodded.

Alan was wondering how he could find out if the Fireclown was here.

'I'm extremely interested in your Order,' he said conversationally. 'I'm something of a student of religions – perhaps you can tell me about yours?'

'Only that we were founded as long ago as 1950, although this Order did not come into existence until 1976 and did not come here until about twenty years ago. We are a branch of the original faith, which did not pay a great deal of attention to its mystical aspects until we founded the Order of St Rene. St Rene is not the true name of our inspired founder – that is secret to almost all – but that is the name we use for him.'

'I should like to see the monastery. Is that possible?' Alan looked around the small room, avoiding the monk's intent gaze.

'Normally it would be possible – but, ah, we have repairs going on in many parts… We are not really prepared for visitors.'

'Oh? Then whose is the ship, other than ours, in the receiving bay?'

'Which one?'

'There are two. The *Pi-meson* and the *Od-Methuselah*.'

'Both ours,' the monk said hastily. 'Both ours.'

'Then why did you ask which one I spoke of?'

The monk smiled. 'We monks have devious minds, I'm afraid. It is the nature of our calling. Excuse me, I'll go and check that the mechanics are repairing your ship.' He rose and left. They heard the door seal itself behind him. They were locked in.

Alan sipped his tea.

'If the Fireclown's here, they're not likely to let on to outsiders who'd take the news back to Earth,' he said.

'We'll have to think of a means of getting a look around this place. Have you noticed the atmosphere? It's weird.'

The atmosphere of the place fitted well with the space-station monastery circling in space, away from the things of Earth. It had a detached air of calm about it, and yet there was a feeling of excitement here, too. It was possible, of course, that he was imagining it, for he was very excited himself.

'Do you think they know what he's up to? Or is he just making use of their habit of affording people sanctuary?' Alan asked her.

'They seem unworldly, to say the least,' she replied, shivering a little, for the room was not well heated.

The door opened and Auditor Kurt came back.

'Your boat has been fixed, my friends. I see from the registration plates that it is owned by Denholm Curtis – an important man on Earth, is he not?'

'He's my brother,' Helen said, wondering if the monk was getting at anything in particular.

Alan became aware at last that they might be in danger. If the Fireclown was here and knew they were here, too, he might decide it was risky to let them go.

'So you are Helen Curtis. Who, then, is this gentleman?'

'I'm Alan Powys.'

'Ah, yes, Simon Powys's grandson. From what I have seen of recent V-casts, Miss Curtis and Minister Powys are at odds over certain issues. Which side do you support, Mr Powys?'

'Neither,' Alan said coldly. 'Just call me a disinterested spectator.'

A peculiar expression came on the monk's face for a second. Alan could not work out what it indicated.

'I should say you were the least disinterested...' the monk mused. Then he said briskly: 'You asked earlier if you could look over the monastery. To tell you the truth we are not always willing to let strangers inspect our home, but I think it would be all right if you wanted to take a quick tour before you leave.'

Why the monk's sudden change? Was he planning to lead them into some sort of trap? Alan had to take the chance.

'Thanks a lot,' he said.

They began to walk along the curving corridor. This part, the monk told them, was reserved for the monks' cells. They turned into a narrower corridor which led them to another similar to the one they'd just left, though the curve was tighter.

'Here is what we term our clearing house.' The monk smiled, opening a door and letting them precede him through. It was a fairly large room. Several monks sat on simple chairs. They were dressed in brown dungarees. The monk in the centre was dressed, like Auditor Kurt, in a blue habit, and was chanting some sort of litany.

'How would you worry somebody?' he chanted.

'By destroying their confidence,' the other monks mumbled in reply.

'How would you make somebody happy?'

'By casting forth their engrams,' said the monks in unison.

'How would you help somebody?'

'Teach them to be clear.'

'By the Spirit of the Eight Dynamics,' intoned the blue-clad monk, 'I command thee to cast forth thy engrams forthwith!'

The monks seemed to freeze, concentrating intently. Above them, behind the monk in the blue habit, a weird machine whirred and buzzed, dials swinging around strangely marked faces, lights flashing.

Alan said respectfully: 'What are they doing?'

'They are attempting to learn the ultimate secret of the Great Triangle,' Auditor Kurt whispered.

'Ah,' Alan nodded intelligently.

They left this room and entered another. Here a great screen was blank and there were comfortable chairs scattered around before it.

'Sit down,' said Kurt. 'We are expecting a special event, today.'

Alan and Helen sat down and watched the screen.

They fidgeted for over half an hour as nothing happened, and Kurt continued to watch the screen impassively, not looking at them.

Alan's sense of danger was heightened and he had a feeling the monk was deliberately keeping them in suspense.

Then, all at once, big letters began to form on the screen until a whole sentence was emblazoned there.

ANOTHER BROTHER CLEAR! said the message. It meant nothing to either of them.

Alan turned to the monk, half-suspicious that a trick had been played on them, but the monk was looking ecstatic and incredibly pleased.

'What does it *mean*?' Alan asked desperately.

'What it says – the hampering engrams have been exorcised from one of our brothers. He is now a clear and ready to become a Brother Auditor, as I am. It is a time for rejoicing in the monastery when this comes about.'

Alan scratched his head and looked at Helen, who was equally perplexed.

'Well,' beamed thin-faced Auditor Kurt, 'now you have seen a little of our monastery.'

Half-convinced that he was the victim of a practical joke, Alan nodded mutely. He was no nearer to finding out if the Fireclown was here, although perhaps a check on the *Pi-meson* when they got back to Earth would help them.

'Thank you for showing us,' Helen said brightly. She, too, was obviously uncertain of what to do next.

'Oh –' the monk seemed to remember something – 'there is one other thing I should like to show you before you leave. Will you follow me?'

They walked until they were close to the centre of the space-wheel and came to a small door in the curved wall of Central Control. Auditor Kurt ordered it open. It hissed back and they stepped through.

'Good afternoon, Mr Powys,' said the Fireclown amiably.

Chapter Nine

'SO YOU DID come here,' Helen blurted out.
      'I have no idea how you deduced it.' He grinned. 'But I
must praise your intelligence. I hope no-one else on Earth thinks
as you do.'

Alan kept silent. They would be safer if they didn't tell the Fireclown how they had worked out his hiding place. He looked
around. Corso and the woman were also there, lounging in their
seats and staring amusedly at the rest.

He felt dwarfed by the Fireclown's bulk, not only physically – the
man stood at least six foot six – but also psychologically. He could
only stare stupidly, unable to say anything. Yet it was peculiar. Now
that they were face to face he did not feel afraid any longer. The
man's strange magnetism was tangible, and once again he found
himself liking the Fireclown, unable to believe that he had committed an act of mass murder and plotted to blow up the Earth.

'So you are Alan Powys,' mused the Fireclown, as if the name
had some special meaning. His face was still heavily painted, with
wide lips and exaggerated eyes, but Alan could make out the features under the paint a little clearer. They seemed thoughtful.

'And why are you here, anyway?' Corso said, moving his repulsive red and glinting body in the chair.

'To ask questions,' Helen said. She was pale and Alan could
understand why – the skinless man took a lot of getting used to.

'Questions!' The clown's body moved in a great shrug. He
turned his back on them and paced towards his seated friends.
'Questions! By the solar firmament! What questions can I answer?'

'They are simple – and demand only simple replies, if you are
truthful with us.'

The Fireclown whirled round and laughed richly. 'I never lie.
Didn't you know that? I never lie!'

'But perhaps you mislead,' Alan said quietly. 'May I sit down?'

'Of course.'

They both sat down.

'We want to know if you planned to blow up the world,' Helen said with a trace of nervousness in her voice.

'Why should I? I wanted to save it, not hurt it.'

'You did a good job with the fire which swept Switzerland,' Alan retorted.

'Am I to blame for that? I warned them not to tamper.'

'Are you trying to tell us you weren't responsible for that fire?' Alan said grimly.

'I've been watching the V-casts. I'm aware of what's being said of me now. They are fickle, those people. If they had really listened to me this would not have happened. But nobody listened properly.'

'I agree with that.' Alan nodded. 'I saw them – they were using you as a means of rousing their own latent emotions. But you should have known what you were doing and stopped!'

'I never know what I am doing. I am...' The Fireclown paused and glared at him. 'I was *not* responsible for the fire. Not directly, at any rate. Some of those policemen must have tampered with my fire-machines. They are very delicate. I have been experimenting with means of controlling chemical and atomic fire. I produced that little artificial sun and could have produced more if I had not been interrupted by those meddlers.'

'Why are you experimenting with fire? What's your purpose?' Helen leaned forward in her chair.

'Why? I have no reasons. I am the Fireclown. I have no purpose save to exist as the Fireclown. You do me too much honour, Miss Curtis, to expect action and plans from me. For a time I spoke to the people in Switzerland. Now that's over I shall do something else.' He roared with laughter again, his grotesque body shaking.

'If you have no plans, no thought for the future, then why did you buy P-bombs from the arms dealers?'

'I know nothing of bombs or dealers! I had no inkling that those bombs were in my cavern!'

Either he was blinded by the Fireclown's overpowering presence or the man was telling the truth, Alan felt. He seemed to have a lusty disregard for all the things that concerned Helen and himself. He did not seem to exist in the time and space that Alan shared with the rest of the human race, seemed to tower over it, observing it with complete and amused detachment. But how far could he trust this impression? Alan wondered. Perhaps the Fireclown was the best actor in the world.

'You must know something of what's happening!' Helen exclaimed. 'Your appearance at a time of acute crisis in society's development could not be mere coincidence.'

'Society has had crises before, young lady.' Again he shrugged. 'It will have others. Crises are good for it!'

'I thought you ingenuous, then I changed my mind. I can't make you out at all.' She sank back into the chair.

'Why should you make me out? Why should you waste time trying to analyse others when you have never bothered to look within yourself? My own argument against machines and machine-living is that it hampers man from really looking into his own being. You have to take him away from it, put him in the wilderness for a short time, before you can see that I speak truth. In my way I worship the sun, as you know. Because the sun is the most tangible of nature's workings!'

'I thought you represented a new breakthrough in ideas,' Helen said quietly. 'I thought you knew where you were going. That is why I supported you, identified myself and my party with you.'

'There is no need to seek salvation in others, young lady!' Again he became disconcertingly convulsed with that weird and enigmatic laughter.

She got up, bridling.

'Very well, I've learned my lesson. I believe you when you say you weren't planning destruction. I'm going back to Earth to tell them that!'

'I'm afraid Mr Corso here, who advises me on such matters, has suggested that you stay for a while, until I am ready to leave.'

Alan saw his logic. 'When are you leaving?' he said.

'A few days, I expect. Perhaps less.'

'You won't, of course, tell us where.' Alan smiled at the Fireclown for the first time and when the man returned his smile, grotesquely exaggerated by the paint around his lips, he felt dazzled, almost petrified with warmth and happiness. It was the Fireclown's only answer.

Why did the Fireclown have this ability to attract and hold people just as if they were moths drawn to a flame?

Auditor Kurt had left the room while they were conversing. Now he returned with another man behind him.

'A visitor for you, Fireclown.'

Both Alan and Helen turned their heads to look at the newcomer. He was a small, dark man with a moody face. A marijuana was between his lips.

'I commend you on your choice of rendezvous,' he said somewhat mockingly. His hooded eyes glanced at the others in the room, stopped for a moment on Alan and Helen. He looked questioningly at the Fireclown. 'I hope you haven't been indiscreet, my friend.'

'No,' said the Fireclown shortly. He chuckled. 'Well, Mr Blas, have you brought what I wanted?'

'Certainly. It is outside in the ship I came with. We must talk. Where?'

'Is this not private enough for you?' the Fireclown asked petulantly.

'No, it is not. I have to be over-cautious, you understand.'

The Fireclown lumbered towards the door, ducking beneath it as he made his way out. 'Corso,' he shouted from the corridor, 'you'd better come, too.'

The skinless man got up and followed Blas from the room. The door closed.

'Blas,' Helen said forlornly. 'So the Fireclown has been lying to us.'

'Who is he?'

'Suspected head of the arms syndicate.' She sighed. '*Damn!* Oh, damn the Fireclown!'

The woman, a full-bodied brunette with a sensuously generous mouth, got up from her seat.

She stared down at Alan, regarding him closely. Helen glared at her.

'And what part do *you* play in this?' she asked.

'A very ordinary one,' she said. 'The Fireclown's my lover.'

'Then your lover's a cunning liar,' Helen snorted.

'I shouldn't condemn him until you know what he's doing,' the woman said sharply.

The three of them were alone together now that Kurt had left too.

'You're disappointed, aren't you?' the woman said, looking candidly at Helen. 'You wanted the Fireclown to be some sort of saviour, pointing the direction for the world to go. Well, you're wrong. And those who think he's a destroyer are wrong also. He is simply what he is – the Fireclown. He acts according to some inner drive which I have never been able to fathom and which I don't think he understands or bothers about himself.'

'How long have you known him?' Helen asked.

'Some years. We met on Mars. My name's Cornelia Fisher.'

'I've heard of you.' Helen stared at the woman in curiosity. 'You were a famous beauty when I was quite young. You disappeared suddenly. So you went to Mars. Hardly the place for a woman like you, was it? You must be over forty but you don't look thirty.'

Cornelia Fisher smiled. 'Thanks to the Fireclown, I suppose. Yes, I went to Mars. The life of a well-known "beauty", as you call me, is rather boring. I wasn't satisfied with it. I wasn't satisfied with anything. I decided that I was leading a shallow existence and thought I'd find a deeper one on Mars. Of course I was wrong. It was merely less comfortable –' she paused, seeming to think back – 'though the peace and quiet helped, and the scenery. I don't know if you've seen it since the revitalisation plan was completed but it is very beautiful now. But I never really lost my ennui until I met the Fireclown.'

'He was a Martian, then?' Alan knew there were a few families of second- and third-generation colonists responsible for working on the revitalisation project.

'No. He came to Mars after a spaceship accident. He's from Earth originally. But I don't know much more about him than you do. Once you've been with the Fireclown for a short time, you learn that it doesn't matter who he is or what he does – he's just the Fireclown, and that's enough. It's enough for him, I think, too, though there are strange currents running beneath that grease-paint. Whether he's in control of them or not, I couldn't say.'

'His connection with Blas seems to disprove part of what you've said.' Alan spoke levelly, unable to decide what to think now.

'I honestly don't know what he and Blas are doing.' Cornelia Fisher folded her arms and walked towards her handbag which lay on the chair she'd vacated. She opened it and took out a packet of cigarettes. Alan tried to look unconcerned but he had never seen a nicotine addict before. She offered them defiantly. They both refused, with rapid shakes of their heads. She lit one and inhaled the smoke greedily. 'I'd swear he's not buying arms. Why should he? He has no plans of the kind Earth condemns him for having.'

'Maybe he doesn't tell you everything,' Helen suggested.

'Maybe he doesn't tell me anything because he hasn't got anything to tell me. I don't know.'

Alan went to the door and tested it. It was shut firmly.

'Judging by the evidence,' he said, 'I can only suppose that the accusations made by my grandfather against the Fireclown are basically correct. Those P-bombs were part of the arms syndicate's stock – and we have seen that the Fireclown already knows Blas, who you say, Helen, is the head of the syndicate.'

'It's never been proved, of course,' she said. 'But I'm pretty sure I'm right.'

'Then the world *is* in danger. I wonder if the Fireclown would listen to reason.'

'His kind of reason is different from ours,' said Cornelia Fisher.

'If I see him again, I'll try. He's too good to get mixed up in this sordid business. He has a tremendous personality – he could use his talents to...' Alan's voice trailed off. What could the Fireclown use his talents for?

Cornelia Fisher raised her eyebrows. 'His talents to do what? What does safe little Terra want with men of talent and vision? Society doesn't need them any more.'

'That's a foolish thing to say.' Helen was angry. 'A complex society like ours needs expert government and leaders more than ever before. We emerged from muddle and disorder over a hundred years ago. We're progressing in a definite direction now. We know what we want to do, and if Blas and his friends don't spoil it with their plots and schemings we'll do it eventually. The only argument today is *how*. Planned progress. It was a dream for ages and now it's a reality. Until this arms trouble blew up there were no random factors. We had turned politics into an exact science, at long last.'

'Random factors have a habit of emerging sooner or later,' Alan pointed out. 'If it wasn't the nuclear stockpiles it would have been something else. And those random factors, if they don't throw us too far out of gear, are what we need to stop us getting complacent and sterile.'

'I'd rather not be blown to smithereens,' Helen said.

'The Fireclown isn't a danger to you, I know.' Cornelia Fisher sounded as if she was less convinced than earlier.

'We'll soon know if the ARP fail to get hold of those stockpiles.' Helen's voice sounded a bit shaky. Alan went over to her and put his arm round her comfortingly.

A short time later the Fireclown returned, seemingly excited. Blas was not with him. Alan couldn't guess at Corso's expression. He could only see the red flesh of his face, looking like so much animated butcher's meat.

'Did you get some more P-bombs?' Helen asked mockingly.

The Fireclown ignored her.

Corso said: 'What are you hinting at, Miss Curtis?'

'I know Blas is head of the arms syndicate.'

'Well, that's more than we do. Blas is supplying us with materials for our ship, the *Pi-meson*, which we badly need. There has been no talk of armaments.'

'Not a very convincing lie,' Helen sneered.

Now Corso also ignored Helen. He watched the Fireclown in a way that a mother cat might watch her young – warily yet tenderly. Corso seemed to play nursemaid to the clown in some ways.

'It will take time to fit,' said the Fireclown suddenly. 'But thank God we could get them. We couldn't possibly have made them ourselves.'

His gaudy red-and-yellow costume swirled around him as he turned to grin at Alan.

'I wonder if you'd want to,' he mused mysteriously.

'Want to what?' Alan asked.

'Come for a trip in the *Pi-meson*. I think it would do you good.'

'Why me? And what kind of good?'

'You could only judge that for yourself.'

'Then you could dispose of us in deep space, is that it?' Helen said. 'We've seen too much, eh?'

The Fireclown heaved a gusty sigh. 'Do as you like, young woman. I've no axe to grind. Whatever takes place on Earth has no importance for me now. I tried to tell the people something, but it's obvious I didn't get through to them. Let the darkness sweep down and engulf your hollow kind. I care not.'

'It's no good.' Helen shook her head. 'I can't believe anything you say. Not now.'

'If you had it wouldn't have made any difference.' Corso's ghastly face grinned. 'The rest of the world lost faith in their idol, and the world hates nothing so much as an idol who turns out to have feet of clay! Not, of course, that the clown wished to be one in the first place.'

'Then why did you start that set-up on the first level? Why did he make speeches to thousands. Why did he let them adore him at his "audiences"?' Helen's voice was high, near-hysterical.

As Alan watched and listened, a mood of absolute detachment filled him. He didn't really care about the pros and cons any more. He only wondered what the Fireclown's reasons were for suggesting the trip.

'The Fireclown was originally living down there in secret. We were working on our machines. We needed help – scientists and technicians – so we asked for it, got it. But the scientists told their friends about the Fireclown. They began to ask him about things. He told them. All he did, in the final analysis, was supply an outlet for their emotional demands.'

Helen fell silent.

Alan came to a decision.

'I'd like to take that trip,' he said – 'if Helen can come, too.'

'Good!' The Fireclown's resonant voice seemed suddenly gay. 'I should like to take you. I'm glad. Yes. Glad.'

Both Alan and Helen waited for the Fireclown to add to this statement, but they were disappointed. He went and leaned against a bulkhead, his great face bent towards his chest, his whole manner abstracted.

Was he thinking of the trip? Alan wondered. Or had he simply forgotten about them now they had agreed to go?

Somehow, he felt the latter was the more likely answer.

The Fireclown seemed a peculiar mixture of idiot and intellectual. Alan decided that he was probably insane, but what this insanity might lead to – the destruction of Earth? – could not easily be assessed. He must wait. And perhaps he would learn from the trip, wherever it took them. Mars, possibly, or Ganymede.

Chapter Ten

HELEN WAS GETTING understandably restless. Five hours had passed and the Fireclown still stood in the position he had taken up against the bulkhead. Corso and Cornelia Fisher had talked sporadically with Alan, but Helen had refused to join in. Alan felt for her. She had placed all her hopes on gaining information from the Fireclown and, he guessed, she had desperately wanted him to disprove the allegations now being made against him on Earth. But, frustratingly, they were no nearer to getting an explanation; were worse confused, if anything.

If he had been studying any other individual, Alan would have suspected the Fireclown of sleeping with his eyes open. But there was no suggestion of slumber about the clown's attitude. He was, it seemed, meditating on some problem that concerned him. Possibly the nature of the problem was such that an ordinary man would see no logic or point in solving it.

The Fireclown seemed to exist in his own time-sphere, and his mind was unfathomable.

At last the grotesque giant moved.

'Now,' he rumbled, 'the *Pi-meson* will be ready. We have been lucky to find shelter with the monks, for they are probably the only men who can come close to understanding the nature of the ship, and doubtless they will have done their work by now. Come.' He moved towards the door.

Alan glanced at Helen and then at the other two. Corso and Cornelia Fisher remained where they were. Helen got up slowly. The Fireclown was already thumping up the corridor before they reached the door.

'I hope you know what you're doing,' she whispered. 'I'm afraid, Alan. What if his plan *is* to kill us?'

'Maybe it is.' He tried to sound self-possessed. 'But he could do that just as easily here as in deep space, couldn't he?'

'There are several ways of dying.' She held his hand and he noticed she was shivering. He had never realised before that anyone could be so afraid of death. Momentarily he felt a sympathy with her fears.

They followed the gaudy figure of the Fireclown until they reached the bay section.

Auditor Kurt was there.

'They have just finished,' he told the Fireclown, spinning the wheel of the manually operated airlock. 'Your equations were perfectly correct – it was we who were at fault. The field is functioning with one hundred per cent accuracy. Five of us were completely exhausted feeding it. Blas being able to supply those parts was a great stroke of luck.'

The Fireclown nodded his thanks and all three stepped through the short tunnel of the airlocks and entered a surprisingly large landing deck. Alan, who had seen the *Pi-meson* from space, wondered how it could be so big, for a considerable portion of spaceships was taken up with engines and fuel.

Touching a stud, the Fireclown closed the ship's lock. A section of the interior wall slid upwards, revealing a short flight of steps. They climbed the steps and were on a big control deck. The covered ports were extremely large, comprising more than half the area of the walls. Controls varied – some familiar, some not. And there were many scarcely functional features – rich, red plush couches and chairs, fittings of gold or brass, heavy velvet curtains of yellow and dark blue hung against the ports. It all looked bizarre and faintly archaic, reminding Alan, in a way, of his grandfather's study.

'I shall darken the room,' the Fireclown announced. 'I can operate the ship better that way. Sit where you will.'

The Fireclown did not sit down as Alan and Helen sat together in one of the comfortable couches. He stood at the controls, his huge bulk blotting out half the instruments from Alan's sight. He stretched a hand towards a switch and flicked it up. The lights dimmed slowly and then they were in cold blackness.

Helen gripped Alan's arm and he patted her knee, his mind on other things as a low whining arose from the floor.

Alan sensed tension in the Fireclown's movements heard from the darkness. He tried to analyse them but failed. He saw a screen suddenly light with bright whiteness, colour flashed and swirled and they saw a vision of space.

But against the darkness of the cosmos, the spheres which rolled on the screen, flashing by like shoals of multicoloured billiard balls, were unrecognisable as any heavenly bodies Alan had ever seen. Not asteroids by any means, not planets – they were too solid in colour and general appearance; they shone, but not with the glitter of reflected sunlight. And they passed swiftly by in hordes.

Moved by the beauty, astonished by the unexpected sight, Alan couldn't voice the questions which flooded into his mind.

In the faint light from the screen the Fireclown's silhouette could be seen in constant motion. The whining had ceased. The spheres on the screen began to jump and progress more slowly. The picture jerked and one sphere, smoky blue in colour, began to grow until the whole screen itself glowed blue. Then it seemed to burst and they flashed towards the fragments, then through them, and saw – a star.

'Sol,' commented the Fireclown.

They were getting closer and closer to the sun.

'We'll burn up!' Alan cried fearfully.

'No – the *Pi-meson* is a special ship. I've avoided any chance of us burning. See the flames!'

The flames... Alan thought that the word scarcely described the curling, writhing wonder of those shooting sheets of fire. The control deck was not noticeably warmer, yet Alan felt hot just looking.

The Fireclown was roaring his enigmatic laughter, his arm pointing at the screen.

'There,' he shouted, his voice too loud in the confines of the cabin. 'There, get used to that for a moment. Look!'

They could not help but look. Both were fascinated, held by the sight. And yet Alan felt his eyes ache and was certain he would be blinded by the brightness.

The Fireclown strode to another panel and turned a knob.

The port coverings began to rise slowly and light flowed in a searing stream into the cabin, brightening everything to an extraordinary degree.

When the ports were fully open, Alan shouted his wonder. It seemed they were in the very heart of the sun. Why weren't they made sightless by the glare? Why didn't they burn?

'This is impossible!' Alan whispered. 'We should have been destroyed in a second. What is this – an illusion of some sort? Have you hypno –?'

'Be quiet,' said the Fireclown, his shape a blob of blackness in the incredible light. 'I'll explain later – if it is possible to make you understand.'

Hushed, they let themselves be drawn out into the dancing glare.

Alan's soul seemed full for the first time, it even seemed natural that he should be here. He felt affinity with the flames. He began to identify with them, until he *was* them.

Time stopped.

Thought stopped.

Life alone remained.

Then blackness swam back. From far away he observed that his rigid body was being shaken, that a voice was bellowing in his ear.

'... you have seen! You have *seen*! Now you know. *Now* you know! Come back – there is more to see!'

Shocked, it seemed, back into his body, he opened his eyes. He could see nothing still, but felt the grip on his shoulders and knew that the Fireclown, his voice excited – perhaps insane – shouted in front of his face. 'That is why I call myself the Fireclown. I am full of the joy of the flames of life!'

'How…?' The word stumbled hoarsely from his lips.

But the Fireclown's hands left his shoulders and he heard the man screaming at Helen, shaking her also.

There could be no fear now, Alan decided. Though, earlier, he might have been perturbed by the Fireclown's ravings, he now half-ignored them, aware that there was no need to listen.

What he demanded now was an explanation.

'How could we have seen that and lived?' he shouted roughly, groping out to seize the Fireclown's tattered clothing and tug at it. '*How*?'

He heard Helen mumble. Satisfied, the Fireclown moved away from her, jerking himself free from Alan's grip.

He got up and followed the Fireclown through the blackness, touched his body again, sensing the tremendous strength in the man.

The Fireclown shook with humour again.

'Give me a moment,' he laughed. 'I have to feed the ship further directions.'

Alan heard him reach the control panel, heard him make adjustments to studs and levers, heard the now familiar whine. He groped his way back to Helen. She put her arms round him. She was crying.

'What's the matter?'

'Nothing. Really – nothing. It's just the – the emotion, I suppose.'

The lights came on.

Arms akimbo, the Fireclown stood grinning down at them.

'I see you are somewhat stunned. I had hoped to turn you mad – but you are obviously too entrenched in your own narrow "sanity" to be helped. That grieves me.'

'You promised me you would explain,' Alan reminded him shakily.

'If you could understand, I said, if you remember. I'll explain a little. I am not yet ready to tell you my full reason for bringing you with me. Now, see…' He turned and depressed a stud and a section of one port slid up to reveal normal space, with the sun flaring – still near, but not so near as to be dangerous. 'We have returned to our ordinary state for a while. Now you see the sun as any traveller would see it from this region of space. What do you think of it?'

'*Think* of it? I don't understand you.'

'Good.'

'What are you getting at?'

'How important do the conflicts taking place on Earth seem to you now?'

'I haven't…' He couldn't find the words. They were important, still. Did the Fireclown think that this experience, transcendental as it might have been, could alter his view of Earth's peril?

Impatiently, the Fireclown turned to Helen.

'Is your ambition to become President of Earth still as strong as it was, Miss Curtis?'

She nodded. 'This – vision or whatever it was – has no bearing on what are, as far as you're concerned, mundane problems relating to our society. I still want to do my best in politics. It has changed nothing. I have probably benefited from the experience. If that's the case, I shall be better equipped to deal with Earth affairs.'

The Fireclown snorted, but Alan felt Helen had never sounded so self-confident as she did now.

'I still want to know how you achieved the effect,' Alan insisted.

'Very well. Put simply, we shunted part of ourselves and part of the ship out of normal time and hovered, as it were, on its edges, unaffected by many of its rules.'

'But that's impossible. Scientists have never…'

'If it was impossible, Alan Powys, it couldn't have happened and you couldn't have experienced it. As for your scientists, they have never bothered to enquire. I discovered the means of doing this after an experience which almost killed me and certainly affected my thought processes.

'The sun almost killed me, realise that. But I bear it no malice. You and I and the ship existed in a kind of time freeze. The ship's computer has a "mind" constructed according to my own definitions – they are meaningless to the rigidly thinking scientists of Earth but they work for me because I am *the Fireclown*!

'I am unique, for I survived death by fire. And fire gave my brain life – brought alive inspiration, knowledge!' He pointed back at the sun, now dwindling behind them.

'There is the fire that gave birth to Earth and fed its denizens with vitality. Worship it – *worship it* in gratitude, for without it you would not and could not exist. *There* is truth – perhaps the sum of truth. It flames, living, and *is*; self-sufficient, careless of *why*, for *why* is a question that need not – cannot – be answered. We are fools to ask it.'

'Would you, then, deny man his intellect?' Alan asked firmly. 'For that is what your logic suggests. Should we have stayed in the caves, not using the brains which –' he shrugged – 'the sun, if you like, gave us? Not using an entire part of ourselves – the part which sets us over the animals, which enabled us to live as weaklings in a world of the strong and the savage, to speculate, to build and to *plan*? You say we should be content merely to exist – I say we should *think*. And if our existence is meaningless then our thoughts might, in time, give it meaning.'

The Fireclown shook his painted head.

'I knew you would not understand,' he said sadly.

'There is no communication between us,' Alan said. 'I am sane, you are mad.'

The Fireclown, for the first time, seemed hurt by Alan's pronouncement. Quietly, without his usual zest, he said: 'I know the truth. I know it.'

'Men down the ages have known a truth such as the one you know. You are not unique, Fireclown. Not in history.'

'I am unique, Alan Powys, for one reason if none other. I have seen the truth for myself. And you shall see it, perhaps. Did you not become absorbed into the fire of the sun? Did you not lose all niggling need for meaning therein?'

'Yes. The forces are overwhelming, I admit. But they are not everything.'

The Fireclown opened his mouth and once more bellowed with laughter. 'Then you shall see more.'

He closed the port and the room darkened.

'Where are we going?' Helen demanded grimly, antagonistically.

But the Fireclown only laughed, and laughed, and laughed, until the strange spheres began to roll across the screen again. Then he was silent.

Chapter Eleven

Hours seemed to pass and Helen dozed in Alan's arms. Alan too, was half-asleep, mesmerised by the coloured spheres on the screen.

He came fully awake as the spheres began to jerk and slow. A bright red filled the screen, divided itself into fragments.

More spheres appeared, but these were suns.

Suns. A profusion of suns as closely packed as the planets to Sol. Huge, blue suns, green, yellow and silver suns.

A thousand suns moving in stately procession around the ship.

The screens slid up from the ports and light, ever changing, flickered through the cabin.

'Where are we?' Helen gasped.

'The centre of the galaxy,' the Fireclown announced grandly.

All around them the huge discs of flame, of all colours and all possible blends of colour, spun at extraordinary speeds, passing by in an orbit about an invisible point.

Alan, once again, could not retain his self-possession. Something within him forced him to look and wonder at the incredible beauty. These were the oldest suns in the galaxy. They had lived and died and lived again for billions of years. Here was the source of life, the beginnings of everything.

Though the Fireclown would probably have denied it, the vision was – profound. It had significance of such magnitude that Alan was unable to grasp it. Philosophically, he resigned himself to never knowing what the experience implied. He felt that the Fireclown's belief of existence without significance beyond itself was preposterous, yet he could see how one could arrive at such a conclusion. He himself was forced to cling to his shredding personality. The whirling stars dwarfed him, dwarfed his ideas, dwarfed the aspirations of humanity.

'Now,' chuckled the Fireclown in his joyous insanity, 'what is Earth and all its works compared with the blazing simplicity of – *this*!'

Helen spoke with difficulty. 'They are – different,' she said. 'They are linked, because they all exist together, but they are different. This is the order of created matter. We seek an order of cognisant matter and the stars, however mighty, however beautiful, have no cognisance. They might perish at some stage. Man, because he thinks, may one day make himself immortal – not personally, perhaps, but through the continuance of his race. I think that is the difference.'

The Fireclown shrugged.

'You have wondered what is real, have you not? You have wondered that we have lost touch with the realities, we human beings; that our language is decadent and that it has produced a double-thinking mentality which no longer allows us contact with the natural facts?'

He waved his hands to take in the circling suns.

'Intelligence! It is nothing, it is unimportant, a freak thrown up by a chance combination of components. Why is intelligence so esteemed? There is no need for it. It cannot change the structure of the multiverse – it can only meddle and spoil it. *Awareness* – now, that's different. Nature is aware of itself, but that is all – it is content. Are we content? No! When I go to Earth and try to convey what I know to the people, I am conscious of entering a dream-world. They cannot understand me because they are unaware! All I do, sadly, is awaken archetypal responses in them which throws them further out, so they run around like randy pigs, destroying. Destroying, building, both acts are equally unimportant. We are at the centre of the galaxy. Here things exist. They are beautiful but their beauty has no purpose. It is *beauty* – it is enough. They are full of natural force but the force has no expression; it is force alone, and that is all it needs to be.

'Why ascribe meaning to all this? The further away from the fundamentals of life we go, the more we quest for their meaning. There *is* no meaning. It is here. It has always been here in some state. It will always be here. That is all we can ever truly know. It is all we should want to know.'

Alan shook his head, speaking vaguely at first. 'A short time ago,' he said, 'I was struck by the pettiness of political disputes, horrified by the ends to which people would go to get power – or "responsibility" as they call it – feeling that the politicians in the Solar House were expending breath on meaningless words...'

'So they were!' the Fireclown bellowed back at him approvingly.

'No.' Alan plugged on, certain he was near the truth. 'If you wished to convince me of this when you took us on this voyage, you have achieved the opposite. Admittedly, as one observes them at the time, the politicians seem to be getting nowhere, society detaches itself further and further from the kind of life its ancestors lived. Yet, seeing these suns, entering the heart of our own sun, has shown me that this stumbling progress – *unaware* gropings in the dark immensity of the universe, if you like – is as much a natural function as any other.'

Gustily, the Fireclown sighed.

'I felt I could help you, Alan Powys. I see you have fled further back into your fortress of prejudice.' He closed the port covers. 'Sit down – sleep if you wish. I am returning to the monastery.'

They berthed and entered the monastery in silence. The Fireclown seemed depressed, even worried. Had he seen that, for all his discoveries, for all his vision and vitality, he was not necessarily right? Alan wondered. There was no knowing. The Fireclown remained still the enigmatic, intellectual madman – the naïve, ingenuous, endearing figure he had been when Alan first saw him.

Auditor Kurt greeted them. 'We are looking at our weekly V-cast. Would you like to come and watch? It might interest you.'

He took them to a small room where several monks were already seated. Corso was there, too, and Cornelia Fisher. At the door the Fireclown seemed to rouse himself from his mood.

'I have things to consider,' he told them, walking away down the corridor.

They went in and sat down. The V-screen was blank. Evidently the amount of viewing allowed the monks was limited.

Corso came and sat next to them. Alan was getting used to his apparently skinless face.

'Well,' he said good-naturedly, 'did your voyage enlighten you?'

'In a way,' Alan admitted.

'But not in the way he intended, I think.' Helen smiled a trifle wistfully, as if she wished the Fireclown had convinced them.

'How did he hit on the discovery that enables him to travel so easily and to such dangerous parts?' Alan said.

'Call it inspiration,' Corso answered. 'I'm not up to understanding him, either, you know. We were co-pilots on an experimental ship years ago. Something went wrong with the ship – the steering devices locked and pushed us towards the sun. We managed, narrowly, to avoid plunging into the sun's heart and went into orbit. But we were fried. Refrigeration collapsed slowly. I suffered worse in some ways. It took my skin off, as you can see. My fellow pilot – the Fireclown to you, these days – didn't suffer so badly physically, but something happened to his mind. You'd say he was mad. I'd say he was sane in a different way from you and me. Whatever happened, he worked out the principle for the *Pi-meson* in the Martian hospital – we were rescued, quite by chance, by a very brave crew of a freighter which had gone slightly off course itself. If that hadn't happened, we'd both be dead now. We were in hospital for years. The clown pretended amnesia and I did the same. For some reason we were never contacted by Spaceflight Research.'

'How did you get the money to build the *Pi-meson*?'

'We got it from Blas, the man you accused of being an arms dealer. He thinks the ship is a super-fast vessel but otherwise ordinary enough. He supplied us with computer parts this time.'

'Where is Blas now?'

'The last I heard he had a suite at the London Dorchester.'

'The Dorchester? That's reasonable – a man could hide in the Mayfair slums and nobody would know.'

'I think you don't do Blas justice. He's an idealist. He wants progress more than anyone. He wouldn't have any part in blowing the world up. At least...' Corso paused. 'He's a funny character, but I don't think so.'

Alan was quiet for a while. Then he said:

'After that trip, I think I do believe you when you say you're not implicated in the arms dealers' plans – not knowingly, anyway. At least the Fireclown has satisfied me on that score, even if he didn't achieve his main object.' He turned to Helen. 'What about you?'

'I agree.' She nodded. 'But I'd give a lot to know Blas's motives in helping you.' She looked at Corso. 'Are you telling us everything?'

'Everything I can,' he said ambiguously.

The V-screen came to life. A news broadcast.

The newscaster bent eagerly towards the camera.

'It's fairly sure who the next President will be, folks. Simon Powys, the one man to recognise the peril we are in from the infamous Fireclown's insane plot to destroy the world, is top of this station's public opinion poll. His niece, the only strong opponent in the elections which begin next week, has dropped right down. Her violent support of the Fireclown hasn't helped a bit. Rumour circulates that Miss Curtis and Minister Powys's grandson, Alan Powys, have disappeared together. Strange that two people who were seen publicly fighting in the recent riots should have teamed up.'

Shot of Simon Powys in his home, a smug expression on his powerful old face.

Reporter: 'Minister Powys, you were the first to discover the bomb plot. How did it happen?'

Powys: 'I suspected the Fireclown from the start. I don't blame people for being duped by his talk – we're all human, after all – but a responsible politician has to look below the surface...'

Reporter (murmuring): 'And we're all very grateful.'

'I made sure that a constant check was kept on his activities,' Simon Powys continued, 'and thus was able to avert what might have been a terrible crime – the ultimate crime, one might say. Even now the threat of this man still trying to bombard the Earth from some secret hiding place is enormous. We must be wary. We must take steps to ensure his capture or, failing that, ensure our own defence.'

'Quite so. Thank you, Minister Powys.'

'Everything's calm again in Swiss City,' announced the newscaster as he faded in, 'and we're back to normal after the riots and subsequent fire which swept sixteen levels yesterday. The Fireclown's victims number over three hundred men, women – and little children. We were all duped, folks, as Minister Powys has pointed out. But we'll know better next time, won't we? The freak hysteria has died as swiftly as it blew up. But now we're watching the skies – for the search for the Fireclown seems to prove that he has left Earth and may now be hiding out on Mars or Ganymede. If he's got bombs up there, too, we must be ready for him!'

Although angered, Alan was also amused by the V-man's double-thinking ability. He, like the rest, had done a quick about-face and now Simon Powys, ex-villain and victimiser, was the hero of the hour.

But the hysteria, he realised, had not, in fact, died down. It had taken a different turn. Now there was a bomb scare. Though he hadn't planned it that way, Alan thought, Simon Powys could easily be falling into the arms syndicate's plot, for this scare was just what they needed to start trouble. As soon as he got the chance he was going to tell the police about Blas and the Dorchester – or else go there himself and confront the arms dealer.

He didn't bother to watch the V-cast but turned to Helen.

'We'd better try to get the Fireclown to let us go as soon as possible,' he said worriedly. 'There's things to be done on Earth.'

'Apart from anything else,' she pointed out, 'I've got an election to fight!'

A chuckle behind her, full-throated and full of humour, made her turn and look up at the Fireclown's gaudy bulk filling the doorway.

'You are persistent, Miss Curtis. Even a journey into the heart of the sun does nothing to change your mind. You'll be pleased to hear that we are leaving very soon and you'll be able to return to Earth. But first...' He looked directly at Alan, stared into his eyes so that Alan felt a strange thrill run through him, partly fear, partly joy. There was no doubt that the Fireclown's magnetism was something apart from his strange ideas. 'I must talk with you, Alan Powys – alone. Will you follow me?'

Alan followed. They entered a room decorated with marvellous oil paintings, all of them depicting the sun seen in different ways.

'Did you do these?' Alan was impressed as the Fireclown nodded. 'You could have put more across to the public by displaying them than with all that talking you did,' he said.

'I didn't think of it. These are private.' The Fireclown indicated a metal bench for Alan to sit on. 'No-one comes here but me. You are the first.'

'I feel honoured,' Alan said ironically. 'But why me?'

The Fireclown's huge chest heaved as he took an enormous breath. 'Because you and I have something in common,' he said.

Alan smiled, but kindly. 'I should say that's extremely unlikely judging by our earlier conversations.'

'I don't mean ideas.' The Fireclown moved about – like a caged lion. There was no other analogy to describe his restless pacing, Alan thought. 'I regret that I've been unable to convince you. I regret it deeply, for I am not normally given to regretting *anything*, you know. What happens, happens – that is all. I should have said we have *someone* in common.'

'Who?' Alan was half-dazed already, for he thought he knew what the Fireclown was going to say.

'Your mother,' grunted the Fireclown. The words took time coming out of this man, normally so verbose.

'*You are my son, Alan.*'

Chapter Twelve

'MY FATHER...' ALAN groped for words, failed, became silent. The Fireclown spread his large hands, his painted fool's face incongruous now.

'I was, in spite of anything you may have heard, much in love with your mother. We planned to marry, though Simon Powys wouldn't hear of it. I was a common space-pilot and she was Miriam Powys. That was before we could find the courage to tell him you were going to be born. We never did tell him – not together, anyway.'

'What happened?' Alan spoke harshly, his heart thumping with almost overwhelming emotion.

'I got sent on a secret project. I couldn't avoid it. I thought it would only last a couple of months but it kept me away for nearly two years. When I got back Simon Powys wouldn't let me near you – and your mother was dead. Powys said she'd died of shame. I sometimes think he shamed her into dying.' The Fireclown broke into a laugh but, unlike his earlier laughter, this was bitter and full of melancholy.

Alan stood up, his body taut.

'What's your real name? What did you do? What did my grandfather say?'

The Fireclown ceased his laughter and shrugged his great shoulders.

'My real name – Emmanuel Blumenthal – Manny Bloom to my friends...'

'And fans,' Alan said softly, remembering a book he'd had confiscated as a child. His grandfather had, meaninglessly he'd thought, taken it from him with no explanation. The book had been called *Heroes of Space*. 'Manny Bloom, test pilot of the *Tearaway*, captain of the Saturn Expedition. That was the secret project, wasn't it? Saviour of Venus Satellite Seven.'

'Co-pilot of the *Solstar*...' the Fireclown added.

'That's right – the *Solstar*, an experimental ship. It was supposed to have gone off course and crashed into the sun. You were reported dead.'

'But a Martian freighter, carrying contraband so that it dare not notify the authorities or land in an official port, rescued us.'

'Corso told me. That was ten years ago, as I remember. Why have you never contacted me? Why didn't you get custody of me when you came back from Saturn and found my mother was dead?'

'Simon Powys threatened to ruin me if I went near you. I was – heartbroken. Heartbroken – yes – but I reckoned you'd have a better chance than any I could give you.'

'I wonder,' Alan said gloomily. 'A kid would have been happy just knowing his father was Manny Bloom – Commander Manny Bloom, frontiersman of space!' The last phrase held a hint of irony.

'I wasn't like the stories, though I thought I was when younger. I loved my own legend then, had it in mind nearly all the time. I wasn't naturally brave. But people behave as other people expect them to – I acted brave.'

'And now you're the Fireclown, shouting and raving against intelligence – championing mindless consciousness with your fingerprints burned off, I suppose, and no records of who you really are. That's part of the general mystery solved, anyway. And part of my own – the main part.'

'And now you know I'm your father, what will you do?'

'What can the knowledge possibly affect?' Alan said sadly.

'Your subconscious.' The Fireclown grinned, half-enjoying a private joke against his son.

'Yes, that, I suppose.' He sighed. 'What are you going to do?'

'I have work that holds me. Soon Corso, Cornelia and I will journey out beyond the Solar System in the *Pi-meson*. There I shall conduct certain experiments on my own mind and on theirs. We shall see what good intelligence serves – and what great good, I suspect, pure consciousness achieves. Then we shall walk the roads between the worlds. Do you want to come, Alan?'

Alan deliberated. He had no place with the Fireclown. There were things to sort out on Earth. He shook his head.

'It grieves me to see you reject a gift – maybe the greatest gift in the multiverse!'

'It is not a gift that suits my taste – Father.'

'So be it,' the Fireclown sighed.

The *Solar Bird* soared down into Earth's atmosphere and streaked across oceans and continents before Helen switched on its braking jets and plunged into Hamburg spaceport.

The berth was ready for her and she steered into it. The water drained from the interior chamber.

Alan preceded her out of the airlock.

As he stepped into the chamber, a man entered through the other door.

'My God, Powys, where've you been?' It was Denholm Curtis, a mixture of worry and anger on his face.

Alan didn't answer immediately but turned to help Helen out of the ship. He didn't need the pause since he had already worked out his answer.

'We've been to see my father.'

'Your father! I didn't know you...'

'I only found out who he was recently.'

'I see. Well...' Curtis was nonplussed. 'I wish you and Helen had told me.'

'Sorry. We had to leave in a hurry. Your ship's perfectly all right.'

'The ship's not important – it was you and Helen...' Curtis pursed his lips. 'Anyway, I'm glad that's all it was. What with the threat of the Fireclown making an attack and everything, I thought you might have been kidnapped or killed.' He smiled at his sister, who didn't respond. Helen had been silent for most of the trip. 'But rumours about the pair of you are rife. Scandal won't do either of you any good – least of all Helen. Uncle Simon's popularity is rising incredibly. Overnight he's become the dominant man in Solar politics. You've got a tough fight on – if you still *intend* to fight.'

'More than ever,' Helen said quietly.

'I've got a car upstairs. Want to come back with me?'

'Thanks,' they said.

As her brother lifted his car into the pale Hamburg sky Helen said to him: 'What do you think of this Fireclown scare, Denholm?'

'It's more than a scare,' he said. 'It's a reality. How can we be sure he hasn't planted bombs all over the world – bombs he can detonate from space?'

Alan felt depressed. If Denholm Curtis, who rebelled habitually against any accepted theory or dogma, was convinced of the Fireclown's guilt then there was little chance of convincing anyone else to the contrary.

'But do you realise, Denholm,' he said, 'that we have only the word of one man – Simon Powys – and circumstantial evidence to go on? What if the Fireclown isn't guilty?'

'The concept's too remote for me, I'm afraid,' Denholm said with a curious glance at Alan. 'I didn't think anyone doubted the Fireclown had planned to detonate his cache. There were enough bombs there to blow the world apart.'

'I doubt if he planned anything,' Helen said.

'So do I.' Alan nodded.

Denholm looked surprised. 'I can understand you being uncertain, Helen, after your support of the Fireclown. It must be hard to find out you've been wrong all the way down the line. But you, Alan – what makes you think there could be a mistake?'

'There's the one big reason – that all the evidence against the Fireclown is circumstantial. He might not have known about the bombs, he might not have been responsible for the holocaust that swept the levels. He might not, in fact, have had any plan to destroy anything at all. We haven't captured him yet, we haven't brought him to trial – but we've all automatically judged him guilty. I want to see my grandfather – he's the man who has convinced the world that the Fireclown is a criminal!'

Curtis was thoughtful. 'I never thought I'd get caught up in hysteria,' he said. 'But, although I'm fairly sure the Fireclown is guilty, I admit there's a possibility of his being innocent. If we could prove him *innocent*, Alan, the war scare would be over. I'm already perturbed about that. You know the government has been approached by the arms syndicate?' This last remark to Helen.

'It's logical.' Helen nodded. 'And we've also considered the chance that this whole thing has been engineered by the dealers – not the clown.'

'That crossed my mind, too, at first,' Denholm agreed. 'But it seems too fantastic.'

'Let's go and have this out with the Man of the Moment,' Alan suggested. 'Can you take us to Grandfather's apartment, Denholm?'

'Take you? I'll come with you.'

As the trio entered Simon Powys's apartment, they were greeted by Junnar.

'Glad to see you're both all right,' he said to Alan and Helen. 'Minister Powys is in conference with the President, Chief Sandai, Minister Petrovich and others.'

'What's it about?' asked Alan, unwilling to be put off.

'The Fireclown situation.'

'So that's what they're calling it now!' Alan said with a faint smile. 'You'd better disturb them, Junnar. Tell them we've got some fresh information for them.'

'Is it important, sir?'

'Yes!' Helen and Alan said in unison.

Junnar took them into the sitting room, where they waited impatiently for a few moments before he came back, nodding affirmatively.

They entered Simon Powys's study. The most powerful politicians in the Solar System sat there – Powys, Benjosef, gloomy-faced Petrovich, Minister in the Event of Defence, hard-featured Gregorius, Minister of Justice, smooth-skinned, red-cheeked Falkoner, Minister of Martian Affairs, and tiny, delicate Madame Ch'u, Minister of Ganymedian Affairs. Beside the mantelpiece, standing relaxed and looking bored, was a man Alan didn't recognise. His eyes were at once amiable and deadly.

Simon Powys said harshly: 'Well, Alan, I hope you've got an explanation for your disappearance. Where have you been?'

'To see the Fireclown.' Alan's voice was calm.

'But you said...' Denholm Curtis broke in.

'I had to tell you something, Denholm. That was before I decided to come here.'

'The Fireclown! You know his whereabouts?' Powys glanced at the tall man by the mantelpiece. 'Why didn't you tell us immediately you knew?'

'I didn't know for certain until I found him.'

'Where is he?' Powys turned to address the tall man. 'Iopedes, be ready to get after him!'

'I met him in space,' Alan said carefully. 'We went aboard his spaceship. He won't be in the same region of space now. He wouldn't let us go until he'd moved on.'

'Damn!' Simon Powys got up. 'We've got every ship of the three planets combing space for him and you discovered him by chance. Did you learn anything?'

'Yes.' Somewhere, in the last few actionful days, Alan had found strength. He was in perfect control of himself. He addressed the entire group, ignoring his fuming grandfather.

'I believe the Fireclown to be innocent of any deliberate act of violence,' he announced calmly.

'You'll have to substantiate that, Mr Powys,' purred Madame Ch'u, looking at him quizzically.

'How do you know?' Simon Powys strode over to his grandson and gripped his arm painfully.

'I know because I spent some hours in the Fireclown's company and he told me he had nothing to do with the bomb plot or the burning of the levels.'

'That's all?' Powys's fingers tightened on Alan's arm.

'That's all I needed,' Alan said, and then in a voice which only his grandfather could hear: 'Let go of my arm, Grandfather. It hurts.'

Simon Powys glared at him and released his grip. 'Don't tell me you're still being gulled by this monster! Helen – you saw him, too – what did you think?'

'I agree with Alan. He says the policemen tampered with his delicate flame-machines and that's what caused the holocaust. He says he knew nothing of the bombs. I suspect they were planted on him by the arms syndicate – in order to start the scare which you're now helping to foster.'

'In short,' Alan said, 'I think this whole business has been engineered by the syndicate.'

The room was silent.

Alan pressed his point. 'I think you've all been blinded by the apparent discovery that the Fireclown wasn't what he at first seemed. Now you've turned completely against him – you believe him capable of any crime!'

'Mr Powys –' Petrovich spoke with an air of assumed patience – 'we are the government of the Solar System. We are not in the habit of jumping to ill-considered and emotional conclusions.'

'Then you're not human,' Alan said sharply. 'Everyone can make mistakes, Minister Petrovich – especially in a heated atmosphere like this.'

Petrovich smiled patronisingly. 'We have considered the place of the arms syndicate in this business. We are sure they are taking advantage of the situation – but we are convinced that they did not "engineer it", as you say.'

Simon Powys roared: 'My grandson's an immature fool! He has no understanding of politics or anything else. When the Fireclown lisps his innocence he believes him without question. Helen Curtis is just as bad. Both of them, to my own knowledge, were on the Fireclown's side from the start. Now they refuse to see the facts!'

The tall man, Iopedes, began to walk towards the door. Simon Powys called after him. 'Iopedes – where are you going?'

'The young people said the Fireclown had left the area of space he was originally occupying. That could indicate he's gone to Mars or Ganymede. It's a better lead than we had, at any rate.' Iopedes left.

'Who's he?' Alan said.

'Nick Iopedes, the ARP's top agent. He's been commissioned to bring the Fireclown to justice – by any means he has to employ.'

'You're turning the system into a police state!' Helen said angrily.

'There's a state of emergency existing!' Simon Powys said coldly. 'The world – perhaps the Solar System – is threatened with destruction.'

'In your mind and in the minds of those you've managed to convince!' Alan retaliated. 'Have any bombs exploded? Has any threat been made?'

'No.' This was Benjosef, who had hitherto seemed detached from the argument taking place around him.

'And the arms syndicate has approached you with a bargain, I hear.' Alan laughed sharply.

'That is true,' Benjosef agreed. Quite obviously, he was no longer in control of his cabinet. Simon Powys dominated it now, as if he had already superseded Benjosef. The old man seemed to accept the situation fatalistically.

'So there's your answer – the syndicate plant the bombs and start the scare. Then they sell you more bombs to "defend" yourselves against a non-existent menace! Then what? Another scare – another move by the syndicate – until the seeds of war have been thoroughly planted. Everybody's armed to the teeth and the possibility of conflict between the planets is increased!'

'Oh, that's very pat,' Simon Powys sneered. 'But it doesn't fit the evidence. You know what you've done? You've been to see the Fireclown and instead of gaining information which could help us capture him, you've listened to his sweet protestations of innocence and thrown away a chance to help save the world!'

'Really?' Alan said in mock surprise. 'Well, I disagree. It seems to me that *you* are taking the world to the brink of destruction, Grandfather, by your blind hatred of the Fireclown.'

'Leave, Alan!' Simon Powys's voice shook with anger. The assembled ministers look disturbed and embarrassed by what was, in the main, a family row.

Alan turned and walked out of the door, Helen following him. Denholm Curtis remained in the room, a frown on his face.

Outside, Helen smiled faintly. 'Well, we seem to have antagonised everyone, don't we?'

'I'm *sure* we're right!' Alan said. 'I'm certain of it, Helen. That trip the Fireclown took us on convinced me. He's too interested in his weird philosophising to be capable of any plots against the system.'

Helen took his arm.

'It's our opinion against theirs, I'm afraid.'

'We've got to do something about convincing the ordinary people,' Alan said as they descended the steps to the ground floor. 'This is still a democracy, and if enough people protest they can be ousted from power and a more sane and rational party can solve the situation better.'

'They're sane and reasonable enough,' she pointed out. 'They just don't happen to believe in the Fireclown's innocence.'

'Then what are we going to do about it?'

She looked up at him. 'What do you expect? I'm still in the running for President, Alan. I'm still leader of my party. We're going to try and win the election.'

Chapter Thirteen

DIRECTOR CARSON, HEAD of City Administration, looked hard at Alan and nodded understandingly.

'It would be best if you resigned,' he agreed. 'Though, as far as it goes, you're the ablest assistant I've ever had, Alan. But with things as they are and with you outspoken against Simon Powys and for the Fireclown, I doubt if the City Council would want you to stay on, anyway.'

'Then we're both in agreement,' Alan said. 'I'll leave right away, if that's all right with you, sir.'

'We'll manage. Your leave is due soon, anyway. We'll settle up your back-pay and send it to you.'

They shook hands. They liked one another and it was obvious that Carson regretted Alan's leaving C.A. But he'd been right.

'What are you going to do now?' Carson said as Alan picked up his briefcase.

'I've got another job. I'm Helen Curtis's personal assistant for the Presidential campaign.'

'You're going to need a great deal of luck, then?'

'A great deal,' Alan agreed. 'Goodbye, sir.'

The Radical Liberal Movement's Campaign Committee met at its headquarters. They sat round a long table in the large, well-lighted room. One of the walls comprised a huge V-screen – a usual feature of the windowless apartments in the City of Switzerland.

Helen sat at the head of the table with Alan on her right, Jordan Kalpis, her campaign organiser, on her left. The two heads of the RLM's Press and Information Department sat near her – Horace Wallace, handsome and blank-faced, Andy Curry, small, freckled, and shifty-eyed – both Scots who had hardly seen Scotland and were yet anachronisms in their pride for their country. National feeling hardly existed these days.

Also at the table were Publicity Chief Mildred Brecht, an angular woman; Vernikoff, Head of Publications and Pamphlets; Sabah, Director of Research, both fat men with unremarkable faces.

Helen said: 'Although you've all advised me against it, I intend to conduct my campaign on these lines. One –' she read off a sheet of paper before her – 'an insistence that other steps be taken to apprehend whoever was responsible for storing those bombs on the first level. Although we'll agree it's possible that the Fireclown was responsible, we must also pursue different lines of investigation, in case he was not. That covers us – the present policy of concentrating on the pre-judged Fireclown does not.'

'That's reasonable,' Sabah murmured. 'Unless someone reveals that you personally believe the Fireclown innocent.'

'Two –' Helen ignored him – 'that more money must be spent on interstellar space-flight research – we are becoming unadventurous in our outlook.'

'That's a good one.' Mildred Brecht nodded.

'It fits our "forward-looking" image.' Curry nodded, too.

'Three, tax concessions to Mars and Ganymede settlers. This will act as an incentive to colonisers. Fourth, price control on sea-farm produce. Fifth, steps must be taken to relocate certain spaceports now occupying parts of the seabed suitable for cultivation...' The list was long and contained many other reforms of a minor nature. There were several short discussions on the exact terms to use for publicising her proposed policy. Then the means of presenting them.

Mildred Brecht had some suggestions: 'I suggest we can stick to old-fashioned handbills for the main policy outline. Worldwide distribution to every home on Earth. Large-size power-posters for display on Earth and the colonies...' She outlined several more means of publicising the campaign.

Jordan Kalpis, a swarthy, black-haired man with prominent facial bones and pale blue eyes, interrupted Mildred Brecht.

'I think, on the whole, we're agreed already on the main points of Miss Curtis's policy as well as the means of publicising them.

We have a sound image, on the whole, and some nice, clear publicity material. The only troublesome issue is that of the Fireclown. I would like to suggest, again, that we drop it – ignore it. Already we have lost a lot of headway by the swing in public opinion from support to condemnation of the Fireclown. We can't afford to lose more.'

'No,' Helen said firmly. 'I intend to make the Fireclown situation one of my main platform points. I am certain we shall soon find evidence of the Fireclown's innocence. If that happens, I shall be proved right. Powys proved the hysteric he seems to be, and public faith in me should be restored.'

'It's too much of a gamble!' Kalpis insisted.

'We've got to gamble now,' Helen said. 'We haven't a chance of winning otherwise.'

Kalpis sighed: 'Very well,' and lapsed into silence.

Alan said: 'When's the first public speech due to be made?'

'Tomorrow.' Helen fidgeted with the papers before her. 'It's at the City Hall and should be well-attended.'

The huge area of City Hall was packed. Every seat was occupied, every inch of standing space crammed to capacity. On the wide platform sat Alan, Helen, Wallace and Curry, staring out at the rows of heads that gaped at them from three sides. Behind them on a great screen pictures were flashed – pictures of Helen talking to members of the public, pictures of Helen with her parents, pictures of Helen visiting hospitals, old people's homes, orphanages. A commentary accompanied the pictures, glowingly praising her virtues. As it finished, Alan got up and addressed the crowd.

'Fellow citizens of the Solar System, in just a few weeks from now you will have voted for the person you want to be President. What will you look for in your President? Intelligence, warmth of heart, capability. These are the basic essentials. But you will want more – you will want someone who is going to lead the Solar nation towards greater freedom, greater prosperity – and a more adventurous life. Such a woman is Helen Curtis...' Unused to this sort of speech-making, Alan found he was quite enjoying himself. Enough of the Powys blood flowed in him, he decided, after all.

He continued in this vein for a quarter of an hour and then presented Helen to the crowd. The applause was not as great as it might have been, but it was satisfactory.

Helen's platform manner was superb. At once alert and confident, she combined femininity with firmness, speaking calmly and with utmost assurance.

She outlined her policy. At this stage she ignored the Fireclown issue entirely, concentrating her attack on the sterile Solrefs and their Presidential candidate Simon Powys. She ignored hecklers and spoke with wit and zest.

When she finished she was applauded and Alan Powys got up, raising his arms for silence.

'Now that you have heard Miss Curtis's precise and far-thinking policy,' he said, 'are there any questions which you would like to ask her?'

Dotted around the auditorium were special stands where the questioner could go and be heard throughout the hall. Each stand had a large red beacon on it. Beacons began to flash everywhere. Alan selected the nearest.

'Number seven,' he said, giving the number of the stand.

'I should like to ask Miss Curtis how she intends to work out the controlled price of sea-farm produce,' said a woman.

Helen went back to the centre of the platform.

'We shall decide the price by assessing cost of production, a fair profit margin, and so on.'

'This will result in lower prices, will it?' the woman asked.

'Certainly.'

The red light went out. Alan called another number.

'What steps does Miss Curtis intend to take towards the present ban on tobacco production?'

'None,' Helen said firmly. 'There are two reasons for keeping the ban. The first is that nicotine is harmful to health. The second is that land previously used for tobacco is now producing cereals and other food produce. Marijuana, on the other hand, is not nearly so habit-forming, has fewer smokers and can be produced with less wastage of land.'

There were several more questions of the same nature, a little heckling, and then Alan called out again: 'Number seventy-nine.'

'Miss Curtis was an ardent supporter of the Fireclown before it was discovered that he was a criminal. Now it's feared that the Fireclown intends to bombard Earth from space, or else detonate already planted bombs. What does she intend to do about this?'

Helen glanced at Alan. He smiled at her encouragingly.

'We are not certain that the Fireclown is guilty of the crimes he has been accused of,' she said.

'He's guilty all right!' someone shouted. A hundred voices agreed.

'We cannot condemn him out of hand,' she went on firmly. 'We have no evidence of a plot to attack or destroy the planet.'

'What would you do if he *was* guilty,' shouted the original speaker – 'sit back and wait?'

Helen had to shout to be heard over the rising noise of the crowd.

'I think that the Fireclown was framed by unscrupulous men who want a war scare,' she insisted. 'I believe we should follow other lines of investigation. Catch the Fireclown, by all means, and bring him to trial if necessary. But meanwhile we should be considering other possibilities as to how the bombs got on the first level!'

'My parents were killed on the eleventh level!' This was someone shouting from another speaking box. 'I don't want the same thing to happen to my kids!'

'It's sure to unless we look at the situation logically,' Helen retaliated.

'Fireclown-lover!' someone screamed. The phrase was taken up in other parts of the hall.

'This is madness, Alan.' She looked at him as if asking for his advice. 'I didn't expect quite so much hysteria.'

'Keep plugging,' he said. 'It's all you can do. Answer them back!'

'Powys for President! Powys for President!' This from the very back of the hall.

'Powys for insanity!' she cried. 'The insanity which some of you are exhibiting tonight. Blind fear of this kind will get you nowhere. I offer you *sanity!*'

'*Madness, more likely!*'

'If you listened to me like sensible adults instead of shouting and screaming, I'd tell you what I mean.' Helen stood, her arms folded, waiting for the noise to die down.

Alan went and placed himself beside her.

'Give her a chance!' he roared. 'Give Miss Curtis a chance!'

When finally the noise had abated somewhat, Helen continued:

'I have seen the Fireclown since the holocaust. He told me that policemen tampered with his machines and caused the fire. He had nothing to do with it!'

'Then he was lying!'

'Calm down!' she begged. 'Listen to me!'

'We listened to the Fireclown's lies for too long. Why listen to yours?'

'The Fireclown told you no lies. You interpreted what he said so that it meant what you wanted it to mean. Now you're doing the same to me! The Fireclown is *innocent!*'

Alan whispered. 'Don't go too far, Helen. You've said enough.'

She must have realised that she had overshot her mark. She had been carried away by the heat of the argument, had admitted she thought the Fireclown innocent. Alan could imagine what the V-casts would say in the morning.

'Are there any other questions?' he called. But his voice was drowned by the angry roar of the crowd.

'Not exactly a successful evening,' he said as he took her home. They had had to wait for hours before the crowd dispersed.

She was depressed. She said nothing.

'What's the next stage in the campaign?' he asked.

'Next stage? Is it worth it, Alan? I'm getting nowhere. I've never known such wild hysteria. I thought we got rid of all that a century ago.'

'It takes longer than a hundred years to educate people to listen to reason when someone tells them their lives are liable to be snuffed out in an instant.'

'I suppose so. But what are we going to do? I didn't expect such a strong reaction. I didn't intend to say that I thought the Fireclown was innocent. I knew that was going too far, that they couldn't take direct opposition to what they now believe. But I got so angry.'

'It's just unfortunate,' he said comfortingly, though inwardly he was slightly annoyed that she had lost her self-control at the last minute. 'And it's early days yet. Maybe, by the time the campaign's over, we'll have more people on our side.'

'Maybe they'll just ignore us,' she said tiredly as they entered her apartment.

'No, I don't think that. We're nothing if not controversial!'

Next day, the RLM Political Headquarters received a deputation.

Two men and two women. The men were both thin and of medium height. One of them, the first to advance into the front office and confront Alan, who had elected to deal with them, was sandy-haired, with a prominent adam's apple and a nervous tic. The other was less remarkable, with brown hair and a mild face in which two fanatical eyes gleamed. The women might have been pretty if they had dressed less dowdily and paid more attention to their hair and make-up. In a word, they were frumps.

The taller woman carried a neat banner which read: THE END OF THE WORLD DRAWS SLOWLY NIGH. LATTER-DAY ADVENTISTS SAY 'NO' TO FALSE GODS. STOP THE FIRECLOWN.

Alan knew what they represented. And he knew of the leader, had seen his face in innumerable broadcasts.

'Good morning, Elder Smod,' he said brightly. 'What can we do for you?'

'We have come as the voice of the Latter-Day Adventists to denounce you,' Elder Smod said sonorously. The Latter-Day Adventists were now the strongest and only influential religious body in existence today, and their ranks were comprised so obviously of bewildered halfwits and pious paranoiacs that public and politicians alike did not pay them the attention that such a large movement would otherwise merit in a democracy. However, they could be a nuisance. And the main nuisance was Elder Smod, second in command to senile Chief Elder Bevis, who was often observed to have fallen asleep during one of his own speeches.

'And why should you wish to denounce me?' Alan raised his eyebrows.

'We've come to denounce the Radical Liberal Movement for its outrageous support of this spawn of Satan, the Fireclown!' said one of the frumps in a surprisingly clear and musical voice.

'But what have the Latter-Day Adventists to do with the Fire-clown?' Alan asked in surprise.

'Young man, we oppose the supporters of Satan.'

'I'm sure you do. But I still don't see what connection...'

'Satan seeks to destroy the world by fire before the good Lord has his chance. We cannot tolerate that!'

Alan remembered now that the original twentieth-century sect had announced that they were the only ones who would be saved when the world was destroyed by fire. They had been a little chary of announcing the date but, egged on by slightly disenchanted supporters, they had finally given an exact date for the end of the world – AD 2000, claiming the Third Millennium would contain only the faithful. Sadly, when the Third Millennium dawned, it contained fewer of the faithful than before, since many had not wholly accepted the fact pointed out to them by the movement's elders, that the Bible had earlier been misread as to the date of Christ's birth. (A speedy and splendid juggling with the Christian, Jewish and Moslem calendars had taken place on 1 January, AD 2000). But, in spite of the discredit, the movement had grown again with the invention of a slightly altered interpretation – i.e., that the world would not perish in a sudden holocaust but that it would begin – and *had* begun – to perish from the year 2000 – giving an almost infinite amount of time for the process to take place. However, the coming of the Fireclown scare, with its talk of destruction, had evidently thrown them out again!

'But why, exactly, have you come to us?' Alan demanded.

'To ask you to side with the righteous against the Fireclown. We were astonished to see that there were still foolish sinners on Earth who could believe him innocent! So we came – to show you the True Way.'

'Thank you,' said Alan, 'but all I say – and I cannot speak for the RLM as a whole – is that the Fireclown is *not* likely to destroy the world by fire. We have no argument.'

Elder Smod seemed a trifle nonplussed. Evidently he considered the Fireclown a sort of johnny-come-lately world-destroyer, whereas his movement had had, for some time, a monopolistic concession on the idea.

Alan decided to humour him and said gently: 'The Fireclown could be an agent for your side, couldn't he?'

'No! He is Satan's spawn. Satan,' said Smod with a morose satisfaction, 'has come amongst us in the shape of the Fireclown.'

'Satan? Yet the clown predicted a return of fire to the world unless, in your terms, the world turned its back on Mammon. And one cannot worship both...'

'A devil's trick. The Fireclown is Satan's answer to the True Word – *our* word!'

It was no good. Alan couldn't grasp his logic – if logic there was. He had to admit defeat.

'What if we don't cease our support of the Fireclown?' he asked.

'Then you will be destroyed in the flames from heaven!'

'We can't win, can we?' Alan said.

'You are like the rest of your kind,' Elder Smod sneered. 'They paid us no attention, either.'

'Who do you mean?'

'You profess not to know! Ha! Are you not one of that band who call themselves the Secret Sons of the Fireclown?'

'I didn't know there was such a group. Where are they?'

'We have already tried to dissuade them from their false worship. A deputation of our English brothers went to them yesterday, but to no avail.'

'They're in England? Where?'

'In the stinking slums of Mayfair, where they belong, of

course!' Elder Smod turned to his followers. 'Come – we have tried to save them, but they heed us not. Let us leave this gateway to Hell!'

They marched primly out.

Mayfair. Wasn't that where Blas had his hideout? Perhaps the two were connected. Perhaps this was the lead that would prove, once and for all, whether the Fireclown planned mammoth arson or whether the syndicate had framed him.

Alan hurriedly made his way into the back room where Helen and Jordan Kalpis were planning her tour.

'Helen, I think I've got a lead. I'm not sure what it is, but if I'm lucky I'll be able to get evidence to prove that we're right about the Fireclown. He's still got some supporters, I just learned, in London. I'm going there.'

'Shall I come with you?'

'No. You've got a lot of ground to make up if you're going to get near to winning this election. Stick at it – and don't lose your self-control over the Fireclown issue. I'll get back as soon as I've got some definite information.'

'Alan, it's probably dangerous. Blas and his like take pains to protect themselves.'

'I'll do the same, don't worry,' he said. He turned to Kalpis. 'Could we have a moment, Jordan?'

Jordan walked tactfully out of the room.

Alan took Helen in his arms, staring down at her face. She had a half-startled look, half-worried. 'Alan…'

'Yes?'

She shook her head, smiling. 'Look after yourself.'

'I've got to,' he said, and kissed her.

Chapter Fourteen

MAYFAIR MOULDERED.
Nowhere on the three planets was there a slum like it, and riches, not poverty, had indirectly created it.

As Alan walked up the festering streets of Park Lane, a light drizzle falling from the overcast afternoon sky, he remembered the story of how it had got like this. Mayfair was the property of one man – a man whose ambition had been to own it, who had achieved his ambition and was now near-senile – Ronald Lowry, the British financier, who refused to let the government buy him out and refused, also, to improve his property. The original residents and business houses had moved out long since, unable to stand Lowry's weird dictatorship. The homeless, and especially the criminal homeless, had moved in. Like Lowry, they weren't interested in improving the property, either. For them, it was fine as it was – a warren of huge, disused hotels, office blocks and apartment buildings. Lowry was rich – perhaps the richest man in the world – and Lowry, in spite of his senility, had power. He would not let a single government official set foot on his property and backed up his wishes by threatening to withdraw his capital from industries which, without it, would flounder and give the government unemployment problems, relocation problems and the like. Until a less cautious party came to power, Mayfair would continue to moulder, at least for as long as Lowry lived.

The scruffy, old-world architecture of the Hilton, the Dorchester and the Millennium Grande towered above Alan as he passed between them and the jungle that grew alongside Hyde Park. Hyde Park itself was public property, neat and orderly, well maintained by London's City Council, but roots had spread and shrubs had flowered, making an almost impenetrable hedge along the borders of the park.

THE WINDS OF LIMBO

Wisely, he did not head immediately for the Dorchester, where Blas was supposed to be, but went instead to a café that still bore the name of the Darlington Grill. The *spécialité de la maison* these days, however, was fish and chips – from the smell.

The majority of the men were gaudily dressed in the latest styles, but some were down at heel – not necessarily criminals, but pridies, people who refused to accept the citizens' grant which the government allowed to all who were unable to work, whether because of physical or emotional reasons. These were extreme emotional cases who, if they had not come to the official-free area of Mayfair, would have been cured by this time and rehabilitated. Mayfair, Alan thought, was indeed a strange anachronism – and a blot on the three planets. Ronald Lowry's vast financial resources had produced the only skid row now in existence!

Alan had taken the precaution of getting himself a green luminous suit and a flowing scarlet cravat which made him feel sick whenever he saw himself in a mirror. On his head was perched, at a jaunty angle, a conical cap of bright and hideous blue, edged with gold sateen.

He saw by the list chalked on a board at the end of the café that his nose hadn't lied. The only food was turbot and chips. The liquor, it seemed, was a product of a local firm – a choice between wheat, parsnip or nettle wine. He ordered a wheat wine and found it clear and good, like a full-bodied Sauternes. It was only spoiled by the disgusting aroma of illicit cigarettes, smoked by several of the nicotine addicts who lounged in what was evidently a drug-induced euphoria at the greasy tables.

Before he had left the City of Switzerland, Alan had procured one of the badges previously worn by the Fireclown's supporters – a small metal sun emblem which the disillusioned Sons of the Sun had rid themselves of when public sympathy for the Fireclown had changed to anger. He wore it inside his cap.

He looked around over the rim of his glass, hoping to see a similar emblem, but he was disappointed.

A sharp-faced little man came in and sat at Alan's table. He ordered a parsnip wine. A few drops spilled on the table as the proprietor brought it.

Alan decided that he would have to chance the possibility that the café fraternity were sufficiently angered against the Fireclown to cause trouble. He took off his hat, lining upward so that the sun emblem was visible.

The sharp-faced man was also sharp-eyed. Alan saw him stare at the badge for a moment. Then he looked at Alan, frowning. In the spilled liquor on the table he drew, with a surprisingly clean finger, a similar design.

'You're one of us, eh?' he grunted.

'Yes.'

'Fresh to Mayfair?'

'Yes.'

'You'd better come to the meeting. It's a masked meeting, naturally. We've got to protect ourselves.'

'Where do I go?'

'South Audley Street – a cellar.' The man told him the number and the time to be there. Then he ignored Alan, who finished his drink and ordered another. A little later he got up and left.

Alan could understand the need for secrecy. The police would be searching for any clue to the Fireclown's whereabouts. He wondered if this group knew. Or did they have any real contact with the Fireclown at all? Perhaps in an hour's time, at six o'clock, he would know.

At six he entered the broken-down doorway in South Audley Street and found himself in a long room that had evidently been a restaurant. Through the gloom he could make out chairs still stacked on tables. He walked over rotting carpets, through the piled furniture to the back of the place. A door led him through a filthy, dilapidated kitchen. At the end of a row of rusted stoves he saw another door. Opening it, he saw that it closed off a flight of concrete steps leading downwards. He advanced into a cellar.

About five or six masked figures were already there. One of them, stocky and languid in his movements, Alan thought he recognised.

One of the others, a woman in a red-and-yellow hood that covered her whole face, came up to him. 'Welcome, newcomer. Sit there.' She pointed to a padded chair in a shadowed corner.

From a brazier at the end of the cellar flames danced. Huge, grotesque shadows were spread along the floor and up the walls as the men and women began to come down the cellar steps and sit on the damp-smelling chairs.

'Thirty-nine, plus the newcomer – forty in all,' the stocky man said. 'Close the door and bar it.'

The stocky man went and stood by the brazier. Alan wished he could place him, but couldn't for the moment.

'We are come here,' he intoned, 'as the last loyal Sons of the Fireclown, to honour our leader and prepare for his return. We are pledged to carry out his work, even if we risk death in so doing!'

Alan realised suddenly that these people were using the Fireclown's name, just as the majority had done earlier, to support some creed or obsession of their own. The whole tone of the meeting did not fit with what he knew of the Fireclown, his father. Probably, he thought, he understood the Fireclown better than anyone – particularly since he could recognise certain traits in the Fireclown that had a milder expression in himself.

Certainly, he decided, this group was worth observing, for it might help clarify the rest of the questions that needed clarifying before he could act in an objective way.

What if the arms syndicate were operating this group for their own purposes? It was possible that they had got hold of these people who seriously wished to put the Fireclown's *outré* philosophy into practice and were making them act against the Fireclown's interests.

Then he had it. The identity of the intoning man – *Blas*!

Now, he felt, there was substance for his theory that the arms syndicate was using the Fireclown as a patsy – a fall guy to carry the can for their devious plans for world conflict. He bent forward as Blas came to the important point.

'You have each been given incendiary bombs to plant in some

of the major buildings around the globe. The burning buildings will act as beacons, heralding the return of the Fireclown with his bolts of fire for the unclean and his gift of a new world for you, the true believers. Are you all sure of what you must do?'

'Yes!' each man and woman responded.

'Now.' Blas's masked face was cocked to one side as he suddenly regarded Alan. 'The newcomer is not yet a full Son of the Fireclown. He must prove himself to us.'

Alan suddenly realised the menace in the words. He sensed, from the atmosphere in the room, that this was not normal procedure.

'Come here, my friend,' Blas said quietly. 'You must be initiated.'

There was a strong chance that Blas recognised him. But what could he do? For the moment he would have to go through with it.

He got up slowly and walked towards the fiery heat of the brazier.

'Do you worship the Flame of the Sun?' Blas asked theatrically.

'Yes,' he said, trying to keep his voice level.

'Do you see the fire as the Fire of Life?'

He nodded.

'Would you bring forth the fires of life in yourself?'

'Yes.'

'Then –' Blas pointed at the brazier – 'plunge your hand into the flames as proof that you are a brother to the Flame of the Sun!'

Ritual! If Alan needed confirmation that these people had nothing to do with the Fireclown in any real sense, he had it now. The Fireclown scorned ritual.

'No, Blas,' he said, and turned to the masked gathering. 'Don't listen to this man. I know the Fireclown – he is my father – he would not want this! He would hate you to debase yourselves as you are doing now. The Fireclown only uses fire as a symbol. He speaks of the human spirit, not –' he gestured at the brazier – 'natural fire!'

'Silence!' Blas commanded. 'You seek to disrupt our gathering! Do not listen to him, brothers!'

The Sons of the Fireclown were glancing at one another uncertainly.

Blas's voice spoke almost good-humouredly in Alan's ear. 'Really, Powys, this is nothing to you. Why do you interfere? Admit to these fools that you lied and I'll let you go. Otherwise I can probably convince them, anyway, and you'll be roasted on that thing there.'

Alan glanced at the blazing brazier, gouting flames. He shuddered. Then he leapt at it and kicked it over in Blas's direction. Blas jumped away from the burning coals, shouting something incoherent.

Alan pushed through the confused crowd and reached the door, wrenched the bar away and fled up the steps. He ran through the darkened restaurant and out into the crumbling street a few seconds ahead of his closest pursuer. He dashed down towards Grosvenor Square, an overgrown tangle of trees and shrubs. In the last of the evening light he saw the monolithic tower of the old American Embassy, fallen into decay long since.

A flight of steps led up to the broken glass doors. He climbed them hurriedly, squeezed through an aperture and saw another flight of steps leading upwards.

By the time he had reached the second floor, let his feet lead him into a maze of corridors, he no longer heard the sounds of pursuit and realised, thankfully, that he had lost them. He cursed himself for not wearing a mask. He should have guessed that Blas and the spurious Sons of the Fireclown had some connection.

And now it was almost certain that Blas, unknown to the Fireclown, was playing both ends against the middle. But he'd still have to find out more before he could prove the Fireclown's innocence.

He had only one course of action. To go to the Dorchester, where Blas had his hideout. He knew he wasn't far from Park Lane, since he had studied a map thoroughly before he left. He waited for two hours before groping his way down to a different exit from the one he'd left and stumbled through the jungle of Grosvenor Square, climbing over fallen masonry and keeping in the shadows as he walked down Grosvenor Street and into Park Lane.

He threw away his hat and reversed his jacket as an afterthought so that the reversible side showed mauve shot with yellow, hunched his shoulders to disguise his outline and hid his face as much as possible, then continued down towards the Dorchester.

Luckily, the street was almost deserted and he passed only a couple of drunks sitting against the wall of a bank, and a pretty young girl who hailed him with pretty old words. She reviled him softly in language even older when he ignored her.

Reaching the side entrance of the Dorchester, he found the door firmly locked. He continued round to the front. Lights were on in the lobby and two tough-looking men lounged outside. He couldn't get past them without them seeing him, so he walked boldly and said:

'I've come to see Mr Blas – he's expecting me. Which suite?'

'First floor,' said the guard unsuspiciously.

Alan found the lobby in surprisingly good repair. Even the elevators looked in working order, although there was a good deal of litter about. He took the stairs, reached the first floor which was in semi-darkness, and saw a light coming from under a pair of big double doors. He paused outside and strained his ear to catch the mumble of voices from within. He was sure he recognised both of them – one was probably Blas's, anyway.

The other, he realised after a moment, was the voice of Junnar, his grandfather's secretary!

He took from his pocket the squat laser-pistol he had brought with him at Helen's request and walked into the room.

'The plot,' he said with forced lightness, 'thickens. Good evening, gentlemen.'

Blas took the cigarette out of his mouth with an expression of surprise. 'Good evening, Powys,' he said amiably. 'I didn't think we'd seen the last of you. If you're not going to be impetuous we can explain everything, I think.'

'Mr Powys,' Junnar said sadly, 'you should have stayed out of this from the start. What's the gun for?'

'Self-protection,' Alan said curtly. 'And I don't need much explanation. I've had an inkling of this for some time. Grandfather put you up to planting the bombs on the Fireclown – am I right?'

Junnar's silence was answer enough. Alan nodded. 'He'd use any means to prove the Fireclown a criminal, even if it meant supplying the proof himself, in a very simple way. You got the bombs from Blas and planted them. But you bit off more than you could chew when you started this war scare. What are you up to now? Doing another deal with Blas over the arms he wants to supply the government with as a "defence" against a non-existent plot?'

'That's about it,' Blas admitted.

Alan felt physically sick. His own grandfather, head of the house of Powys, descendant of a line of strong, honest and fervently dedicated politicians, had descended to faking evidence to prove his own theory about the Fireclown. And, in consequence, he had started a wave of hysteria which he was virtually unable to control. He wondered if Simon Powys now regretted his infamy. He probably did, but it was too late.

And this was the man the public were almost bound to elect President.

'You bloody, treacherous pigs!' he said.

'You'd have to prove all this,' Blas said softly, his self-assurance still apparently maintained.

Alan was still in a quandary. All his life the concept of clan loyalty to the Powyses had been drummed into him. It was hard to shake it off. Could he betray his own grandfather, who in a peculiar way he still loved, at the expense of the father responsible for his bastardy?

Slowly, standing there with the laser-gun in his hand, its unfamiliar grip sticky with sweat, he came unwillingly to a decision.

He waved the gun towards the door. 'After you,' he said.

'Where are we going?' Junnar asked nervously.

'The City of Switzerland,' Alan told them. 'And just remember what a laser can do. I could slice you both in two in a moment. It's going in my pocket, and my hand's going to be on it all the way.'

'You're rather a melodramatic young man,' Blas said resignedly as he walked towards the door.

Chapter Fifteen

UNDER ALAN'S DIRECTION, Junnar brought the car down on the roof of the Powys's apartment block.

'Climb out, both of you,' Alan ordered. They obeyed him.

They descended to Simon Powys's apartment and Junnar made the door open. They went through.

'Is that you, Junnar?' Powys called from his study.

Alan herded them in.

He saw a terrible expression of sheer fear cloud his grandfather's face as they entered.

Hollowly, Alan said: 'I know everything, Grandfather.'

Simon Powys remained seated at his desk. Slowly he put down his stylus and pushed the papers from him.

'What are you going to do then, Alan?'

'Denounce us, I expect,' Blas said cheerfully. 'May I sit down, Powys?' He turned to Alan.

'Both of you sit,' Alan ordered, his hand still on his pocketed gun.

'You'd have to prove it,' Simon Powys said slowly, in an old man's voice. 'It's the word of an emotional young man against that of a respected minister. I could say you were raving. Neither Junnar nor Blas would testify against me.'

'Why?' Alan demanded. 'Why, Grandfather?'

'There are a number of reasons, Alan. It was my last chance to become President. A Powys of every generation has been President at least once. I couldn't let family tradition die – it would have been a disgrace.'

'Isn't what you did a disgrace? Isn't it a crime?'

'You don't understand. Politicians can't always use clean methods. I was right. The Fireclown's no good, Alan. It was the only way to show the public...'

'That was only a matter of opinion. The fact is you framed the Fireclown in order to prove your own theory about him – and because Helen was bound to win the election if you didn't do something desperate. It was the only way to change public opinion radically. Because of that, Sandai's police tampered with the Fireclown's flame-machines – and three hundred people were killed.'

'I didn't want that to happen.'

'But it happened – *you* were responsible for their deaths!'

'I feel guilty...'

'You *are* guilty! And you fell neatly into Blas's plan, didn't you? He supplied you with the bombs with which you framed the Fireclown. And now, because you daren't admit the whole thing was manufactured by you, he's holding the government up to blackmail. There is a possibility of mass destruction if this hysteria builds up – but even if that doesn't happen the money that Blas will demand will impoverish the Solar nation for years. And he's got you neatly in his trap – he can dictate any terms he wants. If you were elected President you would be his puppet. Blas would run the Solar nation. And he nearly succeeded, didn't he?'

'As your grandfather pointed out,' Blas said equably, 'you still have to prove all this, young man.'

'I intend to, Blas. Grandfather – you're going to confess, before it's too late. You're a Powys! You must!'

Simon Powys wet his lips and stared down at the desk.

'Are you going to confess, Grandfather?'

'No,' said Simon Powys. 'No, I am not.'

It had been Alan's only chance, and it had failed. As his grandfather and Blas had said, it was his word against theirs. Already he had the reputation as a diehard supporter of the Fireclown. Who would believe him now that Simon Powys had turned the Solar System against the Fireclown? What could he do now?

His idealism, his belief that his grandfather would act in accordance with the principles he had so plainly shed was shattered. He was drained of emotion and could only stand staring down at the old man.

'Stalemate, Powys.' Blas crossed his legs.

There must be proof, Alan thought. There must be proof somewhere.

He knew that if he could prove his grandfather's guilt he could stop Blas's plan for controlling the Solar System, avert the threat of a war almost bound to come about with so much hysteria in the air, prove the Fireclown innocent and allow Helen to become President.

Everything hinged on what was, in fact, a means of betraying his grandfather.

He gave Blas a disgusted glare.

'Yes, stalemate. But if I walk out of here now, you daren't do anything for fear that I'll say too much. You can't rig evidence against me the same way as you did to the Fireclown.' As an afterthought, he added: 'You could kill me, of course.'

'No!' Simon Powys rose from his chair. 'Alan, come in with us. In a few weeks the world will be ours!'

Alan went towards the door. 'You accused me once of having none of the noble Powys blood, remember? If that's what flows in your veins, thank God I haven't got any!'

He flung down the gun and left.

Outside, he walked slowly towards the elevator cone, brooding and unable to think coherently. All he had was definite knowledge of his grandfather's perfidy, knowledge that he was unable yet to prove. Still, the knowledge itself was something.

He went down to the thirtieth level and made his way to the RLM Headquarters.

He entered the front office, still stacked with posters. Jordan Kalpis was there, his bony face full of worry.

'Powys! What did you find out?'

'Where's Helen? I'll tell you later.'

'At a meeting in the Divisional Hall on forty. There's some pretty bad heckling going on. The crowd has turned nasty.'

'Right. I'm going over there.'

Alan went out into the corridor and took the fastway to the elevator, rose ten levels and took the fastway again to the Divisional Hall. Every ten levels had a Divisional Hall, comprising a meeting hall and the offices of the local sub-council officials. Outside, the posters of Helen had been torn down.

There was a fantastic noise coming from inside. Alan entered the crowded hall and glimpsed Helen at the far end on the platform. A man beside him threw back an arm. Alan saw it held a piece of raw meat. As the man's hand came up to hurl the meat, Alan grabbed it and wrenched it savagely back. He didn't give the man time to see who had stopped him but pushed his way down the aisle. All kinds of refuse flew onto the platform as he hauled himself up.

Helen's face was bleeding and her clothes were torn. She stood rigidly, defiantly shouting at the mob.

'Helen!'

She saw him. 'Alan! What –?'

'Get out of here – they're not listening to you!'

She seemed to pull herself together.

Now the mob surged forward, faces twisted, hands grasping. He heard someone shout: 'She wants us burned to death.'

She – wants – us – burned – to – death!

A gem of a phrase, Alan thought as he kicked the first man who tried to climb the stage. It fed the hysteria which spawned it. He found himself hating humanity and his kicks were savage.

Andy Curry's freckled face appeared from the side exit. 'Quick! Here!'

They ran in and Curry ordered the door locked.

'I can only say I told you so,' Curry said dourly. 'You shouldn't have made the speech in the first place, Miss Curtis.'

'I avoided all mention of the Fireclown,' she said furiously, 'and they didn't give me a chance!'

Curry picked up the VC in the passage. He pressed two studs.

The word *Police* flashed on the screen and an operator's face followed it.

'I'm speaking from Divisional Hall, level forty,' Curry said swiftly. 'There's a riot going on down here. We're besieged. We need help.'

The operator looked at him. 'Helen Curtis meeting – is that right?'

'That's right.'

'We'll have a squad there right away,' the operator told him in a voice that indicated he should have known better than to start trouble.

The police dispersed the crowd and the captain told Alan, Helen and Curry that an escort was ready to see them home. He sounded unsympathetic, as if he was helping them unwillingly.

When they reached Helen's door the leader of the escort said: 'If I were you, Miss Curtis, I should stay inside. You're liable to be attacked otherwise.'

'I've got an election to fight,' she pointed out.

'You'll have people to fight if tonight's trouble's repeated – and I don't doubt it will be if you insist on setting yourself up to resist the whole climate of public opinion! We've got enough on our hands with the Fireclown investigation – crowds demanding to know when we're going to catch him, rabble-rousers shouting that we must prepare for war, and all the rest of it.'

The escort leader shrugged. 'We can't be held responsible if you deliberately risk being mobbed.'

'Thank you, officer.' Alan followed Helen into the apartment. The door closed.

'So I'm supposed to stay boxed in here, am I?' she said bitterly. 'Meanwhile I've got to try and convince people that they're wrong.'

'It's useless,' he said hollowly, going into the sitting room and slumping down in a chair.

'What did you find out in London?'

'Everything.'

'Even what Blas is up to?'

He told her, slowly and wearily, all that had happened.

'So we *were* right,' she said thoughtfully. 'But Uncle Simon – that's incredible.'

'Yes, isn't it?' He smiled cynically. 'And our hands are virtually tied. We've got to do some cool thinking, Helen.'

She was calmer now. She seemed to notice, for the first time, that he was exhausted.

'We'd better sleep on it,' she said. 'We may feel more optimistic in the morning.'

As they breakfasted, Alan switched on the V. 'Let's see what's happened in the world this morning,' he said.

'... petition urging the government to speed up its defence plans,' mouthed the newscaster. Then he leaned forward urgently. 'For those who missed our early edition, the first attacks by the Fireclown have begun. Two nuclear bomb explosions have been observed – one in the Atlantic and one in the Gobi Desert. So far nobody has been reported hurt, but it will be impossible to know for certain for some time yet. Where will the Fireclown's next bomb strike? Swiss City? New York? Berlin? We don't know. Emergency shelters are being erected and bomb detector teams are covering the areas around the main cities to try and discover hidden bombs. Meanwhile, in Britain, mystery fires have devastated important public buildings. The National Gallery is smouldering wreckage – the marvellous architectural beauty of Gateshead Theatre is no more. Precautions are being taken to protect other such buildings throughout the planet. There is little doubt that the Fireclown – or his diehard supporters here – was responsible!'

'That's all Blas's work,' Alan said angrily. 'How are we going to prove it?'

'Look,' Helen pointed at the screen. Simon Powys had appeared, looking dignified and grave.

'My fellow citizens of the Solar System, I am speaking to you in troubled times. As I predicted a short while ago, the Fireclown has attacked the globe. He has been offered no hostility, we have intended him no harm. But nevertheless he has attacked. We must defend ourselves. If we had to manufacture bombs and other weapons for defence we should be wiped out before we had any chance. Luckily the Solar Government has been offered arms.' Powys paused as if saddened by the task he had to perform. 'A group of men – criminals we should have called them but a few hours ago, but now we are more than thankful to them – have offered us a supply of arms. We are going to purchase them, on your behalf, and set them up around the planet. This will have to be done swiftly, and already bodies of volunteers are working on emergency installations. Let us hope we shall be in time to avert our peril. When I next speak to you, perhaps we shall know.'

'The devil!' Helen swore. 'He's obviously completely in Blas's power. He knows that Blas will use him to control Earth – that we're threatened with a military dictatorship, and yet, in his pride, he still refuses to stop. Doesn't he know what he's doing?'

'He's gone so far now that he can't go back. His hate for the Fireclown and love for his own political ambitions have combined and, in a sense I'm sure, turned him insane! Maybe he can't even see the extent of his treachery.'

'We've got to do something to stop him, Alan.' Helen spoke quietly.

'Like what?'

'First we'll try to convince Sandai. Then, if that fails, we'll have to kill him.'

'Helen! Killing him won't do any good. What could we do? Set up another dictatorship to control the people? Don't you see that if we continue this violence we'll breed more violence *ad infinitum*? We've *got* to use legal means against him. Otherwise, society as we know it is finished!'

'Then what other alternative is there?'

'First we'll see Sandai,' he said. 'Then we'll decide.'

Chapter Sixteen

I T TOOK TIME to get to see Sandai. It took over a day. By the time they walked into his office they were looking very tired indeed. So was Sandai.

'If you've come to tell me that the Fireclown's innocent of these outrages,' he said, wiping his olive forehead, 'I'm not interested.'

Alan stood over the seated police chief, his hands resting on the man's desk.

'That's part of it, Chief Sandai. But that's not all. I have heard the man responsible confess his guilt to me!'

'You've what?' Sandai looked up, astonished.

'The man responsible for framing the Fireclown, for setting off the bombs and causing the fires in Britain, is a man named Blas.'

'Blas? François Blas? He's suspected head of the arms syndicate.' Sandai looked thoughtful. 'It's a possibility, Mr Powys. But what proof have you? How did you find out?'

'I heard that Blas had his headquarters in Mayfair. I went there and discovered he was running an organisation calling themselves the Sons of the Fireclown.'

'So Blas is working for the Fireclown?'

'No. The thing was definitely spurious. Blas was using it for his own ends. Later I broke into Blas's apartment and confronted him with what I knew and what I suspected. He denied nothing. He told me to prove it – which I couldn't do. I then brought him and another man back to the capital...'

'Who was the other man?'

'Junnar, my grandfather's secretary.'

'You mean you suspect he's been working against Minister Powys? That's fantastic – if it's true.'

'He's been working with Powys,' Alan said firmly. 'Blas and my grandfather are hand in glove – they plan to use the war scare they've created and the fear of the Fireclown to hold the Earth to ransom. You heard yesterday's announcement – about Powys having to buy bombs from the syndicate. It's a set-up, Chief Sandai!'

'Young man, you're evidently deranged.' Sandai stood up and patted Alan's arm sympathetically.

'Listen to him!' Helen said urgently. 'Listen, Chief Sandai. It sounds impossible, but it's a fact.'

'And the proof?' Sandai said gently.

'As circumstantial as that against the Fireclown,' Alan pointed out.

'But the Fireclown is a renegade – your grandfather is virtually the leader of the Solar System. That's the difference, Powys. I'm sorry, but your defence of the Fireclown doesn't hold up. Why don't you admit that and work with the rest of us to avert the menace?'

'It's the truth,' Alan said. He felt the energy go out of his body, his shoulders slump.

'I'm very busy,' Sandai said. 'You'd better leave now.'

As they crossed the sunny gardens of the Top, Helen said to him: 'That didn't work. What do we do now, Alan?'

'Watch the world die,' he said hopelessly.

'The whole lot of them deserve death for what they're doing,' she said cautiously.

'Maybe. But the law banished the death sentence over a hundred years ago. We want to preserve the law, Helen, not demolish it further!'

'If only we could contact the Fireclown. Maybe he could help us.'

'He's journeying off somewhere in that ship of his, conducting his experiments. There's no hope there, anyway. He's not interested in Earth's problems, you know that.'

They reached the elevator cone and entered it with a dozen others.

As they descended a man stared hard at Helen.

'Aren't you Helen Curtis?' he said roughly.

'I am.'

The man spat in her face.

Alan jumped at him, punching savagely. The attendant shouted for them to stop. Hands grabbed Alan. The man punched him in the stomach and then in the head.

'Stinking firebug!'

Alan felt bile in his throat. Then he passed out.

He came to in a few seconds. The lift was still going down. Helen was bending over him. The lift stopped. 'You'd better get out, both of you,' the attendant said.

Alan got to his feet.

'Why?' he grunted.

'You're making trouble, that's why.'

'We didn't start it.'

'Come on, Alan,' Helen said, taking his arm. 'We'll walk.'

He was weak with pain as they stumbled into the corridor. Also he was insensately angry.

She helped him onto the fastway and supported his weight until his strength returned.

'That shows you how much anything we say is worth,' she said quietly. 'Hatred and violence are everywhere. What harm would a little more do? The good would outweigh the bad, Alan.'

'No,' he gasped. 'No, Helen. Simon Powys sold his principles. I'm not selling mine.'

'So,' she said when they were back in her apartment, 'what do we do? Just wait here and watch the world collapse?'

'Switch on the set so we've got a good view,' he said. She went over and turned on the V.

They watched glumly as the announcer reported another explosion in the Pacific, two more in Central Africa, killing a large number of people who lived in small communities in the blast area. Work was under way on the defence project. Simon Powys was directing the preparations.

'They don't need to bother with the farce of electing him,' Helen said. 'He's as good as President now!'

'You mean Blas is,' Alan told her. 'He's the one pulling the strings.'

Helen reached over to the V and pressed out a number.

'Who are you calling?'

'My brother,' she said. 'Denholm's about the only person who can help us now.'

Her brother's face came on the screen. 'Hello, Helen, I'm rather busy – is it important?'

'Very important, Denholm. Could you come over?'

'If it's another defence of the Fireclown...'

'It is not.'

Her brother's expression changed as he stared at her image. 'Very well. Give me an hour – all right?'

'Okay,' she said.

'How can Denholm help us?' Alan said. 'What's the point?'

'We'll tell him all we know. The more people of importance who are told about it, the better chance we have.'

Denholm came in, placed his gaudy hat on a chair arm and sat down.

'Alan,' Helen said, 'tell Denholm everything – from the time we went to see the Fireclown until our interview with Sandai.'

He told Denholm Curtis everything.

When he had finished, Curtis frowned at him. 'Alan,' he said, 'I think I believe you. Uncle Simon's been behaving a trifle mysteriously in some ways. The alacrity with which he managed to contact the dealers when the government finally decided to buy the arms was astonishing. It could mean that he's abused his position as chairman of the One Hundred Committee!'

'What do you mean?'

'Supposing in some way he had got hold of a list of the dealers and the location of their caches? Supposing he held on to it without letting the other committee members know, contacted Blas and concocted this scheme? Suppose then they worked out a plan to take advantage of the Fireclown, get Simon Powys elected as President, and then run the world as they wanted to run it? Powys might have got in touch with Blas originally with a view to smashing the syndicate. But Blas might have proposed the whole idea. We all know how much Uncle Simon hates the Fireclown. It would have been the perfect means of getting rid of him. Maybe he intended to capture the Fireclown. Maybe the original deal was simply over a few bombs. But Blas has provided the Fireclown with the means of producing a super-ship, and he was fairly certain that the Fireclown would escape when the chips were down. He did. The war scare started, aided by the police tampering with the flame-machines. Simon Powys couldn't back out – and Blas had him where he wanted him.'

'That sounds logical,' Alan agreed.

'But all this needs proof to back it up.' Denholm Curtis pursed his lips thoughtfully.

'It comes back to that every time.' Helen sighed.

'There'd be only one way. To find the man who was Powys's original contact with Blas, and get him to confess.'

'But how?' Alan asked. 'Where do we look?'

'We check the files of the One Hundred Committee – that was probably how Powys found his contact. You're still secretary, Helen. Where are the files?'

'Right here. In the safe.'

'Get them.'

She got them – dozens of spools of microfilm. They fitted them into the projector.

It was more than six hours before they found what they were looking for. A reference to one Nils Benedict, suspected of trying to sell arms to a super-reactionary Crespignite splinter group. They had turned him over to the police. The police had been unable to find any evidence against him. Simon Powys had interviewed him while in custody and reported that, in his opinion, the man was innocent. Simon Powys had been, apart from the police, the only man to question Benedict. Benedict had a Brussels address.

'Do you think that's him?' Alan said, rubbing his eyes.

'It's the only one it could possibly be. What do we do now?'

'Pay Nils Benedict a visit, I suppose,' Helen suggested.

A smaller, less complex version of the City of Switzerland, Brussels had an altogether different character. Every inch of stonework was embellished with red lacquer, and over this bright designs had been laid. Gilt predominated.

The structure rose fourteen levels above the ground, five below, covering an area of five square miles. The roof landing space was limited so that they were forced to land outside the city and take a monorocket which let them off on the tenth level. Benedict lived on level eight.

They reached his apartment. They had already decided that Denholm would do the talking, since he was less likely to be suspect than the other two.

'Nils Benedict,' he said to the blank door, 'this is Denholm Curtis. I've got some good news for you.'

The door opened. A tall, rangy man in a dressing gown of green silk stared curiously at Curtis.

'Are you from Powys?' he asked as the door closed behind them.

Alan took the lead. 'We want to contact Blas in a hurry. Can you arrange it?'

'Sure. But why? I thought he was in direct contact nowadays.'

That was enough. Now they knew for certain.

'Oh, he is,' Alan said. 'But we thought it would be nice for you and Simon Powys to meet again after all this time.'

Benedict had been uncommonly slow, he thought, for a man who was supposed to live by his wits. The man seemed gradually to realise that something was wrong. He backed into his living room. They followed.

The answer was there. Benedict was an addict. The stink of mescaline was in the room; nightmarish murals covered the walls. He was a mescamas who got his kicks from descending into his own psychological hell.

Helen said in a strained voice: 'I'll wait outside.'

'Come on, Benedict,' Denholm said roughly.

'I have rights, you know,' Benedict said thickly. 'Why does Powys want to see me?'

'Are you scared of Powys?'

'He told me I'd be killed if I ever got in touch with him again.'

'There's not a chance of that, I promise,' Alan said.

Benedict was still wary. Alan suddenly hit him under the jaw. He collapsed.

'Let's get him dressed,' Denholm said. 'It wouldn't be proper for him to go out without his correct clothes on.'

They had surprisingly little difficulty getting Benedict to Helen's apartment. Organisation of the usual kind seemed to have gone to pieces during the fake emergency.

While Helen tried to revive Benedict and Denholm tied his hands, the V began to flash. Alan answered it. Chief Sandai looked out at him.

'You're not the only madman in the system, it seems,' he said. 'I thought about what you told me and thought I couldn't do any harm to assign a few men to go undercover to Mayfair and check your story. It held up. We found Blas and Junnar there. We're holding them, under the emergency laws which Simon Powys insisted we make, as suspects in an arson plot. We got one of the Sons of the Fireclown, too. But we're going to need more proof – and I'm still not convinced that your tale about Simon Powys is true!'

Alan stepped aside so Sandai could see Benedict.

'Recognise this man, chief?'

'I've got a feeling I do, but I can't place him. Who is he?'

'He's Simon Powys's original contact with Blas. He's a mescamas. If we withhold his supply for a short time he should tell us everything he knows.'

'If it's true, you've had a big stroke of luck, young man.'

'It'll be the first we've had,' Alan said dryly. 'Can you come over and pick us up? It might be wise to have an escort.'

Sandai nodded. The screen blanked.

Blas alone remained seemingly at ease. Benedict was slumped hopelessly in his chair, perhaps even enjoying the experience of defeat. Junnar had his back to them, staring out of the window over the mountains. The police prison had a wonderful view.

Blas said: 'Chief Sandai, what evidence do you have for these fantastic charges? Confront Simon Powys with them. He will laugh at you!'

Sandai turned to Denholm Curtis. 'Where's Powys now? You've convinced me.'

'He's at a special meeting in the Solar House. Members are asking him questions on his war policy. He's bound to answer since we still retain a vestige of democracy.'

'What are you going to do, chief?' Alan asked.

'Something spectacular,' Sandai said. 'It's probably the only thing we can do now to break Powys's power in front of the assembly. Otherwise it may be too late.'

'After what I've been through in the last day or so,' Helen said grimly, 'I'm beginning to doubt that anyone can topple Uncle Simon!'

Standing nobly before the mighty assembly of Solar Representatives, Simon Powys answered their questions in a grave and sonorous voice. He was the image of the visionary and man of action. The weight of responsibility seemed to rest heavily upon his broad shoulders, but he bore it manfully, not to say hypocritically.

Alan watched him on the screen outside the main entrance to the Assembly Chamber itself. He, Denholm and Helen stood in a group to one side. Chief Sandai, four policemen and the fettered trio of Junnar, Blas and the slobbering Benedict stood to the other.

They chose their moment well, when a member for Afghanistan asked Simon Powys what the police were doing in the Fireclown investigation.

Sandai pushed the button operating the double doors. The doors swept open and the party pushed forward.

'The police,' Sandai called, 'have caught most of the men responsible for the present situation.' He gestured dramatically towards the shackled men. 'Here they are – there is only one man missing!'

Alan saw that Simon Powys's face bore an expression similar to the look he'd had on the night he'd accused him.

But he held up well, Alan decided, considering everything.

'What does this interruption mean, Chief Sandai?'

Sandai spoke laconically. 'Using the emergency powers vested in me by the Government of the Solar System I am holding under arrest the three men you see there – François Blas, suspected arms dealer, Nils Benedict, a contact for the arms syndicate – and Eugene Junnar, personal assistant to Minister Simon Powys. All the men admit to being implicated in a plot, instigated by Minister Powys, to frame the Fireclown, start a war scare by means of nuclear bomb explosions and incendiaries, and thus assure Minister Powys of full political power as President of the Solar System!'

Blas said: 'He's lying, Minister Powys.'

But Nils Benedict, not of Blas's calibre, continued the theme. 'We didn't admit anything, sir! I haven't said a word about the deal!'

Simon Powys thundered: 'Be quiet! You have abused your powers, Sandai. I demand that you leave the hall immediately!'

But the hubbub from the rest of the representatives drowned out anything else he might have wished to say.

Alan walked swiftly down to the central platform and mounted it.

'We have witnesses, now, Grandfather! We have the proof you told us to get!'

Benjosef rose from his seat.

'What's the meaning of this, Mr Powys?'

'My grandfather, sir, has betrayed every trust you and the system have ever put in him.' Briefly, Alan outlined the facts.

Benjosef turned to Simon Powys who stood rigidly, as if petrified, in his place. 'Is this true, Powys?'

'No!' Powys came alive, his face desperate – wretched. 'No! Can't you see this is the work of the Fireclown's supporters, an attempt to disgrace me and confuse us in our hour of peril? My grandson is lying!'

But Simon Powys had lost all self-control. His wild denial had convinced the assembly of his guilt. He knew it. He stared around him, his breathing irregular, his eyes wide. He advanced toward Benjosef.

'I run the Solar System now, Benjosef – not you! You can't do anything. The people are with me!'

'Possibly,' Benjosef said mildly, with a slight air of triumph, 'but evidently this assembly is not.' Benjosef seemed pleased at his would-be successor's downfall. 'I was aware, minister, that you wished to oust me as President – but I did not expect you to take quite so much trouble.' He gestured to the police chief. 'Sandai – I'm afraid you had better arrest Minister Powys.'

Simon Powys leapt from the dais, stumbled and fell. He got up, evidently in pain, and stood there panting as Sandai stepped cautiously towards him.

'You fool! I could have made the world a better place. I knew it was going soft. I could have stopped the rot! You are under my orders, Sandai – don't listen to Benjosef.'

Sandai slipped a pair of electrogyves from his belt.

'No!' Simon Powys was sobbing now. 'The Fireclown will destroy us! He will destroy you all – as he destroyed my daughter!'

Alan looked up in surprise. So his grandfather had known all along that the Fireclown was his father! That explained, even further, his insensate hatred of the Fireclown.

He went up to the old man, pitying him now.

'Grandfather, I know you have suffered, but...'

Old Simon Powys turned his great head and looked into Alan's eyes. His expression was that of a bewildered, tearful child.

'It was for her sake,' he said brokenly. 'For hers and yours, Alan.'

The gyves hummed and curled about Powys's wrists. His head bowed, his seamed face now tear-streaked, he allowed Sandai to lead him out of the assembly hall.

Benjosef stepped from the platform and touched Alan's arm. 'I'm sorry you had to do what you did, my boy. I must admit I never liked your grandfather – always thought him, well, somewhat weak, I suppose. That was why I, and many members of the party, never promoted him to a more prominent position; why he had never, until now, been nominated as a Presidential candidate. Evidently I was right, at least.' He turned to Helen Curtis. 'The world is going to be grateful to you both, I suspect. The climate of opinion is going to take yet another reversal before the elections are finally held. I hope you make a good President, Miss Curtis.'

'Thank you, sir,' said Helen, looking worriedly at Alan.

Alan ran a hand across his face. He swallowed with difficulty and glowered at the ground. Then he shook Benjosef's hand off his arm.

'I'm glad you're all proved right,' he said bitterly. 'I'm bloody glad about the happy ending.'

And he walked straight up the aisle and out of the Solar House, his pace fast as he crossed the lawns. His heart pounding, his eyes warm, his fists clenched and his mind in a mess.

Chapter Seventeen

Two days later Alan emerged from the cavern on the first level, where he had been avoiding everyone, and ascended to the Top, passing a great many power-posters proclaiming Helen Curtis for President. Listening to the conversation, his faith in the stupidity of human nature was fully restored. In the swift movement of events, the public had changed their loyalty from the Fireclown to Simon Powys, and now to Helen Curtis. Why did they need heroes? he wondered. What was wrong in people that they could not find what they needed within themselves? How did they know Helen was any better than the rest?

Vids announced the complete rounding up of the members of the arms syndicate and the discovery of every nuclear cache left in existence. That was one good thing. The Vs also said that order had been completely restored. Alan wondered. On the surface, perhaps, it was true. But what of the disorder that must still exist in the hearts and minds of most members of the public?

He reached the Top and entered Police Headquarters. After a few moments he was shown into Chief Sandai's office.

'Mr Powys! There has been a general search out for you! You and Miss Curtis are the heroes of the hour. Every V station in the Solar System has been after you.'

'In that case,' Alan said coolly, 'I'm glad they couldn't find me. I want to see my grandfather, chief – if that's possible.'

'Of course. He made a full confession, you know. He's been very subdued since his arrest – hasn't given us any trouble.'

'Good. Well, can I see him now?'

Not exactly every home comfort had been provided for Simon Powys, but his room hardly looked like a prison cell with its pleasant view of the clear summer sky, the cloud-wreathed mountain peaks in the distance. It was well furnished. There were books, writing materials and V-prints on the small desk by the window.

His grandfather was staring out at the mountains, his chair pushed back from his desk, when Alan entered.

'Grandfather.'

The old man turned. And it *was* an old man who stared gauntly up at his grandson. All the vitality had left him. He seemed completely enervated.

'Hello, Alan. Glad to see you. Do sit down.' He gestured vaguely towards the only other chair in the room.

'How do you feel?' Alan asked inanely.

Simon Powys smiled thinly. 'As well as can be expected,' he said. 'How are you?'

Alan seated himself on the edge of the chair. 'I'm sorry I had to do it, Grandfather, but you know why it was necessary.'

'Yes. I'm glad, in a way, that you did – though I can hardly bear the shame. I don't know if you'll understand, Alan, but I *was* insane, in a way. I was caught up in a nightmare – my ambition, my hatred, my schemes ran away with me. Do you know that when my fortunes turned after the Fireclown business I seemed to be living in a dream thereafter? I feel as if I've just woken up. I remember I accused you of having none of the good Powys blood. I shouldn't have done that, and I'm sorry. I tried, in my way, to apologise almost as soon as I'd said it. But it seems you had better stuff in you than I. I've always been conscious of my inherent weakness, that I wasn't of the same breed as our ancestors, but I always fought it, Alan. I tried not to let it get the better of me. It did, of course, but in a different way.'

'You didn't really hate the Fireclown for anything he was doing, did you?' Alan spoke softly. 'You hated him for loving my mother, and giving her a son – me. You knew he was Manny Bloom all the time.'

'Yes.' Simon Powys sighed and stared out of the window again. 'I knew he was Manny Bloom. I was responsible for sending him on the Saturn mission. That was my first major mistake, I suppose. But I couldn't see my daughter marrying an ordinary spaceman, however much of a hero he was in the public eye. I didn't realise you were going to be born. He was away for two years. When he came back you were here – and your mother had killed herself.'

'Killed herself! I didn't know...'

'I'd told her Manny Bloom was dead – killed in a space accident. I didn't expect those consequences, of course. That was the first death I was responsible for, indirectly. As Minister for Space Transport I was in the perfect position to send Manny Bloom wherever I chose. I bided my time – then I really *did* try to kill him.'

'What? You mean the rocket that went too near the sun?'

'Yes. I bribed the technician responsible for the final check – had him fix the steering rockets so that the ship would plunge into the sun. I heard the ship had gone off course and I thought I was rid of him. But somehow he survived – and he came back, to haunt me as it were, as the Fireclown.'

'So you really created your own nemesis. You caused my father to drift towards the sun and that experience resulted in his strange mental state. Ultimately he appeared as the Fireclown and, because of your hatred against him, brought about your ruin without ever consciously wishing for vengeance against you.'

Simon Powys nodded. 'I appreciate the irony of it all,' he said. 'It's one of the things I've been thinking about, sitting here and waiting for my trial.'

'When is it to be?'

'They haven't fixed it yet. It's going to be a big one – will probably take place after the Presidential elections.'

'Helen will be able to influence the judges then,' Alan said. 'She'll probably try to get you the lightest possible sentence.'

'The lightest sentence would be death, Alan. And that, I'm afraid, is outside even the President's powers to exact.'

Alan remembered Helen's proposal to assassinate Simon Powys. In many ways, he thought, everyone would have welcomed it. It was painful to see this once respected and powerful man in such a wretched state, no matter how much he deserved it.

Simon Powys got up, extending his hand. 'It was good of you to come, Alan. I wonder if you would mind leaving now. This – this is somewhat hard to...' He broke off, unable to express his shame.

'Yes, of course.' Alan went forward and shook Simon Powys's hand. The old man tried to make the grip firm, but failed.

Feeling considerably more affection for his grandfather than he had ever had in the past, Alan left the cell, left Police Headquarters and stood for a long time by a splashing fountain, staring into the clear water and watching the darting goldfish swimming in the narrow confines of the pool. Did they understand just how narrow their little universe was? he wondered. They seemed happy enough, if fish could be happy. But if they weren't happy, he reflected, neither were they sad. They had no tradition but instinct, no ritual but the quest for food and a mate. He didn't envy them much.

Chapter Eighteen

IN THE FOLLOWING weeks Alan led a fairly solitary life, taking little interest in the elections, scarcely aware of the fact that Helen was almost certain to win since there were no candidates in the field with her popularity. Denholm Curtis, who had played some part in the denunciation of Powys, was now the Solref's candidate for the office, but he didn't stand much of a chance. Helen was busy, but she had tried to contact him from time to time. He would see her when he was ready.

The election date came. The votes were counted. Helen was President.

The day after her election she came to see him and he let her in.

'I thought you were angry with me,' she said as she accepted a drink. 'I thought, perhaps, you'd decided not to see me again. I know you've had a bad series of emotional shocks, Alan – but I could have helped you. I could have been some comfort, surely.'

'I didn't need comfort, Helen. I needed to be alone with myself. And anyway, you couldn't have afforded to waste time on me – you had problems of your own.'

'What do you propose to do now?' She couldn't disguise the fact that she was anxious.

'Ask you to marry me, Helen.'

'I accept,' she said thankfully. 'I thought…'

'We all tend to see other people's emotions as reflecting on ourselves. It's a mistake. People's emotions are rarely created by anyone else. I think we might be happy, don't you?'

'In spite of my work?'

'In spite of that, yes. I don't expect to see much of you for some time. But maybe that's for the best.'

A buzz began to sound on her wrist.

'I'm sorry.' She smiled. 'I get issued with this thing – I'm on call, as it were, all the time. I didn't expect it to start so soon.'

She went to his V and pressed a number.

'President Curtis,' she said to the slightly perturbed-looking man on the screen. She put the drink down on the set.

'Madame – there is probably no danger but I have just received news that a strange spaceship has landed somewhere near Algiers. It's believed to be the Fireclown's.'

'No need for declaring a state of emergency now.' She smiled. 'It will be good to see him again.' She switched out and turned to Alan. 'He's your father – want to be part of a deputation?'

'If it's just the two of us, yes.'

'Come on then. Let's see what his experiments have proved.'

Before Helen could go she was forced to leave notification of her whereabouts. Her Presidential duties had not really begun as yet, but from now on her time would never be her own. In his new state of mind, Alan decided he could bear it so long as she only served one term.

The *Pi-meson* rested on its belly, its pitted hull gleaming in the African sun. As yet, nothing had been heard from the ship. It was as if it was empty, bereft of life.

As their car settled beside it, the huge airlock began to open. But nothing else happened.

'What now?' Helen looked to Alan for guidance.

'Let's go in,' he said, leading the way over to the ship and clambering into the airlock.

On the big landing deck Alan touched the stud operating the sliding wall. It opened and they climbed into the control deck. It was darkened. No light passed the closed ports.

'Father?' Alan spoke into the silence, certain someone was here. 'Fireclown?'

'Alan…' The voice was rumbling, enigmatic, thoughtful.

'Yes – and Helen Curtis. We've got something to tell you.' He was slightly amused at his decision to announce his engagement formally to his strange father.

A single light shone now from the corner. Alan could just make out the slumped bulk of the Fireclown. A short distance away Cornelia Fisher stirred. Corso seemed prone, but Alan thought he heard him mumble under his breath.

'Is anything wrong, Father?'

'No.' The Fireclown raised his huge body up from the couch. His gaudy tatters curled about him, his conical hat still bobbed on his head and his face was still painted. He chuckled. 'I thought you'd come here first. I wouldn't have admitted anyone else.'

'Helen and I are getting married, Father.'

'Ah... really?' The Fireclown didn't sound very interested. His manner had become, if anything, more detached and alien.

'A lot's been happening on Earth, sir,' Helen put in, 'since we last met. You're no longer an outcast.'

The Fireclown's body shook with laughter which he at first suppressed and then let roll from his mouth in roaring gusts. 'No – longer – an – outcast. Ha! Ha! Ha! Good!'

Nonplussed, Alan glanced at Helen, who frowned back at him.

'It is not I who am the outcast, young lady – not in the cosmic sense. It is the human race, with their futile, worthless *intelligence*!'

'I still don't understand...' Helen said bewilderedly.

'I took you to the heart of the sun – I took you even to the heart of the galaxy and you still failed to understand! Consciousness is not the same as intelligence. Consciousness is content to exist as it exists, to be what it is and nothing more. But intelligence – that is a blot on the cosmos! In short, I intend to wipe out that blot. I intend to destroy intelligence!'

'Destroy intelligence? You mean, destroy life in the Solar System!' Alan was horrified.

'No, my son, nothing so unsubtle. For one thing, human life is the only culprit – the only thing that offends against the law of the multiverse. I have journeyed the roads between the worlds and have found nothing like it anywhere else. Intelligence, therefore, is a weed in the garden of infinity, a destroying weed that must be dealt with at once.'

'You are mad!' Alan said desperately. 'It's impossible to destroy intelligence without destroying those who have it!'

'According to human logic, that is true. But according to my logic – the Fireclown's logic – that is false. I have perfected a kind of fire – call it "Time Fire" – which will burn away the minds of those it strikes without consuming them in body. My Time Fire will destroy the ability to think because thought takes time.'

The Fireclown reached out his hand towards a stud and depressed it. The wall hummed down. He went over to the controls and began to operate them. 'I waited for you to arrive because I still retain some human sentiment. I did not want to make my son go with the rest. I will convince you, anon, that I speak truth and you will agree with me. You will want only consciousness!'

Alan strode towards his father and grasped his huge arm. 'It can't work – and even if it could, who are you to take such a task upon yourself?'

'I am the Fireclown!'

The screen in front of them showed that the ship had once again set up its own peculiar field. The spheres began to flash past.

'See those!' The Fireclown pointed. 'They are chronons – Atoms of Time! Just as there are atoms of matter, the same is true of time. And I control those atoms as ably as the physicists control their electrons and protons. They are the stuff of my Time Fire!'

Astounded, Alan could only believe his father. He turned to Corso, who was opening his eyes, a dazed look on his red face. 'Corso! Do you want any part of this? Stop him! Cornelia –' the woman stared at him blankly – 'tell him to cease!'

The Fireclown put his painted, bellowing face close to Alan's. 'They cannot understand you. They hear you – but they hear sound alone! They are the first to gain from the Time Fire. They are fully aware but they have no intelligence to mar their awareness.'

'Oh, God!' Helen looked aghast at the blank-faced pair.

'Where are we going?' Alan yelled at his insane father.

'I intend to put the ship into a time freeze. Then, as the globe passes beneath me, I will unleash the Time Fire, covering the world with its healing flames!'

'No, Father!'

'Don't try to tamper with the controls, Alan. If you do you will disrupt the time field and we might well perish.'

The spheres – the chronons – flashed past. Alan stared at them, fascinated in spite of the danger. Atoms of Time. He had heard the chronon theory before, but had never believed it had any reality in fact. But there was no other explanation he could think of for the Fireclown's ability to ignore the laws of matter and venture into the sun's heart, travel swiftly through the galaxy to its centre and remain unharmed. Unharmed bodily, at least. His mind had obviously been unable to stand up against the impressions it had seen.

Faster and faster the chronons rolled past on the screen.

Concentrating on his controls, the Fireclown ignored them.

'What are we going to do, Alan?' Helen said. 'Do you think he's right about this Time Fire?'

'Yes. Look at Corso and Cornelia for proof. He is a genius – but he's an idiot as well. We've got to stop him, Helen. Heaven knows what destruction he *can* work – even if it isn't as bad as he boasts!'

'How!'

'There's only one way. Destroy the controls!'

'We could be killed – or frozen for ever in this "time freeze" of his!'

'We've got to take the risk.'

'But what can you do? We've no weapon, nothing to destroy them with!'

'There's one thing we can do. I'm going to grapple with him. He's incredibly strong so I won't be able to hold him for long. While I keep him occupied, go to the control panel and press all the studs, change the position of all the levers, twist all the dials. That should do something. Ready?'

Conscious that this might be the last time he saw her before they perished, he gave her a long, eloquent look. She smiled.

He leapt at the Fireclown's back and got his arm around his father's thick neck.

The great arms went up and the hands closed over his wrists. The Fireclown shook him off.

'I've spawned a fool! You could cause us to slip into a time vortex we could never get out of!'

Alan grabbed the Fireclown's legs and, surprisingly, though the clown was still a trifle off balance, pulled him down.

Helen dashed towards the controls and began depressing studs and pulling levers.

'No!'

The Fireclown raised himself on one elbow, his other hand outstretched in a warning gesture.

The light began to fizz, to change colour rapidly. The ship shuddered. He was blinded by the glare, his head ached. He felt the Fireclown move and flung himself at his father. With a movement of his arm and body the Fireclown shook him off again.

Then the deck seemed to vanish and they seemed to hang in space. All around him now Alan saw the spheres whirling. The great chronons, each the size of the moon, spun in a dazzling and random course.

The Fireclown bellowed like a baleful bull from somewhere. He heard Helen's voice shouting. He could make no sense of their words. He tried to move but his body was rigid, would answer none of his commands.

Then the chronons changed colour and began to expand.

They burst! A chaotic display of coloured streamers smeared themselves all around him and dissipated swiftly.

Alan tried to breathe but couldn't.

Instead, he sucked in water!

It took seconds for him to realise that he was under the sea. He struggled upwards and at last reached the surface, drew air into his lungs. He was in the middle of an ocean, no land in sight.

There was no evidence that a ship had crashed. Had it entered the water so smoothly that it hadn't made a ripple?

But – another thought came – he should have been *in* the ship! How had he got out?

Another head broke the surface. He swam towards it. The Fireclown! The paint streaked his face. He was panting and cursing. Then Helen's head came up!

'What happened!' Alan gasped. 'Father – what happened?'

'Damn you! You broke the time field – I've lost my ship!'

Overhead Alan heard the drone of an air car. He looked up, waving frantically. It was an amphibian and it seemed to be looking for them. It came down low and landed.

Puzzled faces stared out of the cabin. Someone emerged onto the small, flat deck and a line flashed out over the water. Alan caught it, swam towards Helen and handed it to her. She was pulled swiftly in and, once aboard, the line was sent back. Alan handed it to the Fireclown.

The man refused to take it. Automatically, he kept himself afloat, but his face had an expression of melancholic suffering.

'Take it, Father!'

'Why should I? What purpose do I fulfil by continuing to live? I have failed.'

Impatiently, Alan tied the rope around the passive Fireclown and watched the great bulk being towed in. The Fireclown made no move to release himself or help himself onto the deck.

Alan took the line as it came out once again.

'How did you know we were here?' he asked the vessel's captain.

'We saw a peculiar kind of explosion in this area. We thought we'd better investigate. Sorry it took us so long. We've been circling over this area for three hours. Can't think how we missed you the first time.'

'Three hours! But...' Alan stopped. 'What time is it now?'

The captain glanced at his chronometer. 'Fourteen hundred, almost.'

Alan was about to ask the date but he decided against it. It seemed that they had been deposited in the ocean exactly half an hour before they entered the Fireclown's ship. But what had happened to the ship? he asked the morose Fireclown who had slumped himself moodily in a corner of the cabin.

'I told you – you broke the time field. What happened was simple – we existed in a different time location, the ship in another. The ship should make its appearance between now and the next million years!'

Thereafter, his father refused to answer further questions.

Chapter Nineteen

THE TRIAL OF Simon Powys and the trial of the Fireclown were held at the same time, but in different courts. The V stations were torn between which should have most prominence.

The *Pi-meson* had been found, intact, in Wyoming. Scientists had already stripped it of its time mechanisms and were investigating them. The Fireclown offered them no help when asked.

The relationship between the late protagonists came out, and scandal blended with sensation to feed the V networks.

Simon Powys was not very entertaining, however. He admitted all charges and was found guilty on all charges. Even the judge did not exercise that strange prerogative which judges seem to think themselves entitled to – his summing up contained no list of his personal biases. It was quick and clean. Simon Powys was banished to a confined bunk in one of the pressure domes in the asteroid belt.

The Fireclown was more verbose, his case harder to try since it had no precedent. He could not be tried for his philosophical beliefs, or even for his unique intentions to destroy intelligence. The charge, when it was finally decided, read: 'Plotting to disrupt human society to a point where it could no longer function'.

His long speeches in his defence – or rather in defence of his creed – agreed with the charge.

'I am the victim of crude intelligence,' he told the bewildered jury. 'Intelligence which has no business to exist in the multiverse. I have been pulled down by it as it will pull down the human race in time. I tried to help you but, for all your vaunted minds, you could not understand. Perish, then, in spirit. Set yourselves against the law of the multiverse! Your punishment will come soon enough and be well merited!'

Though still puzzled, the jury decided the Fireclown's own

punishment soon enough. They found him guilty but insane. He would be sent to a mental hospital on Ganymede.

Meanwhile, the scientists continued to puzzle over his bizarre equations and could arrive at no conclusion. In time, perhaps, they would, for once on the track they would never leave it.

For the time being, public hysteria died down, and society once again settled into an ordered existence. Helen Curtis began to put her reforms to the assembly and they were accepted or rejected after discussion. Progress would be slow and would always follow behind the demands of the reformers, but at least in this manner it might retain its dynamism. Helen was comparatively satisfied.

Their wedding date was fixed.

And then came the final drama.

Alan, once more looking for a job, scanned the list of specialist agencies, and sipped coffee. The V buzzed and he switched it to receive. Helen's face appeared on the screen.

'Alan – the Fireclown's escaped!'

He put down his cup with a clatter. 'What! How?'

'You know how strong he was. He overpowered a guard, got hold of his gun and held up the entire Police Headquarters. He made them release Uncle Simon and they left in a stolen police car together.'

'Where have they gone?'

'We don't know.'

'I'm coming over. Are you at the House?'

'Yes.'

When he reached the Presidential apartments Helen and some of her advisers were staring at the huge wall-screen. A commentary boomed:

'Our cameras have succeeded in tracking the escaping spaceship *Pi-meson*, containing convicts Manny Bloom, better known as the Fireclown, and Simon Powys!'

Deep space. The ship in clear focus.

'The ship, degutted of its weird time devices but retaining its ordinary drive, has so far outdistanced all pursuers.'

'That answers my question,' Alan said from behind Helen. 'Where are they going?'

'They seem to be heading for Venus. They could just about survive there and certainly escape the police. The revitalisation project is two-thirds complete,' said Helen, adding in puzzlement: 'A strange pair to be travelling together!'

'They've got things in common,' Alan pointed out. 'In their different ways they were both reactionary idealists. They wanted things simpler than they in fact are.'

The ship passed Venus.

'Where in the universe are they heading for?' Helen said, baffled.

Alan thought he knew.

He watched helplessly as the ship carrying his father and grandfather plunged on.

'Perhaps it's for the best – for them and for us,' he whispered.

The Pi-meson *passed the orbit of Mercury.*

They watched as it wheeled and sailed in towards the sun.

It vanished, consumed almost immediately, as it followed its unveering course into the heart of Sol.

The watchers were silent. Helen turned her face up towards Alan and studied his expression. She glanced back at the screen.

In a few short weeks a new Age had come to Earth and gone as swiftly. It had left a strange mood behind it – and perhaps a new science. Sociologists and psychologists attempted to explain the sudden ebb of hysteria that had seized the people. There were a dozen theories, all complex, all with their merits. One attempted to explain it as the result of the transition period between 'natural' (or biological) living and 'artificial' (or machine) living. It concluded that until the artificial became the natural and human psychology altered accordingly we should experience many such disturbances.

It was a likely explanation. But there might have been another, far simpler explanation.

Perhaps the world had just been – *bored*.

The Shores of Death

For Harry Harrison

'Let me assert my firm belief that the only thing we have to fear is fear itself.'

– Franklin D. Roosevelt

Prologue

WHEN SHE TOLD her father she was pregnant he said, 'We'll have to get rid of it,' but almost immediately his morbid, introverted mind was fascinated by the idea of permitting the birth; so he put his arm around his daughter's soft shoulders and murmured, 'It is wrong, however, to take life, particularly when life is so scarce in this region of the world. Let us see if the child lives after birth. Let nature decide...'

They lived in a grotesque tower in the twilight region. Moulded several centuries before from steel and glass-alloy by a neo-naturalist architect, its asymmetrical lines gave it the appearance of something that had grown, living, from the ground and then atrophied. Red dust blew around it and sparse brown lichen covered its lower parts.

The tower threw a black shadow across the rock and the shadow never shifted, for the Earth had not turned on its axis since the raid from space ages before, when the space-dwelling creatures had paused with casual ease to stop the world spinning, looted what they required, and passed on in their insane, ceaseless passage through the universe.

One of the birdlike mammalian bipeds had been left behind and from him it was learned that his race was seeking the edge of the universe. When they discovered it, they would fling their ships and themselves into the oblivion of absolute lifelessness. From what could be understood of the alien's explanation, his people were driven by a racial guilt which had existed for aeons. This was all mankind could learn before the alien had killed himself.

After hearing the alien creature's story, the few survivors of the raid had accepted their fate realising the comparative insignificance of their own disaster when compared with the grandiose madness of the space-dwellers.

Now the Earth, with perpetual day on one side, perpetual night on the other, and a twilight and dawn region between the two, circled on around the sun.

Psychological alterations had been bound to result from the drastic environmental changes that had occurred in the different regions of the planet. The alterations had been beneficial to some and not to others. In the sparsely populated twilight region, where Valta Marca and his daughter lived in love, the inhabitants had turned in on themselves, rarely leaving their heavily guarded towers, devoting their time to eccentric pursuits, pleasures and experiments of a dark, narcissistic nature.

Children were scarcely ever born in the twilight region, so

inbred were the inhabitants. It was customary, in the event of conception, to destroy the foetus. Valta Marca's decision to let his incestuous offspring live was the decision of a man whose mental and emotional appetites had become dulled. Having convinced his daughter that she must endure her pregnancy, he waited in morbid anticipation for the birth.

In the season of the winds, in the post-raid year 345, a son was born to Valta Marca and his pale daughter Betild.

It was a lonely, unlucky birth, and Betild died of it after a few months.

Strangely for a child of incest, Clovis Marca clung to his life and grew strong and healthy in time. He flourished in spite of his father's careless and disappointed attitude towards him. His father, expecting a freak of some kind, half hoping that his offspring should be a girl so that he could continue to experiment, lost interest in Clovis as the boy grew healthier and healthier. Clovis was as delicate-boned and slender as Betild and Valta, but there was a toughness about him and a will to survive that was intensified, perhaps, by the unconscious understanding of the circumstances by which he had entered the world. It was this will to live, apparent since birth, that was his most remarkable characteristic.

His brain was good, his intelligence broad, and, because of his father's lack of interest in him, Clovis Marca grew into an independent, self-reliant boy. When he was twelve, his father died. Clovis burned the body, locked up the baroque tower and set off for the daylight region which, for several years, it had been his ambition to visit.

Here, Clovis Marca discovered a world absolutely different from the one he knew. The society was the nearest thing to perfection that had ever existed; vital without being violent, stable without being stagnant. This society had resulted from a number of factors, the most important being a small population served by a sophisticated technology and an equally sophisticated administrative system. The arts were alive, there was universal literacy, the philosophies flourished. To Clovis the world was paradise and he was taken into it kindly and made welcome. He quickly responded to the frank and healthy outlook of the daylight people and had soon adapted to their way of life as if he had always known it.

Only in the deep places of his mind were the dark influences of his first twelve years dormant rather than exorcised. Perhaps it was these that led to his interest in the administrative life of the daylight region so that he sought power whilst thinking he sought to serve. He began by getting elected to local committees, rose to become a member of the upper council and at last supreme administrator, Council Chairman. He was much admired by everyone. He was respected for his understanding, his ability to take the right decisions at all times, his awareness of the processes governing both individual human life and society in general. It was agreed that he was the best Council Chairman there had ever been.

A much respected man, Clovis Marca; famous for his philosophical writings, his easy stoicism, his unselfish energy, his kindness and his wisdom. There were many to match him in most of the qualities, but none who combined them as he did. Clovis Marca was the golden man, almost the god, the darling of his world.

Clovis Marca was in his fifth year of office when the scientists announced the catastrophe.

For several generations no children had been born to the daylight people. With life-spans of up to three hundred years, people did not feel the need to reproduce very often. Those who tried and failed thought little of it. Everyone assumed that the reason for the lack of children was because everyone else had decided not to have any.

Then a couple complained. Other couples complained. It was discovered that a large section of the population had indeed tried to have children and had failed.

Urgent experiments and tests were made.

Physics and biology were fields in which little new research had been done for at least two hundred years; it was felt that there was no need for any more information than was available to assure comfortable living.

The climate of the times had not produced anyone sufficiently interested in the two disciplines to do new research. The increase in harmless omega radiation had been measured and noted in the previous century. It was believed that the radiation was a by-product of the mysterious energies which the space-dwellers had used to stop the world spinning. The radiation had seemed, in fact, beneficial to many plants. It had produced the flower forests, it destroyed weeds, it appeared to contribute to people's youthfulness.

The tests showed that it also affected semen and ova. In short, it had made every man and woman on daylight Earth barren.

This was not at first thought particularly disastrous. Expeditions were sent to the twilight regions to seek people who could still reproduce.

But, whether or not they had resisted the effect of the omega radiation, the denizens of the twilight regions had inbred to the state of impotence. Valta Marca had been the last father, Clovis Marca the last child of the twilight.

A few expeditions were made by robot machines into the cold nightlands, but there, as was already known, nothing lived.

In space, then?

A thousand years before, at great expense and at the cost of many lives, Mars and Ganymede had been transformed into facsimiles of Earth. They were lush worlds and they had supplied food and minerals to Earth when they had been needed. After the raid from space, they had lost their usefulness, for the population had greatly decreased. Now only a few existed on either planet, simply to ensure that they continued to produce food and minerals in case they were ever needed. The wardens of Mars and Ganymede and their small staffs were replaced every three months because three months was almost the maximum time that men could live away from Earth and remain sane.

It was because of this that space travel to distant solar systems had been discontinued not long after man had first gone into space; it had been discovered that in spite of their ability to reproduce exactly Earth atmosphere and other conditions on ship or, as in the case of Mars and Ganymede, even on planets, somehow men could not bear being away from Earth for long.

There were psychological explanations, physiological explanations, semi-mystical explanations for this being so, but the fact remained: Men who were on average away from Earth for little over three months went mad with pain and a terror that welled up from the recesses of their minds and could not be controlled. Even in space, on the journey to Mars, men had to undergo the *space ache*. The word had been coined to describe the indescribable experience of leaving the mother planet. Space ache – a combination of mental and physical agony – came soon after your ship had passed the halfway point on the journey to Mars. It was possible, by complicated methods, to relieve the space ache, but not to avert it.

Thus the faint hope that those men who guarded Earth's colonies for a few months every year would not have received as much omega radiation as those who had never left Earth.

It was proved that they had, while on Earth, received more than enough radiation.

There was a legend – a mere fiction, everyone knew – that a colony had been founded on Titan soon after the raid and that the colonists had managed to adapt, losing something of their humanity in the process. Half-human or not, their seed could be used.

It was an illustration of the point of desperation reached that a volunteer expedition was sent to Titan and did not return.

There was no escape from the truth after that. The space-dwellers had, probably without realising it, effectively destroyed the human race. In two hundred years everyone would be dead. Two hundred years was the life expectancy of the youngest person on Earth. Her name was Fastina Cahmin.

When the realisation dawned that the mortality of the race could not be averted a new mood swept through the society of daylight Earth. The people gave themselves up to pleasure-seeking, and a party began. It was a kind of Wake; a premature Wake held by the soon to be deceased. Too sophisticated to let it control them as yet, the people of the daylight suppressed their hysteria or gave vent to it harmlessly, in their arts and pleasures.

Clovis Marca resigned his chairmanship of the council and mysteriously disappeared.

The shock of realising he was never to propagate himself had reawakened the dormant elements in Marca's psyche.

He became wholly driven by what had caused him to survive his birth and early childhood so successfully. He became wholly driven by his intense will to live.

The long party continued and the signs of the suppressed hysteria began to show – in the fashions, art and in the topics of conversation. From time to time people wondered where Clovis Marca had gone and why he had gone, though it had not taken them long to get used to instances of irrational actions by men once thought completely adjusted. It had been surprising, though, that Clovis Marca, their demigod, should break so soon – unless he was seeking still for a remedy for their plight. They told themselves that this must be so. It was comforting to know that Marca was making this sacrifice, even though it was absolutely certain that no hope was left.

Clovis Marca was gone a year and then he returned to his friends and his people.

They celebrated his homecoming with a party. It was really just part of the ever-present party. It was more elaborate than usual that was all.

Book One

Book One

Chapter One
Something to Fear

I T WAS A noisy party, a colourful party, a splendid, exciting party, and it swirled all around him in the huge hall. It was packed full of life; full of heads and genitals and bellies and breasts, legs and chests and arms and hands; people with pumping hearts under their ribs, rushing blood in their veins, nerves at work, muscles moving. Most of their costumes were colourful and picturesque, though here and there stood a dark-clad sexless individual in heavy clothes, wearing a mask and with its head shaven. But most of them drank down the liquor and ate up the food and they danced and flirted and they talked all the time. It is necessary, he thought.

The walls of the hall were of pseudo-quartz, translucent and coloured like writhing rainbows. Pillars, arches and galleries, rising from the floor, were of the same subtle manufacture. Music filled all parts of the hall and there was laughter, excited voices. The throng seemed in good humour.

He tried to relax and join in the pleasure. A roboid waiter, humanlike but running on hidden casters, paused with a tray of drinks. Clovis Marca reached out from his seat in the corner and took a wine-glass; but as he did so he saw his pursuer again. The enigmatic face was merged with the blackness, but Marca recognised the awkward way in which the man held his head, as if he had weak neck muscles and was keeping the head erect by an effort. Marca stared at him, but there was no response from the dark figure, no sign that he knew Marca was looking at him.

Marca sipped his drink, wondering whether to ignore the man or cross the hall and confront him. But he felt afraid.

To succumb to the fear would be irrational, he realised. Fear could be understood and controlled. There seemed no reason to be afraid of the mysterious figure. Marca frowned and stood up, stepping down from the little dais and joining the heaving, almost solid mass of people on the floor. Being very tall, he could look over their heads and keep his attention on the still figure of the man who stood in the shadow on the far side of the hall.

Almost involuntarily, Marca began to move forward. Everything but himself and the other figure seemed unreal. He was hardly aware of the warm bodies pressing against his and now even the noise of the party seemed distant.

He had held off confronting this man for too long. He had had opportunities on Mars and Ganymede to speak to him face to face. He had seen him more than once on Earth, too; but he had given in, every time, to his irrational reluctance to admit that the man existed, or that his constant presence near him was anything more than coincidence.

He knew the man only as Mr Take. He had discovered that much from the passenger list of the ship they had both taken to Mars. The outdated form of address the man chose to use before his name was another unusual thing about him, smacking of the pointless eccentricities of the twilight people. It was even likely that Mr Take was not his real name.

Repressing his fear, Marca moved more rapidly towards him.

Overhead a fat man levitated, laughing in a way that had not been heard a year ago. The laughter was brittle, hysterical. The fat man ascended erratically towards the nearest gallery where similarly laughing men and women reached out, trying to grab him. He was giggling so much himself that he could hardly control his flight, threatening to crash on the heads of the crowd below. He had a bottle in his hand and, as he veered about in the air like a gigantic, drunken bumblebee, the bottle spilled its contents, raining golden wine down into the hall. Some of it caught Marca in the eyes. He paused to wipe his face, and when he looked at the corner again, Mr Take had gone.

Carefully scanning the hall, Marca saw Take moving slowly towards one of the big oval entrances. The crowd, like the foaming wake of a ship, seemed to divide about him as he walked.

Marca shrugged. He felt relieved that the man was leaving.

Then Take turned. He still held his head in that strange way, but now he looked directly at Clovis Marca. Take's frame was thin; his head was long and pale, his sombre eyes hooded, colourless.

Marca shrugged again, emphatically, and felt someone touch his hand. It was his old friend, Narvo Velusi, the man who had chosen to protect him when, over twenty years before, he had first come to daylight Earth. Narvo Velusi was two hundred and ninety years old; a man nearing death. There were few signs of this on Velusi's face. The flesh was old, but firm, the blue eyes alert and the hair dark. He had a square face and a bulky, wide-shouldered body. When he spoke his tone was mild but vibrant.

'Are you enjoying the party, Clovis?'

Clovis felt slightly offended by the presence of the hand on his arm. He took a step back. He had never considered Velusi's age before, but now he did and the thought was unpleasant. He controlled himself and smiled.

'Wonderful, Narvo. It was good of you...'

'You don't look happy, though. Perhaps I was thoughtless? I should have given you time to rest before I suggested the party. After all, you only got back this afternoon...'

'No, I meant it. It's a relief to be back here and a pleasure to be with so many people.' He looked for Take, but the dark man had gone. 'Did you invite a person who calls himself Mr Take?'

Velusi shook his head. 'Did you hope to meet him? He could be here. It's open house – to welcome you back.'

'No – he was here. He's gone.'

'I still think you seem ill at ease, Clovis.'

Marca tried to smile again. 'I suppose I am a little tired. I'll stay though. It would be ungracious to leave so soon.'

'Not at all. Let's go. Your house has been prepared for you. If you –'

'No. I'll stay. Have you heard of this Mr Take? A strange man.' Marca described him.

'He sounds it. I should know a man like that – but I don't. Why are you so interested in him?'

'I've seen him before. Not just on Earth – on Mars and Gany-mede, too. He seems to have been following me.'

Velusi pursed his lips. Marca knew that he was too polite to ask him directly where he had been and why he had been gone so long. Velusi was evidently hoping to hear more. Marca was half-ashamed of himself for being so secretive with his old friend, but he had long ago made up his mind to share his ideas with no-one else.

'We can find out who and where this Take is tomorrow,' Velusi said with a smile. Once again he took Marca's arm. Once again Marca felt a trace of revulsion at the touch but let Velusi steer him towards the nearest gravichute. 'Come on, Clovis, cheer up. Let's go and meet some friends. I think you know most of them.'

Marca made himself relax as Velusi stood aside to let him enter the gravichute entrance. The gravichute was a circular shaft going from top to bottom of the house. At its base was a force-beam generator. A single button by the entrance could control the strength of the beam so that one could drift gently down or be pushed gently up. Inside the opening was a simple handgrip which could be grasped to halt one's progress.

The harnessing of this power had contributed a great deal to Earth's present civilisation, and all techniques were now based on it, as earlier they had been based on nuclear energy.

They drifted up to the highest gallery, several hundred feet above the floor of the hall. There were only a few people here lying on couches, talking quietly. Most of them were old acquaint-ances. Marca greeted them politely. He sat down on a couch beside Velusi.

Several of the men and women there were ex-officials of the council. Since the disaster, most people had followed Marca's example and resigned their jobs so that now only a skeleton staff looked after the administration. It was all that was needed.

Marca was surprised to see Brand Calax, Warden of Gany-mede, in conversation with Andros Almer, ex-Controller of Public Communications. Calax should have been in the middle of his three-month duty on Ganymede. Why was he here?

Miona Pelva, a red-headed woman running to fat, smiled at Marca. She had been Deputy Chairman under his chairmanship. She had not been fat then. She was not the only person who had let herself go since last year's news.

'How was space?' She was evidently as eager as Velusi to hear him answer the questions they had all been asking about him.

'Awful,' he smiled.

'Isn't it always? Any after-effects of the space ache?' She shook her head in sympathy, her floppy purple headdress waving. 'A *year* away! Was it all spent in space?'

'Not all.'

'Somebody said they thought you'd gone back to the twilight region for a while.' The speaker was a sharp-featured man wearing a golden gauze mask over his upper face. The fashion of wearing masks had grown up since Marca had left. Symptomatic of the suppressed hysteria now dominating daylight Earth, Marca thought.

'Really?' said Marca, thinking that people's manners also seemed to have declined in the year.

Velusi changed the subject. 'Have you been to see Carleon's new novel, Quiro?' he asked the man in the golden mask. 'You must see it, Clovis. The mood mobiles are very impressive.'

Marca felt more comfortable as the conversation went on to more general topics. A little later he rose and went over to speak to Brand Calax and Andros Almer. The men seemed to be arguing quite fiercely but broke off as he greeted them.

'Sit down, Clovis,' Almer said cheerfully. 'The council's gone to pieces since you left – but I suppose there's no need for it any more. Brand and I were discussing this idea of his about sending another expedition to Titan. Do you think it's a good idea?'

Marca shrugged. 'I doubt if it would achieve anything but a few more deaths. Besides, who'd volunteer now?'

Brand Calax was a squat man with a pointed, black beard. He wore an orange turban, a red, knee-length coat, open at the neck and flared at the waist, and low-heeled boots. Some said he had been born in space. Certainly he had a stronger resistance to the space ache than anyone else.

'I would,' Calax said. 'I could take it – I doubt if anyone else could.'

'It's a long journey,' Marca said.

Andros Almer scowled. He had a dark, tanned face, slightly slanting eyes and cheekbones, full lips and a supercilious expression that always seemed a little studied. 'A pointless journey,' he said.

'You agree we should not give up,' Calax growled. 'What else is there to do?'

'Anything would be better than risking your life or your sanity in a voyage through space to a planet that is barely habitable in search of a group of people *thought* to have gone there just after the raid and who would probably be dead if they had!' Almer drew a deep breath and was going to continue when Brand Calax broke in.

'I told you I had found evidence that a large expedition did land on Titan. I circled the world myself. I saw the remains of ships. I saw suggestions that attempts had been made to begin a settlement of some kind.'

'You saw these things from a great distance!' Almer said. 'You brought back no proof that you actually saw ships and buildings. Your eyes might have deceived you. Maybe you saw what you hoped to see! Why didn't you land?'

Marca listened intently to the two men.

'Because I had little fuel left and because the space ache was getting me,' Calax said sharply. 'I was in a converted ferry. They haven't a big range!'

'And that's the only survey you made.' Almer spread his hands. 'Flimsy evidence, surely? Yet you came back to Earth to ask for a special ship to be built so that you can bring some of these "survivors" back to Earth. Even if there were ships and buildings – do you think anyone could have lasted on a world like Titan?'

'It's possible,' Calax said. 'I spent nine months at a stretch away from Earth once.'

'Nine months – and you're scarcely typical of the rest of us. These people are supposed to have been on Titan for four hundred years!'

Calax turned to Clovis Marca. 'It's just possible, isn't it, Clovis?'

Marca shook his head. 'Not likely, though. You want to build a ship, eh, to take you to Titan and bring back the people you think are there?'

'The descendants of the original expedition,' Calax said brusquely. 'It's a chance worth taking, I think. If I hadn't been away when the first expedition was made, I'd have volunteered. I could have made it.'

'Possibly,' said Almer. 'I still think we should be concentrating on something more positive – creating semen and ova artificially, for instance.'

'It's been tried. Not one of our scientists has got anywhere.' Calax helped himself to wine.

Marca sensed that a genuine dislike existed between the two. There seemed no reason for it. There seemed to be no argument, either. If Calax wanted to go to Titan, surely that was his risk?

He started to say as much when suddenly they all looked up. The hubbub of the party, which had been in the background all the time, had cut off sharply.

Marca moved to the edge of the gallery and leaned over the invisible force-rail.

People were streaming rapidly from the hall. All the other galleries had been cleared. Through every exit, people hurried silently. They seemed tense.

Then they had gone and the hall was still and silent.

There was party litter everywhere and the light breeze from the entrances stirred it. That was the only movement.

Almost in the centre of the hall, near a couch, Marca saw a dark shape on the floor. It was the figure of a man.

As Almer, Calax, Velusi and the others reached the rail, Marca turned and made for the gravichute. He descended rapidly, crossed the hall to where the figure lay.

The man was dressed in the high fashion of the moment, his head shaved, his rust-coloured mask obscuring his entire face, belted coat of deep blue spread out around him on the floor.

Marca knelt beside him and felt his pulse.

He was dead.

Velusi and Almer crossed the hall towards him.

'What's the matter with him?' Almer asked.

'Dead,' said Marca. He peeled off the mask. The man was old. Evidently he had died of a heart attack probably brought on by the excitement of the party.

Velusi turned away, clearing his throat. Almer looked embarrassed.

'Why did they all just leave like that?' Marca asked. 'So suddenly – not trying to help him or anything…'

'They probably decided to carry on with the party somewhere else,' Velusi said. 'That's what usually happens – they go on somewhere else…'

'I don't understand,' Marca said. 'You mean they just leave a corpse where it lies?'

'Usually,' said Almer. 'You can't blame them, can you?'

'I can't understand them, either!' Marca said disapprovingly. 'What's happening here nowadays, Andros?'

'Can't you guess?' said Velusi quietly. 'Are you sure you can't understand them, Clovis?'

Chapter Two
Someone to Love

FASTINA CAHMIN HAD waited a year for Clovis Marca to return, but on the day of his arrival she had been asleep. She could go without sleep for extraordinarily long periods and could spend an equally long time catching up on it. She woke, after three days' asleep, to learn that Marca had come home. Andros Almer had told her in a letter he had left while she slept.

Fastina Cahmin was a widow whose husband had been one of the Titan expedition volunteers. She was twenty-eight and the youngest woman in the world. She was the last child of the day side of the Earth as Clovis Marca was the last child of the twilight region.

She was tall, with a slender, full-breasted figure and golden skin. Her hair was black and her eyes were a deep, luminous blue. She had a small, oval face and a wide mouth. Perhaps because her life-span would be so long, she took a sensual pleasure in living that was nowadays rare.

Before her husband's death she had known Clovis Marca only socially, but she had been completely in love with him for several years. Her husband had loved her with similar single-mindedness and she believed, without remorse, that it was because he had realised her own obsession that he had volunteered for the Titan expedition.

She read Almer's letter.

Fastina,
  My selflessness knows no bounds. We heard today that Marca is on the Mars ship and should arrive this afternoon. Remember what you told me. I hope you are unlucky.

  With love,
  Andros

She smiled affectionately. She liked Andros. He had been the one who had brought the news of her husband's presumed death. At the same time, knowing what her feelings had been towards her husband, he suggested that she should come and live with him. She had refused, telling him that she would first propose to Clovis. If he rejected her, which was likely, she would then accept Andros. That was what the letter was about.

She put the letter on the table beside her bed and touched a stud on the control panel. The wall shimmered and became transparent. It was a fine day. The sun, at permanent zenith, shone down on the sea. The tideless expanse of water was completely still and blue. The white beach that led up to her house was deserted, as it almost always was. In daylight Earth, people lived far apart. Their houses were self-sufficient and transport swift. There was no need for cities. The nearest thing to a city had been the few buildings which had housed the administrative offices.

Fastina lived in an area that had once been Greece, although there were no artificial boundaries of that sort any more. The planet's real boundaries were now formed by the twilight region.

She contacted Central Information on her V-screen, and asked: 'Where is Clovis Marca at this moment?'

The screen replied.

'He was last observed half an hour ago entering the south-western flower forest.'

Fastina put on her best dress. Its crimson fabric was virtually weightless and drifted around her like a cloud of blood. She took the gravichute to the roof of her house. There her air carriage waited. Its golden body had been moulded to the shape of a fantastic bird with spreading wings. There was a cavity in the back, lined with deep red cushions. Up to four people could rest in it in comfort.

She climbed into the carriage and put a small, ultrasonic whistle to her lips. She blew a particular signal and the air carriage drifted upwards over the beach and the sea. Like a fabulous creature it swept gracefully towards the south-west and the flower forest.

A little while later she walked through the flower forest, hoping that she might bump into Clovis Marca. She walked with a long, easy stride, smiling as she breathed in the scents of the huge blooms hanging above her and around her.

Everywhere rose the shining green and brown trunks of the flowers and the scents were so heavy that they drugged her into a state of pleasant light-headedness. She looked up at the leaves, the petals, the heat-hazy sky and the sun. Beneath her feet were petals of all colours; large petals of pale purple, small ones of dark purple, pink, pale yellow and mauve. There were petals of yellow, scarlet, cerise and crimson, petals of soft blue and orange, sometimes ankle-deep. And there was every shade of sunlit green, from near-black to near-white, where flower trees stood tall and cool or clustered to the ground.

She turned down a path that was thick with the cerise flowers fallen from the trees above her. It was cooler in this avenue and, although like all her people she had become used to the great heat of the world, she appreciated the shade.

She did not, as she had hoped, bump into Clovis Marca. She bumped into Andros Almer instead and knew at once that it was not accidental. Obviously he had guessed she would come here.

Almer had succumbed to fashion, it seemed. He was wearing a gauze mask that gave his face a blue tinge. He wore a deep blue pleated shirt, black, tight trousers and a loose, black cloak that was gathered in at the waist and belted. He paused, bent and picked up one of the fallen cerise flowers, offering it to her with a smile.

She smiled back and accepted it. 'Hello, Andros. Have you seen Clovis?'

'Ah,' he said lightly. 'If I were vain, I'd be so offended…'

She laughed. 'I hope you are vain, Andros. Didn't Alodios write "Vanity makes for variety in a man, whereas humility offers only the humdrum"? I'd hate you to be humdrum.'

'You hate me anyway,' he said with a mock frown. 'Besides, if what you say is the truth then Clovis should not attract you, for

THE SHORES OF DEATH

his lack of vanity is well known. He's a perfect man, all virtue and no vice – a whole man. A whole man offers no surprises, Fastina. Change your mind or risk his acceptance. He would *bore* you to death!'

'I see you're not completely given to the fashion,' she said lightly. 'You can still force yourself to say the word...'

'Death is all I want if you won't have me, Fastina.'

'Don't die, Andros. It would embarrass all those poor people. After all, it's our duty to stay alive, isn't it? Just in case.'

'Just in case there's a miracle and the world starts spinning and jostles our genes so that overnight we all find ourselves parents of triplets?' Andros laughed, but now his laughter was sharper. 'That's the soundest hope, you know. There are wilder ones about. Brand Calax believes there are people on Titan just throbbing with healthy seeds. The only trouble is the gravity's a bit heavy and they look like walking pancakes. The big bangers might have a better idea – they want to go out in one mighty explosion. They seriously suggested we make a bomb big enough to blow up every human artefact in the world.'

'Why blow them up?'

'They think they've no right to exist. They've gone off sex as well – no love-making without progeny, they say. What a syndrome!'

'Poor things. I'd never have thought people could change so much.'

'It's fear,' he said. 'And they've got every right to be afraid. You're lucky – you don't seem to worry at all.'

'I'm worried, of course, but I can't believe it altogether.'

'You should have been on the council when we gradually realised the whole truth. You'd believe it.' He pulled at his dark clothes, fingered his mask. 'Look at all this – I *like* the fashion, but you can see what's creating it. I must be as scared as anyone else. I haven't started shaving my head, yet, or wearing those sweltering black masks and robes – but don't be surprised if I get to like the idea in a few months.'

'Oh, Andros, you're too intelligent to go that far!' She smiled.

'Intelligence has very little to do with it. Can I take you to the meeting?'

'Is there a meeting?'

'Is there a meeting! Your senses must be more distracted than I guessed. That's why Clovis is here. Everyone interested is in the Great Glade discussing Brand Calax's idea. It'll be decided today whether to let him have the materials to build his ship or not. I hope they laugh him out of the glade!' The last sentence was spoken with such vehemence that she glanced at him in surprise. *Was* Andros becoming unbalanced? She could hardly believe it.

'When does the debate start?' she asked, taking his arm gingerly.

'It's already started. Come on, we'll go there now.' He put the ultrasonic whistle to his lips and shortly afterwards his carriage moved down through the flower trees, hardly disturbing a leaf. It hovered a foot above the ground, its ornate metal scrollwork glistening red and yellow. Andros helped her onto the plush cushions and lay down on the couch opposite her. He blew on the instrument and the carriage rose into the hot sky. Through its transparent floor, she saw the mass of brightly coloured flowers, some measuring twenty feet across, moving swiftly past.

She said nothing as they flew along and Andros seemed to respect her silence and stared with apparent interest at the flowers until the carriage had found a space for itself among the hundreds of other carriages hovering above the Great Glade where that part of Earth's society sufficiently concerned with the problem of a second Titan flight had met to debate. For a moment she thought she saw Andros glance at her in a peculiar way, but she dismissed the idea, guessing that it came from her own abnormal mental state.

'I see you're not wearing a gravstrap,' Andros said, reaching under the couch. He handed her the thin, tubular belt and fitted a similar one under his arms. She did the same, clipping the thing together over her breastbone. They left the carriage and drifted down among the packed tiers until they found two vacant chairs and seated themselves.

Below them, on the central dais, Brand Calax was speaking. He still wore his turban and red coat.

She did not listen closely to Brand Calax until she was sure Marca was there, sitting with his arms folded, dressed in a simple high-collared white shirt, black trousers and with small dark lenses over his eyes to protect them. From his seat in the first tier, he seemed to be listening intently to Calax. Beside Clovis sat old Narvo Velusi, dressed soberly in a russet toga, his high-heeled black boots stretched out before him, his body bent forward slightly. His square, heavy face was turned towards Calax.

Calax's voice seemed harsh to Fastina. He was speaking urgently and bluntly.

'In about two hundred years there won't be any of us left in the world. The human race will be nothing but a few bones and a few buildings. Surely it's better to keep trying to stop that happening? Everyone on Earth seems to have drawn in on themselves – there's an apathy I never expected to see. Do you want to die? From what I've seen in the past few days, that's the last thing you wish. Besides – I'm only saying I want to risk my own life on Titan. I know what the gravity's like and I know that that combined with space ache is too much for the average man to take for more than a day or so. But I'm used to space – I can even live with the space ache for longer than I'd need to stay on Titan, just to make sure there isn't any hope there. I'm asking for materials we'll never need to use for anything else. What's the matter with everyone? Why don't you just let me go ahead? I'm the only one who might be hurt!' Calax wiped his forehead and waited for the response. None came. 'We've got to go on trying,' he said. 'It's a valuable human trait to go on trying. We survived the raid. We can survive this.'

'This is the aftermath of the raid,' said Almer from the audience. The silvery phonoplates hanging in the air around the auditorium picked up his words and amplified them for the others. 'We only *thought* we'd survived it.'

Narvo Velusi got up and looked at the mediator who sat on the dais behind Calax. The mediator was a fair-haired man with a

blond moustache which he kept stroking. He nodded and Velusi
walked onto the dais as Calax left it.

'I think I can tell Brand Calax why we are reluctant to grant
him the resources to build his ship,' said Velusi quietly. 'It is
because we have now become so fearful that we are even afraid to
hope. We are rational people normally – our society is still probably the most perfect in history. Yet we can all sense it going sour
on us – our reason doesn't seem to be helping any more. I think
this is because, though we know why we are behaving unreason-
ably, what has happened to us is bigger than reason. It strikes at
our deep psychic drives – our animal drives, for that matter. We
are no longer immortal as a race. We had always assumed we
would be. We are beginning to behave irrationally and I think this
will get worse, no matter what we do to try to stop it. I feel that
Brand Calax should be allowed to do as he thinks fit – but I share
the general opinion that he will be doing it for nothing.'

Velusi's calm, slow words seemed to impress his listeners. Fastina saw people nodding agreement with him. She too sensed his
sanity, his understanding of the situation they were all in.

Someone else spoke from the audience.

'May we hear what Clovis Marca thinks?'

Velusi glanced at Marca.

Marca remained seated. He said. 'I can add nothing more to
what Narvo Velusi has said. I am sorry.'

People looked disappointed. Evidently the rumour that Marca
had been seeking some solution had been wrong.

Velusi continued:

'There is little hope. It would be stupid to hope. If our destiny
is to die, let us try to do it well.'

A woman laughed shrilly. They saw her rising towards her air
carriage on her gravstrap. A few others followed her. A group of
faceless, sexless people in their masks and dark clothes also
returned to their air carriages. The vehicles wheeled away through
the bright, hot sky.

Brand Calax jumped back onto the dais. 'And let's do it fighting!
Will you give me my spaceship?'

The mediator stopped stroking his moustache and got up. 'Who agrees?' he asked the crowd.

Hands rose. The mediator counted them.

'Who disagrees?'

Fastina watched Andros raise his hand.

The mediator counted again.

'Brand Calax, the resources you need are at your disposal,' said the mediator formally.

Calax nodded his thanks, touched his gravstrap and rose into the air.

Fastina saw Clovis Marca stand up, obviously preparing to leave. He was pointing into the air, towards a white air carriage hovering above him. Narvo Velusi was nodding. They were obviously deciding to travel in that carriage.

Impulsively she touched the control of her gravstrap and was lifted upwards, guiding herself gently towards the white carriage.

Andros shouted after her, but he did not follow.

She reached the carriage before Marca and Velusi. She drifted over the side and sat down on one of the couches.

Clovis was not the first man she had confronted with a proposal of marriage, but her heart was beating rapidly as he and Velusi reached the craft and saw her sitting there.

Clovis recognised her and smiled. 'Hello, Fastina.'

'Hello, Clovis. Welcome back. How are you feeling after your mysterious travels?'

'He's better today,' Velusi said, settling onto a couch and raising a whistle to his lips, 'you should have seen him yesterday, Fastina!'

Marca did feel better that morning, having slept well during the period they still called 'night'. He felt more his old self. He sat down next to Fastina and kissed her lightly on the forehead. They had never been lovers, but she had always flirted with him and he had always responded cheerfully.

Before he blew the appropriate signal, Velusi asked: 'Do you want a lift, Fastina?'

'Not really,' she said. 'I came to see Clovis. If you're busy, I'll wait...'

'That's all right,' Marca told her. 'It's nice to see you again. Come and have some lunch at my house.'

She looked at him, wondering how deep his affection was. She could tell that he was attracted to her, but she knew he was not the man to begin a casual love affair on the strength of a mild attraction.

The carriage was moving away from the flower forest, passing over the occasional house. Now that there was no need for towns, public services were maintained by a big underground computerised network. The houses were mobile and a man and his friends or family could land their buildings in the scenery of their choice. Marca's house was situated at the moment close to the lake that had once been known as Lake Tanganyika. Europe, Africa, the Middle East, India and parts of Russia faced the sun, as did a tiny part of the South American continent. Most of South America, all of North America, nearly all of China, and all of Japan and the Australias lay in the night region. The habitable world was, in fact, what had been the known world before the great explorations of the Renaissance.

Soon they could see the lake ahead, like a sheet of blue steel flanked by hills and forests. Herds of animals grazed below. While the human race had decreased, the animals had proliferated; perhaps because their life cycles were shorter, they had adapted to the omega radiation in time. It was ironic, thought Marca as his carriage dropped towards the mosaic roof of his tall house, that if human longevity had not been increased they would probably be all right as far as the survival of the race was concerned. With what had once been the normal cycle of life and death, genes might have built up a gradual resistance. It was too late to do anything about it now, though.

When the car had landed, Clovis helped Fastina out of it. She smiled, breathing in the rich, heavy air. Africa directly faced the sun and its vegetation was even lusher than it had been. She glanced at Clovis and was about to comment on the view when she thought she caught a peculiar look in his eyes, as if he stared at some secret part of her that she did not know existed – some

physical organ of hers which stored the secrets of her unconscious ambitions and her future.

She thought of him for an instant as an ancient, sombre sha-
man who might cut the organ from her living body and toss it
steaming in the still air to make some unholy divination. He
smiled at her quietly as he gestured for her to precede him into
the gravichute which gaped in the centre of the roof. Perhaps, she
thought, he had not been looking into her soul, but his own.

Dropping into the dark hole of the chute, she felt as if she were
condemning herself to an irrevocable destiny. Whether her destiny would be good or bad she could not tell.

I'm in a funny state of mind, she thought, as she drifted down.
A disordered state of mind, no doubt about that. It must be love...

Later they stood drinking aperitifs on the balcony outside the dining room. It looked out over the lake. A great cloud of pink
flamingoes flew past, high above the lake. There was a sense of
peace now and the silence of the countryside was broken only by
the distant call of some wild canine in the forest.

'When we're gone, at least this will remain,' said Velusi leaning
on the invisible force-rail. 'When people bothered to debate these
abstract issues, some used to think that the human race was a
freak – a sport of nature – that we had no business being here at
all and no place in the scheme of things. Perhaps they were right.'

Fastina smiled. 'It doesn't matter now.'

'Not to us,' Velusi replied, 'but there are people about even
today who think that the space-dwellers were some sort of mystic
agency – you know, like in the old religions – whose purpose was
to eliminate human beings, to straighten the biological record, as
it were. It matters to them – it's becoming their creed.'

'You mean those peculiar people who shave their heads and so
on?' Marca asked.

'Yes, poor things,' Velusi sighed. 'We don't change much, do
we? Only a short time ago we had nothing to fear. Our population
was small, we had everything we wanted, the world was good –
we lived in a paradise, though we didn't know it...'

'I knew it,' Marca murmured.

'Yes, I suppose you did,' Velusi continued. 'I remember when you first came to live with us how you would go on and on telling us how perfect our society was compared with the one you'd just left. I could never properly understand why a certain kind of person actually chose to live in the twilight...'

'Can you now?' Fastina asked.

'In a way, yes. Those people with their shaven heads are living in a kind of mental twilight already. If you have that mentality, then I suppose you choose to live where it can survive best. That's what I was going to say. In a world without fear the human virtues flourish and become dominant. We've had no violence, no major neuroses for centuries. The space-dwellers somehow managed to put us in our place, made us realise our limitations, made us cultivate the best of what we had. But now fear is back, isn't it? Fear was largely responsible for creating the primitive religions, and fear, of one sort or another, was what fostered the unpleasant elements in even the sophisticated religions. Fear produced repressive societies, totalitarian governments, wars, and the major proportion of sexual perversions, as well, of course, as the multitude of mental perversions – perverse philosophical theories, political systems, religious creeds, even artistic expression. Think of the numbers of talented creative people who spent their lives trying to bend their gifts to express some insane notion of the way things should be.' Velusi gestured with his glass. 'Well, it seems we're back where we started. There's nothing we can do about it – when in the past did a really irrational person ever listen to reason? I'm not a pessimistic man, but I get the feeling that we're going to enter a new dark age which will only end when the last man or woman on Earth dies – and at this rate that could be even sooner than we think...'

'You sound like an ancient prophet yourself, Narvo.' Marca drained the remainder of his drink. 'The apocalypse is at hand, eh?'

Chapter Three
Something to Hide

THEY ATE IN Marca's dining room. It was not large. Its walls were decorated with abstract frescoes, vaguely reminiscent of Mayan art. The room was just a little gloomy.

After the meal, Narvo Velusi got up to go. He had guessed the purpose of Fastina's visit.

'I'll see you tomorrow, Clovis,' he said. 'And I'll tell you then about my own equally unreasonable project.' He waved cheerfully and entered the gravichute entrance.

'I wonder what that could be,' Marca murmured when he had gone. 'I hope it's nothing drastic.'

Fastina poured more wine for both of them. 'Narvo wouldn't do anything drastic, would he? Do you think he's right about what he said? It sounded ominous – and it did seem reasonable.'

Marca stretched out in his big chair. 'We haven't changed much in all those thousands of years, Fastina. We have the same drives, the same ambitions – presumably the same fears producing the same results. I know that I've felt afraid at times, recently...'

'But you've been in space. That's different.'

'Not just in space. In fact it's nothing to do with space or any other kind of environment – it's in *me*. I think it always has been.'

'Is that what made you go off so suddenly?'

He laughed. 'You're still trying to find out about that, aren't you? I promised myself I'd tell no-one why I left or what I'm looking for...'

'So you're looking for something.' She smiled back. 'Not someone, by any chance?'

He shook his head. 'Not a woman, Fastina, if that's what you're getting at. I don't need to look, anyway, when the nicest woman I've ever known is sitting opposite me.' He spoke half-jokingly and she looked at him carefully, trying to guess if the statement had been anything more than a pleasant compliment. For an instant he returned her gaze steadily, then looked at the wine. He reached out and refilled their glasses. They were both drinking more than usual.

'It is someone as well,' he continued. 'Someone with something I want – and even then I'm not sure they have it.'

'You're not being fair, Clovis,' she said lightly. 'You're making it sound more and more intriguing!'

'I'm sorry, Fastina. I suppose there's no harm in mentioning the name of the person. It's Orlando Sharvis...'

He glanced at her intently, as if looking for a sign that she recognised the name. It was vaguely familiar, but nothing more.

'No,' she said. 'It doesn't mean anything. I won't press you any further, Clovis. I'm sorry to have sounded so curious. You're back now, that's the main thing.'

He rubbed his lips, nodding abstractedly. 'For the time being, anyway,' he said quietly.

Now she could not disguise her anxiety. She leaned towards him over the table. 'You're not leaving again?'

'It might be necessary.' He touched her hand. 'Don't worry about it, Fastina. My own feelings are as stupid as anyone's. Maybe I'll see sense and forget all about them.'

She held his hand tightly and now they looked directly into each other's faces.

'We should enjoy life,' she said hesitantly. 'Shouldn't we? While we can?'

Still holding her hand, he got up and came round to the couch.

He took her in his arms, pressing her to his body. 'Perhaps you're right,' he said. His voice was trembling, grim, distant.

He kissed her suddenly and she responded, though now she was afraid of him, afraid of something she had released in him. His love-making became urgent, desperate.

'The bedroom,' he murmured and they got up together, walking towards the gravichute.

His frantic and tense manner disturbed her, but she knew it

was far too late to do anything but let him lead her into the shaft. They rose up together. His grasp on her arm was painful.

They reached the bedroom entrance and he caught the handgrip, pulling them both to the side of the shaft. They entered his room. It had been darkened and only a little light came through the outer wall.

Surprised, she saw the silhouette of a man against it. A man who held his head in a peculiar way.

In a world without crime, locks and alarms did not exist, so that the man could have entered the room when and how he chose. He was guilty of a crime; an invasion of privacy at very least.

That was not what shocked Marca so much as his recognition of the man. He paused by the gravichute entrance, still gripping Fastina's arm.

'What do you want here, Mr Take?' he said.

The man did not move, did not speak.

Almost for the first time in his adult life, Clovis Marca allowed anger to get the better of him. He let go of Fastina's arm and plunged across the room towards the dark figure.

'This time I'm getting my explanation,' he said, reaching out towards Take.

The intruder moved just before Marca's hands touched him. He moved faster than it should have been possible for an ordinary man to move. He made for the gravichute, but Fastina blocked the entrance with her body. He veered aside and stood stock-still again. Then he spoke. His voice was melodious and deep.

'You will never be able to touch me, Clovis Marca. Let me leave here. I mean you no harm, I hope.'

'No harm?' Marca was breathing heavily. 'You've been haunting me for months! Who are you? What do you want from me?'

'My name is Take.'

'A good name for a thief. What's your real name?'

'I did not come here to steal anything from you. I merely wished to confirm something.'

'What?'

'What I guessed you are looking for.'

'Be quiet!' Marca glanced anxiously at Fastina.

'You are ashamed?' asked Take.

'No, but it doesn't suit me to reveal what I'm looking for. You can see the sense of that, can't you? Conditions here are no longer normal. I'm not sure you know what it is, anyway.'

'I know.'

Then Take had leapt to where Fastina stood, pushed her gently aside and jumped into the gravichute, so swiftly that it was impossible to follow his movements.

Clovis ran across the room and followed him into the chute. Above him he heard Take's voice calling a warning.

'You are a fool, Clovis Marca – what you're looking for isn't worth the finding!'

Reaching the roof, Marca saw a small carriage taking off.

His own car was back at the Great Glade. He could call it on his ultrasonic whistle, but it would take too long to get here.

He watched Take's car disappear in the direction of the mountains. He shielded his eyes, trying to see exactly where it was heading, but it was no good.

His face clouded with anger, he walked slowly back over the bright, mosaic roof to the gravichute shaft.

Fastina appeared. Her hair was dishevelled, her expression concerned.

'I couldn't stop him,' she said. 'I'm sorry.'

He took her hand gently, controlling his anger. He shrugged.

'That's all right. He moved too quickly.'

'Have you ever seen a man move as fast as that? How does he do it? You know him, don't you?'

'I've seen him – but that was the first time I've spoken to him. I must find out where he comes from. How *could* he know what I'm looking for?'

'If he's staying on daylight Earth, then Central Information could find him for you,' she suggested. 'But he looked like a twilighter to me – there was something about him...'

'I know what you mean. Forget about him. I'll get in touch with Central Information later, as you suggest.'

Then he grasped Fastina, pulling her towards him, bending her head back to kiss her, pushing his hands over her body, feeling her arms circle him and her nails dig into his back.

'Oh, Clovis!'

As they lay in bed later he decided to tell her what he was looking for. Since he had made love to her, his original obsession had become more remote and the need for secrecy, at least with her, less important. Also it would be a relief to talk about it to her.

He began to speak. In the darkness, she listened.

'My father used to talk about Orlando Sharvis,' he said, his voice faint and reminiscent. 'He was a scientist who lived in the days before the raid. There was never a genius like him, my father said. He had mastered every discipline. Sharvis was not a seeker after knowledge in the ordinary sense, but he had a monumental curiosity. He would experiment for its own sake, just to see what could be made to happen. When the world stopped, he built a laboratory in the twilight region and gathered a group of people about him. They were not all scientists. They decided to build a spaceship to Sharvis's specifications and go to Titan, to set up a colony...'

'The Titan expedition – the original one?' She raised herself on her elbow and faced him. 'So there was an expedition.'

'Yes. Sharvis's experiment, so my father said, had revealed a way of staving off the effects of the space ache for long periods. Sharvis believed that they could stay on Titan long enough to adapt to the conditions there even if adaptation had to be artificially aided. Sharvis's biological experiments had already got him into trouble in his youth. There had been a war – the Last War we call it now – between the monopolistic commercial companies. Sharvis had been chief of research with one of the companies and had experimented on living prisoners. When the war was over – you remember that it was responsible for the radical change in our society that led to the establishment of our present one...'

'I know that much. The commercial organisations destroyed one another. Paseda's party stepped in, nationalised everything and abolished the money system. Go on.'

'After it was all over, Sharvis was a wanted criminal, but he managed to go into hiding during the confusion. He would have been caught eventually, I suppose, if it hadn't been for the raid. His experiments, inhuman though they were, had taught him a great deal about human biology. He believed that he could operate surgically to counter the space ache and accelerate adaptation. He made the initial operations on Earth, then they left for Titan.'

'So there is a chance that there are people on Titan?'

'I thought so – but there aren't.'

'How do you know?'

'I went there in a ship I obtained on Ganymede.'

'But surely you couldn't have survived long enough to –?'

'It wasn't pleasant, but I was there long enough to discover that Sharvis's colony had arrived, that it had survived for a while… but when I got there all I discovered were skeletons. They were scarcely human skeletons, either. Surgically, Sharvis had changed his Titanians into monsters. I looked for Sharvis himself – or at least a sign of him – but there was nothing. As far as I could tell Sharvis had left Titan.'

'But he would be dead by now,' she said. 'He must have been born at least a hundred years before the raid.'

'That's what I was coming to. You see, my father told me that Sharvis was immortal. He said that Sharvis had the power to make others immortal as well.'

'And yet you've spent a year looking for him and haven't found a trace. Doesn't that prove that your father was wrong?'

'There *have* been rumours. I believe that Alodios discovered where Sharvis was.'

'Alodios!'

Alodios, the great artist, had disappeared at about the same time as Marca. His disappearance had been even more inexplicable than Marca's.

'Yes. I came back to see if I could pick up the trail again – find out where Alodios went.'

'What about Take?'

'I know nothing of Take – unless he is Sharvis's agent.'

'But you still haven't told me what you want Sharvis for. Do you think he might have a means of reviving our fertility – or creating artificial sperm in some way?'

'He might have. But my reason for finding him is rather more selfish.'

She kissed his shoulder softly, moving her left hand over his chest.

'I can't believe you're selfish, Clovis.'

'Can't you?'

Once again she felt that disturbing, desperate grip on her body as he caressed her.

'I'll tell you what I want from Sharvis,' he began grimly, but she put her mouth to his and kissed him.

She no longer wanted to know what he was looking for. She was afraid for herself and for him.

'Don't tell me,' she murmured. 'Just love me, Clovis. Love me.'

Chapter Four
Something to Forget

As THEY WERE preparing to get up some hours later, the V-screen in the corner signalled. Marca wondered who it was and whether to ignore it. He decided to answer it since he had anyway meant to get up earlier. He went to a cupboard and took a yellow cloak from it, wrapping it round him.

He activated the screen.

Andros Almer's face appeared. He could see into the darkened room and his expression changed as he saw Fastina lying in the bed.

'So you weren't unlucky, after all,' he said to her.

She smiled regretfully. 'Sorry, Andros.'

Marca looked perplexed. 'What do you want, Andros?'

'I've just had news that a ship is heading for the Sector Eight landing field,' Almer said, still looking at Fastina. 'Due to get here soon.'

'What of it?'

'Well, as far as we can tell, the ship's coming from Titan. We think it's the Titan expedition returning.'

'Impossible.'

'Maybe. I'm going to meet it, anyway. Something could have activated the automatic return system. I thought you might like to see it, too, Clovis. I screened Brand Calax, but he's busy, he says, with the plans for his own expedition. My guess is that he just doesn't want to see proof of the truth. Fastina might like to come, too. After all...'

'Thanks, Andros, we'll probably see you at the field.' Marca switched off. 'Your husband could be on it,' he said. 'Do you think you want to see him?'

'I'll come,' she said, swinging her legs to the floor.

*

The ship came silently down. It landed on the deserted field under the blazing, motionless sun. It was a big, complex ship of a golden plastic alloy that was turned to deep red by the sunlight. It landed with a faint whisper of sound like a murmur of apology, as if aware that its presence was unwelcome.

Three figures started forward over the yielding surface of the space field. In the distance, to their right, were the partially abandoned hangars and control rooms: slim buildings in pale yellow and blue.

The voice in Marca's earbead said: 'Shall we open up?'

'You might as well,' he said.

As they reached the spherical ship, the lock began to open, twenty feet above them.

They paused, listening for a familiar sound they did not want to hear.

There was no sound.

Drifting up on their gravstraps, they paused at the open airlock. Marca looked at Fastina. 'Andros and I will go in first – we've seen this sort of thing before. You haven't...'

'I'll go with you.'

The smell from the airlock was nauseating. It was a combination of foul air and rotting tissue.

Andros Almer pursed his lips. 'Let's go, then.' He led the way through the airlock into a short metal tunnel.

The first body was there.

It was a woman's body. It was naked, contorted and it stank. The grey flesh was filthy, the hair was matted, the upturned face was twisted, with wide eyes and lips snarling back from the teeth; the cheeks were hollow. The flesh showed signs of laceration and her fingernails seemed imbedded in her right breast.

'Ierna Colo,' Almer murmured. 'Pyens Colo's daughter. I told the old fool to make her stay behind.'

Fastina turned away. 'I didn't realise...'

'You'd better wait outside,' Marca said.

'No.'

In the main control cabin they found two others. A man's body lay over a woman's. For some reason the man's body had corrupted much faster while the woman's was still almost whole. She seemed to be embracing him, the rictus of her mouth giving her the appearance of revelling in obscene joy – though it was really plain that she had been trying to ward the man off.

'Hamel Berina,' Almer said. It was Fastina's husband.

'The woman's Jara Ferez, isn't it?' Fastina asked weakly. 'Jara Ferez?'

'Yes,' Marca replied. Jara had always liked Hamel. That was probably the reason why she had volunteered for the expedition.

The remains of the rest of the crew were also there. Some of the bones had been gnawed, some split. A skull had been broken open.

Face taut, Andros operated the door to the galley. He glanced inside.

'Enough supplies for at least another six months,' he said. 'We made the controls simple enough, in case things got really bad. All they had to do was break the seals on the packs.'

'But they didn't, did they?' Fastina said, her voice breaking.

'You'd think they'd retain some survival instincts,' Marca murmured.

'Isn't that a definition of madness, Clovis?' Andros cleared his throat. 'Something that makes you act against your natural instincts? Look – that's how we lost contact.'

He pointed at the smashed cameras above. Their protective cases had been torn open. Everything breakable had been destroyed. Machinery was twisted, papers torn, streamers of tape were scattered everywhere.

Andros shook his head. 'All those tests we made on them, all that time we spent training them, conditioning them – all the precautions we took...' He sighed.

Marca picked up a torn length of tape and began twisting it round his finger.

'They were intelligent people,' Andros went on. 'They knew what to expect and how to fight it. They had courage, initiative, common sense and self-control – yet in six months they became insane, bestial travesties of human beings. Look at them – grotesque animals, more debased than we could guess...'

He glanced at a wall. He pointed at the pictures drawn on it in what seemed to be dried human blood. 'That sort of thing was done quite early on, I should think.' He kicked at a pile of filthy rags. 'Titan! We can't survive in space for a matter of months, let alone centuries. These people were sacrificed for nothing.'

Marca sighed. 'We could revive the woman – Jara – for about ten minutes. She's not too far gone.'

Andros rubbed his face. 'Is it worth it, Clovis?'

'No.' Marca's voice was hollow. 'It's unlikely they were able to get at the recorders. They should tell us what happened.'

'We don't really need to check, do we?' Almer said.

Marca shook his head slowly. He put his arm round Fastina's shoulders. 'Let's get out of this ship.'

As they left the airlock and drifted towards the spaceport buildings the voice in Marca's earbead said: 'Any instructions?'

'Destroy it,' Marca said. 'And don't release the news. Morale's bad enough as it is.'

They climbed into Almer's car on the edge of the field.

The ship had an automatic destruction mechanism that could only be operated from base. All ships had the same device in the event of space ache getting out of hand as it had done on the Titan vessel.

Behind them the golden ship crumpled. There was a brilliant flash and they heard the sharp, smacking sound as it was vapourised.

Fastina's face was pale.

'Do you think Calax will change his mind now?' Marca asked Almer.

Almer sneered. 'Calax? Not after we've destroyed the evidence. Mark my words, he just won't believe us.'

'You think we should have kept the ship to show him?'

'I doubt if he'd have let us show it to him,' Almer said. 'Calax doesn't obey any rational instincts as far as I know.'

'You seem to have some personal grudge against Calax,' Marca said. 'It's almost as if you hate him.'

'I hate everyone,' Andros said savagely. 'I hate the whole horrible mess.'

Marca stretched back on his couch, trying to get the images in the ship out of his mind. He could see them all, still; twisted faces, contorted bodies, filth, wreckage, bones.

Memento mori the world could do without, he thought. That was why he had told them to destroy the ship. If they ran away from a dying man at a party, what would that sight do to them?

Fastina was sitting upright, staring over the countryside as they moved along. Marca knew it would be stupid to try to comfort her at this stage. She was in a state of shock.

'What do you want to do now?' Almer was asking him. 'Can I take you both back to your house, Clovis?' His voice sounded ragged.

'No thanks, Andros. Take us to the Great Glade, my car's there.'

The air carriage wheeled in the cloudless sky as Almer accelerated and headed for the south-western flower forest.

Chapter Five
Something Ominous

FOUR DAYS LATER, Clovis Marca left Fastina at his house and went to see Tarn Yoluf of Central Information.

Fastina had recovered from her shock but was still occasionally pensive. She had been unable completely to rid her mind of the sight of her dead husband in the spaceship and at length Marca had decided to leave her alone for a while so that she could, as she had suggested, sleep for a couple of days and hope that that would be enough to clear her head of the images in the ship and the guilt that she felt when she remembered them.

The horror he had witnessed had, for the moment at least, convinced Clovis Marca of the futility of his own search for the legendary Orlando Sharvis. Doubtless Sharvis had died on Titan, too.

Situated on the edge of a flower forest, the Central Information building stood two storeys above ground and fifty storeys below. Tarn Yoluf's big, computer-lined office looked out over the sunlit forest and a smooth intervening lawn.

Yoluf sat at his desk surrounded by V-screens and control consoles. He was a tall, slim man in middle age. He had very fair hair and a pale, anaemic face. His eyes were pale blue and in contrast to the rest of his features his very full red lips looked as if they had been painted. He was wearing a high-collared lilac shirt and green tights.

Marca told him that he wanted to know the whereabouts of Take. Yoluf started at once. He punched buttons and operated controls but after an hour his records had come up with nothing.

'I'll try my sections, Clovis,' he said. His voice was extremely high-pitched. 'But not all of them are operating these days.'

Later he sat back in his chair and spread his long hands in apology.

'No trace yet, Clovis.'

Marca shrugged. The problem of Take had become less important since he had made his decision. 'I'm sorry to have troubled you, Tarn. The man's made me uncomfortable, that's all. As I said, he seems to have been following me for some time. The other day I discovered him in my house...'

'Surely not?' Yoluf looked shocked. 'Uninvited?'

'Yes. I thought if I could find him and warn him about doing anything like it again, it would be sufficient to make him leave me in peace. For all I know he's vanished for good, anyway.'

'You mentioned that his reflexes were abnormally fast. Your description of him could hardly fit anyone – but we're stumped, Clovis. He sounds like a twilight man, but we've records of all surviving twilight people and he's not amongst them. Twilighters are about the only people who'd invade a man's house like that...'

Marca nodded. 'Thanks, anyway, Tarn.'

Yoluf chewed his lower lip. 'Hang on for a moment, Clovis. There's still a chance...'

'It's not really important...'

'I'd rather make sure we've checked everywhere.' He turned to one of his consoles and began pressing more buttons. 'You know what we need? A passport system like the old days. To hell with the freedom of the individual. How am I supposed to run an information centre without a decent system?'

Marca smiled and sat down in the chair opposite Yoluf. 'You're a frustrated bureaucrat.'

'We wouldn't be where we are today without the bureaucrats, Clovis.' Yoluf jokingly wagged his finger. 'It was the civil servants who helped turn over the State from its old restrictive form into the present one. Don't underestimate the bureaucratic mentality. You might think that the administration's decision to wind itself up was a good idea – I don't.'

'It simply happened that way,' Marca said good-humouredly. 'Since we only had a short time to go we suggested that anyone who wished to give up their work could do so. Many are still continuing. You are, for one.'

'It's not the same, Clovis. Where's yesterday's smooth-running administrative machine? Bits! Bits without links or a properly working motor. If the machine were running right do you think it would take this long to find your mysterious friend?'

'I suppose not,' Marca admitted as Yoluf fussed with his controls. 'You think some sort of emergency government should be formed?'

'I don't make decisions of that order. That's up to you. But anyone can see that our civilisation's crumbling to pieces day by day. We need a firmer government – not none at all!'

'Firmer government? You're really beginning to sound like someone from pre-raid days. What good do firmer governments ever do that isn't overbalanced by the harm they cause.'

'You used the word "emergency" yourself, Clovis. Isn't this one? Ah, here's Mars...'

A light was blinking above one of the V-screens and a face appeared on it. The colours were in bad register and the man's face was a dirty green.

Yoluf pointed at the screen. 'There's another example of what's happening. See that colour? We can't get a mechanic to fix it. At this rate there'll be complete chaos in a matter of months. Didn't they always say that when communications began to break down that was a sign of the beginning of the end? We'll all be dead sooner than we think...' The signal buzzed and Yoluf flicked a switch. 'Yes?'

The man on the screen was already talking. '... no information regarding the man you call Mr Take. No ship registered to him. No-one of his description or name has landed in a passenger ship. We haven't checked everywhere. Some of the old mine pits are deep enough to hide a small ship...'

Yoluf's tone was exasperated. 'Then keep trying.' He broke contact well before his message could get to Mars. He shook his head. 'I used to be all but omniscient a year ago – as far as people's public lives were concerned. Now all I get are mysteries! We were asked about your whereabouts and lost you half the time. We're still being asked about Alodios and we can't find *him*. Now this man Take can't be traced. You're looking at a broken man, Clovis! Somebody who's gone from omniscience to impotence in less than twelve months. I'm going insane!'

'Aren't we all?' smiled Marca. 'What did happen to Alodios?'

'I told you, we don't know. We found his air carriage without any trouble. It was in the twilight region. Sector 119.'

'I know the area – near the sea, isn't it?'

'Yes. South American continent.'

'Do you think he killed himself?' Marca was now almost certain that this was what had happened to the great artist. There had been one or two other suicides, especially among artists.

'That's what I do think,' Yoluf said emphatically, 'but not everyone will have it. I have to keep trying with the best means at my disposal, which isn't saying a great deal these days...'

'Ah, well,' said Marca as he got up to leave, 'struggle on as best you can, Tarn.'

Yoluf shrugged. 'What's the point?'

'None, I suppose. If you do hear anything of Take you'll let me know, will you?'

'If I can get in touch with you,' said Yoluf bitterly, turning his attention back to his instruments.

On his way to visit Narvo Velusi, Marca saw smoke rising in the distance. He was crossing a great, grassy plain that covered the region once known as northern France. The breeze whispered through the grass and around the air car and a few white clouds moved slowly through the deep blue sky. As always, the sun hung motionless above him. In this area it was in a position of mid-afternoon.

It was definitely thick, black smoke he could see ahead. It was very unusual to see smoke at all. Curious, he guided the car towards it.

Later he saw that it was a building; an ordinary mobile house. Strictly speaking the house was not burning, but its contents were. Marca took the car down to see if there was anyone in trouble.

On the far side of the building, obscured at first by the billowing smoke, he saw a small group of figures standing watching the blaze. There were about eight people there, all dressed in black robes like ancient monks' habits, their heads shaven and their faces covered in masks of the same black material.

There was little doubt, Marca decided, that the fire had been started deliberately.

As he circled closer the bald skulls went back and masked faces peered at him. He felt bound to shout to them.

'Anything wrong? Can I help?'

One of them called back: 'You can help cleanse the universe of evil by joining us, brother.'

Marca was astonished. The word 'evil' was an archaic term rarely heard these days.

'What are you doing?' he called.

'We are ridding the world of the artefacts of mankind,' answered another tonelessly.

'Who are you?' Marca could hardly believe that these people were from daylight Earth. Twilight Earth had had, at one time, its share of peculiar cults, but that was normal and even the cults had died out in later years as the twilight folk became more and more introverted.

'We are the guilty!' a new voice screamed up at him.

With a shudder, Marca took the car into a rapid climb and fled away.

He looked back once at the smoke. It seemed to him that it came from the first signal fire that heralded the apocalypse he had joked about a few days earlier.

He knew that, unless it was checked, it would soon be one of many fires. His own upbringing in the twilight region had made him familiar with the darker side of human nature, but he had never expected to see anything like it in the daylight world.

How could this cult's activities be checked? There was no method known to his society; there had been no violence there for centuries. To take the reactionary step, as Yoluf had half-jokingly suggested, of forming a 'firmer' government was unthinkable to people trained to respect the freedom of the individual at all costs.

Yet here was a situation that could only be fought by a society of the old sort.

There was no doubt about it, he thought, as he passed over the forests of the Rhine and neared Narvo Velusi's house, Narvo had been right: Fear created fear and violence created violence.

It was with a feeling of despair that he landed on the roof of his old friend's house.

No-one more than himself had appreciated the social and natural paradise of daylight Earth, no-one had valued it more or realised how ideal it had been.

Now, it seemed, the world he had loved was not even to die gracefully.

Fear was back and with it the old terrors, the old mental aberrations, the old superstitions, the old religions. He knew the pattern. He had studied it in the text books. He knew how little power rational argument had when faced with minds turned sick by fear. He knew how quickly a cult of the kind he had seen could proliferate and dominate a society and then split internally and become several warring sects. And his society, without means of fighting the cult, was probably the most vulnerable in history.

His paradise threatened to become a hell and there was little he could think of doing that would stop the process now that it had begun.

Chapter Six
Something to Hope For

'THEY CALL THEMSELVES the Brotherhood of Guilt,' Narvo Velusi said, pouring Marca a drink. 'Originally they simply decided to give up sexual relations because it was pointless – though it hadn't stopped anyone in the past. Well, you can guess what followed that decision, can't you? The masks and the rest were explained by them as being necessary so that a person's sex could not be distinguished. Up to now they have been harmless, in that they haven't actually done anything violent. This burning you mention must be the first – we'd have heard of others. I suspect that the house belongs to one of their number. It's an odd syndrome, Clovis, but one we could have anticipated if we had not been so obsessed with the idea of our ultimate fate.'

'What do you mean?' Marca noticed his hand was trembling as he took the drink and walked towards the window to look out over the forest of dark pines that lay below the hill on which Narvo Velusi had sited his house.

'Well, while denying nature in themselves, they say that what is not "natural" is "evil" – you're quite right, that is the word you heard them use – and that therefore all human artefacts are evil.'

Marca shook his head. 'It doesn't make sense, Narvo.' He took a sip of his drink. 'I know these peculiar ideas never do, but it's not that I really meant. I can't understand how a well-adjusted society could go rotten in such a brief time. Even in the past things didn't happen so rapidly.'

Narvo joined him at the window. 'You're quite right – but in the past they had various means of resisting and controlling such outbreaks. They were a recurring cancer in the body of society, but usually they were promptly cauterised from the main body –

segregated in some way. Sometimes they were not cut out in time – so you got the fanatical Christianity of what the Christian society later called their "middle ages" – and the equally fanatical black magic cults and secret societies. A few hundred years later, when non-religious leaders were dominating the world, you got the madness of Nazism; still later there was the meritocratic system which virtually controlled the whole world at one stage. And every time, of course, human society managed, through violence and struggle, to rectify itself and destroy the cancer. But now, Clovis, there will not be time to do any such thing...'

'Are you sure?' Marca's tone was bleak.

'The only thing that would save us,' Narvo smiled ironically, 'is salvation itself. If our poisoned cells could be revived. It is a pattern, you see. There's always a pattern.'

'Isn't there something positive we can do, Narvo? Isn't there some goal we could give people – even...?' He broke off and stared at his friend miserably.

'Even if it means lying to them?' Velusi said gently. 'Perhaps there is, but you can see what's happening, can't you? A lie or two might halt the process for a little while, but it wouldn't stop it for long enough. And how would lying affect us, Clovis? There's no doubt in my mind that we should find ourselves corrupted, needing to gather more and more personal power in order to control the means of communication, keep the truth from the majority. It has started, you see. Even we are affected by what is happening. We can't fail to be.'

Marca threw down his glass. It bounced across the sunlit room and struck a wall. 'Can't we divert them? Can't we appeal to their better instincts? All these people were sane, rational human beings up to a few months ago. Their ethical instincts have only been buried. If we can revive them...'

'An ethic is simply a system of survival,' Velusi said. 'What does an ethic mean when there is no chance of survival?'

Marca put his hands to his face, shaking his head mutely.

Velusi went over and picked up his glass. It was unbroken. He filled it and took it back to Marca.

'Clovis,' he said after a while, 'I mentioned the other day that I had a scheme – a scheme as irrational as Brand Calax's, but one that might work to some extent.'

'What is it?'

'It's a stupid plan. It seems ludicrous even to me when I think about it. It is just something I thought of. I want to build a big transmitter – a bigger radio transmitter than any that has ever existed. And then I want to send a message on it.'

'A message? Why? What message?' Marca tried to clear his head and give his attention to the old man.

'Just a message that will travel through space – that will go to the other intelligent races in other star systems and galaxies. We know they exist – the space-dwellers told us that much. It will be a message that will survive long after we have perished. It'll be a kind of monument – it'll just say that we once lived. They probably won't even be able to understand the message...'

'What will it say?'

Velusi went over to a deep, high-backed chair and sat down.

'Just "We are here",' he said.

'Just that?' Marca shrugged: 'But we won't be...'

'I know, but someone might follow the message back – the transmitter will continue to work after we are dead, you see. Another race might find us, discover our records, and we'll live on in a way – in their minds and their books. Do you see, Clovis?' Velusi looked up eagerly at him.

Clovis nodded. 'I do, Narvo, but is there any point? I mean, could you convince the others that the transmitter would be worth building?'

'I'm going to try at the Great Glade tomorrow. The message could be picked up by all manner of creatures, you see. Perhaps some of them will be like us. The message will convey our pride in our existence, our gratitude to the biological accident that gave us the ability to reason.' Velusi sighed, looking up at Marca. 'I know it's pathetic, Clovis, but it's the best thing I could think of.'

'It's better than anything I can think of,' Marca said, putting his hand on the old man's shoulder. He saw that Narvo Velusi was crying. 'I'll come with you to the glade tomorrow. I'll back you up. Work on the transmitter will employ hundreds of people. It will be therapeutic at very least, eh?' He made an effort and smiled at his friend.

'It will be a kind of immortality,' Velusi said, weeping openly now. 'Won't it, Clovis?'

'Yes,' Marca said in pity, 'a kind of immortality.'

Chapter Seven
Somewhere to Go

FASTINA SAT IN bed eating the meal Marca had brought her. 'So Narvo convinced them?' she said with her mouth full.

'Many of them. Obviously I don't know as much about human nature as I thought. They're wondering where to site the transmitter and everything.' He sat down beside her on the bed. 'How do you feel?'

She grinned at him. 'Fine. How are you? Have you given up the search for Sharvis?'

'There doesn't seem any point in going on with it.'

She put down her fork and took his hand. 'I'm glad, Clovis. We've got the best part of two centuries together. We should be grateful.'

He smiled. 'Do you think we can stay together that long?'

'The first hundred years are the worst,' she laughed. 'Anyway, you're a very mysterious person and I'm sure it will take that long to get to know you. I'm not as simple as I look, either.' She gave him the tray. 'I'd like to get up and go out now. Where shall we go?'

'Anywhere,' he said. 'Anywhere you like.'

Lying side by side, naked under the hot sun, they let the air car drift out above the sea. Virtually tideless now, the South Atlantic went sparkling to the edge of the world.

They talked idly, holding hands. He spoke of his childhood and his morbid, melancholy father; of his mother, who had also been his sister. He spoke without rancour or embarrassment, for the times were now distant and unreal. The twilight world had become the same strange place to him as it had always been to her. He told her how Velusi had had his house in Kashmir the year he had walked towards the sun. He had arrived there, almost dead with fatigue and starvation.

Velusi and his wife had liked him. Velusi had probably been a little amused by him, too. They had adopted him and Velusi had begun to teach him all that the old man knew himself; though Clovis had already known a great deal from his own reading in his father's tower. Velusi was then deputy chairman of the council and had been able to instruct Clovis Marca in the ideas and methods of the politics of the daylight region. He had encouraged him to go into public life when the time came.

'I wanted to, anyway. I admired this world so much, you see.'

The carriage drifted on. They raised the canopy and made love. They ate and drank. Later, they settled the car on the water so that it rocked on the gentle waves. They swam in the warm ocean, splashing and laughing in the salt sea, making it foam around the hull of the carriage.

Time passed and they did not care. They became filled with a euphoric happiness and a pleasure in each other's company that could only be felt away from society. They both experienced a love that they knew to be elemental and probably never to be repeated. They wanted it to last. They had brought no means of telling the time and they had all they needed to eat. They sailed on across the calm Atlantic, hardly even talking now, but smiling a great deal and laughing sometimes, too, and staying very close together as if they feared that once they parted they would not find each other again.

There were no strong winds on the ocean, no cold nights, no wild tides. The sea was at peace and so were they. They saw a whale. It was a huge adult blue whale, nearly a hundred and twenty feet long, the largest beast that had ever lived. It was moving over the surface at speed, sometimes lifting its great bulk clean out of the water. They followed it. It swam along gently for a while and then dived deep into the ocean. They saw a school of fifty or so dolphins not long after, chasing one another through the sea.

Still later, they saw seabirds wheeling in flocks in the distance.

The sun was far behind them now, not far from the horizon, and it was a little cooler but still pleasant.

The carriage was swept by a sudden current towards an island. It was thickly wooded and a yellow beach ran down to the sea. The sky behind the island was orange and darkening and they knew that this was almost the twilight region; but the island was pleasant and they ran about in the sand, picking up sea-shells and pieces of coral. They went to sleep on the beach, with their toes pointing towards the sea.

When they woke up, it seemed colder, and an animal was screaming from behind them in the jungle. They laughed, but ran down to the air carriage and wrapped themselves in cloaks.

Then he took the carriage into the sky and headed swiftly towards the sun.

They landed on the ocean again when they were back, and swam and made love again, but their earlier pleasure was gone and soon they went home into Africa and his house beside Lake Tanganyika.

Even here they ignored the V when it signalled and spent a great deal of their time together in bed, or walking along the shore of the lake arm in arm.

One day Fastina sighed. 'If only we could have children,' she said, dabbling her bare foot in the lake and looking out over the tree-covered hills that were framed against the hot sky. 'Look what there is for them to enjoy.'

Marca decided to go to Narvo Velusi's house and see how the work on his transmitter was going.

A month had passed.

The time, he thought, as he headed towards Europe in the air carriage shaped like a golden bird in flight, meant nothing to Fastina, with her barren womb.

It seemed, however, that they were bound together now, perhaps until death. How the link had been forged, he did not understand, but it *had* been forged and neither would ever be able to stay away from the other for long. There might never be pleasure again, only pain, but that would not matter.

He could not explain his knowledge: Love, as he understood it, was not what they had, but love was there in all its forms. Hate was there, too, now, and anger and a melancholy bitterness, and a need for her body that was not any sort of love or hate, but a blind hunger that terrified him. He could understand how such unbearable emotion could drive lovers to suicide.

It was unbearable now. That was why he needed to go away from her and yet seek other company than his own.

The automatic force-screen leapt around the carriage as he pushed it to its maximum speed.

The tension had begun to leave him as he saw the Rhineland ahead and reached Velusi's house.

Chapter Eight
Something to Fight

T HE HUGE APPARATUS took the form of a gigantic sculpture in blue steel and gold wire. It overlooked the Black Sea, rising hundreds of feet high, each piece shining and vibrating slightly in the breeze. It was still surrounded by its tall scaffolding. Its central sections at base were almost half a mile in diameter; between them ran delicate webs, threads of copper, coils of silver, triangles and squares of shimmering greens and reds.

On a high platform above the apparatus stood two figures dwarfed by the great structure.

'There's still a lot to do,' Narvo Velusi said to Clovis Marca. 'We haven't begun to install the power yet.'

Marca folded his arms and looked down at the transmitter. He knew that it could have been built in a more compact form and cased in some kind of cabinet, but he understood why Velusi had chosen to build it this way. It was not only visible to all those involved in working on it, it was also extremely beautiful, somehow complementing the simplicity of the message they intended to send.

'It's very impressive, Narvo,' he said.

'Thank you. It really does seem to have cheered a lot of people up.' He smiled. 'The work's going faster than I anticipated. We might have to invent a few technical hitches.'

A black air carriage began to circle down towards them. It came level with the platform. In it stood a man wearing a loose, flowing black cloak that enclosed his whole body. Attached to the cloak was a hood of the same material. The hood hid the man's face in shadow.

'May I join you?'

Marca recognised the voice as Andros Almer's.

'Hello, Andros,' he said, as the man stepped from the car and onto the platform.

Andros nodded to them and pushed his hood back slightly to peer down at the transmitter. Far below tiny figures could be seen at work.

Marca saw that he was wearing a dark blue mask over the top half of his pale face. The mask was edged in scarlet and like the hooded cloak was of heavy, rich material. On Almer's hands there were matching gloves in dark blue, worked with scarlet, and on his feet were soft, red, knee-length boots.

'"We are here", eh?' Almer's voice was dry. 'Perhaps "We were here" would be a better message, Narvo?'

Velusi looked uncomfortably at Marca. 'Andros thinks there are better uses for the transmitter, Clovis.'

Almer turned with a swirl of his heavy cloak, raising one gloved hand. 'I have no intention of interfering, Narvo. It is your project. It simply seemed a good idea to broadcast rather more information, to give whoever heard it a better idea of who we were and where to find us.'

'That would defeat the whole spirit of the idea, surely?' Clovis frowned. 'Can't you see that, Andros?'

'It simply seems a waste, that's all, Clovis.' Almer's voice was acid now. 'To build this great contrivance and make so little use of it.' Almer shrugged. 'I wonder what other projects of this kind we'll see in the near future?'

'What do you mean?' Velusi said, pushing his old hand through his hair. Marca noticed that it was beginning to grey. 'Other projects?'

'I'd admit that this one isn't as hopeless as Calax's Titan ship – at least it has a definite, understandable purpose...'

'The Titan ship has a purpose,' Marca interrupted, 'if only to occupy Calax's mind. How's the building going?'

'Oh, rapidly, rapidly. Yes, soon Calax will be off for Titan and that's the last we shall see of him – unless he returns in the manner of the first expedition.' Almer moved arrogantly towards his air car. 'Well, give my regards to Fastina, Clovis. I must get back to my own affairs. My men are waiting...'

'Your *what*?' Marca was incredulous. He had only heard a phrase like that in an historical V-drama.

Andros ignored him, stepped into his air car and swept away.

'What did he say, Narvo?' he asked.

'His men.' Narvo repeated quietly, looking down at the transmitter to avoid Marca's eyes.

'*His!*' The concept of other people 'belonging' to a particular person was even more archaic than the term 'evil' which he had heard a month earlier. 'Was he joking, Narvo? What's he doing?'

Velusi's tone was over-controlled when he replied. 'The Brotherhood of Guilt fired several more houses while you were away. They didn't actually burn the houses, of course, because they won't catch fire, but they destroyed everything that could be burned inside them. And the last two houses they set fire to didn't belong to their own members – a woman was badly burned trying to put the blaze out in her house. Some people, particularly Andros, didn't see why the Brotherhood should be allowed to go about destroying at will while everyone looked on passively...'

'So they formed themselves into a group against the Brotherhood, is that it?'

Velusi nodded. 'I think *vigilante* is the term they found from somewhere. Andros became their leader – he seemed to like the idea, Clovis.'

'I see you were right,' Marca sighed. 'It was bound to happen, as you said. But I find it hard to believe a man of Andros's training and intelligence would give himself over to such an idea...'

'He argues an old theme, Clovis. Desperate times, he says, require desperate measures.'

'So now there are two sources of that cancer you mentioned,' Marca murmured, 'and if the pattern stays true, there will be more.'

'Well, the way it was in the past was that the cancers helped destroy one another, but, as I told you, I doubt if there will be time left for that now.' Velusi touched his gravstrap. 'Come, let's get back to the ground. You've seen the transmitter. What about coming to my house for a meal?'

As they sank down gently, Marca said: 'I think I'd like to have a look at Brand's spaceship, if you don't mind, Narvo.'

'Very well. It's only a couple of hundred miles from here.'

They were using Fastina's air car and when Velusi had walked around talking to some of the people working on the transmitter, they got into it and headed for the mountains of Turkey where Calax's Titan ship was under construction.

As they rode towards Turkey, Velusi said: 'It's not a question of knowledge and reason, you see, Clovis – it's essentially a question of temperament and strength of mind. Andros had given up. Brand, in his way, has given up, too. In the past we were always ruled by our unconscious drives – even when we knew they were there – reason simply tempered instinct. Andros knows what's happening to him, but he doesn't seem to care any more. I think it's because of Fastina...'

'She told me that he was attracted to her, but I didn't think it was a very strong attraction.'

'Deep enough, perhaps. Ah, we're nearing the mountains.'

In a wide valley, the heavy outlines of Calax's ship could be seen as they descended. The sharp peaks of the mountains, formed into their present shape by the upheavals that had come with the raid, surrounded the valley. The spaceship hull was complete and men were currently fitting its machinery.

They found Brand Calax inside the ship directing the positioning of the compact drive unit. Marca was surprised to see how gaunt and grim-faced he had become. He greeted them civilly enough. 'Hello Narvo – Clovis. It's coming along. When we're finished she'll be the best ship ever built. I've got complete simulated Earth environment which will help stave off the space ache. She's about the fastest thing there is, which will help get me there and back quicker and allow me to spend more time on Titan. If there's –' they all stood aside to let the mechanics through as they carried various pieces of equipment into the drive chamber – 'if there's anyone on Titan, I'll find 'em.'

Marca could have told Brand Calax the truth about Titan, but he had decided that it would not be fair to spoil the man's dream. Even if he died, Calax had the right to die in the manner he chose.

Calax peered into the drive chamber, checking something against the plans he held in his hand. He straightened up, leaning on his other hand against the cold, dark metal of the bulkhead. Later, the interior would be coated with several layers of other materials, and the shell itself was in fact three divided layers with force-fields between them.

'People have been really kind,' Calax said. 'I've had more than I need volunteering to help put the ship together. I'm going to call her the *Orlando Sharvis*, after the man who commanded the colonising expedition...'

Though startled to hear the name, Marca said calmly: 'Sharvis wasn't a particularly heroic figure, by all accounts. Didn't he do biological experiments on living human beings, things like that?'

'Maybe he had to,' Calax said. 'Besides, it depends how you look at it. Sharvis had vision and guts. I don't care about the rest of his character, good or bad.'

Marca walked around the ship. It was relatively cold in there and he shivered slightly as he went to the entrance and peered out. The airlock had not been installed as yet. He blinked in the strong sunlight, reached into a pocket and brushed darkened lenses over his eyes.

In the foothills of the mountains he thought he saw some people standing motionless, watching the ship.

'Who are those men over there?' he called to Calax.

Brand Calax joined him. 'They're from that damned Brotherhood of Guilt cult. They've been there for days. They don't do anything but stare at us, but I'm afraid they may try some sort of attack. From what I've heard they've already done damage. I'll say that for Andros Almer, he was wise to act swiftly and protect us against them.'

'Have they shown any sign that they would attack?' Velusi asked from behind him.

'No, but you know what they think of machinery and the like. A ship like this would be a prime target for them I shouldn't wonder.'

'You're probably right.' Marca touched his gravstrap and drifted down to the ground. The other two followed him.

'Miona Pelva and Quiro Beni have joined them, I heard,' said Velusi, referring to two ex-councillors they had known.

'Incredible!' said Calax. 'Decent, intelligent people.'

The masked, bald, heavily robed men and women stared in their direction. Whereas earlier they had worn clothes of any dark material, now they all wore brown.

'Some of them flog one another, by all accounts,' Calax said as he led them towards a temporary building where he had his living quarters. 'It's part of the punishment for their guilt apparently. I may be stupid, but I can't see what they feel to be guilty about. Still, so long as they don't interfere with me, they can stand there for the next two hundred years for all I care.'

'You think they might start something?' Marca asked as they reached the single-storey building and went inside. The room they entered was functional and undecorated. They sat on hard chairs while Calax operated the food dispenser in the corner.

'They might,' Calax nodded, 'but they've no weapons as yet, only fire. If they want weapons, of course, they'll have to manufacture them in some way and luckily Andros is keeping a firm check on the stores of supplies they'd need. I think we'll be all right.'

Marca turned to Velusi. 'What authority has Andros to do all this? Has anything been voted on at all?'

'More or less,' Velusi said. 'A lot of people agreed to give him temporary powers to deal with the emergency.'

'I see.' Marca accepted the plate Calax put before him.

'There's only one way of countering this that I can see,' Velusi told Marca as they ate. 'And that's for you to re-form the official council before it's too late.'

'How many of us are there left?' Marca asked cynically. 'If some of them have joined the Brotherhood and Andros is going it alone, there can't be many.'

'We can hold a new election or co-opt fresh members,' Velusi suggested.

Marca nodded reluctantly. He did not like to admit to his old friend that his heart was no longer in politics, that, in spite of the threat of the Brotherhood and Andros Almer's vigilantes, he was too obsessed with his personal affairs to consider seriously becoming chairman of the council again.

'You are still the most respected man in public life, Clovis,' Velusi told him. 'The majority of the people would follow your leadership willingly. It would give us the chance to put a stop to Almer's ambitions before he gained too much power.'

'Are you sure the people would be behind me, Narvo?' he asked. 'And would there be time to stop Almer?'

'You could find out!' Brand Calax had been listening. He leaned across his plate, gesticulating with his spoon. 'Narvo's thinking straight at last. My feeling is that someone like Almer's needed to deal with the Brotherhood, but we could find ourselves needing someone to deal with Almer in time. Let's act now.'

'It would mean restricting people's liberty...' Marca shook his head, perplexed. 'I couldn't do it. My conscience...'

'We've got to make the best of a bad situation, Clovis,' Velusi reminded him. 'Now Almer's evidently got an appetite for power he'll want more. It's obvious.'

'I'd have to think more seriously about it,' Marca said. He was playing for time, he knew. He did not want the responsibility any longer.

'You'd better make up your mind soon, Clovis,' Calax warned

him. 'When I come back from Titan with my good news I want to find a few people still alive to hear it.'

They left a short time later. The little group of Brotherhood members were still standing there, watching them impassively.

Brand Calax returned to his ship, the *Orlando Sharvis*.

Book Two

Chapter One
Men of Action

MARCA SOON DISCOVERED that he could not stay away from Fastina for long and he decided to return home after only three days at Narvo Velusi's house. A further incentive to leave was offered by Velusi's somewhat accusing eye; the old man was plainly waiting impatiently for Marca to make his decision.

He left for Lake Tanganyika.

'I'll decide what to do once I'm there,' he told Velusi.

The golden air car took him home and he found Fastina asleep.

Resisting an urge to wake her, he wandered around the house and along the lakeside for several hours, trying to justify to himself the decision he had already made not to become chairman again. He ought to agree to Velusi's idea if he felt badly about the state of things, he knew. He was being as selfish and irrational as those he despised. It was as if there were a tangible poison in the air that destroyed one's strength of mind.

Yet he could not face Velusi if it was to tell the old man that he was not going to help form a government. Perhaps he could act as a token chairman, and let Velusi do the real work? But that was no good; the people would soon realise he was not active.

He had made the right ethical decisions all his life, up until the news of the race's sterility. First he had gone off on that wild-goose chase after Orlando Sharvis, thus indirectly affecting the morale of the public, and now he was taking no pains to rectify the situation while he could.

Was there some instinct in him that was driving him to help destroy the society he valued? An instinct that had been buried since he had left the twilight regions? An instinct inherited, perhaps, from his father?

Fear was encouraging the dark side of human nature to flourish again. Was it also reviving a dark side of his own nature that he had thought to be dead?

He could now sympathise, to some extent, with the feelings that had led people to join the new cult. First came the fear, then the dark thoughts, then the guilt in having the thoughts. It had been a common enough syndrome in the past.

He sat down on a rock and stared into the calm water of the lake.

Perhaps it would be best for himself if he agreed to Narvo's suggestion? The practical problems of organising a new administration might divert his mind into healthier channels. He had already given in to one selfish impulse and it did not seem to have benefited himself or anyone else.

He decided to do nothing for a couple of days and then contact Narvo to say that he was ready to head a new government.

He felt more at ease as he walked back towards his house.

After he had prepared himself a light meal and eaten it, he went back up to the bedroom. Fastina was still sleeping. There was a slight smile on her lips and she seemed very much at peace. He envied her.

He took off his clothes and had a shower, then he moved desultorily around the house, sorting through his Vs for something to look at or read, but nothing appealed to him.

A little later he got into bed beside Fastina. She stirred slightly and he put his arm around her shoulders, enjoying the sensation of her soft skin and hair against his body, feeling the old affection returning.

Soon he was also asleep.

Fastina was not beside him when he awoke, but she returned shortly with warm drinks for them both. She handed him his and came back to bed. They sipped their drinks in silence. Both were thoughtful and relaxed.

After a while he kissed her and they made love gently, handling each other carefully as if each was infinitely precious and fragile.

Some hours later, when they were eating breakfast on the balcony overlooking the lake, he told her what he had been doing and what he had seen. He mentioned Almer and she did not seem surprised to learn what had happened to him.

'Andros even anticipated it himself,' she said. 'He seemed to like the idea in a way, I think. He was always a little perverse.'

Marca told her about Velusi's suggestion that he become chairman of a new government.

She frowned. 'It would be a good idea, I suppose. It would be useful to have some sort of mediating influence between those vigilantes of Andros's and the Brotherhood. But it would take up a lot of your time, wouldn't it, Clovis? I think you ought to do as Narvo suggests – but I don't really want you to.'

'I don't want to. Every instinct is against it. I'd prefer simply to retire here, or move the house to some other spot where it would be hard to find.'

'Run away, Clovis? That's not like you.'

'I ran away once, Fastina, when I was a child. I ran away a second time just over a year ago – though I told myself I was looking for something. I could run away a third time, couldn't I? It *is* like me...'

'Like all of us,' she said. 'Sometimes. What do you want to do, Clovis? Which impulse is strongest?'

'That's the trouble – I'm completely torn between my emotional need to keep away from it all, and my feeling that it is my duty to get involved. Oh, there are easy roads out – I could indulge in a spot of self-pity, I could argue that in the long run it all comes to the same thing – death. I could build up a bit of resentment, I suppose, at their foolishness. Perhaps, eventually, I will take one of those ways out – if the situation gets worse for me. But really, if I'm to remain true to my own ideals, I must join with Narvo and form the damned government. It's partly a question of self-interest, anyway. The more power Andros gets, the more he'll want to use it – and I have the impression he doesn't feel particularly friendly towards me.'

'You know why that is...'

'I know.' He stared gloomily at the great flight of flamingoes wading in the shallows of the lake. In this timeless world of ever-lasting day it seemed impossible that violence and hatred could intrude and, what was more, begin to hold sway so rapidly.

'I can't help,' she said.

'You don't have to. It's my problem. I'll do what I decided earlier. I'll leave it for a day or two until I feel calmer about it. Then I'll probably go and see Narvo.'

He walked into the room, leaving the balcony. 'I don't want to stay in the house, though. What shall we do?'

She joined him in the room. 'We'll go to my house,' she suggested, 'and then we'll decide. All right?'

He sighed. 'All right. A good idea. You're coddling me, Fastina. There's no need to – but it's kind of you.'

'Come on,' she said. 'Let's go to the car.'

He went up to her and hugged her. 'Don't worry.' he said. 'I'm just off balance at the moment, that's all.'

She kissed him lightly on the chin and took his hand, leading him towards the gravichute. He followed passively, like a tired child.

He spent much longer than he had intended at her house in Greece. He took to going for protracted walks along the beach, thinking about nothing in particular. He put off contacting Narvo day after day. He dozed or slept a great deal of the time. He hardly spoke to Fastina at all, but she was there whenever he was hungry or wished to make love and if she was disturbed by the remote look in his eyes, the impassive features, she kept her feelings hidden.

One day, just after he had returned from the beach, she gave him a drink and said: 'Narvo called earlier. He asked if you were here. I told him you were. He said that it was even more important than ever that you get in touch with him.'

He nodded abstractedly.

'Will you contact him?' she asked.

'Yes, I'd better.'

He walked slowly to the screen and spoke Velusi's name into the console. Narvo's face appeared almost immediately.

'I expected to hear from you earlier, Clovis. Is anything wrong?'

'No. I meant to talk to you, but...' He cleared his throat. 'Why did you ask me to call you? Fastina said it was important.'

'There's fighting going on, Clovis – between Almer's vigilantes and the Brotherhood people. Outside my house at this minute!'

'What?' Marca began to feel more alert. 'How did it happen?'

'The Brotherhood tried to set fire to the house. I was asleep. They were running about everywhere with brands when I woke up. I tried to get them to leave. They wouldn't listen – they set hands on me – threatened me. I panicked, I'm afraid. I called Almer. Could you come over, Clovis?'

Marca nodded grimly. 'Yes, of course. At once.'

The fire had not really had time to get a grip on the relatively few things that were inflammable, but the stink of burning was coming up through the gravichute as Marca landed the air car on the roof.

Down the hillside, among the trees, he could see the brown-clad Brotherhood struggling with men in black, hooded cloaks like the one he had seen Almer wearing. In the general manner of their dress, there did not seem to be much difference between them.

He dropped through the gravichute and found Narvo Velusi in his living room. The old man was trembling violently, sitting in his deep armchair and staring through the transparent wall at the fighting men in the woods below. Velusi looked older than he had ever seemed before. His clothes were smudged and torn, his hands dirty and bleeding.

Horrified, Marca knelt down beside the chair and looked into his friend's face.

'Narvo?'

Velusi was in a state of shock. He turned his head slightly and his lips moved and even tried to smile.

The room was disordered. Furniture was overturned, fabric charred and water saturated the floor coverings. Marca had never seen such a sight at close hand. He patted Velusi's arm and went to the wall to look out at the battle.

Men were rolling about on the ground punching one another. Others were using sticks torn from the trees to strike one another. Marca was horrified. He touched the appropriate control and the wall became blank and solid again.

In the semi-darkness, he drew up a chair beside Velusi and sat down, trying to comfort the old man. He fetched him a drink and put it into his hand.

After a while, Velusi raised the glass to his lips and sipped the drink. A long, infinitely tired sigh escaped him.

'Oh, Clovis,' he murmured, 'I blamed you for your apathy, but now I feel that it's not worth continuing to try to do anything. You knew it was too late, didn't you?'

'Nothing of the sort. I was just trying to come to grips with my conscience, that was all. Later, when you feel better, we'll go to the Great Glade and tell the people we intend to re-form the council.'

There was a sound from behind them and a tall, black-cloaked figure emerged from the gravichute. His chest was rising and falling rapidly. He was dressed exactly as Almer had been, save that his mask was without the scarlet edging and his boots were black, his gloves undecorated.

He walked over to the cabinet and, unasked, poured himself a drink. He drained the glass and put it down with a thump.

'We've dealt with them,' he said harshly. 'I'm glad you called us in time. This is the first real chance we've had to have a proper go at them.'

'What happened?' Marca asked hesitantly, not really wanting to hear.

'We captured a couple of the maniacs. We'll put them in a safe place somewhere where they can't affect anybody any more.'

Marca no longer questioned the archaic terms the man used so freely. It would not be long, he thought, before the words 'arrest' and 'prison' would become familiar again. He felt afraid of this masked, earnest man with his brisk manner. The state of mind, reflected in the fact that he and his fellows wore uniform clothing, was one of basic insecurity.

'Was anyone badly hurt?' Velusi asked.

'Only one of them. He is no longer with us.'

'Where is he?'

'He – he is no longer with us.' The masked man helped himself to another drink.

'You don't mean he's dead?' Marca got up. 'You killed him?'

'If you insist on the term, yes, he's dead. There was no intention of taking his life. It was accidental. But it has its advantages now that it's happened. It will warn the cult off from further violence...'

'Or incite them to vengeance,' Marca said scornfully. 'What's happened to your education, man? Remember your history, your psychology, your sociology!'

'The present situation is unique as you well know,' the vigilante replied forcefully.

'Only in one respect – certainly not in any other.'

'We shall see. I must say I expected more gratitude when I came here. We probably saved your friend's life.' The man's tone was deliberately rude and there had not been quite such a breach of manners before in all Marca's experience. He felt unable to deal with the man's impoliteness; he had no precedent.

'This is Narvo Velusi...' he began.

'I know very well who he is. You are Clovis Marca. I'm supposed to respect you, I gather. Well, I did once, but what have you done to help the present situation? Velusi has embarked upon a useless, time-wasting project with that transmitter of his – and you have done nothing at all. Very well, I accept that you are men of peace and enlightenment. Such men are not particularly useful these days. Men of action are needed – like our leader.'

'Andros Almer?'

'We do not use personal names. We have dispensed with the old associations until the Brotherhood is under control. You seem ill-informed for men of affairs. Perhaps things have moved too rapidly for you – perhaps you are unused to people making rapid decisions?'

'Hasty decisions, perhaps?' Marca suggested coolly.

The man laughed harshly and turned to go. 'Decisions, anyway.' He gestured with one gloved hand. 'Look down on us from your remote height if you wish, but, if it weren't for our decisions and our action, Narvo Velusi might be badly injured, at very least, by now. You should be grateful to us. We are giving you the security to continue with your pleasant philosophising!'

'I came here today to discuss reforming the administration,' Marca told him angrily. 'We intend to hold a meeting in the Great Glade today and co-opt new members onto the council.'

'Noble of you. But a little belated, I would say.'

The man drew his hood further over his face and entered the gravichute.

'Tell Almer we shall need him there!' Marca called after the man, half-placatingly. He realised he should have responded rather more neutrally than he had done. There was no point in angering Almer or his vigilantes. The best thing to do would be to get Almer onto the council and also, perhaps, a member of the Brotherhood cult, since it would be only fair to have all sides represented.

He smiled ironically, then.

When, in the past, had such attempted conciliations worked when the parties concerned were so full of anger and distrust?

Chapter Two
Men of Judgement

As soon as the meeting began, Marca realised that it was all but useless. The proportion of black-cloaked vigilantes and brown-habited cult members in the auditorium was slightly higher than the proportion of ordinary men and women. He had not realised how quickly groups of that sort could grow.

Hovering above, in their black air cars, were several more of Almer's vigilantes. Almer himself sat on the platform with Narvo Velusi and Marca. He leaned back casually, with his arms folded and his legs crossed; the very picture of arrogance. His hood was flung back, but he wore his mask still.

Looking around the auditorium, Marca saw that the fashion for wearing masks – albeit brightly coloured ones – had also increased. There were scarcely twenty people there who did not wear a mask of some kind.

Velusi had recovered. His hands were still bruised and his shoulders were not held as straight as normal, but he gave the appearance of being relaxed. He stood up to open the meeting.

'As you have heard,' he began, 'Clovis Marca has agreed to head a new administration which will be specifically concerned with dealing with the various problems that have arisen since the old council disbanded.'

He was speaking very carefully, Marca thought, making sure he offended no-one.

'The new administration,' Velusi continued, 'will attempt to ensure that people will have security and, perhaps, a sense of purpose…'

He went on in this vein for some time, but Marca could tell that Velusi's diplomatic words were making no impression at all. The Brotherhood of Guilt was fanatical and convinced of their own right to act as they saw fit. The vigilantes evidently despised the kind of argument Velusi was using. As for the ordinary people, they could look around them and see how useless it was to try to reconcile the opposed groups by means of placatory words.

'And so we require volunteers,' Velusi concluded. 'Preferably people who have served on a council of some kind in the past. Would those willing raise their hands?'

All the Brotherhood members raised their hands. Most of the vigilantes raised their hands. Two ordinary people raised their hands, glanced about, and lowered them again.

Marca realised that a mockery was being made of the whole anarchic-democratic system they had lived by for so long.

The idea of forming a new administration on a sane and rational basis had been doomed from the start, it was now plain. Perhaps he had instinctively realised this and for that reason had been slow to act?

Velusi was evidently at a loss.

'Perhaps if you could remove your masks...' he began.

Marca got up. He thought he heard Almer chuckle from where he sat, still in the same casual posture.

'We want a balanced representation,' said Marca as levelly as he could. 'Could we have a few more volunteers from the –' he pretended to smile – 'non-aligned men and women here?'

No more hands were raised.

Suddenly there was a scream from above them. Everyone looked into the air. A black-cloaked man was falling towards the ground. He landed with a smack just short of the platform. Marca rushed towards him but he could tell from the way the body lay that he was dead. He began to peel off the mask, to see who it was.

The man seemed to have fallen from his air car, yet he was wearing a gravstrap. It had not been switched on.

He heard a shout. People were still looking upwards.

There, drifting away from the air car on a gravstrap, was a brown-habited member of the Brotherhood.

It was evident that he had come up behind the vigilante and pushed him out of his car before he could operate his gravstrap.

Vigilantes were now rising into the air to give chase, others were grappling with Brotherhood members in the tiers of the auditorium.

Marca still had his hand on the dead man's mask and now he felt someone touch his shoulder. He looked up into the shadowed face of Andros Almer.

'Don't remove his mask,' Almer said icily. 'Didn't you know that that was one of the reasons for wearing them – so we shall not know who are dead and who are living?'

Marca straightened and stood looking at Almer.

'This is superstition, Andros!'

'Is it? We think it is practical.' There was a triumphant, bantering note in Almer's voice now. 'We are a practical group of men. It was a worthy decision to make, Clovis, about forming a government, but as you can see it is unnecessary. I suggest you and Narvo go home and stay out of all this. We can look after things perfectly well.'

Marca looked to where a great mass of men were fighting. The whole auditorium was in confusion. In the air two cars crashed head on with a great splintering sound. Men dropped out of them and began fighting in mid-air.

'As you can see, there is too much violence for a man like yourself to cope with, Clovis,' Almer said patronisingly, with soft amusement. 'There's a new order now – one well-equipped to deal with this sort of thing. I would rather see you safely away from the unpleasantness...'

Marca felt the anger coming back with renewed strength. He wanted to strike Almer.

'You helped produce this situation, Andros – you are doing nothing to get rid of it! Look what happened earlier. Your men killed a Brotherhood member. Now a Brotherhood member kills one of your men. You can only make things worse!'

'We shall see.'

As Narvo Velusi and Clovis Marca flew back towards their air car, a voice from below cried 'Cowards!'

Bewildered and outraged by the turn of events, the two men headed towards Fastina's house on the Greek coast, hurrying away from the noise and confusion in the Great Glade.

They flew over the flower forest. Its heavy scents and richly coloured flowers half-surprised them as they looked down.

'There is nothing we can do, after all,' Velusi said after a while. 'That was the defeat of reason you saw back there – symbolised and displayed.'

Marca nodded.

'What do we do now, Narvo?'

'I don't know. Stay out of it for a while. What else can we do?'

'It depends what happens,' Marca said. 'For how long will Almer confine himself to fighting only the Brotherhood? When will he begin to arrest those he suspects of being "secret" members? There is even the chance that the Brotherhood will get the upper hand and destroy him and his vigilantes. It would not matter.'

'At least Almer speaks for order,' Velusi said.

'Of a sort,' Marca agreed. 'But there will be no difference between them in a short while.'

'I suppose not.' Velusi seemed no longer interested. His voice was heavy with despair.

'Perhaps we should take Almer's advice and stay out of things,' Marca said. 'It's not our world now, Narvo – it's becoming unrecognisable. Let them sort out their own problems.'

Velusi nodded.

A little later the old man said: 'We can ignore them, Clovis, easily enough. But will they ignore us?'

A month later, lying on the white beach, half-submerged in the warm sea, Clovis Marca heard the thump of someone running towards him.

It was Fastina. He stretched out a hand to her, smiling, but she shook her head. 'It's the news, Clovis. Narvo said you'd want to see it.'

She began to run back and he followed her more slowly.

Velusi was hunched forward, watching the V-screen on which, lately, news bulletins had begun to be broadcast. The screens had not been used for such things since Central Information had been set up to serve anyone who wished to know something. But information was now restricted and channelled into the regular hourly bulletins operated from the old Central Information building, which was under the control of Almer's vigilantes.

The scene on the screen showed the Great Glade. The glade was now surrounded by a force-wall nearly a mile high. This was to restrict passage to and from it.

On the enlarged platform stood three members of the Brotherhood. They had been stripped naked, but their shaven heads were sufficient to tell what they were. Two were men and one was a woman. They were dirty and there were recent scars on their bodies. By the look of them, they could hardly stand with exhaustion and starvation.

Black-cloaked vigilantes ringed the platform. They all bore

swords in their hands; long blades of bright steel. So far these were the only weapons that had been manufactured, but in a world otherwise without weapons, they were sufficient to suit the vigilantes' purpose.

In a high chair, raised above the floor of the platform, sat a man who could be recognised as Almer by his red boots and scarlet-trimmed mask and gloves.

He was not called Almer now, by his men, but simply 'leader'.

Almer's voice came from the V-screen.

'I judge you guilty of complicity in the murder of another citizen,' Almer was saying. 'And sentence you to die so that your fellows will learn by your example.'

'No!' Marca looked incredulously at his friends. 'Has it reached this stage already?'

'I said it would be rapid,' Velusi said tonelessly. 'In a society not equipped to withstand this sort of thing, people like Almer and his vigilantes can develop as quickly as they wish to.'

Marca saw the ring of vigilantes turn inwards, their swords raised.

The Brotherhood people fell to their knees, making no attempt to rise.

The swords fell, rose, and fell again, sparkling with blood in the strong sunlight.

Then the vigilantes stepped back from the corpses.

They had been butchered beyond recognition.

Marca controlled his need to vomit. He could not move to switch off the set, but watched in fascination as Almer stepped haughtily down from his chair and stood near the bloody pile of flesh and bone.

Almer looked down at it for a moment and then disdainfully drew in his cloak and walked around it, leaving the platform and crossing to a specially cleared space in the auditorium where his black air car stood guarded by four of his men.

The auditorium, Marca could now see, was packed.

Chapter Three
Men of Conscience

AFTER THAT, THEY switched off the V-screen for good. They moved the house from Greece to the deep jungles of Sri Lanka, close to Anuradhapura, the ancient city of the Mahavansa, with its great domes and ziggurats dating from almost five hundred years before the Christian era. Thousands of years old, the buildings had survived tidal waves and earthquakes and the encroachment of the jungle. No-one lived there now. No-one visited the city. They could site the house in the shade of a temple, disguise it with tree branches, and be invisible from the air.

Months passed and they found comparative happiness in the jungle city. It was everlasting afternoon, mild and golden. Monkeys and brightly coloured birds moved through the foliage and over the old, vine-covered stones of the buildings. Jungle and city seemed merged into one ancient entity.

Occasionally Narvo Velusi would take the air car and go to the Black Sea to supervise work on his transmitter. Almost a colony had formed there, he told the others, of people who wanted nothing to do with Almer or the Brotherhood. He would bring back extra supplies every time he visited the transmitter and once he made a point of calling on Brand Calax, who had not been bothered by the Brotherhood since Almer had come to power and had been full of praise for the vigilantes' system.

One day, when they were picnicking on the grassy slope of a ziggurat, they saw an air car come drifting down through the trees. Instinctively they looked for cover, but then Velusi recognised the carriage.

'It's Brand. He asked where we were and I had to tell him. He promised he would keep the secret.'

They knew that if anyone really wished to seek them out it could be done systematically, using instruments, but they hoped that the old maxim 'out of sight, out of mind' would hold true as far as Almer or the Brotherhood were concerned. They were simply being cautious, they told themselves.

Brand guided his car down until he was hovering beside them.

'I tried to get you on the screen,' he said, 'but I couldn't get through. So I thought I'd come personally and say goodbye.'

He was paler and gaunter still, but he seemed very cheerful.

'The ship is complete, is it?' Marca said. Like the other two, he wore a loose kilt around his middle and he was very brown.

'Yes. We blast off tomorrow. I'll be back in six months of course...'

'Of course,' said Marca.

'... and I shouldn't wonder if I won't have a couple of healthy Titanians with me in the *Orlando Sharvis*.'

Velusi, who still did not know that Marca had already been to Titan, said slowly: 'Are you sure you'll manage the voyage both ways, Brand?'

Calax laughed. 'Surer than ever. I'll make you all eat your words when I come back.'

Fastina smiled. 'You'll do a lot of good if you do find some Titanians, Brand.' The smile trembled and her expression was pitying before she turned her head away, pretending to pack up the picnic things.

Calax had not noticed her face and he grinned. 'I know it.'

He brought the air car a little closer, so that they could climb aboard. 'I hope you'll offer me a drink to celebrate. You guide me, and I'll take you back to your house.'

In the main room, which was full of the golden-green light of the forest, Calax sat down and stretched his legs.

'You know, I'm in agreement with a lot that Almer's doing. He's got strength and conviction and he knows what he wants to do. A few people have got hurt, I realise, but it was no more than they deserved. I can't understand his constant antipathy towards my Titan project. It's such a negative attitude for such a positive man to hold.'

'I would have said his whole attitude was negative,' Fastina said, leaning against the transparent wall and looking at the trees which grew right up to the house. They were gnarled old trees and had probably been there since before the raid.

'I don't see that,' Calax told her. He looked back at Marca and Velusi who were standing together behind his chair. 'And I don't understand why you're hiding from him like this. What harm would he do you? He's only interested in controlling the madmen who've joined this cult. I know he's had to take emergency measures to check the thing growing and so on, and I don't say he has to kill these people, but someone like him was needed. He filled a demand, you know. He was what everyone but the Brotherhood wanted.'

'Yes,' said Velusi, 'you're probably right. But better safe than sorry, eh?'

'He won't try to do anything to people like you – ex-members of the council! He wouldn't dare, for one thing, and he wouldn't need to for another. I just don't know why you're worrying.'

'Neither do we,' Marca put in. 'Just call it the example of history. We're probably being over-pessimistic. But when a man like Almer goes insane, anything that conflicts with his view of things is likely to be regarded as a threat.'

'Almer insane? He's not insane, Clovis. He follows this fashion of masking and so on, and maybe he's a bit more brutal than he should be, but that's not insanity – not strictly.'

Velusi laughed. The laugh was a little strained. 'Let's not argue any more. We should be drinking to the success of your trip, Brand.'

After Calax had left, the three of them sat in the room looking at the monkeys playing over the half-ruined temple. They chattered and squawked, knocking one another from their perches, leaping wildly from level to level and from stone to stone.

As they watched the monkeys they began to relax and smile.

'I think I'll reconnect the V tomorrow,' Marca said, 'just to see Brand taking off. I don't think he'll be back.'

'There's a chance,' Velusi said.

'I don't think so.' Marca got up. 'When he finds that there's no human colony on Titan, I don't think he'll want to come back. I think he knows there isn't a chance. He wants to go there to die, that's my guess.'

'He could die just as easily here if he wanted to kill himself,' Fastina said.

'That's not the point. He wants to die trying – doing something. You can't blame him.'

When he and Fastina went to bed that night, their love-making was cruel and desperate.

The next day they sat down to watch the take-off on the V-screen. It was not being covered on Almer's official broadcasts, but there were cameras trained on the ship. The cameras were of the ordinary domestic kind, but they were sufficient to show the mountain valley and the great steel ship ready on its launching pad.

There was no commentary, no countdown that they could hear, as the ship began to warm up.

The ship was built to a design that was nowadays unusual. It was a slender, tapering thing, with circular fins at its base.

Its drive began to murmur, its hull began to tremble slightly, and then it was rising slowly into the air.

They said nothing as they watched the *Orlando Sharvis* climb upwards, beginning to gather speed; but they gasped when the explosion came.

The whole hull burst apart in blue and orange flames. Pieces of the ship were flung in all directions and they saw them begin to fall while the antigravity drive unit continued alone to sail upwards, as if unaware that the ship it had powered had broken into a thousand fragments.

They heard the roar of the explosion and the screen rattled and reverberated as its speakers were unable to take the strain. They could almost feel the heat of the blast.

'Sabotaged,' whispered Fastina. 'It must have been.'

'But by whom?' Velusi was badly shaken. 'Who killed him?'

The scene faded and a masked member of the vigilantes appeared on the screen.

'We have just received news that Brand Calax's Titan ship, the *Orlando Sharvis*, has blown up,' said the man. 'It is suspected that members of the notorious Brotherhood of Guilt or their sympathisers were responsible for this destruction. Brand Calax, the heroic ex-Warden of Ganymede who was embarking on a lone expedition to seek survivors of the rumoured Titan colony...'

'Too quick,' Marca said. 'What do you say, Narvo?'

The old man nodded. 'They were expecting it. They knew it was going to happen. They're the ones who did it. Almer did not want Calax to build the ship in the first place. I thought it was strange that he didn't interfere with him. They sabotaged the ship, unquestionably.'

'... those responsible will be found and punished,' the vigilante was saying. 'This is perhaps the worst crime the so-called Brotherhood has yet committed. Be certain, however, that we shall protect you against further outrages of this kind.'

'They don't need further outrages,' Fastina said. 'And there can't be anything like it. Why has Almer done this?'

'For several reasons,' Velusi murmured, 'to consolidate his own position because he probably wants a reason for extending his power, to make the people even more reliant on him than they are already, to punish Brand Calax for his "obstinacy" and not listening to "reason"... The man's clever and psychotic at once. The combination is pretty rare, by all accounts.' Velusi shook his head sorrowfully. 'Poor Brand – he wanted to die, but not like that.'

'I'm going to see Almer,' Marca said suddenly.

Velusi did not take him seriously. 'What good would that do?'

'He still has his conscience. He still has to justify these actions to himself.'

'He's too far gone – he can justify anything now.'

'I might as well try, anyway. And I might get the chance to see Yoluf at Central Information. He would possibly give me a chance to broadcast the truth. This can't go on unchecked...'

'You think you can check him now? We tried and failed. Now he has more power than ever.'

Fastina broke in. 'It would be dangerous, Clovis. Don't go.'

'I'm afraid of him, Fastina – as we all are. I must try to face him nonetheless.'

Velusi shook his head. 'We must be more subtle, Clovis. The only thing we could do would be to get together a group of our own and undermine Almer's power gradually.'

'While he murders at will?'

Velusi sighed. 'Very well, go to see him, but be on your guard, Clovis.'

Chapter Four

Men of Reason

ALMER'S HEADQUARTERS WERE in the old Main Administration Building just south of the flower forest that enclosed the Great Glade. Though still surrounded by its smooth lawns, it seemed to have been turned into a fortress, guarded by vigilantes armed with swords and a force-field that was partially visible; the shimmering air that indicated its presence gave it extra menace.

Strangest of all, a flag flew from the roof of the building. The letter 'M' had been worked on it and beneath this were the smaller words 'For Order'. The M could stand for militia or even, Marca guessed, for some dead-language word. Although not personally familiar with such things, he had seen enough similar examples in his history Vs.

Well before he had reached the force-barrier an amplified voice roared from a phonoplate close by.

'Stop! It's forbidden to approach Main Admin by air!'

Marca stopped the car as two vigilantes on gravstraps came speeding up from the ground. They dropped into his car and stood looking down at him. He rose, frowning.

'I have come to see An – your leader,' he said. 'Tell him that Clovis Marca is here.' He spoke with deliberate firmness.

They both seemed to relax a trifle then and one of them spoke apparently into the air. Marca knew that his voice was picked up by the tiny earbead transceiver in his ear. The man relayed Marca's message and then waited for a reply.

Marca stood there impatiently for several minutes until at length the vigilante looked up and said: 'It's all right. They'll make an opening in the screen. Go through carefully – the thing's charged with enough energy to stun you badly.'

The two men left his air car and returned to the ground. Marca saw a gap appear in the screen well above the level of the lawn and he guided his air car through it to land on the roof of the building.

Two more guards were waiting for him there. They were swathed, like the others, in their heavy black hoods and cloaks, but their masks and gloves were edged in yellow braid. This was evidently some sign of rank or function. This evidence of further erosion of individuality depressed Marca. He let them lead him to the gravichute.

They fell several storeys and then entered what had once been the big council meeting room. Where there had been seats for almost a hundred people, there was now only one chair at the far end near the darkened wall. It was the same black, high-backed chair that Marca had seen on his V-screen several months before when Almer had had his men murder the Brotherhood members. The chair was equipped with an antigravity generator, for it hovered about a foot off the floor.

The walls were now lined with scores of V-screens and just in front of Almer's chair was a console that evidently controlled them.

Almer sat in the chair, even more arrogant in posture than ever. He signalled to the guards and they left.

Marca faced Almer alone.

He began to walk down towards the masked man.

When he had covered half the distance, Almer drawled: 'No further please, Clovis.'

Marca stopped, puzzled. 'Why is that?'

'I have enemies. It is impossible to trust anyone. Besides, after today's wanton murder of Brand Calax and the destruction of his ship...'

'That's what I came to see you about.'

'You know, perhaps, which members of the Brotherhood were responsible?' Almer's tone was sardonic.

'I know that they were not responsible.'

'Oh? Then who was it?' Almer crossed his legs and settled deeper in his chair. 'You? Have you come to confess, Clovis?'

'You were responsible, Andros. It was quite plain – your news bulletin came too rapidly and too fluently after the explosion...'

'Did it now? We live and learn. Thank you, Clovis.'

'All these lies! This myth you are building! Your evasion of reality, both personally and publicly, is almost unbelievable, Andros. You hide in your hoods and masks, you hide in half-baked ideas, you hide, now, in outright lies. For your own sake, listen to me!'

'I'm listening,' said Almer banteringly.

'There comes a point in a situation like this where you become so far removed from actuality that your own system of lies defeats you. It has happened often enough in the past. Your lie becomes your reality – but it is only yours. You begin to operate according to a set of self-formulated laws that conflict with the actual laws of existence. If you continue, you will realise that eventually. But if you listen to me now, you will be able to rectify the position and...'

Almer began to laugh. 'Thank you, Clovis, thank you. What a sweet-hearted man you are. You have come to save me from myself, eh?'

'I suppose so.'

'Oh, Clovis, don't you see that it doesn't matter about *my* reality and *the* reality any more? We have only so long to live. We can do what we like. I can play kings here – you can play hermits wherever you've hidden yourself. We are both in hiding – but you hide in your detachment while I hide in my *attachment*.'

'I don't see...'

'Yes you do, yes you do. You hide by refusing to become involved in all this – I hide, if you like, by involving myself in it up to the chin. More than that, Clovis, I act as the catalyst, do you see? I cause things to happen that much faster!' Andros began to laugh again.

'You aren't as insane as I thought you were,' Clovis said quietly. 'Or at least...'

'I know I am? Is that what you want to say?'

'It will do.'

Almer chuckled. 'You don't have to tell me that this process will result in mutual destruction eventually. But I am following the rules, Clovis. I am doing all the things I should. I am repressive, I aggravate a situation by publicly murdering people, I sabotage spaceships, I lie and distort the truth and then arrest people on false charges.' He leaned forward, still smiling. 'And I wait to see how far I can go before some resistance is offered by thoughtful people like yourself, Clovis…'

'You expected me here?'

'Sooner or later. I've been disappointed on the whole – I expected opposition earlier. My public killings were actually popular. I had underestimated the people. I had underestimated the power of fear.'

'So I am here. And obviously I cannot appeal to you to stop.'

'I have anticipated all your arguments, I believe.'

'All but one. Haven't we a duty to help people lead happier lives than these?'

'Duty? I am no Messiah, Clovis. But you are, perhaps?' Andros Almer's tone not only mocked him but somehow struck an unpleasant chord deep inside Marca. He began to wish very much that he had not come to see Almer.

'You are an arrogant man, Andros Almer.'

'Arrogant? Arrogant? Oh, come now, Clovis!'

'You imply that I'm arrogant…'

'Aren't you? Clovis – I am merely moving with the tide of events.'

'And turning them to your advantage.'

'Someone would have done. You, under other circumstances, perhaps?'

'Perhaps.'

'Well, then?'

Marca shrugged. 'I left things too late. If I had stayed…'

'Things might be the same today – only you would be sitting in this fine chair.' Almer slapped the arm.

'I don't think so.'

'Maybe not. But they would be the same tomorrow or the next day. You are slower to accept the obvious, that's all.'

'I like to think you're wrong, Andros.' Marca sighed. 'But I suppose it is possible that I would have found myself forced into the position you now occupy. I did anticipate that – and that was one of the reasons I chose to do nothing until too late.'

'There you are then!'

A signal on one of the central V-screens had been blinking urgently for some moments. Almer had ignored it up to now. He drifted in his chair to the console and reached out a gloved hand to touch a stud.

A masked and hooded vigilante appeared on the screen.

'About twenty suspects have been rounded up, leader,' said the man. 'Half are actual Brotherhood members and the rest are thought to be secret sympathisers.'

'They are the ones on the list I gave you?' Almer asked.

'Most of them. We still have to locate one or two.'

'Good work. Find them soon.'

Marca shook his head. 'I take it these are people you regard as dangerous. You intend to accuse them of destroying the spaceship?'

'Quite so.' Almer turned his attention back to the vigilante who was still on the screen. "And the other matter? How is that progressing?"

'We expect the result very soon, leader.'

'Excellent!'

The man faded from the screen.

'What "other matter"?' Marca asked.

'Oh, I expect you will hear of it shortly,' Almer told him. 'Now, Clovis, I must supervise the questioning of our suspects. If there is nothing else…?'

'Plainly there is nothing I can do?'

'Certainly there is nothing you can *say*, Clovis, that will affect me. Goodbye.'

Marca turned and went to the gravichute entrance. The guards were still there, hovering just inside. They escorted him back to the roof.

Almer's last statement seemed to have been something of a challenge.

As Marca flew back towards Sri Lanka, he let the golden air car drift slowly while he tried to gather his thoughts. Almer seemed to want him to take some sort of positive action against the vigilantes and Almer himself. In short, Almer wanted to fight Marca, perhaps to test himself and almost certainly to 'win' Fastina from his rival.

Marca had no intention of playing this game, but Almer might try to force him to in some way. Almer had impressed Marca with one thing; the man could only be brought down by violent means now.

Marca was still horrified at the idea of using violence and yet could think of no subtle method.

About half an hour after he had left Almer's fortress, he glanced behind him and noticed several flying objects coming closer. They were probably air cars and they were moving very rapidly. Soon they could be seen plainly. There were five black air cars, and standing in them, their cloaks billowing out behind them, were vigilantes.

Marca frowned. Was Almer already trying to force his hand?

The cars caught up with him and began to surround him and Marca saw the men draw the straight swords with which they were all armed.

'What's going on?' he called.

'We have been ordered to take you into custody, Clovis Marca!' one of them shouted back. 'Turn your car about and come with us.'

'What is the reason?'

'Suspicion of complicity in sabotage.'

'Oh, this is stupid. I was nowhere near Calax's spaceship for months. Even Almer can't make that sound right!'

'The charge is not connected with the Titan ship. You are thought to have helped sabotage the giant radio transmitter project initiated by Narvo Velusi.'

Now Marca knew what the other matter was that Almer had mentioned earlier.

'You have destroyed Velusi's transmitter, is that it?' he said levelly. 'You are contemptible.'

'Come with us.'

Marca touched the control that operated the car's force-shield and instantly the car was enclosed in an invisible bubble of force.

The vigilantes did not seem to have noticed this action. Marca felt in his pocket and took out the ultrasonic whistle there, trying to remember the code he needed. He had never had occasion to use it before.

One of the vigilantes gestured impatiently with his sword and his voice was muffled now by the screen.

'We are prepared to use violence if you do not come willingly,' he said.

Marca took the whistle from his pocket and blew three long blasts on it.

The car began to hurtle upwards and he was flung to the couch as it went into an emergency climb. If he had not been protected by the screen, Marca could not have survived the rapid ascent into the ionosphere. As it was the only air he had was that trapped inside the bubble.

He looked down. The cars were climbing very slowly it seemed.

His chest felt sore and he could hardly get to his feet again. He looked out over the planet, searching for what he needed. Then he saw them. A group of cumulus clouds to his west. If he could dive into them, he might stand a chance of evading the vigilantes.

The clouds were travelling in roughly the same direction he had been going before the vigilantes turned up.

He settled himself back into the couch and felt under the ledge of the car to find the manually operated control board. He swung it out and his fingers moved over the studs, giving the car its directions.

The car dipped and began to dive, like the huge bird it resembled.

Marca was again pressed deep into the cushions as the car hurtled downwards. He could not see if the vigilantes were following him.

Then he was in the obscuring mist of the clouds. He quickly cut the car's speed and calculated the speed at which the clouds were travelling.

Gently, he began to move along, using the clouds as a cover.

He would have to wait and see if the vigilantes had discovered his trick.

Several hours later, Marca knew that it had worked. He had been forced to switch off the screen and let the cold, clammy mist into the car, but it was the only way he could breathe.

The quality of the light told him that he was entering the twilight region and he judged that it was safe to leave the clouds and descend into the warmer air.

Dropping from the clouds, he saw that he was over the ocean and he guessed that it was probably the Bay of Bengal. He checked his instruments and set his course for Sri Lanka, travelling rapidly.

Soon the island was in sight and he swept lower and lower over the jungles until he could make out the buildings of Anurad-hapura below.

With a feeling of relief, he circled into the jungle, guiding the car among the trees to land on the mosaic roof of the house.

There were two other air cars already there. They were black and they were familiar. He was sure that one of them was Andros Almer's.

Panic-stricken, Marca dashed for the gravichute. It now seemed likely that the attempt to arrest him had been designed to keep him away from the house while Almer and some of his vigilantes went there. Perhaps the vigilantes had even let him escape.

He dropped into the shaft and drifted down to the entrance of the main room. He could hear voices. He reached out and grabbed the handgrip, hanging there and peering cautiously into the room.

Almer only had two others with him. They were holding Fastina who was struggling.

Almer himself stood over Narvo Velusi. There was a sword in Almer's hand and there was blood on the sword.

It took Marca a while to realise the truth that Velusi was in fact dead and that Almer was his murderer.

Almer was chuckling. 'If that doesn't force Marca to do something desperate, nothing will.' He turned to Fastina who looked away from him in disgust. 'It's quite traditional, really, Fastina.

Now we take you off with us – and the noble prince has to rescue the fair princess from the wicked baron.' He laughed again. 'What a game!'

Marca was trembling with rage as he entered the room, unseen as yet by any of them.

Then he flung himself at Andros Almer, grabbing him clumsily around the throat with one arm and punching at his body with his free fist.

Almer shouted and tried to release himself. Marca was weeping as he punched. Almer's sword fell to the floor as he turned and began to grapple with Marca.

One of the men let go of Fastina and came forward, drawing his sword. Marca managed to swing Almer round so that the vigilante leader formed a shield between himself and the other swordsman, but Almer twisted away and broke free.

For a little while they stood there, panting and glaring at one another. Almer's man seemed uncertain what to do and kept looking to his leader for instructions.

Marca dived for the fallen sword, picked it up and aimed an awkward blow at Almer who skipped aside.

Marca found himself confronting the other swordsman. He had no idea how to use the weapon he had in his hand and knew that he had no chance against the vigilante who was now beginning to edge around him, crouched and feinting. There was a smile on Almer's face now.

'I'll have your blade,' he told his man. 'This really will be quite dramatic.'

Almer took the sword from the vigilante and clashed it lightly against Marca's. He half turned his head, his smile broadening, and spoke to Fastina who was looking on, her expression tragic.

'There's a bargain, Fastina,' Almer said. 'He who wins this duel shall have your hand. What do you say?'

She said nothing. She knew there was nothing to say which would make Almer stop.

Marca now held his sword out clumsily before him, backing away as Almer advanced.

Almer grinned and lunged, pulling the point of his sword just short of Marca's heart. Marca had made a defensive movement with his sword, but it would have been too late to save him if Almer had been in earnest. He swung the sword out in an arc, slashing at Almer who leapt lightly backwards.

'You haven't the same interest in these romantic old customs, Clovis – if you had, you would stand a better chance.'

He thrust again with the sword and again Marca parried it too late. Grinning, Almer moved his sword from side to side as Marca tried to return a lunge. Marca knew that Almer was going to kill him eventually.

He lowered the sword.

'You will have to butcher me as you butchered Narvo,' he said quietly. 'I still refuse to play your game, Andros.'

Almer assumed an expression of mock disappointment.

'Oh, Clovis – where's your sense of fun?'

'When you have killed me, what do you intend to do with Fastina?'

Almer put his masked head on one side, his eyes gleaming from behind the cloth.

'What does a villain always do? He *rapes* and he *humiliates* and then he *slays!*' He chuckled as he saw Marca raise the sword again. 'That's better, Clovis. That's better.'

Slashing wildly, Marca attacked and then, quite suddenly, the sword was gone from his hand. Almer had twisted it away.

Almer was grinning no longer. Hatred was there now as he drew back his sword arm to finish Marca.

There was a movement from behind them and a new figure could be seen standing in the gravichute. He held an object in his hand, a bulbous instrument from which extended a tube. Marca thought he recognised it. It was probably a gun. Almer lowered his sword.

'Who are you?' one of the vigilantes said.

'My name is Mr Take. This thing in my hand is a weapon. It fires a poison charge which kills as soon as it touches any part of your body. It will be my pleasure to use it unless you release Clovis Marca and the girl at once.'

'A gun! Where did you get a gun?' Almer took a step forward, staring at the object.

'I have had it for a very long time. I am a soldier – or was once. This is one of many guns of all kinds I had.'

One of the vigilantes sneered. 'He's mad. We haven't made any guns yet ourselves. I'll soon…' He lunged at Take with his sword. Take's hand moved abnormally fast. There was a brief hissing sound, the vigilante groaned, clutched his chest and fell to the floor.

'A gun, as I said,' Take continued. 'I have no feelings of mercy for you, Andros Almer. I will kill you without reluctance if you do not obey. Throw that sword thing down.'

The sword clattered to the floor. Marca and Fastina moved to join Take at the gravichute entrance.

Almer shouted: 'I'll find you! Where are you from?'

'Titan,' Take replied as he followed Marca and Fastina up towards the roof.

Chapter Five

Men of Vision

Take took them away in Fastina's golden bird-shaped air car, heading east.

All were silent; Take because he was concentrating on the instruments and Marca and Fastina because they were too stunned by recent events.

Gradually, the light began to change in quality as they crossed the Bay of Bengal and left the sun behind.

Below, the water darkened to deep blue, reflecting the red rays of the sun. The air car cast a long, black shadow ahead and the sky was full of rich, hazy yellows, reds and purples.

Marca spoke, eventually, in a low voice. 'Where are we going?'

'Home, Clovis Marca.' Take's own tone was as vibrant and deep as it had been when they had first confronted each other in the house at Lake Tanganyika.

Land was ahead; the coastline of Burma. The dark jungles of the twilight were soon beneath them and from time to time they passed over the ruins of cities, mysterious in the perpetual half-light. Sometimes, too, they saw a tower standing alone in a clearing. The towers looked as if they had been formed of molten rock that had cooled so that it was impossible to tell if they were natural or man-made. They were familiar to Marca, for he had been born in one.

Take changed course slightly and began to drop lower. Marca now recognised the land area as the region where once the borders of Burma, China and Thailand had met. Now Take was heading north, towards the country that had once been Mongolia, and Marca realised what Take had meant.

'We're going to my father's house, is that it?'

'Yes.'

'Why?'

'You will be safe there. You know the house.'

'Of course!' Marca said. 'The defences.'

'Exactly.'

All the old towers had defences, though there had never been any use for them. It was just one effect of the introverted character of the twilight people who had hidden themselves in their towers and taken every possible precaution to see that they were never disturbed.

It was quite true that they would be safe there, even if Almer followed them, for the armaments of the tower would still be in working condition and could be used to repel any attack Almer could make.

Soon the landscape below changed from forests to mountains and then to desert.

Red dust and brown lichen were now all that could be seen for miles. A light, cool wind blew over the desert, rustling the lichen, stirring the dust; and then a tower came into sight.

The tower was tall and bulky, and though its materials were primarily of steel and glass-alloy, it, like the other towers they had passed, had the appearance of a strange volcanic rock formation. Darkly shining greens and yellows merged with gullies of orange and blue and thin frozen bubbles of pink covered the openings of windows. There were no straight lines or angles in the building. Everything flowed and spread and curved like living matter that had suddenly petrified. There was no symmetry to the tower. Even the main doorway was an irregular shape, rather like a crudely drawn letter 'G' on its side, resembling the entrance to some undersea grotto.

Take landed the air car. Fastina shivered as she looked around at the dead landscape and the looming, twisted tower that was illuminated by the mellow sunlight.

'Only you can open the tower, I believe,' said Take.

'How do you know that?' Marca asked as they trod across the soft, sighing dust towards the entrance.

'I know a great deal about you,' Take said.

Marca had begun to notice that Take's voice was always deep and vibrant and that the basic tone never changed so that while the voice was pleasant, it was also almost expressionless.

They reached the entrance. It was protected by a sheet of smooth material that looked like a thin membrane but was actually impervious to anything that tried to destroy it. Only Marca's touch on it could make it ripple downwards to the ground.

Marca touched the warm membrane and it responded at once. The entrance was open.

They walked through.

Marca put his arm around Fastina's shoulders and stretched out his free hand to touch the stud to reawake the tower's heating and lighting system.

Faint, yellow light now filled a passage walled by dark, veined crystal. The light actually emanated from the walls, floors and ceiling. They stepped from the passage into an oddly shaped room with a roof that slanted close to the floor at the far end.

Two low, oval passages led from this room. The passages had walls of a soft, pinkish colour. The furniture of the whitish room was as asymmetrical as the rest of the tower and took odd forms. Here a chair was designed to look like a crouching gargoyle with open arms, there a table resembled a kneeling, grinning beast with a broad flat back.

The grotesque, half-barbaric ornamentation of the tower so contrasted with the simplicity of the daylight houses that Fastina was obviously finding it hard to get used to the place. The design everywhere as they wandered through the upper parts of the tower was like the brilliant imaginings of a certain kind of surrealist painter; morbid, yet moving, fantastic, but inspired. Not one room looked the same. All were contorted to resemble nothing so much as the innards of an animal, save that every room had its particular colour, though all the walls resembled silicon or crystal.

In a top room Marca found the controls for the tower's armament. In keeping with the rest of the place, the control panel was ornate, in beaten brass and heavily worked gold and silver. Each individual control was in the form of a fierce fantastic beast's head and the instruments were arranged to look like eyes and open mouths, with dials, meters and indicators inset.

He found a book beside the panel, written in his father's hand. It was a manual for operating the force-screens, laser-cannon, energy-guns and other armament both offensive and defensive.

He worked the controls and saw the panel registering activation all over the tower. The defences were in good order.

Take and Fastina were watching him from near the doorway.

'All the towers in the twilight region are similarly equipped,' Take said, his voice reverberating through the place. 'If anyone wished to oppose Almer they would have a great arsenal at their disposal. Almer could not match it. It would take too long to redevelop weapons on this scale.'

'Are you suggesting I use this stuff to carry a war into the daylight region?' Marca asked.

'Not at all, Clovis Marca. My comment was merely a comment, nothing more.'

'What was your purpose in rescuing us, then?' Fastina asked. She looked a little less pale now.

'None, other than that I knew how much Clovis Marca valued life. I have been watching you in Anuradhapura, you know, for some time. I saw the black-cloaked ones arrive, I saw Clovis Marca arrive. It occurred to me that you would be in danger, so I came to help.'

'Why have you been watching?' Marca asked. There was no anger in his question, only curiosity now.

'I was not sure that you had given up your earlier quest.'

'The one for Orlando Sharvis?' Fastina said.

Take nodded. His head still lolled slightly, as if kept up by an effort.

'What would you have done if I had taken up the search again?' Marca asked.

'If you had got close to him, I should have killed you,' Take replied.

'And yet you saved our lives...?' Fastina began.

'So Orlando Sharvis does still exist!' Marca's tone was eager.

'I saved your lives,' Take agreed, 'but I would have killed Clovis Marca to save him from something else – from Sharvis.'

'Where is Sharvis?' Marca left the control panel and approached Take. 'On Titan? You said you were from Titan...'

'I am, in a sense,' Take answered, 'but I told Almer that partly to confuse him. I am the only survivor of Sharvis's colony.'

'Other than Sharvis, himself,' Marca said. 'Where is he, Take?'

'At this moment? I don't know.'

'Where does he live? On the night side? That's where Alodios went and I know that Alodios was looking for him, too.'

'Alodios was following an old trail.'

'He didn't find Sharvis, after all?' Marca moved to look through the window that faced the night. The red sunlight poured in from the window opposite, throwing dark shadows on the twisted walls of the room. All their faces were tinted by it.

Take seemed to be deep in thought.

'Alodios did find Sharvis eventually,' he said.

'Did he give him what he wanted?'

'Sharvis gave him what he thought he wanted, just as he gave me what I thought I wanted once. That is Sharvis's sense of humour, you see. He always gives people what they think they want.'

'Did you and Alodios want what I wanted?' Marca faced Take. 'Did you?'

'More or less, yes. We both wanted immortality, as you did. But Alodios and I did not escape. Luckily, I gather, you saw reason in time.'

'So immortality is possible!' Marca exclaimed.

Fastina looked up at Take. 'Then why can't Sharvis be found? If the world knew this, the things that have been happening would stop soon enough. If everyone were immortal...'

'Sharvis is not idealistic,' Take said with a slight, ironic smile. 'He would not go to the world with the offer of immortality. If anyone went to him, he would give it to them willingly, but his gift would not be appreciated by many.'

'I don't understand,' Fastina said. 'Why won't you tell us where Sharvis is – so that we can tell others?'

Take laughed humourlessly. The sound was a frightening one and Fastina moved closer to Marca.

'I hate no-one sufficiently to send them to Orlando Sharvis and I would advise you, very strongly, never to think of Sharvis again, to assume that he is dead. If I underestimated his power, I would show you things that he had done to warn you away from him, but I know from experience that even these sights are not enough to overcome the fascination Sharvis can exert on the strongest of wills. Listen to my advice – particularly you, Clovis Marca. Stay here where you are safe. You are in love – you can live here together for the rest of your lives. Be as happy as you can be – enjoy each other's love and the life you have.' Take's voice was still rich and vibrant, still essentially without expression. He was trying to give his words urgency, trying to use his eyes to emphasise his words, but, strangely, he could not. He spoke emotional words without emotion.

He obviously realised this, for he added: 'Consider my words. Take them seriously. Do not become like me.'

He began to walk back down the passage, his pace quickening until his movements were a blur of speed.

Marca knew that this time Take could not escape him. Only he could open the membrane at the entrance to the tower.

He followed the man, shouting after him. The tower and its associations, his conversation with Take, his experiences at the house in Sri Lanka, all had combined to revive the old, dark thoughts that he had managed to submerge in Fastina's company.

As Marca ran after Take, Fastina ran behind him, calling: 'Clovis! Clovis! I'm sure he's right. We'll stay here. Let him go.'

Marca caught up with Take at the entrance. The man was trying to force his way through the membrane but it would not yield.

Marca said: 'Tell me where Sharvis is, Take! I am my own man – I won't be deceived by him or whatever it is you fear will happen to me. I don't even want what I wanted before when I searched Earth and space for him. But he is a brilliant biologist and physicist. Can't you see that there is a chance he can help the race somehow? He might know of a way to revive the poisoned sperm and ova, to...'

Take leapt forward so quickly that Marca did not realise anything had happened until he felt Take's hand gripping his wrist in a hold that could not be broken.

'Do as I told you,' Take said. 'Stay here. Forget everything but that girl behind you. Make her happy and let her make you happy. Stay in the tower!'

'And go mad as my father and sister went mad?'

'If it happens, it will be a human madness. Accept it!'

Take hauled Marca forward. Marca tried to resist but Take's strength was incredible. He forced Marca's hand towards the entrance and pushed it flat against the barrier. The membrane dropped down. Take dropped Marca's wrist and sped towards the air car.

'You have stocks of food here,' he shouted as he took the car upwards. 'I will bring you more when I can. I will visit you when I can. I am your friend, Clovis Marca!'

They stood together in the twilight, watching the air car disappear.

'We haven't any gravstraps,' Marca murmured as Fastina put her hand in his. 'And he's taken the car. We couldn't go back if we wanted to – except by walking and the journey is almost impossible as I well know. He has marooned us!'

'He means well, Clovis. Take his advice, please.'

'Whether he means well or not, what I said to him I meant, Fastina. I am my own man. I will not be given orders by Take or anyone else.'

'You are proud, Clovis. You are proud, after all.'

He sighed as they went back into the tower. 'I suppose so. Arrogant, Almer said – more arrogant than himself. Does it matter to you, Fastina?'

'Does it to you?' she said.

'It would have done just a little while ago,' he told her. 'But I'm not so sure now.'

'Then I don't mind,' she smiled. 'I don't mind what you are, Clovis. We are together, we are secure, we have each other for all our lives. Isn't that enough for you?'

He drew a deep breath. 'You're right,' he said. 'I can do nothing in the world Almer has created. I should appreciate my exile. Yes, it's enough.'

Book Three

Chapter One
The Tower

B UT IT WAS not enough. Not eventually.

For over two years they lived together in the tower. They never went out, for there was nowhere to go on that red, barren plain. They were in love; that did not change. If anything, their love became fiercer, though their love-making became a shade stranger. They spent the greater part of their time in the huge bed in the deep yellow room. In that bed Clovis's father had been born; in it his wife had conceived and borne a daughter; in it father and daughter had coupled and conceived a son. Now the son sported there, but this time there would be no issue.

True to his word, Take visited them from time to time, bringing them food and other things they needed. He came fairly regularly, about once every three months. Marca gave up trying to discover from Take where Sharvis was.

Take was reticent, also, about the state of affairs in the daylight world. He mentioned that Andros Almer was now in complete power and that the Brotherhood of Guilt was all but extinguished. On a more personal note he told them that Almer had blamed them not only for the destruction of Narvo's transmitter, but also for Velusi's murder. According to Almer, they had perished by crashing deliberately into the sea.

When not in bed, Marca would read his father's books, or look through tapes of his family history since his ancestors had settled in the twilight region. There was a strong resemblance between all the men and many of the women towards the end. Valta Marca and his daughter Betild might have been twins as far as appearance was concerned, and for that matter Clovis Marca could have been a twin to either. They all had the same tall, delicate-boned bodies, the large eyes and heavy brows and broad cheekbones. Marca began to identify with them again and think that he was a fool to have left the tower for the daylight region and that there was only one good thing that had resulted from that boyhood decision – Fastina.

He would wander back through the twisting, crystal corridors that were bathed in dim, shifting light, and seek her out.

Their need for each other was almost always so strong that they could not bear to be apart for more than an hour at a time.

Sometimes they quarrelled, but not often and never for long. Sometimes, more frequently, they would lie side by side hating each other with such an intensity that they would have to make love or kill the other person, and the love-making then was brutal and selfish.

Marca devised a trap for Take. It was modelled on something his father had made for slaughtering animals. There was no game in this part of the twilight region, so it had never been used. It was one of many such useless inventions of his father, who had turned his attention to such things after Betild's death.

It was a couch now. It had been a bench. The couch was broad, but could curl up on itself rather like a Venus flytrap and crush or stifle whatever lay in it. It would not be strong enough to kill a man like Take, but it would hold him and give Marca a chance to question him.

Marca's desire to question Take was no longer based on any particular wish to act on the information he might get; he had lost sight of that. His single obsession now was somehow to get his jailer at a disadvantage – get him in his power if only for a short time.

The couch could be controlled by a little device that Marca kept in his pocket when dressed.

He had tried to get Take to sit on the couch the last time the man had visited them, but Take had not stayed long enough.

Fastina did not know about the couch. He kept it in his father's room, where he kept the books and the tapes.

Time passed, though they had no record of its passing and there were no signs outside until the rains came.

The rains came infrequently to this part of the world, but when they came it was for days at a time. They welcomed the change in the climate and would sit by the windows watching the water mingle with the dust and turn it to mud. It fell without pause in a great, pounding sheet.

It was during this rainfall that the vigilante found the tower.

Chapter Two
The Pursuit

THE VIGILANTE LANDED his small, one-man air car close to the entrance of the tower. The rain fell on the force-bubble protecting him and washed over it.

They watched from a small window as the man drew his cloak about him, switched off his force-screen and dashed for the entrance.

'What shall we do?' Fastina said to Marca who was thoughtfully rubbing his lips with his fingers.

Marca had suddenly thought of a new plan.

'We must let him in,' he told her, getting up and making for the entrance. 'Perhaps Almer found a record of this place as my family home and sent him to investigate.'

'We can't let him in. He's armed. He might kill us.'

'An assassin would have come more cautiously. I'll let him in.' He paused for a moment. 'You stay out of sight, Fastina. I'll take him to my father's room. If you think I'm in trouble, you'll be able to help better if he doesn't know you're here.'

She nodded mutely, her large eyes full of anxiety.

Marca went along the passage and saw the outline of the vigilante as the man tried to push his way through the protecting membrane.

Marca stared through at the black masked, hooded face. The mask was edged with light blue.

The vigilante spread his hands, making gestures to show that he came in peace.

Marca put his palm against the membrane and it folded down to the floor.

The vigilante recovered himself and swaggered through, one

gloved hand on his sword hilt. There was another weapon at his belt. Marca recognised it as a gun of some kind.

There was a damp, musty smell from the vigilante's cloak as he entered and watched as the membrane shimmered back into place.

'A peculiar sort of device,' the stranger said, indicating the membrane. 'I've seen nothing like it before.'

Marca said, with a trace of humour, 'It was an invention of my father's. Only members of my family can make it open or close. Since I'm the last surviving member of my family, you would do well to remember that only my *living* hand can open it and let you out.'

The stranger shrugged.

'I haven't come to offer you any harm, Clovis Marca. On the contrary. I have come...'

'Tell me in my study,' Marca said. He led the way up the winding, sloping crystal passage until they reached his father's room.

'A strange, bizarre sort of place,' the stranger said as Marca poured him a drink. He sat on the couch, lounging back and raising a hand to refuse the drink. 'No thanks – old habit – never trust an offer of food or drink in my job.'

Marca drank the wine himself. 'What is your job?'

'I am Security Scout 008, especially commissioned to find you by our leader himself.'

'Almer knew where I was? How long has he known?'

'Our leader suspected you could be here. Since you did not seem to offer him much immediate harm, he did not bother to check his suspicion. He has more important things on his mind.'

'What kind of things? What has been happening back there?'

'I'm coming to that, Clovis Marca. The Control has succeeded in establishing order and peace throughout the daylight world. It is a tribute to Chief Control, our leader, that the old Brotherhood of Guilt has been virtually stamped out or driven underground and now offers no threat to the security of the people. The birth struggles, perhaps, were what you witnessed and, looking back, we can see that these might well have horrified you...'

Marca interrupted suspiciously. 'The Control? Is this the term you now use to describe the vigilantes?'

'It is. Having established the Rule of Law, we decided the old term was no longer functional.' The man's pale lips smiled. 'We were forced to do certain things at the beginning, but they enabled us to bring peace and security to a disordered society. You would not recognise it now, Clovis Marca...'

'I'm sure I wouldn't.' The terms and phrasing were familiar to Marca from his reading. He could imagine the repression that must now exist throughout the daylight world.

'Instead of the old, hard to administer, system of living, we now have all houses grouped in strictly defined areas. This enables us to deal with the needs of the people with greater efficiency and also makes it more difficult for violent elements to threaten...'

'Don't go on,' Marca told him. 'Just explain why you're here.'

The security scout looked down at his hands and cleared his throat gently. 'Your old friend needs your help,' he said.

'My old friend? You mean Almer?' Marca laughed.

'I am told to say that he realises he did you harm in the past, but that he thinks you will now recognise the difficulty he was in, establishing order in the world. Some people have to suffer in order that the majority...'

'He killed my closest friend,' Marca said. 'He killed Brand Calax, too. He killed people working on Velusi's transmitter – idealistic, innocent people. He murdered scores...'

'Hundreds,' said the scout, with a touch of pride. 'But it was necessary for the common good.'

'And now he has mellowed, has he?' Marca said sardonically. 'He only kills a few every so often. Soon only Andros Almer will be left...'

'He appreciates the anger you must feel,' the scout continued imperturbably. 'But he thinks your sense of duty – always marked in the past – will make you understand that now he needs your help in order to control the ordered society he has created...'

'He has created nothing but ignorance and misery. The race

will peter out of existence in fear and despair. That is all he has done for the world.'

'It is a matter of opinion. Please let me finish, Clovis Marca.'

'Very well.'

'Chief Control has discovered recalcitrant elements amongst his upper echelon officers...'

'Only to be expected. He knew this would happen, surely?'

'... and the officers have managed to get a great deal of support in the more naïve sections of the community. They have used your name...'

'My name?'

'... your name to convince the people that they are guided only by idealism and wish to return the world to what they call the paradise it was before our leader restored order. They tell the people that you have returned and are secretly in charge of this splinter group.'

'So they plan to overthrow Almer and set themselves up in his place – and continue in the same way as Almer.'

'They have not our leader's principles and strength of mind. Society will collapse as they war among themselves...'

'I know the pattern. What does Almer want of me?'

'He offers you joint command with him as Chief Control if you will return and give your support to him.'

Marca did not reply immediately. He had the feeling that the story was just a little too glib. If Almer had already blackened his name as Velusi's murderer, why did that name now carry weight amongst the ordinary people? He was almost certain that this was a trap of Almer's to get him out of his tower and into a position where he could be killed easily. He must still represent a threat to Almer – and Almer must still want Fastina Cahmin.

'So Almer needs my help,' he smiled. 'I can't believe that. What are you to do if I refuse?'

'Take your message back to our leader.'

'And what then?'

'He has another plan – to tell the people where you are hiding and then launch a heavily publicised attack on this place and destroy you – thus checking his officers' plans. You would do better to accept his offer. If you accept he will send a carriage to collect you.'

'This tower is invulnerable. He would waste his time attacking it.'

'That's as may be – but we are developing strong weapons nowadays. You are not as secure as you think.'

'You said Almer was not sure I was here?'

'I did.' The scout placed a hand on the butt of his gun. 'I have a commission to try here and then try the other towers in the region. If I do not return in a month or so, he will check to see what has happened to me.'

'A month?'

The scout tightened his grip on the gun butt, looking into Marca's eyes, obviously guessing why Marca was asking these questions.

'And if I am offered violence, Clovis Marca, I am instructed to kill you.'

'You forget that you cannot get out of here unless I am alive.'

The man hesitated, glancing instinctively towards the door.

Marca reached into his pocket and pressed the single stud on the little device he had there.

The sides of the couch curled in on the scout well before he could drag the gun from its holster. Slowly, they began to squeeze in on the frightened man.

The couch had been designed to have enough force to hold but not harm a man of outstanding strength like Take.

The black-masked scout had only ordinary strength. The couch began to crush him and he began to scream.

Marca turned away. This was the first creature he had ever knowingly killed.

He covered his ears as the man's screams changed to a panting gurgle and bones crunched as the couch slowly squeezed him to death.

Marca shuddered. Tears ran down his face, but he knew he could not stop what he was doing. The man was as good as dead already.

In a short while the man stopped making any noise at all.

Marca looked back at the couch. It was folded neatly in on itself.

A little blood seeped out of it, but that was the only sign of what had happened.

Then he looked towards the entrance of the room and saw Fastina leaning there, her face covered by her hands. She must have heard the screams and come to the room, thinking Marca was in trouble. She must have seen the scout's death.

Marca crossed the room and guided her out of it, up the sloping, winding passage to the yellow room. He made her lie down on the disordered bed. He went to the window and, for the first time since he had been here, opened it.

The rain swept into the room, and the cold air came with it. The water washed over the floor and Marca stood by the window, the rain beating at his face, running down hands and body, soaking his clothing.

Fastina began to sob from where she lay with her face buried in the bedclothes, but Marca did not hear her, and eventually Fastina fell asleep while Marca continued to stand stock-still by the window, letting the rain lash his face.

After a long while, he turned, closed the window, covered Fastina with dry blankets from a cupboard, and went to dispose of the couch and what it contained.

The couch went into the incinerator easily enough. The last corpse Marca had put in it had been his father's.

He wrapped a heavy cloak about him and went to the entrance of the tower, opening it and slopping through the thin, red mud to the air car. He reached into it and activated its controls so that it drifted just above the ground. Then he began to drag it towards the tower.

The rain made it difficult to see, and twice he slipped in the mud, but eventually he got the air car into the tower and began guiding it through the passages to his father's room where he put it where the couch had been and covered it with a large cloth.

Now he was ready for Take's next visit. He went to bed.

*

Take came a week later, with his car full of provisions.

The rain had stopped and the mud had hardened to earth which would soon become dust again. It was already cracking as Take, his shadow long and black behind him, hauled the sack of foodstuffs from the landed air car and stumbled towards the tower.

Marca greeted him with apparent cheerfulness. Fastina was still in bed, where she had been since Marca had murdered the scout. She had recovered a little and evidently did not blame him for what he had done, since she believed the scout had tried to kill Marca, but she had not been willing to talk much and this had suited him as he had waited impatiently for Take's arrival.

Take noticed the difference in Marca's manner as he entered the tower. 'You seem in better spirits,' he said.

Together they dragged the provisions into the nearest room and Take sat down in one of the grotesque chairs.

'I don't feel too badly, for a prisoner,' Marca replied. 'Perhaps the rain washed my depression away. Have you seen Orlando Sharvis recently?'

'Not recently – only the effects of his work. You are well off here, my friend.'

'I wish you would let me decide that,' Marca replied equably.

'How is Fastina Cahmin?'

'In bed. She's sleeping.'

'Sleeping? She's lucky. Do you sleep often?'

It was a strange question. 'Frequently,' smiled Marca. He sat down opposite Take. 'Why do you ask?'

'I envy you, that's all.' Take's head began to sink forward in the familiar, lopsided way, and he straightened it slowly. It was almost as if his neck were broken, Marca thought.

'You don't sleep well, Mr Take?'

'I don't sleep at all, Clovis Marca. You are a very lucky man. I wish I were the "prisoner" and someone else the "jailer", as you put it...'

'I would be the first to agree,' Marca smiled. 'Can I offer you something to eat? A drink?'

'No. Is there anything you particularly want me to bring on my next visit?'

'Nothing.'

'Then I will get back.' Take raised himself to his feet.

Marca escorted him to the door and opened it for Take. He did not close it again, but said hurriedly, 'I think I heard Fastina call. Goodbye, Mr Take.'

'Goodbye.' Take began to trudge towards the golden air car he was still using.

Marca ran rapidly through the corridors to his father's room, tore off the coverings from the small one-man air car and jumped into it.

At a crazy speed, he drove it through the passages, twisting down and down until he reached the entrance. He slowed the car. There was a glint of gold in the dark sky.

The air car was equipped with a fixing device. Marca adjusted his speed, homed the air car on the one above, and began to climb into the air, leaving the tower, and Fastina, behind him.

This had been his reason for murdering the scout. Now he could follow Take to wherever the man came from.

He suspected that Take would lead him to Orlando Sharvis.

Chapter Three
The Cage

Take's air car was heading deeper and deeper into the night.
Marca had suspected that it would, which was partly why
he had not relied on keeping the golden car in sight but had made
sure his own car's instruments would follow it. As the light got
fainter, the shadows lengthened until they merged into a general
darkness and the air became cold.

The car, built only to be used in the daylight and twilight, had
no heater and Marca huddled in his cloak wishing he had brought
more clothing.

At last it became pitch-black and Marca could see nothing of
the land below and above him were only massive clouds and the
occasional stars. The moon had been dragged down into the sea
by the space-dwellers when they had brought the Earth to a gradual stop. It now lay in the North Pacific somewhere, with much of
its bulk below the surface.

The air became damper and even colder. Unable to see his
instruments, Marca had no clear idea where he was now, although,
judging by the air, he was probably over one of the many ice-fields
that covered both land and sea on the night side of Earth.

As he travelled his perceptions became dulled and his contact
with reality so tenuous that it did not occur to him to protect himself by means of the car's force-screen.

Much later, when his body was numb with cold and he was
half-certain he was going to die, the car began to fall in a gradual
dive.

Looking over the side of the craft, he just made out the glint of
ice reflecting the sparse starlight, and ahead was a dark outline that
seemed to be a great mountain range, though it was peculiarly
rounded. The car was heading straight for this. Marca wondered if

Take had led him into a trap and if he was going to crash into the side of the curved mountain that protruded from the ice-flats. The air car sped nearer. It was only then that Marca switched on his force-screen to help cushion the impact he anticipated.

No impact came. Instead the car reached the cliff and kept going. It had entered a great cave in the face of the cliff.

The air car continued to sweep downward through the utter darkness of the gigantic tunnel and Marca's air became foul in time so that he was forced to switch off the force-screen.

To Marca's relief, it was much warmer in the tunnel.

Deeper and deeper down the tunnel went the air car, banking occasionally to take turns, until a faint light could be seen ahead.

As the light increased, Marca could see the walls of the tunnel, far away on both sides of him. The tunnel was obviously artificial and could take a large spaceship.

The air car began to slow as it reached the source of light and eventually stopped altogether, moving in to the side of the tunnel. There, in a niche, Marca saw the golden air car that had once belonged to Fastina. Take seemed to have hidden it there.

Running his hand over the rock, Marca gradually realised where he was.

He was in the moon itself, now far below the surface of the Pacific.

He searched through the little air car until he found a gravstrap in a locker. He fitted it under his arms and left the air car, drifting cautiously forward towards the blaze of light ahead.

The light hurt his eyes for a while, as the tunnel opened out into a vast, artificial cavern.

Shielding his eyes, Marca looked upwards into the 'sky' and saw the source of both the heat and the light. It was a globe of energy, pulsating slightly, a man-made sun.

Below was a rolling landscape of what appeared to be scarlet and black moss that was relieved in the distance by slim, jagged crags of brown rock. The 'sky' itself was a lurid orange colour, fading to pink near the horizon.

It was a world of rudimentary and primordial colours, like a planet half-created and then abandoned. But this place had been created by a man – or at least some intelligent agency. Marca guessed who the man had been. He thought he had found where Orlando Sharvis lived.

How long had it taken to hollow out the moon and make this tiny world within it? Why had Sharvis made the world in the first place?

Marca began to feel afraid. He could see nothing of Take, and the rest of the place seemed deserted. Ahead of him now was a tall mass of rock, a plateau rising suddenly out of the scarlet and black moss surrounding it.

Through the warm, utterly still air, Marca drifted along on his gravstrap, heading towards the bluff.

As he rose above the level of the cliff-top, the first thing he saw was the metal. In the distance it looked like a great, static mobile, only momentarily at rest. Multi-angled surfaces flashed and glared.

The thing lay in a depression on the plateau, ringed by rocks that all leaned inwards so that the object seemed to lie in the gullet of some sharp-toothed beast. The rocks were long, black fangs, casting a network of shadows into the depression. Sometimes the individual surfaces would merge as he turned his head, and then the whole would combine – a blaze of bright metal – and as suddenly disintegrate again.

Only as he got closer did Marca realise that this was a settlement of some kind; a peculiar shanty town with shacks of gold, silver, ruby, emerald and diamond, built from sheets of harder-than-steel plastic and metal. They all seemed to lean against one another for support; were placed at random, forming a cluttered jungle of artificial materials on the barren rock.

Soon Marca could make out individual buildings. All were single-storeyed. There too were patches of cultivated land, small, deep reservoirs, featureless cabinets of machinery, and thin cables.

There seemed to have been no design to this strange village. It appeared to have grown little by little and it was quite plain that whoever lived there existed in conditions far more primitive than anyone else on the planet. Why? Surely they had a choice? They did not need to live in an artificial world, artificially maintained.

Marca dropped to the ground, within the circle of black rocks but beyond the limits of the village.

Now he could see one or two figures moving slowly between the shanties.

From the ground, the place did not look quite so makeshift, though it was also evident that the shanties were not made of pre-fabricated parts but constructed from the plates of spaceships and other large machines.

Marca walked cautiously forward.

And then a tall old man, with curling white hair, a cream-coloured cloak, yellow tights and a huge box strapped to his naked chest, appeared from behind the nearest building and greeted him.

'Stranger, you are welcome,' he said gravely, dropping his chin to his chest and staring hard at Marca. 'You enter a holy place, the Seat of the Centre, Influencer of the Spheres – come, pilgrim!' With a great show of dignity he swept his arm to indicate a low, narrow doorway.

Marca did not move. He recognised the jargon. The man was a member of the new Deistic Church of the Zodiac, a cult that had flourished before the raid but which had died out after it.

'Who are you?' he said. 'How long have you been here?'

'I have no name. I am the guardian of the Seat of the Centre and I have been here for eternity.'

The man was mad.

'What's that box fixed to your chest?' Marca peered at it. Wires seemed to leave the box and enter the man's body. 'What is it?'

'Box? There is no "box"!' The demented old man bent and dis-appeared into the doorway.

Marca continued to move through the village. From the shanties he heard stirrings and soft voices, low moans and whines that were either human or mechanical, heard a scraping noise once or twice, but saw no-one until he entered a small clearing.

There, to one side, in the shade of a building, sat a man. Marca went up to him. The man stared out at him but his eyes did not move as Marca knelt beside him.

'Can you tell me what this place is?' Marca asked.

'Heaven,' said the man tonelessly, without looking at Marca. He began to laugh in a dry, hopeless voice. Marca straightened up.

Further on he saw something that appeared at first to be nothing but a tangle of coils and thin cables, a dark, static web standing nearly two metres high and some sixty centimetres in diameter, of a dull, red colour with threads of blue, gold and silver closer to its centre. As he got closer Marca saw the outlines of a human figure inside the web. A clear, pleasant voice came from it.

'Good morning, newcomer. I saw you approaching across the fields. What a warm day it is.'

'Fields?' Marca said. 'There are no fields. You mean the moss?'

The voice chuckled. 'You must have been in a daze. You have only just left them. You came past the farm and walked along the lane and came through the gate there and now you are here. I like visitors.'

Marca began to realise that the man was living an illusion, just as the other old man he had first met. Was this the function of the village? Did people come here to have their illusions made into some sort of reality? He recognised the basic design of the machine in which the man sat. It was one of many invented in an effort to defeat the effects of the space ache. Every function of a man's mind and body was controlled by the machine which completely simulated an earthly environment for him. The thing had worked quite well, except it left a man all but useless for anything but piloting a spaceship and, it was discovered later, it spread a peculiar kind of cancer through the spinal fluid and the resulting death was worse than the space ache. Also once the thing was connected, it had to stay connected, for disconnection generally resulted in an acute psychic shock that brought death instantly.

The cage of metal moved jerkily forward. From inside it an emaciated hand reached out and touched Marca's arm. 'You,' said the clear voice. 'You. You. You.' It paused. 'Me,' it said at length. Then the encaged figure turned and went back to its original position.

Marca moved on. The man he had questioned had called the place heaven, but it seemed more like hell. This was like somewhere that might have existed in pre-raid days. The village seemed populated only by the insane.

He knocked on the wall of the nearest shack. He called: 'Is anyone in?' He bent his head and entered the room. The smell was terrible. Inside the room, on a big, square mattress, a young man sat up suddenly. Beside him lay a young woman.

But were they young? Looking closer, Marca could see that they had the appearance of old people whose flesh had somehow been artificially padded and whose skin had been worked to remove all signs of age.

'Get out!' said the man.

Outside, Marca sighed and looked around him. He began to feel that it would be wiser to leave the village and return to his air car and then make his way back to the tower and Fastina.

Why had these people come here? Why had they subjected themselves to such a dreadful existence?

He found another man. This one's skull was open to reveal his brain. Electrodes poked out of it and were fixed to a box on his back. The brain was protected by some kind of force-screen. The man himself looked quite normal.

'Why are you here?' Marca asked him.

The man's smile was melancholy. 'Because I wanted to be.'

'Did Orlando Sharvis do this to you?'

'Yes.'

'As punishment?'

The man's smile broadened. 'Of course not. I asked him to do it. Do you realise that I am probably the most intelligent man in the world thanks to all this?' He pointed a thumb at the box on his back. Then an expression of fear came over his face.

'You mustn't delay me, I must hurry.'

'Why?'

'The power-pack uses an enormous amount of energy. It must be recharged every twenty minutes, or I die.' The man stumbled away between the shanties.

'Sharvis giveth and Sharvis taketh away,' said a maliciously amused voice behind Marca. Marca did not recognise the quotation, but he recognised the face as he turned.

The man was pale-faced and thin-lipped and he had bitter eyes. He was dressed in a loose black toga and on his hands were a great many rings. The jewels in the rings were Ganymedian dream-gems. By concentrating on them, one could rapidly hypnotise oneself.

The man's name was Philas Damiago who had once had the reputation of being the world's last murderer, though his victim had been revived in time and lived to die of old age. Damiago had disappeared a hundred and fifty years before, but his face was familiar to Marca from the history Vs. Marca thought ironically that Damiago would now be merely one among many if he returned to the daylight.

'Philas Damiago?'

'I am, indeed. Do you recognise the origin of the quotation?'

'I'm afraid not.'

'You are not a literary man?'

'I think I'm well-read, but...'

'It comes from the old Christian Bible – the English translation. I used to read that a lot, as well as more or less contemporary works – Shakespeare, Milton, Tolstoy, Hëdsen. You know them?'

'I know of them. I have read a little of them all, I think.'

'I was a scholar, you know. Ancient literature was my speciality. I became too absorbed in it, I suppose...'

'You murdered your brother...'

'Exactly. All that blood and death, my friend. It went to my head.'

'You've been here ever since?'

Damiago shook his head. 'No. Originally I went to the twilight region. I was there for some time. Then I came here.'

'Looking for Orlando Sharvis, I suppose.'

'Yes. As these others had done before me – and since.'

'You do not seem as affected as they are.'

Damiago smiled. 'Not externally.'

'What did you want from Sharvis?'

'Time. I wanted time to study every work of literature that had ever been written and time in which to write my history of literature.'

'Sharvis gave you time?'

'Oh, yes. He operated on me. I can now live for at least another five hundred years.'

'Surely that is enough time to do what you want to do.'

'Certainly.' Damiago's mouth moved as if to add something.

'Then what's the trouble?' Marca felt impatient. He wanted to find Take.

'The operation affected my brain – my eyes. I am word blind.'

Marca felt sorry for Damiago. 'In the circumstances you have kept remarkably sane. You must be very strong-minded, Damiago.'

Damiago shrugged. 'I have ways of staying sane. I have my work – new work. Would you like to see it?'

Damiago strode towards a hut and entered it. Marca followed him. The place was well lit and bigger than he expected. In the centre, on a plinth, surrounded by tools and furniture, stood a great half-finished sculpture. It was a crude thing, yet powerful. The whole thing was constructed from human bones.

Marca changed his opinion of Damiago. The man was only apparently sane.

'Do you hunt for your materials...?' Marca asked harshly, try-ing to humour the man.

'Oh, no. They come to me eventually. I'm the most valuable member of the community, really. They want to die – I need their bones. Perhaps, in time, you, too, will come to me?'

'I don't think so.'

'You never know. You are looking for Orlando Sharvis, are you not? You will not go away, having seen what will happen to you?'

'I might well go away.'

'Sensible.' Damiago sat on the edge of the plinth. 'Go away, then. Goodbye.'

'First I want to find out more about this place. I think Alodios, the artist, came here. And a man called Take...'

'You're hesitating already. I advised Alodios against going to see Orlando Sharvis, and I advise you, likewise. But it will do no good.'

'Does Sharvis resent visitors?'

'On the contrary, he welcomes them. He will welcome you, particularly when you tell him what you want. You do want some-thing from him, of course?'

'I suppose so. But I did not really come to see Sharvis. I'm not even sure now why I came at all. But now I'm here, I'd like to see Alodios, at least. I knew him well...'

'If you did, then don't go to see him.'

'Where is he?'

Damiago spread his hands and then pointed. 'He lives about a hundred kilometres to the right over there. You'll see a cluster of high rocks. Alodios lives there. Sharvis lives in the mountains to the north-east of there – you will see the mountains from the cliff.

His laboratories extend throughout the mountains. You will see a tall shaft of polished stone. That will show you where the entrance to the laboratories lies.'

'I told you – I didn't think I wanted to see Sharvis now.'

Damiago nodded. 'If you say so.'

Clovis Marca stood on the edge of the cliff beneath the artificial sun. Next to him was a high-backed chair in which sat a silent man.

For the second time, Marca said politely: 'Alodios? Am I disturbing you?' But the seated figure did not reply or move.

Nervously, Marca stepped closer.

'Alodios. It is Clovis Marca.'

He moved around the chair. He was careful where he put his feet for he was very close to the edge. It was a long, sheer drop to the red and black moss below.

Alodios continued to stare fixedly outwards. The sun in his eyes did not seem to bother him. Marca wondered if he were dead.

'Alodios?'

There was great character written in the old man's face and hands, in the very shape of his body. He was a big man, with great hard muscles, a broad chest and huge arms and hands. His head was of similar proportions, strong and massive, with thick dark hair framing it. Heavy black eyebrows bristled on his jutting brow, heavily lidded eyes were half-closed, but the black eyes could be seen. The nose was aquiline and the mouth seemed the mouth of a bird of prey, also. The full lips were turned downwards in a way that was at once cruel, sensitive and sardonic. But it was all frozen, as if Alodios were a living statue. Only the eyes lived. Suddenly, they looked at him.

In his horror Marca almost lost his footing on the cliff. There was absolute torment in the eyes. From that frozen face they stared out at him, without self-pity, without any true intelligence. It was as if some mute, uncomprehending beast were trapped in the skull, for it was not the look of a man at all. It was the look of a tortured animal.

Alodios plainly did not think now. He felt, only. Sense was

gone, leaving only sensibility. Marca could not bear to look into the eyes for long. He turned away.

Alodios had been a genius. His intellect and sensitivity, his creative powers, had been unmatched in history. He had created great novels – combinations of poetry, prose, pictures, sculpture, music and acted drama that had reached the peak of artistic expression. Now it was as if something had destroyed the intelligence but left the sensitive core unsullied. He was still receptive, still aware – but with no mind to rationalise the impressions.

Marca thought that there could be no worse experience than this. For Alodios's sake, he began to push the chair towards the very edge of the cliff. Alodios would crash to the bottom and die.

A voice came from behind him, then. 'I doubt if that will do any good, Clovis Marca.' It was Take's rich voice.

Marca turned. Take stood there with his head on one side, dressed in his dark clothes, with his white hands clasped before him.

'Why won't it do any good?'

'He has what you wanted.'

'This? This isn't what I wanted!'

'He has immortality. Alodios went to Orlando Sharvis and Orlando Sharvis played a joke on him. Alodios found immortality, but he lost the sense of passing time.'

'A *joke*?' Marca could hardly speak. 'Alodios was the greatest...'

'Yes, Sharvis knew what he was. That, you see, was the joke.'

After a moment, Marca said: 'Isn't there any way of killing Alodios?'

'I think you would find him invulnerable, as I am.'

'You are immortal, Mr Take? I thought so.'

Take laughed flatly. 'I am immortal. I am a superman. My reflexes are ten times faster, my strength ten times greater, my reasoning powers ten times better than they were. I cannot be destroyed – I cannot destroy myself, even! Only Sharvis, who made me, can destroy me. And he refuses. I was his first immortal. I was a soldier, originally, who escaped with him after the Last

War. I was his chief lieutenant when he had gathered his Titan expedition together. By that time he had experimented on myself and two others. They had died, but I had survived. I wanted immortality at the time. It may sound strange, but I was prepared to risk dying for it. We went to Titan after he had operated on himself in the same way. It was because of these operations that we were able to survive Titan.'

'The others?'

'In spite of more and more experiments on their bodies, they died one by one. Sharvis and I returned to Earth – to the night side and the moon.'

'How did you create this world?'

'We had begun work on it before we left. This was where the Titan ship was built. He has machines – they can do anything. He gets his raw materials either from the moon itself, or else from the seabeds.'

'And you found immortality unbearable. Why was that?'

'He gave me immortality, but took my life.'

'Sharvis giveth and Sharvis taketh away,' murmured Marca. 'That's what Damiago said. You know Damiago?'

'I know them all. It is I who look after them. Sharvis does not.'

Marca looked towards the mountains far away. 'That's where Sharvis has his laboratories, Damiago said. Surely, Take, he has the means to do anything – to revive our diseased cells – make the world well again... If I paid Sharvis a visit...'

Take lunged forward, arms outstretched, and, before Marca realised it, the man had hurled him over the cliff.

Marca, as he fell, almost welcomed the fact that he was going to die. In killing him, Take had absolved him from all responsibility. Then, automatically, he had squeezed his gravstrap and began to float gently downward. More pressure on the strap and he was rising again.

Take was waiting for him, arms folded.

'As you see, Clovis Marca, I am in earnest. I would kill you rather than let you go to Sharvis. You do not understand the fascination that he can exert.'

Marca sank back to the ground. Nearby he saw a piece of loose rock. He stooped and picked it up.

'The only point you have made, Take, is to prove yourself as irrational as anyone. How do I know that your judgement of Sharvis is the correct one? You hate him because he gave you something you wanted. Is he to blame for that?'

'You see,' Take said. 'Your mind is already twisting. If you persist, if you will not return to the tower with me, I must kill you. It will be an act of mercy.'

'I still wish to decide for myself.'

'I will not let you.'

Marca flung the jagged rock at Take.

Take reached out and caught it. Then he moved towards Marca, his arm raised.

Marca pressed his gravstrap and began to rise into the air, but Take seized his ankle and hauled him to the ground. He swung the rock and smashed it down on Marca's head. Marca felt nothing, but he knew he was dead.

Chapter Four
The Resurrection

IN HIS LAST moment of life, Clovis Marca had realised how much he wanted to live and had at the same time been reconciled to the fact that he was dead; yet now he was conscious again and full of infinite relief.

He opened his eyes and saw nothing but a milky whiteness. He became frightened suddenly and shut his eyes tightly. Was he dead, after all? He seemed to be drifting weightlessly, unable to feel the presence of his own body.

It seemed that he remained with his eyes shut for hours before he opened them again, curiosity overcoming his fear.

Now in front of him something crystalline winked and shimmered. Beyond the crystal a shape moved, but he could not define what it was. He turned his head and saw more crystal, with dim outlines behind it. He tried to move a leg, but could feel nothing. Something happened, however. His body began to turn slowly and he could see that he was completely surrounded by the crystal. Attached to his mouth was a muzzle and leading away from it were several slender tubes which seemed imbedded in the crystal. He could look down and see the rest of his body.

With some difficulty he stretched out his hand and touched the irregular surface of the crystal. It tingled and made him feel less intangible. He tried to make some sound with his mouth. The muzzle stopped him from speaking, but he managed a muffled murmur. The awareness that at least he retained his senses of sight, touch and hearing reassured him.

He closed his eyes again and lifted his hand to his head, but could feel nothing.

Far away, a voice said softly, 'Ah, good. You will be out of there soon, now.'

Then Marca fell asleep.

He woke up and he was lying on a couch in a small, featureless room. It was warm and he felt very comfortable. He looked around, but could not see a door in the room. He looked up. There were indications that the room's entrance was in the roof directly above the couch. He could make out fine indentations forming a square.

He swung himself off the couch. He felt very fit and relaxed, but there was the slight feeling of being watched. Perhaps the walls of his room could be seen through from the other side.

He saw that he was dressed in a one-piece garment of soft, blue material.

He touched his head. It had been partly shaven where Take's rock had struck it and there was an indication of an old, healed scar, but nothing more.

He had been dead and someone had revived him. Had this been a second warning from Take? His brain must have been damaged, he was sure, and only a few surgeons in the world were capable of the operation necessary to revive a man with a bad head injury of that kind.

Orlando Sharvis? It could only have been the mysterious immortal.

A voice whispered and hissed through the room. At first it sounded like a wind sighing through trees, but then Marca recognised words.

'Yes, Clovis Marca. It is Sharvis who has saved you. Sit back – sleep – and soon, I assure you, Sharvis will be at your service...'

Marca returned to the couch, aware, but somehow not surprised, that Sharvis could read his thoughts. He lay down and slept again.

The next time he awoke he was still on the couch but it was rising towards the ceiling and the ceiling was opening upward to let him pass. He entered a far larger room, adorned with fluorescent walls of a constantly changing variety of colours. The walls moved like flames and dimly lighted the room.

'Forgive the rather gloomy appearance,' said a voice only slightly less sibilant than the one he had first heard, 'but I find it hard to bear too much direct light these days. As you guessed, I am Orlando Sharvis. You have been seeking me a long time, I gather, then you gave up, but now you are here. Your unconscious mind was taking you towards me all the time. You realise that now, of course.'

'Of course,' Marca agreed.

'Then it is a mutual pleasure that we are able to meet at last. As I said, I am at your service...'

Marca turned and looked up at Orlando Sharvis.

He had expected to see a man, but he saw a monster; albeit a beautiful monster.

Orlando Sharvis's head resembled a snake's. He had a long tapering face of mottled red and pink. He had faceted eyes like a fly, a flat, well-shaped nose and a shrunken, toothless mouth.

His body was not at all snakelike. It was almost square and very heavy. His legs were short and firm. His arms and hands, when he moved them, seemed sinuously boneless.

Marca's first impression, however, was one of height, for Orlando Sharvis was nearly ten feet tall.

Bizarre as he was, there was something attractive about him; something, as Take had said, completely fascinating. He could not always have looked like this...

'You are right,' whispered Sharvis, 'my body is the result of extended experiments over a great many years. I have made alterations not merely for convenience, but also to satisfy my own aesthetic tastes and curiosity.'

Sharvis was casually reading his mind.

'Another of my experiments that succeeded quite well,' Sharvis told him. 'Although I must admit that my ability is not perfect. Your mind is, in fact, something of a mystery to me – it harbours so many paradoxical thoughts...'

'How did you find me?' Marca asked. His speech was slightly slurred.

'A minor invention of mine to bring me information from not only everywhere in the moon, but everywhere in the world. It is a device a little larger than a poppy seed. Call it a micro-eye. I use many thousands of them. I saw what the ungrateful Take did to you and I sent one of my machines to pick you up and bring you here.'

'How long have I been here?'

'About a month, I'm afraid. The initial operation failed. I nearly lost you. You need not worry, incidentally, that I have tampered with your mind or body in any way. If you find you are a little numb or that speaking is at first difficult, be assured that the effects will soon disappear. I pride myself that I have done a perfect repair. Your hair growth has been accelerated as you will discover.'

Marca touched the top of his head. The bald part of his scalp was now covered in hair again.

'How do you feel generally?' Sharvis asked.

'Very well.' But now memories were returning – the colony outside, Alodios, what Take had told him about Sharvis.

'Again, I must be candid,' Sharvis said. 'Perhaps I will lose your trust, but I must tell you the truth. I did perform an operation on your artist friend, although I warned him of the consequences. Yet he still insisted. Every one of those others you saw were also warned that there would probably be side effects to their operations – and every one begged me to continue.' The tiny mouth smiled. 'I am an equable soul, Clovis Marca. I only do for people what they ask. I use no coercion. If you are thinking of my Last War days, please realise that I was young and headstrong then. I knew no humility. Now I know much. The Titan expedition and its failure taught me that.'

'You could give me immortality, then?'

'If you wanted it.'

'And what's the price?'

Sharvis laughed softly. 'Price? Not your "soul", if that's what you mean – and I see you have some such thought in your mind. You mean your individuality – something like that? I assure you it would remain intact. I am here only to serve you, as I said; to give you your heart's desire.'

'Take seemed to think you were guided more by malice than by idealism...'

'Take and I have known each other too long for me to regard him with complete objectivity, and the same is true of him. Perhaps we hate each other – but it is an old, sentimental hatred, you understand. I gave Take his freedom. I gave him immortality. Are those the actions of a malicious man?'

Sharvis had a power that was almost hypnotic. Marca found himself unable to think with anything like his old clarity. It was probably the after-effects of the operation.

'You have been guilty of many crimes in the past...' Marca began heavily.

'Crimes? No. I serve no abstract Good or Evil. I have no time for mysticism. I am entirely neutral – a scientist. When called upon, I do only what is asked of me. It is the truth.'

Marca frowned. 'But good and evil are not abstract – ethics are necessary, there are fundamental things which...'

'I have no ethic other than my will to serve. Do you believe me?'

'Yes, I believe that.'

'Well, then?'

'I see your point of view...'

'Good. I am not pressing you to accept any gift of mine, Clovis Marca. I have revived you, you are well, you may leave here whenever you wish...'

Marca said uncertainly: 'Could I possibly stay for a while – to make up my mind?'

'You are free to go wherever you like in my laboratories. You are my guest.'

'And if I decided to ask you for immortality...?'

Orlando Sharvis raised a sinuous hand. 'To tell you the truth, I lack all the materials to give you an absolutely perfect chance of immortality.'

'So even if I asked you, you could not do it?'

'Oh, yes. I could make you immortal after a fashion, but I would not guarantee you a normal life.'

'Could you get the materials you need?'

'There is a chance, yes.' Orlando Sharvis seemed to consider carefully. 'I see from your thoughts that you are torn between seeking immortality for yourself and asking me to "cure" humanity in general. I doubt my ability to do the latter. I am not omnipotent, Clovis Marca. Besides, what if most of the human race dies eventually? There are others who will never die living here, inside the moon.'

'Freaks,' said Marca without thinking.

'You fear the end of the "normal" human race, is that it?'

'Yes.'

'I can't appreciate your fears, I'm afraid. However, I will think about this. Meanwhile I should tell you that enemies of yours seem to be everywhere at the moment, both within the moon and on its surface.'

'What enemies?'

'Take for one. He is your enemy, though he thought himself your friend...'

'I have always known that much.'

'And Andros Almer and his gang are currently running about all over the surface trying to find you. They have your woman – Fastina – with them.'

'Is she safe?'

'Extremely. I take it that Almer regards the girl as his chief piece in the game he is playing with you...'

'Not a game I have any willing part in. How did he get to the moon? Why hasn't he discovered your tunnel?'

'I gather that his men's air cars all have tracer devices planted in them. This is to guard against them making any move that is contrary to what Almer wants them to do. Almer became suspicious after his scout had been gone longer than he expected. He traced the air car to your tower. He found Fastina there and you gone. He seized her and discovered that his air car had disappeared into the night region. It did not take him long to equip an expedition and come in search of you. The air car was traced to the moon, but now they are puzzled. I have sealed off and disguised my tunnel. Almer's instruments show that your air car is deep within the moon – but he cannot discover how it got there.' Sharvis laughed softly. 'He is extremely perplexed. They have begun boring into the moon, but I have managed to damage their instruments in one way or another. I shall have to think of a way of dealing with them soon. They are threatening my privacy.'

'You'll make sure Fastina's safe. She's innocent...'

'There was never a woman so innocent, I agree. Yes, I will make sure she is safe. I was not planning any sort of spectacular destruction of Almer and his crew, Clovis Marca. No, I am subtler than that, I hope.'

'And what of Take?'

'Actually he is outside my laboratories now. He has been trying to get in for ten days without my noticing. I don't know what he wants here. He knows that he is free to come and go as he pleases, but he is a narrow, suspicious man. I expect we shall see him soon.'

Sharvis turned gracefully. 'I will leave you now, if you will excuse me. I have more than your particular problem on my mind. Go where you will – you may find my home interesting.'

Apparently without the aid of any mechanical device, Sharvis began to drift towards the flickering wall and sink into it until he disappeared.

Marca began to see that Take had been wrong, after all, in attributing malice to Sharvis's actions. The scientist's actions were neither good nor bad as he had said. It was what one made of them that counted.

Chapter Five
The Truth

ORLANDO SHARVIS'S VAST network of laboratories impressed Clovis Marca as he wandered around them in the days that followed. Marca had seen similar places on daylight Earth, but none so spectacular. Orlando Sharvis's laboratories had been designed not simply for function, but also for beauty. The complex building, carved from the interior of mountains Sharvis had himself created, had been built by Sharvis alone. It was difficult to realise this as he explored room after room, passage after passage.

The laboratories were only part of the system. Some rooms seemed to have been designed merely as rooms, with no other purpose than to exist for their own sake. The building was, in fact, a palace of incredible beauty. There were galleries and chambers in it which, in their sweeping architecture and colours, were unmatched by anything in the history of the world. Clovis Marca was moved profoundly, and he felt that no-one capable of such work could be evil.

In one very large chamber he found several works that were not by Sharvis. They were unmistakeably by Alodios.

Marca went to look for Sharvis and found the self-deformed giant at last, sitting thoughtfully in a chair in a room that twirled with soft, dark colours. He asked Sharvis about Alodios's work.

'Normally,' Sharvis told him, 'I ask no price for my gifts – but Alodios insisted. He was the only modern artist I admired, so I was pleased to accept them. I hope you enjoy them. I hope that someday others will come to see them.'

'You would welcome visitors, then?'

'Particularly men and women of taste and intellect, yes. Alodios was with me for some time here. I enjoyed our talks very much.'

Memory of Alodios's trapped, tormented eyes returned to Marca, and he felt troubled.

Sharvis's shrivelled mouth smiled as if in sadness. 'I can refuse no-one, Clovis. In many ways I would have enjoyed Alodios's company, but, in the end, I had to do what he demanded of me. I fear that you will not stay long, for one reason or another.'

Still confused, Marca left the room.

Sharvis's palace was timeless. There were no clocks or chronometers to tell Marca how long he had been there, but it was probably a day or two later that the scientist sought Marca out as he listened to the singing words of the mobiles in the Alodios chamber.

'You must hate me for interrupting,' whispered Sharvis, 'but our friend Take has arrived at last. He finally took the simple way in and entered by the main door. I am glad he has arrived, for I wanted to speak to you both together. I will leave you to finish the novel if you like…'

Marca glanced up at the red-and-pink mottled face that seemed to look at him anxiously, although it was impossible to tell from the faceted eyes what Sharvis's feelings were.

'No. I'll come,' said Marca getting up.

Leaving the novel, Marca went with Orlando Sharvis to the room of flame where they had first confronted each other.

Take was there, standing in the middle of the room, the coloured shadows playing across his face. He had his hands clasped behind his back and there was a defeated look about him.

He raised his strange head and nodded to Marca.

'I should have battered your skull to pulp and taken your corpse with me,' he said. 'I'm sorry, Clovis Marca.'

Marca felt disturbed and hostile as he confronted the man who had twice tried to murder him. 'I think you're misguided, Take. I've been talking to Orlando Sharvis and…'

'And you are as gullible as all the others. I told you that you would be. He has deadened your brain. What have you said to him, Orlando?'

The giant spread his sinuous hands. 'I have only answered his questions truthfully, Ezek.'

'Glibly, you mean. Your truth and mine are very different!'

Marca began to feel sorry for Take. 'What Sharvis says is correct,' he said. 'He has been fair with me. He hasn't lied. He hasn't tried to encourage me to do anything I do not want to do. In fact, to some degree, he has tried to discourage me.'

'To some degree?' Take's deep voice rose until it bore a hint of despair. 'You fool, Clovis Marca. I wasted my time when I tried to protect you.'

'I told you – I am my own man. I need no protection.'

'You are no longer your own man, whether you realise it now or not. Already you are Sharvis's – you cretin!'

'Please, Ezek, this is unworthy of you,' Sharvis interrupted, gliding forward. 'When have I ever tried to exert my will on others – at least since the Titan failure? Have I ever tricked you, Ezek? I have always been straightforward with you.'

'You devious man – you destroyed me!'

'In those early days I was still learning. You wanted what I could give you. Why blame me for my ignorance? These outbursts only do you discredit.'

'You were never ignorant. You were born with knowledge – and it made you the evil monstrosity…'

'Take!' Marca put his hand on the man's arm. 'He has a point.'

'You know nothing of all this, of all he has done. Not only to me, but to all who have ever had any dealings with him. He is subtle, persuasive and malevolent. Do not believe anything he tells you. He gave me immortality, but he robbed me of any ability to appreciate life. Happiness and love are denied me. There is only one thing that moves me now – and that is suffering. I am dead, but he won't give me proper death. All his "gifts" are like that – all are flawed. He pretends to exert no power over you – and you find yourself a creation of his warped need to make others like himself!'

'You want me to kill you, Ezek?' Sharvis said. 'Is that it? You must understand what that implies. Death. It is final. I could not revive you.'

'Now you are trying to raise my hope,' Take said, turning away. 'Then you will say you have not the conscience to kill me.'

'It depends...' Sharvis mused. 'It depends on Clovis Marca's decision.' Before Marca could ask what he meant, he continued, 'Almer and your woman, Fastina, are here.'

'Here? How did they get here!'

'Almer had Fastina Cahmin with him in his air car as he went on yet another circuit of the area of the moon above the ice. I had waited for this to happen, as it had to eventually. I opened the tunnel a little way. Almer entered it to investigate. I closed the tunnel. Almer came here. It was the only way he could go. After that, my robots escorted them to my laboratories. They are at the entrance now.'

'And his men are still outside?'

'Yes. I was forced to remove all sources of heat from the area. They are not dead – merely in suspended animation of sorts.'

'Frozen?' Marca asked.

'In a way. Now, you must tell me what you want me to do with Almer and the girl. Do you want to see them?'

'Almer might try something violent...'

Sharvis chuckled. 'He could try all he wanted, but I doubt if he could do much damage here.'

'I would like to see Fastina. I would like to ask what she thinks of my accepting immortality from you. And there's one other thing I would like to ask you...'

'What's that?'

'Could you give her immortality as well?'

'I could give you both immortality, yes – with the materials I have at hand now.'

'You have got hold of them.'

'I might have done, yes.'

Marca could not puzzle out exactly what Sharvis meant. He turned to Take. 'You've spoken very melodramatically just recently, Take. Do you really want death?'

Take still had his back to them. 'Ask Sharvis how many times I have begged him to destroy me properly,' he said.

Sharvis pursed his shrivelled lips. 'Who knows?' he said. 'Perhaps everyone's wish can be made to come true today. I will go and fetch the new arrivals.'

Sharvis glided into the wall and disappeared. Take turned back to face Marca. 'Come to your senses while you have time,' he said urgently. 'Leave with Fastina. I will deal with Almer, if Sharvis does not. You will be free.'

Marca shook his head impatiently. 'Sharvis is obviously not normal in any way,' he said, 'but I am sure your judgement of him is biased...'

'Of course it is – by all I've seen. He is wiser than any man has ever been. He knows how to trick someone of your intelligence. He means you nothing but harm. If he gives you immortality as he gave it to me, you will feel nothing except despair – *eternally*. Don't you realise that?'

'Surely your emotions are only dead because you have refused to awaken them?' Marca said. 'Have you never thought that the fault lies with you and not with Sharvis?'

'Your mind has already been turned by his logic,' Take said. 'I have tried to save you from an eternity of misery. You will not listen. I'll say no more.'

'Misery for you? It need not be for me. Besides, I have not decided yet.'

'You decided the first day you heard of Orlando Sharvis. Don't deceive yourself, Clovis Marca.'

Sharvis came back through the walls of flame. Behind him, looking about him warily, stepped Almer and behind Almer came a pale-faced Fastina.

Almer still wore his heavy black hooded cloak and mask. There was still a sword at his side. He was still arrogant in his manner, though his arrogance was now plainly inspired by fear.

'What is this place?' he asked as soon as he saw Marca. 'Who is this creature?'

Fastina moved uncertainly towards Marca, her expression changing from despair to relief. 'Oh, Clovis!'

He took her in his arms and kissed her as she trembled there.

'Whatever happens, we are safe together now,' he assured her. 'I'm sorry I left you as I did – but I had to. And it was for the best, as you'll find out.'

She looked up at him. There were tears in her deep blue eyes. 'Are you sure?'

'I'm sure.'

Almer pointed a gloved finger at Sharvis. 'I warn you, whoever you are – I rule Earth, even the night side. I have an army at my command...'

Sharvis smiled. 'I have offered you no harm, I believe, Andros Almer. I see from your mind that you are afraid; that you are afraid of your own weakness more than anything else. I will do nothing to you. All who visit me are welcome. All who ask something of me are granted it. Take off your armour and relax.'

Almer dropped his hand to his sword hilt and turned to Marca. 'Is he some ally of yours, Marca?'

'He's no-one's ally,' Marca told him. 'Do as he says. Relax.'

'That world out there,' Almer said, walking to a couch and ostentatiously leaning back on it. 'How was it created? I never heard...'

'Orlando Sharvis created it,' Marca told him.

Almer looked at the giant with the pink-and-red mottled skin and the expressionless, faceted eyes. 'You are Orlando Sharvis? The scientist? I thought you were dead. What happened to you? How did you become like that?'

Sharvis shrugged. 'Clovis Marca will answer your questions. I must leave for a while.'

When Sharvis had gone, Marca explained everything to Almer and Fastina. As he finished, Almer said: 'He's neutral, you say. He'll do anything for anyone who asks?'

'Anything within his power.'

In the shadows Take stirred. 'You deserve a gift from Sharvis, Almer,' he said.

'What does he mean?' Almer asked.

'He's demented – he has an old grudge against Sharvis,' Marca told him. He now realised that Sharvis was indeed neutral. If he granted a request from Almer, what would the consequences be?

Sharvis returned to the room of flame.

'Well, Ezek,' he said to Take, 'here is what I can do. I can use certain elements in your body to give Clovis Marca immortality. It will mean, of course, that I shall have to destroy you. So there it is – his immortality for your life, and everyone gets what they want.'

'I haven't yet said I want immortality,' Marca said, 'unless Fastina can have it too.'

'I promised you both immortality,' Sharvis reminded him.

'What do you say, Fastina?' Marca asked her.

'Would you want me for all that time?'

'Shall we accept Sharvis's gift and become immortal?'

She hesitated. Then she whispered: 'Yes.'

Sharvis looked at Take. 'What do you say, Ezek? Marca's immortality for your life?'

Take shook his head. 'Another of your jokes, Orlando. You know I would not do that...'

Marca broke in. 'I thought so. You have talked about the horror of immortality, but, now it comes to it, you want to keep your life, after all. Very well.'

Take moved into the centre of the room and grasped Marca by the shoulder. 'You were once admired for your intelligence, Clovis Marca – look what you have become. Selfish and stupid! My desire for death probably far outweighs your desire for immortality. You have missed the subtlety of Orlando's bargain.'

'And what would that be?'

'He knows that I have tried to prevent you from doing something that will cause you terrible misery, that I would have no other human being suffer what I suffer. I sought only to prevent that suffering in you. Now he offers me peace at the price of letting you become what I am. Do you see now?'

'I think you are over-complicating the matter,' Marca said, coolly. 'I will have immortality. I will make use of it, if you dare not!'

Take moved away again, towards the shifting wall. The dancing shadows seemed to give his face an expression of anguish.

'Very well,' he said quietly. 'Take it and hope that one day Orlando Sharvis makes you the offer he has made me!'

Concentrating on this argument, no-one had noticed Andros Almer draw his sword and stalk towards Orlando Sharvis to press the tip against the scientist's great chest.

Sharvis was not surprised. It was evident that he had read Almer's mind before the man crossed the room.

He reached forward, displaying the same rapid reflexes as Take, and snatched the sword from Almer's hand. He snapped the sword in two and then into four and dropped the pieces casually in front of the astonished man.

'What did you intend to do?' Sharvis asked gently.

'I intended to force you to release me.'

'Why?'

'Because you are in league with Marca.'

'I have told you, and he has told you, that I am in league with no-one, I merely do what I am asked, if I can.'

'Could you turn the world again?' Almer asked suddenly.

Sharvis smiled thoughtfully. 'Is that what you want me to do? I see from your mind that you could claim credit for the action, that you think it would give you an advantage to seem some sort of miracle worker. You are full of superstition, aren't you?'

'Could you turn the world? Have you that power?'

'You think if I did it would give you mastery over it all, don't you?'

'I think it would. I would be able to control it all, then. I would leave you in peace. It would not be in my interest to reveal your presence in the world.'

Orlando Sharvis looked down at Almer and smiled again.

'Would you interfere with Clovis Marca and Fastina Cahmin?'

'No, I swear. Give me the opportunity – and I will do the rest.'

'I have had a project ready for some time,' Sharvis said. 'It is as yet untested. Since the raid I have been fascinated by the space-dwellers and the forces they commanded. I have discovered something of their secret. I might be able to do it.'

'Try!' Almer said eagerly. 'I will give you anything in return.'

Sharvis shook his head. 'I ask no price for my gifts and services. We shall see what we can do when we have settled Clovis Marca's problem.' He glanced at Marca, Fastina and Take.

'You are sure you are willing to make this sacrifice, Ezek?'

'It is no sacrifice. Marca will be the sufferer, not I.'

'And you two – Marca? Fastina?'

'I'm ready,' Marca said.

Fastina nodded hesitantly.

'Then we can begin at once,' said Sharvis, with a trace of eagerness. 'You will wait here, Almer, and we will discuss your request later. Go where you like in my laboratories. I will seek you out when I have finished.'

Take, Marca and Fastina followed him through the wall of flame and into an arched corridor.

'I have already prepared my equipment,' he told them. 'The operation itself will not take too long.'

Fastina gripped Marca's hand and trembled, but she said nothing.

Chapter Six
The Turn

WHEN MARCA EVENTUALLY awoke it was with a feeling of increased numbness through his body, as if he were paralysed. But when he tried to move his limbs, he found that they responded perfectly. He smiled up at Orlando Sharvis who was looking down at him. Behind Sharvis were the blank cabinets in which his equipment was housed.

'Thank you,' Marca said. 'Is it done?'

'It is. Poor Ezek's few remains were flushed away a couple of hours ago. It was a pity that that was the only way.'

'And Fastina?'

'She, too, has been operated on. With her it was an altogether easier job. She is perfectly well as you will see when you join her.'

'Were there any difficulties in my operation?'

'There could be some side effects. We shall have to see. Come, we'll go to find Fastina.'

Fastina was in the Alodios room. The novel was in progress, with abstract colours and delicate music mingling with the voice of Alodios himself narrating the prose sequences. She turned it off and ran towards him, her face alight with pleasure. She looked now as she had first looked when they had met on his return to daylight Earth. He felt something like pleasure, himself, as he reached out with his insensitive fingers and took her hands.

'Oh,' she said, 'you *are* all right. I wasn't sure...' She glanced at the scientist. 'Did Orlando Sharvis tell you the good news? He didn't tell me until after the operation!'

'What's that?'

'I can have children. My ovaries weren't badly affected by the omega radiation. He was able to make them healthy again. That's what he meant by immortality. He is a good man, after all!'

Marca was puzzled. 'But you alone being able to bear children isn't enough…'

'You, too, are now capable of fathering children,' Sharvis told him. 'I hope you call your first son Orlando.'

Marca did not feel the emotion he expected. He tried to smile at Fastina, but it was difficult. He had to make his lips move in a smile. She looked at him in alarm. 'What's wrong, Clovis?'

'I don't know.' His voice now sounded just a little flat.

Behind them there was a rustle of cloth as Sharvis folded his strange arms.

'I'm feeling numb, that's all,' he said. 'The operation did it. It will wear off soon, won't it, Sharvis?'

Sharvis shook his mottled head. 'I'm afraid not. That was the side effect I mentioned. In using various glands and organs extracted from Take, I somehow made the same mistake I made on him. You will not be able to feel anything very strongly, Clovis Marca. I'm sorry.'

'You knew this would happen!' He turned on the scientist. 'You knew! Take was right!'

'Nonsense. You will get used to it. I have.'

'You are like this all the time?'

'Exactly. I have been for centuries. Mental sensations soon replace the physical kind. I find much that is stimulating still.' Sharvis smiled. 'What you have lost will be made up for by what you have gained.'

'Damiago was right. You give and take away at the same time. I should have listened to Take.' Marca struck at his body and felt nothing. He bit his tongue and there was only a little pain.

'I must live for ever like this?' he said. 'It defeats the whole thing.'

'You knew the dangers. Take told you of them. But Take was weak. You are strong. Besides, you can now have children.'

'How, when I feel nothing?'

'I have done my best. I have seen to it that certain stimuli will still have certain effects.'

Marca nodded despairingly and looked at Fastina.

'I still love you, Clovis,' she said. 'I'll stay with you.'

'It would be wise,' Sharvis agreed, 'if you wish to continue your race. Clovis Marca, I have given you both the things you asked of me.'

'I suppose so,' said Marca. 'It is a sacrifice I should be proud to make. But I wish I had known I was to sacrifice something...'

'An unknowing martyr is no martyr at all,' Sharvis agreed. 'For your own sake, I would not make you that.'

'Are you so neutral?' Marca said. 'Are you not simply a complicated mixture of good and evil?'

Sharvis laughed. 'You describe me as if I were an ordinary man. I assure you, I am entirely neutral.'

'You have forced this girl to live with a man who cannot respond to her, cannot love her except in a strange way – a way he cannot demonstrate...'

'I have forced her to do no such thing. She is free to do as she wishes. She will bear your children – that is her immortality. You will live on. Her life will be short enough...'

'Am I invulnerable – like Take?'

'That happened, yes, in the transference of Take's parts to your body.'

'I see.' Marca sighed. 'What do we do now?'

'You are free to leave. However, if you wish to stay and see me try to answer Almer's request...'

'You can do it? You can make the world turn?'

'I think so. Do you want to come with me, back to the flame room?'

They went with him to the flame room and found Almer there. He looked as if he had not moved since they left him.

'Why didn't you do as I suggested?' Sharvis asked him. 'You could have seen everything there is to see in my laboratories.'

'I didn't trust you,' Almer mumbled. 'Are those two immortal now? They don't look any different.'

'He's sulking, Clovis,' said Fastina with a smile. In spite of what had happened to her lover, she seemed elated still.

'They are,' Sharvis told Almer.

'I'm hungry,' Almer said.

'I've been a poor host. Let's go and have something to eat.'

After they had eaten, Sharvis led them through a door and down to a hall which was empty save for two bronze air cars covered in baroque decoration. They climbed into one.

They began to descend through a tunnel narrower than the one which led into the hollow world of the moon, but which wound downwards at a much greater incline. The air became thick and salty. The tunnel was lit by dim strips in its sides and they felt the blood pound in their ears as the pressure increased.

'We are just about to reach the level of the ocean bottom,' Sharvis told them. 'This tunnel leads from the moon to the rock below it.' He continued to talk, but Marca could hear very little but the booming in his eardrums. Sharvis seemed to be explaining how he had managed to build the tunnel.

At last they left the tunnel and entered a huge, dark cavern. Sharvis guided the air car to the side and turned on the lights.

Water seeped down all the walls of the great grotto. The place seemed of natural origin. On its floor stood a machine.

The machine was large and had been coated in some kind of yellow protective plastic. In its centre was a gigantic power unit. From this led a structure of rigid pipes and cables attached to a grid which encircled the whole apparatus.

'As you can imagine,' Sharvis's voice said over the pounding heartbeats that filled Marca's ears, 'I have had no chance to test this device. The model seemed to work successfully enough, but I was never sure that the power was sufficient to do the job. The thing is, in effect, an engine which will push in a given direction. It will, with luck, begin to turn the world sufficiently rapidly to restore the planet's momentum.'

Sharvis took the air car down to the slimy floor of the cavern and stepped out of it, gliding across to the machine. 'The only control is on the machine itself. I thought it unwise to risk connecting another control that could be operated from my laboratories.

I only invent, as I told you. I never use my inventions for any specific purpose unless asked to do so. I am grateful for the opportunity you have given me, Andros Almer.'

Dimly, Marca saw Almer huddled in his cloak, his hood drawn about his face. The man seemed to be watching Sharvis intently as the scientist stepped over to the machine and, after hesitating for a moment, depressed a stud on the small control panel.

Nothing happened.

Sharvis came back to the air car and clambered in, his huge bulk dominating them.

'It has a timing mechanism so that we can return without undue haste to my laboratories.' He turned the air car back into the tunnel.

Later, they sat looking up at the huge screen which showed a view of the Earth from above, evidently transmitted from an old weather control satellite.

Sharvis swung a chronometer from a hidden panel below the screen, watching closely as the seconds indicator swept around it.

A faint tremor began to be sensed in the room.

'It will be gradual,' Sharvis told them. 'It will take quite a few hours. This is to ensure that no major upheavals take place on the planet. The whole operation should be quite smooth, if I have judged correctly.'

The laboratory shook violently for a few seconds and then subsided.

The picture on the screen showed the day side of Earth. They could see no indication of movement as yet.

'Of course,' Sharvis said casually, 'there is just a chance that the engine will begin to push in another direction and carry the Earth out of her normal orbit. I hope it is not towards the sun.' He chuckled.

'It's moving,' whispered Fastina.

It was moving. A shadow was beginning to inch across the outline of Asia.

The laboratory trembled, but this time the vibration was steady.

They watched in silence as the shadow lengthened over Asia and touched Africa. The coastline of South America came into view.

As the hours passed and the vibration in the laboratory became familiar, the shadow reached Europe and spread into the Atlantic.

Later they saw the whole of the American continent appear. The vibrations increased, as if the engine were labouring.

Sharvis looked calmly at the instruments below the screen.

They could now see the blinding whiteness of the ice-covered Pacific and then they could make out the visible surface of the moon rising from the ice in clear daylight.

The vibrations increased. The laboratory rocked. They were flung to the floor and the picture above them wavered and then became steady again.

From far below them they heard a deep, echoing sound and again the laboratory shook.

Then everything was still.

They looked at one another and at the screen.

The world had stopped turning.

Almer turned to Sharvis. 'What's happened? Start the thing up again.'

Sharvis chuckled. 'Well, well. I've turned the world for you, Andros Almer. But the engine must have reversed its thrust...'

'Keep it turning!' Almer bellowed.

'I'm not sure that I can. Come, we'll investigate.'

They followed him as he glided from the laboratory and back to the place where the air cars were.

Again they flew down the tunnel, through the moon and beneath it through the ocean floor until they entered the cave.

The air was scorching hot and there was no longer any moisture on the grotto walls.

They saw the machine. It was now merely a fused tangle of blackened metal.

'Overloaded,' Sharvis shouted, and began to laugh.

'You expected this?' Almer called over the roar of his own heartbeats. 'Did you?'

Sharvis looked around. 'We'd better leave immediately. The section joining the tunnel from the moon to the bed of the sea has been weakened. You can imagine the pressure outside it. If we don't go, we'll be crushed or drowned.'

Almer stood up in the air car. 'You did this deliberately! You knew the machine was incapable of turning the Earth!'

Sharvis swung the air car into the tunnel. Water was already running in a steady river down its sides.

Almer beat at Sharvis's heavy body, but the scientist continued to chuckle while he guided the air car upwards.

Marca and Fastina clung together as Sharvis increased the speed. There was a strange creaking noise filling the tunnel now.

Eventually they returned to the chamber below the laboratories and Sharvis hurried to the door, with Almer still clinging to him and repeating again and again, 'Did you? Did you? Did you?'

Sharvis ignored Almer and entered another room. The wall slid back at his touch and he began to run his seemingly boneless fingers over a console, his eyes on the indicators above. Again the room trembled slightly.

A little later he stepped back.

'I've sealed off the tunnel,' he said. 'There'll be no trouble there.'

Sharvis seemed to be relieved. He turned his pink-and-red mottled face towards Marca and Fastina and regarded them with his expressionless, faceted eyes.

Almer appeared to have exhausted himself. He lay against a wall mumbling.

'Did you know the engine could not work properly?' Fastina asked Sharvis innocently.

'I have given Almer what he really wanted, I'm sure,' Sharvis replied enigmatically. 'He wanted the world turned. I turned it. Now his empire lies in the night. Could that be where it belongs?'

'The people,' Fastina said. 'The ordinary people...'

'Those who wish to escape him may now do so. But few will, I think. The darkness is safe. They can huddle in it until death comes. Isn't that what they want? Haven't I given everyone what they really wish?'

Marca looked at him unemotionally. 'Certainly the darkness mirrors the darkness in their minds,' he said. 'But do they deserve it?'

'Who is to say?' shrugged Sharvis.

Almer stepped forward. 'I wish to go home,' he said levelly. Apparently he had recovered and had accepted what had happened. It seemed strange to Marca that he should do so with such apparent equanimity.

'You may do as you please,' said Sharvis with a trace of malicious humour. It was almost as if he felt he had paid Almer back for the pitiful attempt the man had made on his life. 'Will you find your own way out?'

Almer marched from the room. 'I have found it, thanks to you,' he called as he left.

'And what of you, Clovis Marca?' asked Sharvis. 'What will you do now?'

'We will return to my father's tower,' Marca said stiffly.

'And raise your children?' Sharvis said. 'I trust you will think in time that your sacrifice was worthwhile.'

'Maybe.' Marca glanced sadly at Fastina. 'But will you think the same, Fastina?'

She shook her head. 'I don't know, Clovis.'

Marca looked suddenly up at Sharvis. 'I have just realised,' he said. 'You have played another joke on us, I believe.'

'No,' said Sharvis, reading his mind. 'The radiation still exists, certainly. But your children's life cycle will be shorter since you will now lack the means to induce longevity. They will have time to adapt and reproduce. And I have made sure that you will never be affected by the radiation. Doubtless you will help father your children's children. It appears to be an established tradition in your family already.'

Fastina took Marca's arm. 'Let's go, Clovis,' she said. 'Back to the tower.'

'If it means anything,' Sharvis told them as they left, 'something has changed which might give you encouragement. It is a sentimental thing to say, I know...'

'What's that?' said Fastina, looking back at him.

'You once faced the evening. Now you face the morning. I wish you and your offspring well. Perhaps I will come to see them sometime, or you will send them to see me?'

Even then, as he walked away from the strange scientist, Marca was still unsure if Sharvis was moved by malice or charity, or whether the neutrality he claimed was founded on some deep understanding of life which was available only to him.

Epilogue

THE TOWER NOW existed in the dawn, but the quality of the light had not altered. The red dust continued to blow and the brown lichen grew around the base of the tower.

The tower's shadow lay behind it now, and the shadow never moved, but one day Fastina told Clovis Marca that she was pregnant.

'Good,' he said as he sat immobile by the window watching the distant sun on the horizon, and Fastina put her arms around his neck and kissed his cold face and stroked his unresponsive body, and loved him with a love that now had pity in it.

Mechanically, he reached up with one of his numb hands and touched her arm and continued to stare out at the sun and thought about Orlando Sharvis, wondering still whether the scientist had acted from good intentions or evil, or neither; wondering about himself and what he was; wondering why his wife cried so silently; wondering vaguely why he could not and never would cry with her. He wanted nothing, regretted nothing; feared nothing.